THE SHIELD
BEFORE ME

JAMISON WHITEMAN

To my junior high school principal, Sister Mary Romuald Nedwecka, S.S.N.D., and my high school principal, Friar Knute Kenlon, O.F.M. Cap, in memory.

Prologue
Time Travel

They said that it couldn't be done; the entire scientific community said that it was just a theory, an unprovable one at that. It couldn't be proven. But Murray Edgeton did. Einstein's Theory of Relativity and the Einstein-Rosen Bridge. He demonstrated that both theories were correct by actually accessing the Space-Time Continuum. And he was just thirty years old when he did it. But he had two problems. His work was so highly classified that only a handful of people knew about it. Secondly, the personal goal that he wanted to accomplish with his work was thwarted by what had occurred. Two years later, he was still seething.

Murray Edgeton was the most brilliant and creative physicist in at least three generations. He received his doctorate in physics from the Massachusetts Institute of Technology, MIT, at twenty-two and then went to work at the Jet Propulsion Laboratory, JPL, in Pasadena. At the JPL, he achieved his most significant professional and personal accomplishment: He demonstrated that traveling through time was a reality and not the stuff of science fiction. He worked with a team that was comprised of physicists, astrophysicists, engineers, and mathematicians. This team, dubbed "The Einstein Project," uncovered the secrets of the Space-Time Continuum, wormholes, and closed timelike curves. Further research and experimentation resulted in their discovering a "portal" that allowed them to access the Space-Time Continuum. With their understanding of this phenomenon, they inserted a team of U.S. Military Special Operations members into the portal. This team was transported to first-century Palestine, where they witnessed the crucifixion of Jesus of Nazareth. This was the source of one of Murray's problems. He was an avowed anti-theist who, along with not believing in a Supreme Being, despised all things religious. He blamed Christianity for the world's woes, and his unstated goal in sending the team back to first-century Jerusalem was to expose Christianity as a fraud. He planned to prove that Jesus was nothing more than a Jewish preacher from the backwaters of Nazareth, a minor historical figure. He wanted to rub the Christian world's collective face into this fact. But what the team had witnessed at the crucifixion left no doubt as to the divinity of Jesus.

And while professionally and personally frustrated by that turn of events, Murray had the proverbial ace "up his sleeve." Although he may not have been able to disprove Jesus' divinity, he could still realize his goal of ridding the world of Christianity by thwarting its spread. He had to send a team back through the portal for a different mission to do this. This became his singular goal, and he dedicated his incredible intellect to accomplishing this task, and so begins our story.

Chapter One
Early March, The Present Day

West Texas

Murray had to think about this: How could he pull this off? He decided that the best way that he could sort this out would be to go back to where it all started, West Texas. He wanted to get that fire back in his belly, stoke the flames of that crucible of hate. Yep, heading back to the Permian Basin would get those feelings back.

Murray hadn't been home for seventeen years. He left for MIT when he was sixteen and never came back. There was nothing left for him here after his mother died. His mother, RaeAnn, was killed by the people in this town; well, maybe not killed in the literal sense, but they killed her, nonetheless. His mother was a sweet young thing, working at the local diner one summer between her junior and senior year in high school when she ran into a smooth-talking roughneck from Oklahoma named Johnny. Well, Johnny got her pregnant that summer and then left her high and dry. The townsfolk in this tiny West Texas town, a town that happened to be the Texas-sized buckle of the Bible Belt, turned their backs on RaeAnn. They turned their backs on her when she needed them the most. While a response like that might be expected, it shouldn't have happened here. These people were all supposed to be "good Christian folk" who should have supported RaeAnn. It was that "holier than thou" attitude of these people and the way that they ostracized both RaeAnn and her little boy that led to RaeAnn dying of a broken heart and also led to his becoming an atheist and eventually an anti-theist.

Driving into town, he noticed it had grown quite a bit since he left. There was a medium-sized shopping mall, several restaurants of the big chain variety, and several nice hotels. Back when he was a young lad, all that they had were diners and the typical Mom and Pop stores. He walked into the empty lobby of the hotel that he had made reservations for earlier in the week. He noticed that they had everything that one would find at a local hotel on the coast: Internet access and a business center. This little Podunk oil town had come a long way in seventeen years.

"Good afternoon, sir, checking in?" asked the young and very pretty desk clerk at the counter. Looking at her name tag, Murray noticed her name.

"Yes, Kristin, I am. You should have a set of reservations for Murray Edgeton."

Kristin completed a few keystrokes on her keyboard, "Oh, yes. Dr. Edgeton, I see that you're here for two nights. May I please see some form of identification and a credit card?" Murray handed his driver license and his American Express over to Kristin.

"Here you go. I need to ask you a quick question, Kristin: Where is a good place to eat around here? I noticed a few chains driving up here, but I hoped to try something more local. One of my friends back at work used to have family out here, and he mentioned that when he visited, they would all eat at Metzger's Family Diner. Is that still open?"

Kristin looked up from her computer with a surprised look on her face. "Wow, the old Metzger Diner. I haven't heard anyone talk about that for years. No, it's gone. It closed down about, let me see, I was in junior high school, so about a dozen years ago. It's incredible that someone from California would mention that. It was a nice little diner. We used to have Sunday dinners there after church when I was a little girl. I remember that they had great milkshakes. OK, here you go. We will have you in Room 212 for two nights. The elevator to the second floor is down the hall to the right. If you want to go ahead and get settled, I can have a list of some restaurants ready for you in about five minutes. Shall I get the list sent up to your room, or do you want to come down and get it here at the desk at your convenience?"

"No, I'll come down and get it in a bit; let me get my stuff up. Thanks for your help."

"Of course. Dr. Edgeton, might I ask you a question? I saw on your reservation that you are a Ph.D. What kind of work are you involved in? Does your work bring you here?"

Smiling at Kristin, he said, "I'm involved with the Space program back in California, but it's nothing glamorous. We just validate the numbers that we get from the engineers. I'm just passing through but taking my time doing it."

"Well, I hope you enjoy your short stay here; this is a very nice town with nice, friendly people. Let me put your list together, and please let me know if there is anything else I can get for you."

He smiled at her, grabbed his briefcase and roll-along bag, and headed to his room. "Those Bible-thumping morons were none too nice and friendly to me and my mom when I was here. I honestly doubt that they've changed," he said as he walked away, "I guess I'll find out in short order."

About an hour later, he returned downstairs and walked to the front desk. Kristin was helping a couple to check in, but when she saw him, she gave him a smile and an "I'll be right with you" wave. As soon as she was done, Murray walked up, and she had the list of restaurants ready for him, along with a nice recommendation. "There is one place on this list I should have mentioned earlier. We have a new brew pub here in town that has turned out to be pretty popular. I don't know if you're into the microbrew scene, but their food is excellent. I guess that you can call it high-class pub grub. The chef went to culinary school in Ft. Worth and has done some interesting work with some of our local game. He has this appetizer, "Snake Bites," made from real snakes. You'd be surprised at how good they are. I haven't been there for a couple of weeks, but I was going to pop by after I get off. Maybe I'll see you there," Kristin offered with another dazzling smile.

"Well, let me give it a try, thanks. And if you get off within the next hour, you might run into me," he answered with a grin. Along with being a brilliant physicist, he was a very handsome man. His mother's exquisitely beautiful features, and his father's rugged handsomeness were passed onto him as he won the genetic lottery for physical attractiveness. Besides a few college romances and a year-long relationship with one of his colleagues, he did not often find himself involved romantically. He discovered that romantic involvements interfered with his work, but he saw something most appealing about the very pretty Kristin.

Without skipping a beat, she answered him, "I'm off in fifteen minutes. See you there?" And with that, Murray smiled as he walked out of the set of sliding glass electric doors to his BMW. It took him five minutes to get to the pub, and when he walked in, he noticed that this place wasn't just popular; it was packed. He got a high-top pub table with two chairs in the bar area and was lucky to get it. His waitress came up after a few minutes and handed him a menu. She had this screwed-on smile that said, "I'm cute; how much will you be tipping me tonight?" She then asked him if someone else would be joining him.

"Yes, I am. She should be here within the next fifteen to twenty minutes. If I could get another menu, a glass of water with a lemon, and a list of what's on tap, that would be great." The smile walked away, happy that there were two at this table. That meant a larger tip. He sat back and checked out the people in the place. The crowd appeared to be a mix of young adults, an office-type crowd, with a crowd of oil workers that seemed to be a bit rougher around the edges. For the most part, they all seemed to get along well enough. After a few minutes, the smile returned with Murray's water, a lemon wedge, the second menu, and the beer list.

"Can I get you anything while you're waiting, or should I come back when your friend gets here?"

He answered back, "Thanks. Just give me a few, and

we'll order them when she gets here." He kept his eye on the door, and about twenty minutes after he arrived at the pub, Kristin appeared. She changed her clothes and was now wearing a pair of jeans and a nice blouse under a denim jacket. He noticed that she put on a bit of make-up. All in all, she looked incredible. The double-takes she was getting from the men she passed by confirmed that. She looked around the pub and spotted Murray semaphoring her from his high-top table. He stood as she walked up, and as she sat down, she touched his forearm, sending a quick shock right through him.

"Sorry that I'm a bit late. I had some difficulty with my changeover. Well, what do you think?" Kristin asked as she looked around the bar.

Murray nodded as he looked around, "Not bad, but then again, I haven't sampled any of their brews or pub grub. What can I get you?"

She replied, "Well, I'm sure that your girls out there in Southern Cal all like their foo-foo wines and such, but I'm a country girl at heart. I'm happy with a cold beer after my shift."

"My kind of girl, Lee Jeans and all. Please take a look at this beer list, and let's order up. I've memorized the menu, and you're right; it looks pretty interesting." Murray caught his server's eye, and she popped over; the smile was instantly put back on.

"Y'all had a chance to take a look? Is there anything that I can help you with?"

"I think that we're ready to order a few beers right now to start. What looks good to you, Kristin?"

Besides you? she thought, then she answered, "Thanks, let me go with your Golden Pilsner; that sounds like it will blow the dust off."

"Great, and how about you, sir?"

"I normally like IPAs, but let me try something with a bit more Texas flavor. How about your Shiner Bock on tap."

"You bet. I'll get those right up and then come back and get your dinner orders whenever you're ready."

"OK, that takes care of that. Thanks for recommending

this place, and I'm glad I ran into you. I'd much rather have dinner with a pretty girl than eat alone. So, tell me, I know that you grew up here, from what you told me about eating at Metzger's, but have you ever ventured off from town?" he asked.

"After graduating high school, I couldn't wait to get out of here. I went up to Lubbock as an undergrad, got my degree from Texas Tech in Business with an emphasis in marketing, and went right to work for the hotel firm. I worked in Lubbock for a year, and then they opened this property up. They asked me if I'd like to transfer back home and be the front-end manager. It was a good career move; honestly, after spending five years in Lubbock, I got homesick for the small-town atmosphere. It was good to come back. How about you? You don't seem or sound like the typical Southern California kind of guy."

He let out a short laugh. "You must be psychic or a detective in training. I thought I lost most of my accent, but you must have picked it up. I'm not like your 'typical Southern California kind of guy' because I'm not. I was born right here in this little town about thirty-some years ago and haven't been back home since I went to school. As I said, I'm just passing through on my way back to Pasadena, but I thought I'd stop and see if Thomas Wolfe was right."

"Oh, wow, a literary reference, you mean 'You can't go home again'? Well, was he right?"

He was becoming more and more impressed with this 'Country Girl.' "Exactly. Can I ever go home again? So far, things are quite different from when I left. This place was a wide spot in the middle of the road, but it has grown, and the population has exploded. I thought I'd see if Metzger's were still here and if I could see my high school. I'll do that tomorrow."

"Did you go to Travis Union High also? Damn, go Oilers! That's where I went. You know, tomorrow is my day off. Would you like some company while you're traveling down memory lane? It might be fun, and you can tell me what life is like outside of West Texas."

"Ah, sure, I guess, if you don't mind. You might be able to answer a few questions about the town. I've forgotten, or tried to forget, a lot about this town. Yeah, that would be great; let's plan on it. Oh, here's our beer."

The ever-smiling waitress, she never gave Murray and Kristin her name, brought their beers over. Kristin quaffed some down and said, "I tell you *what*, damn, that's good beer!"

Murray threw his head back and laughed. "You know, I never thought I would say this, but it is so good to hear that again. 'I tell you what.' I used to say that in almost every sentence but fell out of the habit. That brought back a lot of memories. Please tell me that you'll keep saying that; it sounded great. I tell you *what*."

They both started laughing so hard that people were looking over at them. Murray then noticed a man at the table next to him. He was about fifty to sixty years old, and he kept straining to hear their conversation. He saw that the man was looking at him very intently. It was a bit unnerving, but he let it go. There was something about him that seemed vaguely familiar.

Regaining their composure, Kristin asked Murray, "So tell me, what did you do when you left here, and why haven't you returned until now?"

"I graduated from Travis when I was sixteen and was accepted to MIT…"

Kristin jumped in, "Is that the Missouri Institute of Trucking?" She smiled at him and then gave a quick chuckle.

Smiling back, he continued, "No, the other one. I earned my undergraduate degree in physics and my doctorate three years later. I did a year of research and then went to work for the JPL in Pasadena, the one in California, not the one here in Texas."

"Wow, I am impressed, brains and good looks, that's a deadly combination. But why haven't you come back until now?" Kristin asked.

"Well, that's a story for another time, but for now, let's just say that I have no family left here. My mother died right as

I got my Ph.D., and both of my grandparents are gone. I may still have some cousins and some other relatives here. I haven't been in contact with anyone for who knows how long, so I don't really know."

Kristin downed more of her pilsner and asked Murray, "You've mentioned Metzger's a few times. Do you have any connection to the old diner?"

He tipped his glass to her in salute, "I told you that you were good. Yeah, Metzger's Diner. My mother was a waitress there. She worked there full-time. She'd also hold down part-time jobs whenever she could get the work. I spent many an afternoon doing homework after school while Mom waited on tables. I had some very nice memories of that little place. In addition to their milkshakes, and you were right, they were good; Old Man Metzger used to make some incredible chili. I have never had chili like his anywhere. Along with seeing if the diner was still here, I'd like to see if Mr. and Mrs. Metzger were still in the area. But Metzger's also..."

The man at the table Murray saw earlier got up and walked right up to him. "I thought that was you. You're RaeAnn's boy, aren't you?"

Murray was slightly startled by this guy accosting him, but he answered politely, "Yes, sir, I am. Did you happen to know my mother?" He also noticed that between the slurred speech and the overwhelming smell of beer, this guy had a belly full of what the barkeeper was drawing out of the tap.

"Yeah, I knew her all right. I also knew your old man, old Johnny. Well, he sure picked right up when the goin' got tough, now didn't he? Leavin' your ma and all. There are guys like that all over the place in this business, but I tell you *what*, that old boy sure knew how to work a rig: old Johnny and me. We put more damned drillin' mud down into boreholes all over this whole basin than anybody I know. I was a worm on a few rigs where Johnny worked the chain, and we could outwork any ten guys. Yep, old Johnny sure knew his way around a rig. But your ma, yeah, she was somethin', right nice woman, old RaeAnn. She never gave up, and she sure took care of you. She did it all by herself, too. Sorry that you lost her, boy, she was a right nice woman."

Murray was stunned by this. He didn't know his father as he left his mother when she was pregnant. But he was interested in discovering what this man knew about his mother. "Thank you for your condolences, sir. I appreciate that, but how did you know my mother?"

"Damn, son, I'm her big brother, I'm your Uncle Randall. Randall Edgeton, that's me. Next to your ma, I guess that I was the black sheep of our family. I never did like what Ma and Pa did to RaeAnn. I mean, you sure as hell couldn't help it, you know, being a bastard boy and all that, damn, son, that sure in the hell weren't your fault, now was it? But no, Ma and Pa sure took it out on you, didn't they? Now, are you going to ask me to sit down here with you and your pretty lady or what? You owe it to me, bein' blood and all."

Murray sat there, stunned. He couldn't say a word, but you could feel that in the hesitation of Murray's not answering, there was tension growing rapidly between Murray and the man who claimed to be his uncle. He recalled how Randall treated him when he was a little boy: Randall used to enjoy tormenting him, and those feelings of his being powerless to stop Randall were welling back up in him. Finally, Kristin broke the awkward silence and said, "I'm sorry, Mr. Edgeton, Murray, and I were going to be leaving, but thank you for stopping by. Murray, are you almost ready?"

Randall barked back, "Well, ain't that typical. You come back here with your nice clothes and your fancy college degree, and you can't even give your uncle the time of day. Well, maybe I wasn't entirely honest. Let me tell you somethin', boy; maybe your ma wasn't a right nice woman, no, sir, maybe your ma was a little slut who thought that she was better than all of us, and what did she do? She got herself all knocked up and gave birth to some little bastard boy. I guess that boy is you. And you know what else she did? She turned her back on the Good Lord is what she did. Go ahead, get the hell out of here, go on, get a move on, and don't come back. We don't need your kind out here. Get on, boy, get out of here before I show you what a real man can do, kin or not, boy, I'm ready to show you."

Kristin grabbed Murray by his arm, "Let's go, we'll pay the tab up at the bar." He could not move; it was as if he were transported back in time to when he was the young outcast boy shunned and shamed by everyone in this town. Finally, Kristin shook him from his stupor, and he got up and walked away.

Randall couldn't give it up. "Yeah, that's right, walk away. You've been doin' that ever since you were a little boy, hidin' behind a woman. Go on, get on with yourself, get the hell out of here."

By this time, everyone in the bar was watching what was happening, but Kristin dragged Murray away. She threw a twenty-dollar bill on the bar and got him outside and into her car. She pulled out of the parking lot and just started driving. "What in the world was that all about? Good grief, that guy was a maniac. What was he talking about? Murray, are you OK?"

He was still in what looked to be a state of shock. Kristin could not believe the rapid turn of events that she just witnessed. One minute, the old drunk was just happy to stand there and talk with Murray, and in the next instant, it looked as if he were ready to become violent. She could not understand why Murray had just sat there; he hadn't even moved when she tried to defuse the situation. Then he slowly turned to face her as she was navigating through traffic. "We have to get my car. Can we go back and get it, please?"

Kristin looked at him briefly and then went back to driving. "We'll head back in a bit. I just wanted to get you out of there, but what happened back there? I have never seen anything like that. Is that Randall, your relative? And what was he saying about your mother?"

He seemed to come out of his trance and opened up a bit. "Kristin, is there a place we can go where I can talk to you? Do you want to head back to the hotel?"

"No, I don't think that would be a good idea right now. Let's head over to my place; my roommate is still working, but she should be home soon. Are you OK with that?"

"Sure, no worries." They didn't say another word to each other until they got into Kristin's apartment. Kristin got Murray to sit down, and then she poured him a cup of tea; within a few minutes, he opened up. "I was born on the kitchen table at my grandmother's house. They lived on what was then the northwest side of town. I don't know what that part of town would be considered now. But as you heard from Randall, my mother got pregnant with me when she was still in high school. She was a single mom who worked two to three jobs at once to support us because no one else in this town would help us. Her whole family and the entire community turned their backs on us. I can understand that with the social mores being what they were, but you know what, do you know what I could never understand? These people preached about 'Jesus loves you' and 'Jesus forgives all of your sins.' Well, if they put so much stock in this Jesus and were being charitable and all of that nonsense, shouldn't they have been loving and charitable to one of their own, even though she may have made a life-changing mistake? Well, they didn't. I must tell you that Randall, and yes, I am fairly sure he is my uncle, did me a huge favor. He reinforced my belief that everything that the Christian religion touches, or any religion for that matter, turns to shit, and pardon my French. But look at human history. How many wars and persecutions have taken place because of religion? Nope, it's all a giant scam. According to their scriptures, money is the root of all evil, but it's not. Their religion is the root of all evil."

Kristin sat there watching him. After he finished talking, she sat there and let him sit silently. She then reached over and took his hand. "I'm so sorry, Murray, that Randall did that to you. That was uncalled for. For a moment there, I thought he was just happy to see you and be happy for you because you have become so successful. But then his entire tone, demeanor, everything, it was like someone threw a switch, and this man turned into a maniac who lit right into you. I have never seen anything like that. I am so sorry. But please understand that his actions and those of all of those other people were not something from God. The actions of those people are not what

God wants from us. I am so sorry that you had to experience hate instead of love and support from your family. You were a little boy; you never did anything wrong."

Murray answered her very quickly; the shock or stupor he was in five minutes before was gone entirely. "So, I take it that you believe in Christianity, is that it? You believe that someone up in the sky is pulling strings, and we're like a bunch of puppets responding to spiritual machinations. Do you believe in that? Every move that we make is predetermined. Does anyone have proof of this Supreme Deity, the big puppet master in the sky? I believe in science, Kristin. I can subject my data to quantification and testing. Can anyone quantify the 'blessings from above'? No. No one can; they can't because the only thing we get from above is precipitation, which, as you know, can be quantified."

Kristin sat back; now it was her turn to be stunned. "I brought you over here to get you away from a situation that looked like it would go from bad to worse. I was trying to help you. Right now, it looks as if you're repaying my trying to help you with anger. Can I ask you why you're reacting this way? I can't figure this out from you, and I don't think I need to bear the brunt of your anger."

Something must have clicked in his head because he realized he was acting irrationally. "I'm very sorry, Kristin. I have many years of anger and heartache that just reared its ugly head, and I don't know why, but it just overtook me; I could not control it. You're right; you do not deserve to be treated like that, and I must ask you for your understanding and forgiveness. I am truly sorry; if you can find it in your heart, can you forget all of the angry things that I said? Maybe we can pick up from where we left off at the bar before Randall walked over."

"Of course, Murray, I realize that you must be in a lot of pain. We can stay here and talk for a while, or if you want, I can take you back to your car, and we can spend part of our day tomorrow talking. It's up to you, but you might be emotionally exhausted and want to wind down at your hotel. Whatever you want to do is fine with me. I do want to help you."

Murray answered, "You're too kind of a person. Thank you for understanding. You may be right. Maybe I should head back and try and calm down. I wasn't expecting that to happen tonight, and I apologize for putting you through that. Why don't you drop me off at my car, and we can catch up tomorrow? It would be nice to have your company tomorrow if you'll still have me."

His candor and heartfelt apology wholly disarmed Kristin; smiling, she said, "Let me grab my coat, and we'll be on our way."

Chapter Two
The Next Day

West Texas

The following day, Murray swung by Kristin's apartment and picked her up. They drove to a small café to have breakfast and then drove out toward their old high school. Kristin offered, "You know, I was very active in a number of activities at Travis, and every time that I came back home, they always asked me to talk to some of the young girls who were thinking of college. I have a lot of contacts there in the school office. Let's pop by and see if they'll let me give you a quick tour, sort of like a homecoming week for a couple of alums. What do you think?"

He thought about this for a second and said, "Sounds good, but can we swing up by Miller's Lake first? That's where my grandparents used to live."

"You bet. Would you like to see where you and your mother used to live? Do you remember where that was?"

"Yeah, I remember where it was. My Mom and I lived in a single-wide trailer out there by Egg City. Can you imagine growing up next to a commercial egg farm and all that you could hear all day long was the sound of chickens clucking, and all you could smell was the stench of chicken waste? That's where I grew up. After my mother died, I had the trailer demolished."

Kristin asked him, "Didn't you tell me you haven't been back here since leaving for school? Didn't you come here for your mother's funeral?"

He shook his head and snorted in disgust. "This is

where it gets ugly. My mother died as a young woman; she was forty years old. I was getting ready for my hooding ceremony when my mother died. She was supposed to come out for the ceremony when one of my cousins called me to let me know that my mother died three days ago. I couldn't believe it. I had talked to my mom no more than four or five days before that, and everything was fine. It looked as if she had a massive stroke with a significant cranial bleed, and she was dead before she hit the floor. Now here is where I will not forgive any of these cretins. I asked my cousin what the funeral plans were; I could be out there by the day's end and help plan things if necessary. My cousin told me over the phone, and I'll never forget this, he said, 'I guess you are out of the loop. Your mom was cremated. The Church won't bury her in hallowed ground. I guess that we can send you her cremains if you want them.' I could not believe it, Kristin. I was my mother's next of kin, and I would never have consented to a cremation. I don't know how that snake of a grandmother pulled it off, but as I was 'the illegitimate child of a lustful union' and my mother died without a will, my grandmother convinced her church pastor and the town magistrate, who happened to be one of the church elders; to consider my grandmother as her legitimate next of kin. She could make any and all decisions regarding my mother. So, my mother was cremated, and I never had a chance to say goodbye to her. But you see, it all goes back to that church of theirs. That church ran every single aspect of everyone's lives out here, and let me tell you something, that church was full of sick, vile people. I loathe them all."

"Are you telling me that you belonged to the Lakefront Community Church?"

Murray shook his head and laughed derisively, "Yep, that was it. They'd have their Sunday meetings and then their 'Fellowship Socials,' but we were never invited. So much for their Christian Charity."

"Murray, I had no idea that you belonged to that congregation. Those people were nuts! We belonged to the First Baptist Church, and we had a good bunch of folks there; we were always involved in helping people in our community. But you're right; the Lakefront folks had their fingers in everything going on in town. But that has tapered off a bit. Most of the people at that church are all gone now. When the oil fracking started, the energy industry in this area boomed, and with it came new businesses and new people. The demographics in this area have changed, and the 'old guard,' as it were, is not the force around here that it used to be. Of course, some of those folks are still here, but nothing like before."

Murray thought about that. "That's good, they were evil people. Look at Randall, a prime example right there. When he said he wanted to sit with us, I could only think about how those people treated me and my mom. I wanted absolutely nothing to do with him, but for some crazy reason, I could not move. Thanks for getting me out of there."

Kristin looked over at him and smiled, "You are most welcome. Turn right on this next road; it will take us towards Miller's Lake."

A few minutes later, Murray pulled off the road, sat, and looked across an open field at an old house. He got out of the car and just stood there, looking at the house. Kristin came up behind him and took his hand in hers. After some time, Kristin looked up at him and asked, "Are you doing OK?"

He stood there just looking at the house. "I don't think I could loathe anyone more than my grandparents and the rest of my mother's family. I don't know how I feel about them. I'm just empty. The world is a better place now that they're gone from it."

"You know, you said something to me last night at my apartment. You asked me if I were a believer or a Christian. I am, and I am very sorry that you were mistreated by people who profess to be Christians. Do you believe in God, Murray?"

"I used to be an anti-theist, not simply an atheist in that I did not believe in a Supreme Being, but I was also against all things religious. I hated the Christian religion, and I did not much care for people who adhered to its principles, but despite what we saw with Randall and with what I told you about my grandparents, those clowns epitomized the Christian religion to me; I have mellowed a bit as far as not caring for Christian people. I have also experienced a few things in the last few years that made me reconsider my position. My thoughts now are more like Albert Einstein's in that I do not believe in a god who takes a personal interest in the fate of individuals or the actions of people. I don't think anyone up in the clouds listens to my pleadings and takes direct action in our everyday affairs. But I have come to believe that some 'prime mover' may be involved in creating the Universe."

"But I once read something that Einstein said; I think that he said something like, 'You can live your life in one of two ways: you can believe that nothing is a miracle, or you can live your life as if everything is a miracle,'" Kristin said. "That sort of lets me know that Einstein believed in God."

"That's true, he did say that, but he also said that belief in a Deity that would be concerned with us as individuals is naïve at best," Murray countered. "We're not that important in the grand scheme of things if you think about it. I mean, *Homo sapiens sapiens* has been around for what, fewer than 100,000 years? That's a drop in the bucket. To put this into perspective, the dinosaurs walked the Earth for over 300 *million* years; now, that's biologically successful, a lot more successful than our species. But going back to your original question, I do not believe in God the way that Christians, Jews, and Muslims believe in God. I do believe there has to be some Prime Mover. Still, there is one thing that I do know: There are very few Christian people who live by the teachings of that rabbi from Palestine, and I think that the world would be a better place if Christianity did not take root in our sociological development. History has shown that the followers of Jesus are responsible for more wars and hardship than any other religion."

"I don't know about that, Murray, but look at the good that Christian people have done in the World; look at Mother Teresa, Albert Schweitzer, or Billy Graham; those are just a few examples. Christian people do a lot of good in this world!"

"True enough," Murray replied. "But Hindus do a lot

of good in this world, as do Buddhists and others. I think that people will do good regardless of their religious affiliation, but I'm more inclined to say that people will do good *despite* their religious affiliation. But why are we arguing about this? I'm just letting you know what my thoughts are. What do you say we drop all of this for now and head over to Travis Union High School? If I remember correctly, you wanted me to tell you what life was like outside of West Texas. Are you up for that?"

"You bet." She took his arm, and they walked back to the car.

They drove slowly up the long, curved driveway that led to the school's front office. Kristin had Murray pull into one of the visitor's parking spaces, and they walked up the steps to the school. Some students recognized Kristin, and they yelled out to her. Waving back to them, she whispered to Murray, "You see, I told you I had friends in high places out here." They walked into the administration office, where the secretary at the front desk, Mrs. Garber, looked up at Kristin. Mrs. Garber adjusted her glasses and then made a great show about Kristin not coming by more often.

"Thanks, Mrs. Garber, but I'm here now! Mrs. Garber, this is another alum, Murray Edgeton. We're wondering if it would be OK if Murray and I had a chance to walk around a bit and look at some of the school's improvements." Then Kristin stopped talking and looked at how Mrs. Garber looked at Murray as she cleaned her glasses and put them back up to her eyes.

"As I live and breathe, Murray Edgeton, I didn't recognize you at first. I need to get a new set of glasses. How are you? It is so nice to see you. It's been what, maybe ten years since you graduated?" Mrs. Garber asked.

Murray smiled at the elderly lady. "Hello, Mrs. Garber. Yes, ma'am, it is very nice to see you, too. Kristin, there were so many times that Mrs. Garber would help me when I was a student here. I would work in the labs after school to try and make a little extra money, but on many occasions, my mom would get stuck at work and couldn't pick me up. I tried to walk home a few times at night after working late in the labs, but some local boys would track me down and put a nice beat down on me. As I said, I was not a very popular boy at school and was a target for some of the young boys' entertainment. Mrs. Garber got me home many a time. Do you remember that Mrs. Garber?"

"I do indeed. And some of those boys came from nice families. I never understood why they did that to you, Murray." Then, looking more closely at him, Mrs. Garber continued, "But you don't look worse for wear. And you're such a scholar! Your dear mother, may God rest her soul, would brag about you whenever my late husband, Josh, and I would have lunch at Metzger's. She was so proud of you, Murray. I never had the chance to say this to you, but I am sorry that you lost your mom."

"Thank you, Mrs. Garber. Kristin, you'll never guess where the young lads who used to wail on me went to church on Sundays."

"Oh, that." Mrs. Garber said. "Yes, they should have known better, being good Christian boys. Oh well, we should not dwell on things from the past. Here, let me get you two a couple of passes, and let me tell Mr. Todd that you two are here. I'm sure he'd love to see some of our successful students."

Murray and Kristin walked out of the office and headed down the wide hallway. Murray told Kristin, "Mrs. Garber is still as sweet as ever, but did you see how she mentioned that those good Christian boys should have known better? Well, let me tell you, the 'fine families' they came from were very active in Lakefront Community Church. That's why they never got in trouble for hitting me like a pinata. It was a sanctioned activity. Unbelievable. They're probably working on a rig, plotting their next wave of mayhem. They are a bunch of jerk-offs. Oh well, let's look at some of the new improvements to these hallowed halls of academia."

They turned right and almost ran into an older man carrying an armful of papers. Kristin recognized the man, "Oops, excuse us, Mr. Walker, are you all right?"

Mr. Walker adjusted the papers in his arms, "Thank you, my dear, I'm fine, and you two are…"

"Sorry, Mr. Walker, I'm Kristin Graham. I was in your class about ten years ago. And this is Murray Edgeton, Murray, did you have Mr. Walker?"

"Oh, yes, Mr. Walker and I know each other very well, don't we, Mr. Walker?" Murray looked at the older man, and you could see him wither under Murray's glare.

"Yes, we do, I know Mr. Edgeton, or should I say, Dr. Edgeton. Murray, it is nice to see you again, and we must say that we are all very proud of you and your academic accomplishments. What brings you back here?"

"I was simply passing through on my way back home to California, and I thought I would spend a couple of days here just to see the old town again. It has been an interesting time, to say the least."

"Well, Murray," Mr. Walker continued, "I hope you will find the time to pay your respects to your grandparents while you are here. They are resting in Evergreen Park, and it would be a blessing for a grandson to pay his respects to his grandparents, who loved him so much."

Murray was amazed that the old man would say something like that. "So, you believe that my grandparents loved me? That's funny. Mr. Walker, I cannot recall a single nice thing they ever said to me. They certainly had an unusual way of showing their love and affection."

"Of course, they loved you. And they loved your mother, too. As an elder of the Church, I had the opportunity to talk with and counsel them regularly. You and your mother were a tremendous source of heartache and sorrow for your grandparents, with everything that your mother did to shame them. Consider this, Murray, even for all you and your mother did to your grandparents. Look at how well you turned out to be, a leader in your field and a respected scientist. How could you achieve that without the love and guidance from your grandparents? Something else you should consider is that your grandparents prayed non-stop that Our Lord and Savior would pity you because of who you were. You should thank Jesus for that. Every bit of success you have is due to your grandparents and a loving and merciful Lord."

Murray was looking at Mr. Walker like a biologist might look at an interesting but repulsive specimen. "Exactly what am I, Mr. Walker? And what was it that an innocent little boy could do to shame two adults? Please explain that to me. Mr. Walker, you're an elder of a church and, in your eyes, a righteous and moral man. Please let me know how an innocent child would be required to be pitied for being born. I don't believe that innocent child had much to say in the matter, do you?"

The old man was flustered and became very agitated when he answered Murray. "You know exactly what you are! You know exactly what you and your mother did. She was a Jezebel and should have received the punishment that Jezebel received, and you along with her. Now, if you two young people will excuse me, I have work to do. Good day to you both." He walked hurriedly down the hall.

"Kristin, can you see what I'm saying? When they sit there and talk down their noses at everyone who doesn't fit into their mold, how can any halfway intelligent person give any credence to their religion? They're nuts. And I have to tell you, a lot of these so-called Christian people all act the same way. It just reinforces my belief that this religion is a sham and that the world would be better without it. Can we get out of here now? I've seen enough in the last two days to confirm my thoughts on Christianity."

Kristin answered, "Sure, let's go, Murray, but can we talk later? Can we try and have dinner again? I'd hate to see you leave like this."

They both turned to walk away, "Let's just go, Kristin. We'll try dinner later, but please, let's go."

Chapter Three
Five days later

Pasadena, California

Murray sat in his office, waiting for his colleague, Ignatius Joseph, to meet with him. Dr. Joseph was a brilliant particle physicist who had researched the quark substructure of matter before his involvement with the Einstein Project. Dr. Joseph was from the southern Indian state of Kerala and was a devout Syro-Malabar Rite Catholic, a very ancient rite within the Catholic Church. Murray and Ignatius, known as "Nate," had developed a very close, albeit unlikely, friendship considering their perspectives on religion. "Hi, Nate, thanks for coming in." He greeted his friend as Nate walked into the office. "Can I get you a coffee or some tea?" Murray moved over to his conference table.

"No, thanks, I'm fine. So, how was your trip?"

Murray grabbed a cup of coffee, "It was great, thanks. I thought a lot about you while I was out there. I met a fascinating young woman on my trip who gave me some interesting insights. We spent a lot of time together; we went to the same high school but at different times, and her talks and sincerity made me think about things. She's thinking of coming out here for a trip next month, and I think you would like to meet her."

Nate got up, poured himself a cup of coffee, and asked, "What did you all talk about? You seem to be excited about it, whatever it was."

"Interestingly enough, Nate, she talked to me about

religion and forgiveness. While there, I had a couple of bizarre encounters with people from my past. Kristin, that's her name, was there when the encounters happened. I also told her a few things about my growing up and what the town was like back then.

She came from a solid Christian background and had a few simple explanations about her Christian faith. We talked at length during my second day there. We kept talking the next day, and after that, I came back home. But after talking with her, I had to go back and think about some of the things you told me. For instance, how religion and science can complement each other. And then, after what happened when Declan and Toma gave their outbrief to the team, some things that Kristin said tripped a switch. Finally, I thought about how we analyzed the sponge that Toma brought back. I couldn't even begin to explain what had happened to me. I want to discuss what you have wanted to talk with me about for years."

Nate sat there at the table, just looking at his friend. After about a minute, he asked, "What does Kristin look like?"

"She's a knock-out if that's what you're asking."

Nate laughed and then said, "That's what I figured. As your best friend, I have been witnessing to you for the last four years, to no avail, I should add. You go back home to Texas, meet a pretty young woman, and in three days, she convinces you to at least open your mind to our faith, is that right?"

"In a nutshell, that's about what happened."

Nate mused for a bit longer. "The three-day period interests me. 'Three days' has theological significance to Christians. But let me see if I can sum up the past four years for us. Because of your brainchild, the Einstein Project, we were able to demonstrate that Einstein's theory of relativity was right. Your work enabled us to access the Space-Time Continuum, and you sent a team of military special operators back into time, specifically, first-century Palestine. While there, they encountered Jesus of Nazareth. Upon their return to the present, they presented you with some very compelling evidence of who Jesus of Nazareth was. Am I correct so far?"

Murray sat there with his hands steepled in front of him and nodded in the affirmative.

Nate continued. "OK. This compelling evidence, first, the narratives provided by two very credible witnesses and second, the physical evidence, did not convince you to at least question these findings. Am I correct again?"

Murray nodded again, "Yes, Nate, you're on a roll."

"But one young woman convinced you to question these things, correct? She must be a brilliant theologian or one of the most successful evangelists of our time. Is Kristin either of these?"

Murray smiled at his friend. "Nope. She worked at the front desk at the hotel where I stayed. And one last thing, as I know that this must be on your mind, Kristin thinks my work involves validating what our engineers do at JPL. She has no idea about the Einstein Project."

"Murray, that's good. I'm glad she's in the dark about what we do, but can you see how I'm stymied by all of this? I will gladly talk with you; I'll even bring in my brother to talk with you." Nate's brother was a Catholic priest and a professor at one of the Catholic universities in Southern California. "Don't get me wrong, I'm happy to hear that you are open to a discussion, and I do want to talk with you, but after four years of hearing you say some hurtful things about my religion, something that is very personal to me, it's a bit of a shock to hear you saying what you're saying now."

"Nate, I hear you, and believe me, I can understand your skepticism. I'd be surprised if you weren't skeptical of my change of heart, but I have to let you know that Kristin talked with me about Paul, and I was interested in his story. I did a bit of research on him, and I have to say that I can see a lot of similarities between my story and Paul's. You also mentioned something about Kristin a few moments ago. You said that she must be a 'successful evangelist.' That's one of the things that I wanted to talk with you about, the first evangelists who spread the Word. How did they do what they did? Look at the impact of what those people did. Christianity is a worldwide religion with over a billion believers. How did those evangelists accomplish this? I want to discuss God, your faith, and many other things with you. Can we carve some time out of our schedules to hold our own 'mini-retreat?' I'm not joking about this, Nate; I would like to hear your thoughts."

To say that Nate was dumbfounded would be an understatement, but he was looking at his friend in a different light. "You seem sincere, Murray, and yes, of course, I would like to talk with you. My time is yours. Let me know when we can sit undisturbed for about an hour to start. Do you want to try and do something this weekend?"

"I'd like that, Nate; I'd like that quite a bit. Maybe we can take a walk in that park by your house. Let's firm this up by this Friday. Does that sound OK?" Murray asked.

"Yes, of course, Murray. I will keep my entire Saturday open for us. If you don't mind, I will call my brother and ask him a few questions. He has significant experience in dialogue with non-Christians and other folks. I want to bounce a few questions off of him. I'll call you in a bit." Nate got up from the table and headed back to his office.

As soon as he left, Murray sat back at his desk, smiled, and thought, *There's one of the pieces in place.*

*****

Murray and Nate were on the walking path in the park, discussing Murray's recent change of heart. It was a beautiful spring morning in Southern California, with a gentle breeze from the northeast over the San Gabriel Mountains. It was early enough in the morning that the shadows were still long, and a quarter moon was still visible in the western sky. Nate asked, "So when did you say your friend Kristin will head out this way for a visit? From what you've said about her and what she has been able to do to change your mind a bit, I'd like to meet this remarkable young woman."

"She'll be out around mid-May. She's never been to California and wanted to spend time on the ocean, so I have her at a condo rental in Ventura. We'll do the tourist thing for a bit, but I thought that taking her out to a smaller city might ease the shock she'll be experiencing in the LA basin. But you two have a lot in common. She looks for the good in everything. Even when she saw how brutally I was treated by those morons back in West Texas, she kept telling me that what those guys did had nothing to do with Christianity. I was impressed with her defending her faith while at the same time telling me that I needed to forgive the guys who mistreated me. And then I recall some things you told me about forgiving people. Then, what struck me was listening to Declan and Toma talk about their experiences at Calvary. I mean, something has to be there. This can't be two millennia of mass hypnosis. So, I've decided to consider at least some of what you have been trying to tell me. Do you remember before we launched the team back to first-century Palestine? You asked me if the team brought back something that proved that God does exist, and would I consider it? Do you remember that? And then I told you I would consider it, but I wasn't worried because I said, and I quote, 'there ain't nothin' there,' remember?"

Nate answered, "I remember that very clearly."

"I have to tell you, I'm not so sure that 'there ain't nothin' there,' I'm still a bit skeptical about a lot of all this, but I'm willing to listen to you, Kristin and your brother, what was his name, Anthony?"

"Yes, his name is Anthony, and I discussed your situation with him. Do you know what he said? He quoted an old line, 'Remember that St. Paul persecuted and beat Christians before he became one.' He didn't even know what you told me, that Kristin talked with you about St. Paul, and that is what caught your interest; you could identify with him."

Murray chuckled, "Yeah, me and Paul. It took a pretty powerful event to make him see the light, and the light blinded him. At this point, I'm just seeing small flashes of light."

Nate turned towards Murray and stopped, "I'm being very frank with you. I have always been honest with you and spoken the truth to you when you were determined to go down the wrong path, even when everyone else was too afraid to speak the truth to you. I'm being honest with you; I am still stunned by your change of heart, happy but stunned. I hope this is not some game you are playing. I will gladly share what I know if you truly wish to hear and learn about Christianity. I will try to be a good Christian example to you."

Murray jumped in and said, "You have been. You have always been kind and good to me. It's just that for years and years, I had been subjected to unbelievable meanness and ugliness from people who confessed to being Christians. I was also taught that it was my fault for being born an illegitimate child and that I had no place among the 'good Christian folk' in my hometown. After a while, you begin to hate God and all those who believe in Him. Kristin's quiet and simple explanation of things, combined with what you have been doing for the past four years, has made me realize that maybe I need to reevaluate things. Let me try to put your mind at rest. I am only asking to learn a bit about your faith. Baby steps, OK? Is that a deal?"

While unconvinced, Nate was touched by his friend's sincerity, "Of course, it's a deal. Just know that I am concerned about your mortal soul. I will gladly take some 'baby steps' with you." They continued to walk down the path.

"You know, Nate, the one thing that impressed me about the early Christians was their ability to, how did Kristin say it, to spread the story of Jesus. I had a chance to read up on that and those early, what would you call them, missionaries? They spread this story to almost every part of the known world at the time, from Western Europe to India. Considering what transportation and communication were like two thousand years ago, that effort was nothing short of incredible. What motivated them to do that? That is one of the questions I'd like to discuss with you."

Nate listened politely to his friend and thought about Murray's question. "You asked, 'What motivated them to do what they did?' Think of the story that they were spreading. It's the same story that Declan and Toma tried to share with you when they returned through the portal. They talked about what

Jesus had done, what Jesus had taught, and most importantly, what Jesus offered us. Salvation and eternal life. That's a story worth spreading, don't you think?"

"Yes, it is. But let me ask you a question or two. Didn't Declan and Toma say that Jesus ordered them from the cross to 'spread the Word?' Why did they hide away in monasteries if they were ordered to do that?"

"Great questions. You have to understand things from a Christian's perspective. Jesus taught us that we must 'render unto Caesar what is his and render unto God what is God's.' Declan and Toma know they are under penalty of prosecution not to disclose their mission as it is highly classified; as such, you have prohibited them from spreading the Word. Maybe they're not spreading the Word now. Maybe they're waiting for the right time. They're both Naval Officers, and they know their duty. Plus, we don't know exactly what they're doing in their monasteries. I need to tell you something else. I felt something when I talked with them before they resigned from the project. God is working through them and has greater things planned for them; we don't know what it is now, do we?"

Murray replied, "No, I guess not. I don't think I allowed them to discuss everything they had seen. I have to tell you, after what I have learned this past week, maybe I should revisit their outbrief. Maybe you and I can go over their transcript together, and maybe you can explain a few things to me."

"Sounds good. You may be reading the transcript with different eyes; I'm interested in seeing how you feel about it now. What do you think? Do you want to jog for the next fifteen minutes or so? I've got ten years on you; you should be able to keep up with me; let's go."

The walking path took them up a small hill, and they got away from the manicured landscape of the city park and into more natural vegetation. As they were jogging, Nate began to think of how similar the vegetation was in the Middle East to Southern California, the various sage plants, scrub oak, manzanita, olive trees, and wild mustard. Nate mused that he would feel very much at home in Judea during the time of Jesus.

He began to reflect on what Declan and Toma told him during their time back in the first century. His mind began to go back to the initial selection and training of the team that traveled through time.

They were heady times indeed. The research and experimentation that unlocked the secrets of the Space-Time Continuum. And then the discovery of the access portal into the continuum...

The Einstein Project Team discovered an access point into the Space-Time Continuum by researching certain astrophysical phenomena. A group of highly trained U.S. Military Special Operators became members of a "time travel team" to determine if time travel was possible. They were successful, but what happened during their trip to the past was entirely unexpected for Murray. What the time travel team experienced ran completely counter to his deeply held views of the existence of God. The time travelers tried their best to convince Murray and the other Einstein Project Team members to declassify the project so the world would learn of their discovery. The Einstein Project Team denied their request. Declan and Toma decided to leave the military and entered a Catholic monastery. Declan became a Cistercian monk, also known as the Trappists, and Toma entered the Antonian Order of St. Ormizda of the Chaldeans.

Nate tried to keep in contact with them, but none of his letters were answered. As he continued his jog with Murray, he thought of Declan and Toma. *What would they think of Murray's change of heart?* "Murray, I was wondering about something. You mentioned wanting to review Declan's and Toma's transcript again. What do you think about getting them out here again to re-brief us in person? Is that something that you might consider?"

Murray smiled to himself and then looked at Nate, "That's a great idea, but do you think you can get a hold of them? From what I remember you telling me, they're both difficult to get to, right?"

"Declan is at a monastery in South Carolina, and Toma

is at a monastery in Baghdad. Let me try and see what I can do to get a hold of them. Let's cross that bridge first, and then we can talk about who you may want to have in the meeting. Another thing, if I'm trying to get a couple of Catholic monks out of their monasteries for a meeting, it might be a good idea to bring my brother with me. His being a priest might help open a few doors for me. Do you have the budget for that?"

"Let me take care of that, Nate; in the meantime, see if you can catch up with me." Murray started sprinting towards the parking lot with Nate hot on his heels. Nate couldn't see the smile on Murray's face as Murray thought to himself, *Looks as if the second piece will be falling into place.*

Chapter Four
Early April

Mepkin Abbey, South Carolina

Brother Declan was working in the carpentry shop at Mepkin Abbey, a Trappist Monastery located near the South Carolina town of Moncks Corner, northwest of Charleston, where the two forks of the Cooper River meet. The Trappists, officially The Order of the Cistercians of the Strict Observance, are a Catholic Religious Order of Monks. There are also Trappist nuns called "Trappistines" who live in convents worldwide. Like their male counterparts, they follow the Rule of St. Benedict, the Father of Western Christian Monasticism, very closely. Declan had left the Navy a year after his mission with the Einstein Project and then joined the Trappist Order; he had been with them for almost a year. He had finished his initial candidacy and postulancy and was now in his novitiate phase of becoming a professed monk.

Brother Declan was helping one of his brothers, Brother Clement, build wooden trays and shelving systems for their mushroom farm. Another one of his responsibilities was moving all the lumber from the warehouse to the carpentry shop. Since Declan was one of the younger members of the monastery and a former world-class athlete, he had competed in the 2008 Olympics as a gymnast; his physical strength was well-suited for some of the more laborious tasks. Declan loved it. According to the Rule of St. Benedict, the monks must "live by the work of their hands," and each monastery must provide for itself and be self-supporting. Each monastery makes various products that they sell to the public. The most renowned product produced by the Trappists is their famous Trappist Beer, which is known internationally as one of the best-brewed beers in the world. But Mepkin Abbey was known for their fruit preserves, fruitcakes, honey, and, most famously, for their mushrooms. In addition to helping build the trays and shelves, Brother Declan enjoyed preparing and pasteurizing the compost. His presence at the Abbey for the past year did have a positive impact in that their mushroom farming had seen a nice uptick in their productivity, but for Brother Declan, the hard, physical work served to allow him to reflect on the most essential part of his monastic life—prayer.

The life of a monk has been characterized as one of "a steady rhythm" of prayer, worship, the study of sacred texts, and hard work to sustain themselves and their mission in God's world. A monk's daily activities can be described as being meditative. Working to achieve that meditative quiet and silence allows each monk to be more receptive to God. Brother Declan and all the monks in his community would arise each day before daybreak, and in that quiet and solitude, they would welcome the Lord back into their hearts and minds as they prepared for a new day of God's creation. Seven times daily, the monks stop their work and gather in Church to sing to Our Heavenly Father and listen to the Word of God. The most important part of each day was the Celebration of the Holy Eucharist. As night would fall at the end of each day, the monks would retire to their cells, surrendering themselves to God's mercy for the night until they would welcome Him back the next morning.

It was in this rhythm that Brother Declan found peace. This life of prayer gave significant meaning to his life. In his letters to his parents, he often joked that his spiritual exercises were for him, "BUD/S for the soul," referring to "Basic Underwater Demolition/SEALs," the unbelievably physically demanding initial training for the U.S. Navy SEALs. During the early morning hours of "The Grand Silence," Brother Declan focused all his mental energies on contemplating the sublime mysteries of God. He found this effort to focus his entire mind extremely demanding, but he found that each day, he became much more receptive to God. He also found that this spiritual training made him much more aware of the presence of God in every aspect of his life.

And one of his greatest prayers throughout his daily activity was to ask God for guidance. Brother Declan had stood at the foot of the Cross on Calvary as Jesus of Nazareth was crucified. At the zenith of Jesus' agony on the Cross, He looked down at Declan and Toma and spoke to them. Jesus knew what brought Declan, Toma, and the other team members to Calvary. Jesus commissioned them, as He would later commission His Apostles, to spread the Good News of Salvation to the people of their own time. Declan and Toma tried to have themselves released from their confidentiality agreement, but they were not released. Resigning his officer's commission, Declan felt drawn to serve God in a life of prayer, so he joined the Trappists. A year earlier, he had the rare opportunity to communicate by mail with his friend and teammate, Toma. They joked that Declan was more like Moses in that he could not speak, but Toma was more like Aaron, who had the gift of communicating clearly and convincingly. Declan discussed with Toma that while Declan was not involved with spreading the Word of God to the outside world, he was praying for the world, which was sorely needed. But every night, at the close of the day, he would ask God what He wanted of him. He knew that the answer would come in God's time, not his, but one day in early spring, there was a hint as to what God's answer may be.

Father Abbot Blaise called for Brother Declan one morning to meet with him in the Abbot's office. Entering the office, Brother Declan greeted the Abbot, "Good morning, Father Abbot."

"Yes, yes, good morning, Brother Declan. I trust that all is well with you. How is the repair of our greenhouse coming along? Please, have a seat."

Sitting down, Declan answered, "It is coming along

very well, Father. Brother Ephraim is an amazing carpenter. He can do more with an axe, a hammer, and a chisel than most carpenters can with a shop full of power tools."

"He is amazing, isn't he? Indeed. Declan, listen, my son, I received a most interesting phone call today from the Jet Propulsion Laboratory in Pasadena, California. A Dr. Ignatius Joseph is asking of you. He asked me permission if he could come out here and meet with you. I know you were in the Navy before you came to us here. The Navy does not work with the Jet Propulsion Laboratory, do they? Do you know what this is about?"

"Yes, Father, I do."

The Abbot nodded his head. "This Dr. Joseph asked if he could see you as soon as possible. He said that he was traveling with his brother, a bi-ritual priest, Latin Rite, and Syro-Malabar Rite, and that his brother would enjoy concelebrating with our other priests here and me. I would enjoy learning some of the Syro-Malabar Rubrics... I'm sorry, I'm getting a bit far afield here. Before I grant Dr. Joseph permission to meet with you, I need to ask you if it is acceptable for you to meet with someone from the outside. Would this meeting with Dr. Joseph be something you are amenable to, or shall I tell them that you are not receiving anyone?"

"Thank you, Father. Yes, Dr. Joseph is a very devout man. I have not met his brother, Father Joseph, but he is a professor at Thomas Aquinas College in Southern California. Yes, Father, I would like to meet with him if that is acceptable to you."

"Of course, my son, shall we invite them to stay with us? We are known for our hospitality, aren't we?"

"Father Abbot, I think that they would enjoy that very much. Dr. Joseph is one of the world's most brilliant physicists, and I think he would enjoy being here for a time to feel God's presence in our silence. Thank you again. Now, with your permission, may I return to work?"

"Please do, and thank you for coming. Now please kneel for my blessing. Benedicat te omnipotens Deus, Pater,

Filius, et Spiritus Sanctus,"

"Amen." Brother Declan then returned to work thinking to himself, *What in the world is going on? Why does Nate want to see me?* That question nagged him until that evening when he prayed in his cell. And then, in a rare moment of non-charitable thinking, he thought, *I bet that Murray is up to something.*

*****

Brother Declan continued with his weekly routine until he received notice that Father Abbot Blaise wanted to have him join him and two guests in the Visitors' Center. It was difficult for Declan to keep his interest and excitement in check, but he displayed an air of equanimity as he walked into the Visitors' Center. As he walked in, he saw Nate dressed casually in a sports coat and a pair of chinos, and sitting next to him was his brother, Friar Anthony, in his brown Capuchin Franciscan Habit. Nate was all smiles as he walked up to Declan and embraced him warmly. "How good it is to see you again, Deck, or should I say, Brother Declan? Let me look at you. Monastic life agrees with you. Brother Declan, please let me introduce you to my brother, Anthony."

Brother Declan extended his hand to Nate's brother, "Friar Anthony, welcome to Mepkin Abbey. It is finally nice to meet you. I remember how Nate spoke of you all the time."

Reverend Father Anthony Joseph, O.F.M. Cap, shook hands with Declan, "Brother Declan, well, let me tell you, Nate talked about you non-stop all the way out from LAX. It is a pleasure to finally meet you, too."

"Thank you, Father, and I believe you and Nate have met Father Abbot Blaise?" With all of the introductions complete, Father Abbot Blaise and Friar Anthony went to the Abbot's office while Nate and Declan had a chance to visit. Declan asked Nate to walk through the monastery's gardens where they could be alone to talk. Declan still had no idea why Nate came out, but he felt it had to do with the Einstein Project. However, regarding their talking, there is a broad misconception that Trappist Monks take a vow of silence and are not allowed to talk, but that is not the case. There are certain areas in the monastery where talking is prohibited, for example, in common hallways or the church. Monks receive visitors and relatives, and during their visits, the monks will converse. But it is the topic of "idle talk" that is discouraged. So, as Nate and Declan were walking along the garden pathways, they could talk at length.

"Deck, you're probably wondering why I'm here, but I would imagine that that is a bit of an understatement."

Declan had a chance to laugh out loud, "You could say that, yeah, I've been wondering what's going on, but I have a sneaking feeling that our dear Dr. Edgeton has something to do with this."

Nate smiled at his friend, "It's not what you think. There may be a chance that Murray may have had a change of heart."

Declan stopped and touched Nate's shoulder, "Excuse me if I don't jump on board with that right yet. You have to remember what he said to all of us in our outbrief. He couldn't have been more insulting to us if he tried, and you have to remember, many of the Einstein Project Team members were interested in what we were saying. I do not contradict what you're saying, but I don't trust Murray."

Nate was quiet for a moment, "I know how frustrated you must be after what you went through and how he treated you. But I'd like you to hear me out. Is that OK?"

"Of course, Nate. You came all this way, and I don't think you would have done it if you didn't have something important to tell me; what's going on?"

"Let me preface what I'm going to say by telling you that, like you, I'm a bit skeptical about what Murray told me, but he may be sincere; he does appear to be. Several months back, Murray had seemed very angry with everything. He did not confide in me, nor do I believe he confided in anyone else; at least, no one at the JPL has said anything. Then, in early March, he took some time off and went back to West Texas. He came back, and I saw him the following week. We had a nice long talk.

It seems that he met several people from his past while he was back there. The people he met were the same group of people who treated him so horribly when he was growing up and who turned him against God and all things religious, but while he was there, he met a young woman. From what I can gather from what he told me, this young woman is a fellow believer in Christ, and she apparently had a huge impact on him. Murray said that this young woman has caused him to rethink his position on a number of issues, namely, his complete denial of God. The way that he explained it is that after talking to this woman, her name is Kristin, an appropriate name for this young woman, he began to reflect on all of our talks together about how religion and science are not mutually exclusive. He then told me he was thinking of the outbrief you and Toma gave the group. He said that he has to reconsider what you two said. He and I later met and had a nice walk through a city park in my community. During that time, Murray asked me more questions, but he seemed very interested in how Christianity spread in the first century. But he did bring up an interesting point. He said that you and Toma said in your brief that you two were commissioned by Jesus from the Cross to spread the Word of God to the people of your time. If you two were indeed ordered by Jesus to spread the Word, why are you, as Murray said, 'hiding away in a monastery?' I think that that's a fair question."

Declan continued walking in silence, just thinking about what Nate said. "I can't talk for Toma, even though he and I write to each other when we can. With the war and turmoil that are going on in Iraq, it's tough to get through to him. But speaking for myself, I struggle with that question all the time. Every night when I am alone in my cell, I ask Our Heavenly Father to please let me know what He wants of me. Am I spreading God's Word the way His Son asked me to? Am I frustrating His will? I don't know, but I feel as if I am. Remember what St. Francis said? He said, 'Preach the Gospel daily, speak only when necessary.' Through my hard work and example to my brothers and the visitors we receive here, am I spreading the Gospel? I hope so, but I feel God pulling at me.

One of the things I've done here is study Latin, not ecclesiastical Latin, but the Latin spoken in the Roman Empire. I thought that with my learning Aramaic and Classical Greek during our team training and as I learned Spanish growing up, I had enough language skills under my belt. But something was telling me to learn Latin. Is that God telling me something? It may be. Is He telling me that I may be doing something else for Him? It may be. All that I know is that after six years as a SEAL and then the two years with the Einstein Project, I had to get away from the world after what I had seen, but I could not leave God. This, to me, presented the best opportunity. Lately, however, I have felt as if I am being pulled back into something. Your coming here confirms that for me." They walked for a few minutes in silence, and then Declan continued, "So, what brings you here besides coming here to tell me that Murray has had a change of heart? There has to be something more than that. What is it, Nate? What does he want? I know that he is behind this."

Nate was pleasantly surprised at how perceptive Declan was. He knew that the monastery had changed him and that Declan going to the monastery was part of God's plan. "Declan, Murray is asking that you come back, both you and Toma, to present your findings and your experiences in first-century Palestine once again. He is willing to hear what you both briefed us on. What I'm praying for is that he will petition to declassify your mission so that we can proclaim to the world who Jesus is, this time with incontrovertible proof. Could this be what Our Lord asked, for you and Toma to spread the Word to the people of our time? This could be what God wants of you. Deck. I am humbled by His choosing me to bring this message to you."

Declan stopped and looked at his friend, "This is a lot to consider. Can you give me some time to think about this?"

"Father Abbot Blaise has offered to put Anthony and me up for a week. Do you think that you can let us know your answer by then?"

Declan thought about this and then answered, "Nate, you are asking me to leave the Abbey. I have a home here; my brothers are here, and I love them." The anguish on Declan's face was visible. He was torn between what he had grown to love and what he felt was God pulling him. "Let me pray on this and talk with Father Abbot Blaise. I will let you know in a week. Let's head back to the Church. It's time for prayer." Nate and Brother Declan walked back towards the Visitors' Center.

Late that afternoon, Nate and his brother, Friar Anthony, joined the monks for Vespers and Benediction. Nate and Father Anthony then retired to their guest rooms as the monks returned to their cells to prepare for bed. In his cell, Brother Declan was deep in contemplative prayer. By the time he was ready for sleep, he felt that God may have answered him.

Later in the week, Declan took a break from his routine to meet with Nate and walk through the grounds again. Declan said, "I have to let you know that I have told no one outside of our Project Team what we did, but you are asking me to do something that is tearing me apart. I need to talk with Fr. Abbot to let him know about my past. I realize our work has the highest classification level, but I need guidance on this. I know that my telling Father Abbot anything will not go any further than the two of us. If I am to do what I think I am going to do, I owe this to my Abbot to let him know why I may leave my home. Can you understand this, Nate?"

"Of course I do, Deck, and if I were in your shoes, I would do the same thing. But I have to tell you, I am sorry that I had to cause you so much internal strife. I can see how you could come to love it here. We do not get much silence in our hectic world, but you all enjoy the silence for most of your day. I envy you all for that, although I know that envy is a sin. This time with you here at the Abbey has proven so rewarding and worth it. I should recommend this to Murray. Fr. Abbot Blaise told me that they welcome people of all faiths to visit here, even those without faith. What do you think? Should I tell Murray to consider a retreat here?"

Declan laughed, "The buildings are all very well built, structurally and seismically sound. I think that the Abbey could withstand a visit from him." Laughing with each other, they headed back for prayer. After their mid-day prayer, Brother

Declan asked Fr. Abbot Blaise if he could schedule some time to meet with him. The Abbot agreed, and they were to meet the next day.

*****

Brother Declan met Father Abbot in his office the following day after Mass. The Abbot knew that there was something on Brother Declan's mind. It was evident that Dr. Joseph had discussed something with him that was causing a tremendous amount of anxiety in the young novice's soul. Father Abbot Blaise invited Brother Declan to come in and have a seat. "Good morning, my son. I trust you are having a nice visit with your friend, Dr. Joseph, and his brother?"

"Yes, Father, it has been wonderful to see my old friend. And you, Father, have you had a chance to discuss things with Friar Anthony? I know that you and Friar Anthony have been concelebrating Mass together. Did you have the opportunity to learn any of the Syro-Malabar Rite rubrics from him?"

The Abbot replied, "Yes, he has invited me to attend Mass with him at St. Thomas Church in Santa Ana, California. He knows I do not travel much, but it is a standing invitation. He is a wonderful priest and friar; I am happy to have met him. But tell me, my son, I can tell that something has been bothering you. Is there something that you need to share with me?"

"Yes, Father Abbot, there is. I must confess that I have not been completely honest with you."

The Abbot reached over and put his stole on, the symbol of his office as a priest, "Continue, my son."

"Forgive me, Father, for I have sinned. It has been one week since my last confession. I have acted non-charitably toward others, and as I said earlier, I have not been completely honest with you or the Novice Master."

The Abbot interrupted and asked, "Are you here under false pretenses, my son?"

"No, Father, not false pretenses. I came here as a

devout Catholic with no outstanding obligations. I am also convinced that Our Heavenly Father called me here, so no, Father, I did not come here under false pretenses. You know of my professional background as a U.S. Naval Officer and a SEAL. That is all true. But what I did not tell you or the Novice Master is that while I was in the Navy, I was involved in a highly secret and classified mission. Under penalty of law and subject to severe sanctions, I have not been able to disclose my mission to anyone outside of our project team."

The Abbot asked, "Am I correct in assuming Dr. Joseph was involved in this project?"

"Yes, Father, he was and still is. When you asked me about Nate, Dr. Joseph, coming out here, you asked me if the Navy had any dealings with the Jet Propulsion Laboratory. I did not answer you. That is a sin of omission. But I was still torn between my legal obligation and my relationship with you. I talked with Nate and told him that I have to tell you about my past as it has a bearing on what I need to do now. Father Abbot, what I am going to tell you is going to strain credulity, but everything that I will tell you is true. The people at the JPL, Dr. Joseph included, have embarked on a most incredible project. They have uncovered some of the most amazing secrets of the Universe. My degree at the Naval Academy was in Physics, and I am still in disbelief as to how those geniuses at the JPL accomplished what they did. The driving force behind this project is Dr. Murray Edgeton, the most gifted physicist on the planet. Unfortunately, he is a very forceful anti-theist and atheist. From what I understand, some people in his past blamed him for being born illegitimate and ostracized him and his mother for his whole life. From what I can gather, it was a very scarring and terrible ordeal. Dr. Edgeton blames the world's troubles on those of us who are believers.

"Getting back to the team, they significantly researched Einstein's Theory of Relativity. The bottom line, Father, is that this team opened up a portal to travel through time. I was part of the team that was selected to travel through time. The project team at the JPL sent us back to the time of Jesus' crucifixion. I was there when Lazarus was raised from the dead. I was there when Our Lord stood before Pilate, and I saw Our Lord crucified. Father, I spoke with Our Lord and He gave me what we call in the military my 'marching orders.'

The Abbot looked at Brother Declan with a look of his being wholly mystified. He stared at Declan, who continued.

"But let me get back to the mission as the JPL project team planned. The mission purpose, as defined, was to demonstrate that time travel was possible. We were to bring back artifacts proving that we traveled through time. But we found out through back channels that the real reason why Dr. Edgeton wanted us to go back there was to 'prove' that Jesus of Nazareth was nothing more than some Jewish preacher from a backwater province. If we were to come back and claim that Jesus was a minor preacher from the hinterlands, Dr. Edgeton would release our findings to the scientific community and the world."

Father Abbot sat there pensively for a moment and then said, "But it appears that you brought back evidence contrary to what this Dr. Edgeton wanted. Am I correct in saying that?"

"Yes, Father, we did. We brought back several artifacts with significant archeological value, but we were able to bring back something even more astounding. When Our Lord was upon the Cross, and He cried out that He was thirsty, the Centurion, his name was Gaius Valerius Crispinus, took a sponge soaked in wine and offered it to Him. After he had finished, my colleague Toma, who is currently a monk in Iraq, took the sponge and put it in his bag. That bag was transported back with us. It contained a sample of Our Lord's DNA. It was checked at one of the government labs and demonstrated properties that had never been seen before in human DNA.

"Even with all of this physical evidence in addition to our sworn testimony, the Einstein Project Team decided to maintain an air of complete secrecy on what our time travel team discovered, just as we knew they would. I became so frustrated, personally and professionally, that I decided to leave my work and come here and search for peace. As I told my friend Nate, I had to escape the world and the evil in it. But, Father, I have been feeling something, something telling me that I need to finish what was started. Nate came here with his brother to talk with me. It appears that Dr. Edgeton has had a change of heart and wants to have Toma and me come back and re-present our findings. Nate's coming here confirms what I have been feeling. Father, I am very conflicted and do not know what to do now."

The Abbot touched Brother Declan on the shoulder. "Do you want to leave the Abbey? As a novice, you are free to leave at any time. You may leave and come back if you so wish. If God wants you to come back, that's a discussion for another time.

"What you have told me, my son, is astounding, to say the least. It confirms what we already knew as Christians, but this work confirms it *scientifically*. But what do you think Dr. Edgeton wants to do at this point? You know this man. Do you think that his motives are sincere? Do you think that his change of heart is genuine?"

He looked up at his Abbot, "I do not know, Father. Nate thinks he is, but I would have to see Murray myself to make a call on that. But I must go back. I have this sinking feeling in my soul that my coming here may have frustrated the will of God. I cannot do that again."

Father Abbot Blaise smiled. "No, you did not frustrate the will of God. Don't you think that God put you here for a reason? God has a plan for all of us. He has you marked to do something amazing. That is why God has had your life's path as it has played out. He wanted you here at this point in time to make this decision. Open your heart, Brother Declan. You will see that God will nudge you the right way." With that, the Abbot smiled at Declan with a knowing air.

"What has God planned for you, Father Abbot?" asked Declan.

"That's the simplest question: He put me here to be with you at this time and place. He put me here to train you to be more receptive to God; my work is done. Now, let us continue this Sacrament of Penance. Are you sorry for your sins, and can you resolve yourself to sin no more?"

Brother Declan looked at his Abbot and replied, "Yes, Father, I am."

"Then please make your Act of Contrition." The Abbot stood over Brother Declan and put his hands on Declan's head. Declan recited the ancient Act of Contrition. As soon as he was done, Father Abbot Blaise recited the formula of absolution, "God, the Father of mercies, through the death and resurrection of His Son, has reconciled the world to Himself and sent the Holy Spirit among us for the forgiveness of sins; through the ministry of the Church may God give you pardon and peace, and I absolve you from your sins in the name of the Father, and of the Son, and of the Holy Spirit."

Blessing himself, Declan responded, "Amen."

Father Abbot then asked, "When must you leave? I am sure your brothers would enjoy wishing you a safe journey and God's blessings upon you as you embark on this new journey in your life. Do you think that you can stay one more night with us?"

"Yes, Father, I will tell Nate and Friar Anthony that we will leave in the morning. Both Nate and Friar Anthony told me that they enjoyed being here. I was concerned that they would not take too well to our vegetarian diet, but they both laughed. They said that as long as we had lentils, beans, and rice, they would be happy."

"Then let us go into Church and offer our prayers to God." The Abbot and Brother Declan then walked back into the cloisters.

Chapter Five
Mid-April

Pasadena, California

Dr. Joseph and Declan walked into Dr. Edgeton's office at their appointed time. Murray got up and warmly greeted the two of them. "Nate, Declan, please sit down. What might I get you, coffee, tea, some juice?"

Nate and Declan declined, and Murray continued, "Nice to see you, Declan, but I have a feeling you might be less than thrilled to see me. Am I correct in that?"

"Well, I didn't leave here under the best terms," Declan pointed out. "And to be completely frank, I'm more intrigued by being back here than anything, and I have a lot of questions rolling around in my brain housing group."

Murray lifted his arms with both hands out in a gesture of mock surrender, "I understand, Declan, believe me, I understand. But first things first, what was it like living as a contemplative monk? Not that long ago, I would have laughed at someone who pursued that life, but now I find myself asking *why* a man or woman would follow that path to God, not questioning their motives, but honestly asking why a person would decide to live a life like that. No judgment, as they say, but I would be truly interested in finding that out."

Declan sat back and reflected on what Murray just said. "Dr. Edgeton-"

Murray interrupted, "Please, Declan, please make it 'Murray.'"

"Thank you. Murray, you said something a few seconds ago, which brings me to my first question, you said 'why someone would follow that path to God.' When I was here, you never mentioned the name 'God' or acknowledged that there would be a path to God. To me, it sounds as if you're acknowledging the possibility of the existence of God. Am I reading that right?"

Murray smiled at Nate and then at Declan, "You're reading it right. Declan. I will tell you that earlier, well, I should say, for almost my entire life, I have been shaking my fist at God, denying Him at every opportunity, and showing unbridled and open disgust to believers. But something happened recently that has awakened a, how can you say it, a 'questioning' about the existence of God? Don't count me among the flock yet, but please consider that I have had a life-changing experience."

"In all fairness, Declan," Nate jumped in, "Murray told me straightaway that he is still 'skeptical' about all of this but wants to sit down and talk to us about our faith journey. Murray knows because I told him I am a bit skeptical, but there is nothing wrong with honest skepticism."

"None indeed," Murray continued. "As Nate may have told you, I met an extraordinary woman, Kristin, who showed me what being a Christian was all about. She talked about love and forgiveness after I had experienced the trauma of my childhood all over again. Maybe it's maturity, or maybe it's a sense of inquiry, I don't know, but what I do know is that I have decided that maybe I should be a bit more flexible in my thinking and a bit more open to at least learning something about Christianity. As I said, I'm not a member of the flock; I'm on the outside, but at least I'm looking in."

Nate and Declan looked at each other and shook their heads, not in dismissal, but more of a feeling of "wow," then they adjusted their positions as they sat on the couch. Declan replied, "I am glad to hear that you're open to learning something. I also like how you said you're outside of the flock but willing to look in on the rest of us. That's an interesting visual, Murray." Murray smiled at that, and Declan continued,

"But you have an entire group of people who could answer your questions better than Nate and I could. There are schools of Theology all over the LA basin and even bible study groups in various churches all over Pasadena. Have you considered asking them for some basic info or a basic catechism? Why bring me back?"

Murray leaned forward in his chair, "I could have done as you said, get some scholar or religious studies expert out here to talk with me, but how many of them have traveled back in time to where Jesus ministered? Here's the thing, Declan, you have first-hand knowledge of what happened: you, Toma, and the rest of your team. Plus, we here with the Einstein Project have information that no one else does. But let me cut to the chase. Here's why we invited you back here, I would like you to present your findings to the group again. Nate and I talked about this earlier. I said I wanted to review the entire transcript and the "after-action report" you put together. Then Nate asked if we could get you and possibly Toma to come back, meet with the team, and give your briefs. We could read the transcripts ourselves, but I would prefer to hear them in person; a transcript won't be able to answer a question in real-time or explain something. You can."

Declan thought, "If I understand you, and please take this the right way, you want me, and hopefully, Toma, to re-brief you on our mission, and this may be part of your journey to understanding Christianity. Am I right so far?"

"Yes, you are, Declan, partially, but there's more to it than that. Understand that due to my hatred of the Christian faith, I did not think objectively of what you and Toma presented to us; I was looking at everything through the prism of a young boy who made up his mind early in life that there is no God." Murray stopped and composed himself while he drank some of his coffee. "As scientists, we are trained to consider every possibility, you know that from your background in physics, but what I did countered the basic concept of the scientific method; I refused, selfishly I should add, to consider anything that you said. But now, you may find that instead of

53

looking at and analyzing your transcript and your presentation through the prism of a young boy, I may be looking at things through a different pair of eyes. At least that's what Nate thinks."

Nate again jumped into the conversation, "I remember saying that to you. That's when we decided that we should try to get you and Toma back here so that we can revisit everything. Declan, what do you think?"

Declan thought about this for a bit. "Murray, you have to forgive me for being skeptical. I am reminded of the passage from Scripture about the sower and the seed. Some seeds will fall on rocky ground with rapid growth, but since they have no roots, they wither and die very quickly. I am being very blunt with you, but as you said, we must consider every possibility. Is it possible that you do have a sincere desire to learn about God, or is this the proverbial 'flash in the pan,' the energetic plants that grow, but without solid grounding, they wither and die? I don't know, Murray. I am not trying to impugn your motives or judge you; I have to give some thought to this. I think that the better way to say it is that I have to try and wrap my head around this."

Murray answered quickly, "I understand how you feel; I was not the nicest person to you when you came back. We all agreed that a little honest skepticism is a good thing, which it is, but please don't dismiss everything. Do you know what got me thinking about this? Kristin told me about the evangelist Paul. I read up on him and became fascinated with his story, and then Nate followed up with his brother, Father Anthony, and he said something interesting. Do you remember that, Nate?"

Nate replied, "I told my brother about Murray's interest in the faith and my skepticism about his about-face. Anthony related that old line, 'Remember that St. Paul persecuted and beat Christians before he became one.'"

Murray continued, "Declan, I would never presume to put myself in the same league as Paul, but recall how after Saul's conversion, those Saul came to persecute were very skeptical of him. But Saul, now Paul, worked hard to convince them. I'm not trying to convince you of my sincerity; I told you I'm on the outside, but I have decided to look in. As I said to Nate, can you two help me with some 'baby steps'? That's all that I'm asking for at this time."

Murray's sincerity moved both Nate and Declan; moved, but not entirely convinced. "Murray," Declan said, "I have to tell you I am touched by what you are saying. It is not for me to judge anyone's faith or even their lack of faith. My duty as a Christian is to help you if you need my help. If you'd like help with baby steps, I'm all in, but I'm also interested in working with you and Nate on revisiting our mission briefing since this appears to be part of your journey. When were you considering doing this, and whom did you want to attend?"

"I was hoping to get our briefing done as soon as we can get the right people involved and set everything up. Jill McAllister is one of the people I need to reach out to; you may remember her. Her background in chaos theory will help answer a few of my questions." Nate and Declan looked at each other, thinking, *"Chaos theory?"* Then Murray continued, "But one of the important things that we need to address is how to get Toma back here. Things are volatile in that part of the world right now, and this is another reason you were asked to come back here; I need to ask you to go to Iraq and get Toma out."

Declan thought about this. He wondered how Murray would get Toma out of a volatile region, and he had his answer. He looked at Murray and Nate, "What do you propose, gentlemen?"

Murray replied, "In all fairness, Nate and I discussed getting Toma out of Iraq, but we never discussed anything concrete. I thought about your background in combat and covert operations and thought you would be well suited for this."

Declan said, "I have spent the last year living as a contemplative monk. My combat days are over. I went to the Abbey searching for peace, and I found it. Part of my journey is that since my time in the Abbey, I have embraced pacifism; I cannot take another person's life."

"I'm sorry, Declan, I'm not explaining myself very well. I do not anticipate your going to Iraq on a military mission, but more of an 'undercover' operation. You have to make contact with Toma; I already have several leads regarding his present whereabouts. I was hoping you could let him know our plan and convince him to return. This is something that I don't believe can be accomplished by phone or email; this is something that would best be accomplished in person. Plus, I'm finding that trying to write to Toma or email him has proven to be next to impossible. Have you had much luck communicating with Toma?"

He shook his head, "I've received one letter in the past year."

"So, you do know that it is difficult. Declan, if you successfully convince Toma to come back, I need your help getting him out of the country. Movement of people in and out of Iraq right now is difficult at best, even though the war is over and ISIS has been somewhat neutralized. If Toma is found to be an American citizen, some low-level bureaucrats might make it difficult to leave. We think the two of you former Navy SEALs working together would have a good chance of getting out of the country unscathed. I was thinking of having you go to Iraq under the cover as a Spanish businessman. Specifically, a businessman from Catalonia, as I know that you speak Catalan and your mother is from Barcelona. Your cover could be a Spanish businessman involved in underwater construction, dredging, and salvage operations. Your purpose for going to Iraq is to offer your innovative services to perform dredging work on the *Tigris*. The *Tigris* River runs from the north past Mosul, where Toma may be. I can get you letters of introduction to various salvage companies in Iraq. Your cover will be pretty solid."

Declan asked, "Who have you been working with on this? I thought we were keeping this in-house, but it sounds like you have done some work outside of the JPL."

"Good point, but actually, our head of internal security is a retired Special Agent from the FBI. During his tenure at the

FBI, he worked with the CIA overseas in an operation involved in rescuing kidnapped U.S. hostages. He also spent a few years as an FBI agent assigned to the CIA, so he has some experience in such situations. We can meet with him if you like, but as of now, this is all the initial planning I'm talking about. I have to tell you that our head of internal security has a wide range of contacts and lots of connections. He has assured me that he can get you and Toma in and out with no or very few problems."

Declan seemed satisfied with this. "What's my cover name going to be? Can I pick my own?"

Murray and Nate laughed at this, and then Murray answered, "I think that's the least we can do for you; go ahead; what do you think?"

"Easy, I'll use my middle name, Antoni, and my mother's last name, Coixet i Ocuna. Antoni Coixet i Ocuna, a typical Catalonian name."

After Declan had returned to his hotel for the evening, Murray asked Nate to meet him in his office. "Nate, thanks for all of the work that you have done to get Declan to come and meet with us. I hope we can work this out to get Toma back here, but we'll have to see. I didn't mean to blindside you with my talking about his heading to Iraq to get Toma back here; I did all that background work when you were in South Carolina. But I think Declan is willing to reengage with us and give his brief to the team. Speaking of which, I need to see if I can get Jill back here. We were not on the best of terms when she left here, but I'm hoping she will hear me out."

Nate asked, "Have you talked to her since she left to return to Georgia? And for my information, why do you think she needs to be back here? You mentioned something about chaos theory; I'm a bit puzzled; is there something else going on?"

"I don't know where this is going right now, but I want Jill to talk about the time travelers' experiences in Judea. What if they had done something to affect events from the past? How far-reaching could that unintended consequence be?"

Nate was quiet, and then he asked, "Are you thinking of accessing the portal again? Is that what this is all about? Level with me, Murray, what is really on your mind?"

"I'm just brainstorming with myself, that's all. We learned so much from the last mission. One of the things that I learned was that it's better to have all of the right people at the table in the beginning to flesh out a better plan. That's why I want Jill here. I will try to reach her later today, but I'm in a tough position. I'm going to ask someone to help me after I treated them so terribly. What's that old Brooks and Dunn song, 'We'll burn that bridge when we get there'? I feel like I've burned a pretty good-sized bridge with Jill. Damn, I can be so stupid at times."

Nate chuckled. "You said it, Boss, not me. Anything else? If not, I'm going to go ahead and head home."

"No, we're done, and thanks again for everything, Nate. None of this could have been done without you. See you tomorrow morning."

After Nate left, Murray thought about his conversation with him. Accessing the portal was precisely what he had in mind, but the reason why was not something that Nate or Declan would approve of; he had to try to deflect Nate's suspicions about this. Secondly, he had to think about how he would approach Jill. They had been quite the item a couple of years ago. They had dated for about a year, but they were very discreet. Jill was a brilliant mathematician whose field of study was chaos theory. Jill and Murray were both very nice-looking, but as their primary focus in life was on their work, they never realized how physically attractive they were. They never took the time to develop personal relationships; they thought that "romantic entanglements" distracted them from their professional pursuits. They worked together on the Einstein Project and then spent time together out of town during a meeting at the Lawrence Livermore National Laboratory. They met for dinner one evening, where they had the opportunity to open up to each other about their personal lives. One thing led to another, and together, they learned the joy romantic entanglements bring. They stopped seeing each other after that one year together, and their break was less than amicable. She resigned from the Einstein project before the time travel team embarked on their mission, but Murray would need her involvement in what he was planning next; he just needed to find a way to approach her and ask for her help.

Later that afternoon, he called Jill. She was surprised to hear from him, but she was cordial. "Hello, Murray, what a surprise to hear from you. How are things going for you?"

"Pretty well, Jill, how are you? How are things out there in the Peach State?"

She laughed, "All is well out here in the Penal Colony. So, to what do I owe this phone call, Murray? What's up?"

"I imagined that you would be surprised to get a call from me. I half expected you not to answer once you saw that it was me calling. Thank you for taking my call. There is a lot to talk about. You left Pasadena right before things got interesting—"

Jill broke in, "You know, I always wondered how the project went. I tried to find out from some of the old team, but everyone reminded me that we were all obligated to maintain confidentiality about the project. Will you be able to let me know what happened?"

"To be honest, that's why I'm calling. Is there a chance that you'd be willing to head out this way? I can schedule you on a flight out here and back, and we can put you up locally. Would you be able to come out if I could give you a bit of a heads-up? You know I can't discuss the project over the phone; I don't know how secure our phones are."

"Classes are out in about five to six weeks. I'm not teaching this summer," she was teaching mathematics at the University of Georgia, "so I will have some free time. But is it pressing? Do you want me to see if I can come out earlier? Why, what's going on?"

Murray was looking at his calendar on his computer, "We're waiting for one of our team members to get some work done in the Mid-East. Once he returns, we'll be able to schedule our meeting. Our team member has yet to leave but should be on his way within the week. You know, five to six weeks might work."

"Yeah, but now you've got my interest piqued. Can you at least give me a hint about what's going on? I can come out for a long weekend to discuss this with you preliminarily if you are OK with that. I do find myself thinking of you from time to time."

Murray's stomach started doing flip-flops. "That might work, but besides school, do you have any other obligations that would hold you back from flying out at a moment's notice?"

Jill was smiling, "Hmmm, what are you asking, Murray? Are you asking if I have a special *friend* that I might have to consider before I jet off to Southern Cal?"

"Well, no, I mean, uh, not really, it's none of my business, but for planning purposes, I just need to see if your schedule is flexible enough to fly out on short notice," he felt like an idiot.

She was still smiling, "Planning purposes, of course. Actually, I am seeing someone, but he would understand if I had to attend a conference on the coast. He knows that I worked with the government on a sensitive project, but that's the extent of what he knows of my time with the Einstein Project. Don't worry, I can get away on short notice if I need to, OK?"

"Thanks, Jill. Once you see what's going on, you will be on board. It will be nice to see you again, so I hope to catch up soon; bye, Jill."

"Goodbye to you also, Murray. I'm looking forward to hearing about this project." When she put her phone down, she sat at her breakfast bar and asked her cat, "What was that all about? He didn't sound like himself. He wouldn't call me out of the blue like that; I bet something big must be up. I have Nate's phone number around here somewhere. I'm going to give him a call tomorrow."

The following morning, right before noon, Jill called Nate at his office, "Hi, Nate, it's Jill McAllister. Do you have a moment to chat?"

"Hello, Jill! So nice to hear from you. Of *course,* I have a moment to chat with you; how are you?"

She smiled, "I'm doing well, Nate, and I hope you and your family are all doing well. I would hazard to guess that you're a bit surprised to hear from me, or is that putting it mildly?"

"A bit surprised, yeah, of course, but I take it that you heard from Murray?"

Jill chuckled, "So, you're in on this too? What's going on, Nate? I was floored when Murray called me. He told me he wanted me to head out to Pasadena and meet with you and the team. Very strange."

"What all did he tell you, Jill?"

She thought for a second, "I thought about that last night. We talked briefly, and he didn't say what he wanted me to come out to the coast for; there was an air of secrecy in everything he talked about. He said that he couldn't talk about the project on the phone. I can understand that, but here's what puzzled me: He didn't seem like himself. What's going on?"

"Like Murray, I can't discuss the project on the phone, but I can tell you that he has changed. He's still Murray, but something has happened to him recently. He went back to his old hometown in West Texas, where he met a young woman who may have changed him. He met me when he returned from vacation and told me about this person. She seems to have made him reevaluate his life, specifically, his being an atheist. Murray told me that after meeting this woman and hearing me preach to him all these years, he is open to learning about the Christian Faith."

Jill was a bit stunned, "You're kidding me, right? Murray is open to learning about Christianity. He used to mock us to the dogs and back. He never hid the fact that he did not need God, religion, and people who believed in God. I find it hard to believe someone like Murray would be open to this now. I should be rejoicing that someone like Murray has come to God—"

Nate interrupted, "I didn't say that, Jill. I told you that he is open to *learning* about God. As Murray says, he's not part of the flock, but he's on the outside, taking an interest in looking in."

Jill replied, "I guess I was a bit eager. Sorry for jumping to conclusions. Well, at least that's a start. Do you think that this is genuine?"

"I hope so, I really do, but we'll have to see. In the meantime, I shouldn't go into what Murray is planning because I don't know exactly what he is planning, but I do know that whatever it is, he was hoping to get you involved with it. You know Murray, his mind is working on a different plane, so we'll have to wait until he gets us all in a conference room and tells us what he has planned. Did he give you any inkling of when he wanted you out here?"

"He said maybe within the next five to six weeks, but he is waiting until someone heads out to the Mid-East and then returns. He said that this might take some time. Do you have any clue how long this might take?"

"Hopefully, not too long. But I'm like you. I'm wondering what he's got brewing in that big brain of his. Either way, seeing and hopefully working with you again will be nice."

"Yes, it will be, Nate, it really will. OK, let me get back to the salt mines, but before I go, if you hear anything that you think I should know, please let me know, OK?"

You bet," Nate replied, "Looking forward to seeing you; until then, please be well, and may God bless and keep you, my dear."

"May God bless you, too, Nate. Bye for now." Jill got up from her desk, grabbed her lunch, and headed outside to eat in the quad. As she sat down on a bench, all she could think was, *What is he up to this time?*

Chapter Six
Late April

Baghdad, Iraq

It was early evening, right before sunset on a Wednesday in late April, and it was still almost ninety degrees outside. He arrived the evening before, trying to get over the jet lag. Declan walked out onto the balcony of his suite at the Babylon Rotana Hotel; the hotel was in downtown Baghdad, overlooking the *Tigris* River, and he was enjoying the view. The sun was setting to the west, well past the *Euphrates* River, where the sky was pink but quickly turning red. Even though it was approaching dusk, the sky overhead was still a brilliant blue. To the east, where the sky was filled with dust from the desert, the color had already turned from indigo to a deep purple. Looking east towards the *Tigris*, he watched as waterfowl took wing. Geese and ducks were in the air, while herons and egrets fed in the shallows. While a significant part of Baghdad had been destroyed in their four-year war with America that started in 2003, reconstruction efforts began in 2008 and were still ongoing. Still, the city had made significant strides in rebuilding.

Baghdad. The second largest city in the Arab world after Cairo, Egypt. A description of Baghdad can be as varied as the people associated with the city, from the literary figure of Sinbad the Sailor to the political figures of Saddam Hussein and Abu Bakr al-Baghdadi. In the eighth century, Baghdad was the capital of the Abbasid Caliphate. Under the Caliph al-Mansur, the city was built to be seen as an example of paradise, as described in the Qur'an. For much of the Abbasid Caliphate, Baghdad was the world's largest city, boasting a population of over one million people. Baghdad had also become known as one of the foremost intellectual centers of the Islamic World. Still, the city declined in the thirteenth century following Baghdad's destruction by the Mongol Invasion. This led to a steady decline in the city's prominence due to various plagues and occupations by other civilizations. By the twentieth century, Baghdad had regained some of its prominence in the Arab World, only to experience massive damage caused by the Iran-Iraq War of the 1980s, the First Gulf War of 1990, the US-Iraq War of 2003, and the War in Iraq against the Islamic State that lasted until 2017.

By 2018, Baghdad had a population of over eight million residents, and one more person added to the city's population that day was one Declan O'Sullivan. Ten days earlier, he agreed to Murray's proposal to go to Iraq to locate Toma, and he realized that he had a tremendous amount to get done before his flying out. Having worn nothing but Navy uniforms since his entrance to the U.S. Naval Academy and then a monk's habit for the past year, he needed to obtain a new wardrobe to maintain the appearance of his cover of a Spanish businessman. Murray had an acquaintance who managed Battistoni's Men's Fashions on Rodeo Drive in Beverly Hills, and he arranged for Declan to spend the day at Battistoni's to have himself completely outfitted with suits, shoes, and accessories to complete his portrayal of a successful European businessman. He then spent time at another store in Los Angeles, where he was outfitted with suitable working attire. He met with Murray and Nate for a day, and they provided him with everything he would need to support his cover. The three of them then discussed the plan at length.

During the Iraqi wars with Iran and the United States, ports, oil pumping stations, bridges, and other structures along the *Tigris* River had been destroyed. Bombing along the river had resulted in underwater obstructions such as sandbars and small islets. Due to these obstructions, water flow and the efficiency of water intakes along the *Tigris* became severely impeded. While several dredging operations had improved water flow along the *Tigris,* significant work still needed to be done.

Declan's background as a Navy SEAL provided him with training in advanced diving techniques, underwater demolition, and hydrographic surveying. His cover was to be the founder of a start-up Spanish company that had developed an innovative approach to dredging and underwater construction. Historically, the Spanish had good relations with Iraq, so as a "Spaniard," he could have relatively free movement within the country. As promised, Murray got letters of introduction to various salvage companies in Iraq. Before Declan went to Iraq, he had a preliminary meeting with one of the engineers with Estuarial Engineering Company, Limited, out of Chicago. This company had a contract with the Provisional Government of Iraq to dredge the main port of Umm Qasr, as it had been severely damaged during the periods of war. The port city of Umm Qasr had an interesting and storied history: It was Iraq's only deep-water port, but it was also the site where Alexander the Great of Macedonia landed in Mesopotamia in 325 B.C. In March 2003, Umm Qasr was the site of one of the first operations during the US-Iraq War. Once the coalition forces took control of Umm Qasr, the Spanish Army, operating with the British Royal Marines, garrisoned the port. In May 2003, control of the port was turned over to a private corporation charged with restoring and renovating the port facilities.

Before he left the States, he met a second time with the Estuarial Engineering team at their corporate offices. To introduce Declan, the team transmitted this meeting via a videoconference call with the local team at Umm Qasr. As the Spanish Army had a history in Umm Qasr, having a Spanish company bidding on dredging and hydrographic surveying would hopefully not raise any red flags. Declan's discussion with the team at Estuarial Engineering was centered around his "proposal" to perform some work on improving water flow in affected areas along the *Tigris* with his innovative technology. His proposal included the possibility of a partnership with

Estuarial Engineering, but as he had stressed, everything was still in the planning phase. Declan made it clear to the Estuarial Engineering team that he was requesting assistance in performing the initial site survey along the affected areas of the river. The Estuarial Engineering team succeeded in deepening the Umm Qasr port and repairing parts of their shoreline. Still, they had no luck convincing the Provisional Government to award them additional contracts to improve water flow in other parts of the *Tigris* River. As a partnership with Declan's "company" might offer the team the possibility of being awarded a new contract, they were more than happy to work with Declan.

With this introductory meeting complete, Declan returned to his home in Boston, where he spent time with his family. He spent as much time as he could speaking with his mother in Catalonian to have his accent polished, or as he used to joke with his mother, to get his accent recycled.

But that evening, as he was on his balcony watching the birds feed in the river, the phone in his room rang. He was given a small device back in Pasadena that would act as a "scrambler" for his phone. Prior to any calls, he had strict instructions to attach this device to the handset; this way, he could have secure communications with Pasadena. Ensuring the device was attached, he answered his phone and was happy to hear Nate's voice. "Hi, Declan, how are you doing this, what is it, evening, right?"

"Yeah, hi Nate, yeah, it's 6 PM local right now. I was just outside on my balcony overlooking the *Tigris* River and thinking of all the world's history outside my window. I can't get over how many birds are around here, but it makes sense with this huge river rolling along outside. But to answer your question, things are fine. I am just trying to get over my jet lag. Eight time zones from Boston is pretty tough to take. I had a long nap, but now I'm just trying to stay awake so that I can try to reset my internal clock. What's going on?"

Nate replied, "Just checking in to see how you're doing and if you have any questions regarding this week and next."

"Yeah, I had a chance to review everything on the flight. I think everything looks OK. I did have a message at the front desk that the local team from Estuarial Engineering will have a car ready to pick me up tomorrow morning at nine. I have the second meeting with the team from Gulf Cobla at two o'clock tomorrow afternoon. All systems are a go from my end."

"Sounds good, Declan. How is your Spanish coming along? Are you all ready for a little *Como esta Usted* tomorrow?" Nate asked.

"Well, *llengua Catalana* is slightly different. We would say '*Com aquesta vostè*,' Catalonian is much prettier than Castilian Spanish but not as pretty as Portuguese, but that's just me. And yes, I'm ready to speak Catalonian as long as needed, but it looks as if tomorrow's meetings will all be in English. No worries, my Catalonian accent is ready to go."

Nate gave a short laugh. "You all are like us Indians; we have different dialects throughout the country. There is something else that I wanted to discuss with you. I just got this firmed up. Don't ask me how I set this up, but I have a point of contact with the Chaldean Catholic Archeparchy of Baghdad. I spoke with them regarding your visit to Iraq. Don't worry; absolutely nothing has been compromised about your real identity to them. You are only known by your cover, but they know you are devout and may want to attend Mass, Vespers, or something with them. They might be able to help run some interference for you if things get sticky, but I just wanted to let you know that you have someone in your corner in Baghdad. If asked, you and I met through my brother, Anthony, and we became friends. You and I talked a few weeks back, and you told me about your business trip to Iraq; that's it."

"That's good to know, Nate. Do you have a name for me there at the Archeparchy? Is it one of the priests?"

"Sorry, Declan. Yes, Father Simon Hanna is your point of contact. He speaks English well, along with Arabic and Aramaic. Just in case, I'll text you his particulars."

"That'll work," Declan said. "Right now, I know that the folks at Estuarial Engineering talked about heading north up the *Tigris*, actually alongside the *Tigris*, starting on Sunday. If so, I'd like to attend Mass on Saturday if possible. I'll give Fr. Simon a call."

Nate asked, "I'm not too familiar with the geography of that part of Iraq. What do you mean by saying you'll travel alongside the *Tigris*? That's a big body of water. Wouldn't it be better to travel by watercraft up the river?"

"Great question, but no. From the Persian Gulf up to Baghdad, you can travel fairly well by boat, but you'd have to take a raft north of here as the waters become shallower. Then, with all of the damage done during the war, sandbars, and such, the water flow is still not what it should be, so navigating upriver will be difficult. I have all of my equipment to do a survey and lots of gear. Going by raft would be tough with everything that I have. The tentative plan so far is to drive up to Tikrit and then up to Mosul. I'll find out more tomorrow. My point of contact at Estuarial Engineering mentioned something about taking a helo. That would be more to my liking. Changing the subject here, any luck in trying to get a better read on Toma's whereabouts?"

Nate hesitated for a second. "We learned that he left Baghdad and is now working at St. George's Church in a small town called Telskuf, north of Mosul. Supposed to be a town populated by Chaldeans. I'll try to firm this up as soon as possible, but right now, that looks pretty solid. Let me know if our plan of extricating Toma still looks good after you go on the road with the Estuarial Engineering folks."

"Thanks, Nate, I will. I appreciate the call and am looking forward to catching up soon."

Declan met with both companies the following day, and as Murray and Nate had planned, he decided to continue his site visits with Estuarial Engineering. Steve Tracy, one of the firm's site engineers, was his point of contact. He met Declan at his hotel on Sunday morning, where they loaded his survey equipment into a company truck.

"*Buenas Dias, Senor Ocuna!*" Steve greeted Declan upon picking him up at his hotel.

"And good morning to you, too, Mr. Tracy. Your Spanish is good, but in our language, *Catalan*, we pronounce it '*Bones dies*,'" subtly different. And we would use my father's last name, 'Coixet,' instead of my mother's, Ocuna. It may be confusing, but you'll get used to it. In the meantime, please call me Antoni. And thank you for collecting me this morning, that plus all of my equipment, most appreciated."

"You're more than welcome, Antoni, and please call me Steve. Sorry for the confusion; I was told I would escort a Spanish businessman. I'll have to plead ignorance; I was not aware of the language differences between Spanish and, what was it, *Catalan*? Is that the same as 'Catalonian'?"

"Yes, Steve, one and the same. And please, there is no reason to apologize. Most people do not know that Spain is comprised of various ethnic and linguistic groups. But your Spanish pronunciation is excellent. Did you study Spanish in school when you were younger?"

Steve replied, "Well, I'm from South Texas, and we had a large Hispanic population there. Most of my friends were of Mexican descent, so I picked up quite a bit of Spanish from them. But I do have to say that your English is perfect. It sounds like you have a European accent, but you must speak English quite a bit. It makes it pretty easy for me. I can't carry on a technical conversation in Spanish, but I can order off of the menu pretty easily."

Declan/Antoni smiled, "I don't think we'll be ordering any tacos out here, but eating tacos sounds good."

Steve laughed at that. "Some tacos, chili rellenos, beans and rice, and a few beers. Man, I do like Mexican food! Have you spent much time in the States?"

"Oh yes, quite a bit. Mostly in California, but quite a bit of time on your eastern coast. So, what is our plan for our survey of the river?"

"We'll be driving up to a town right on the river, Al-Khalis, about seventy miles from here. We can take a look, and then we'll head up north to another small town on the river, Balad, about another twenty-five miles or so. Both areas appear to have experienced significant problems with their flow. From there, we'll head up another fifty miles upriver to Tikrit. Then, we have a helicopter to pick us up, and we'll head north to Mosul. Mosul is way up there, about 150 miles from Tikrit. Now I understand that you'll be staying up in Mosul for a couple of days, and then we'll be coming back up north to bring you back?"

"Yes, Steve, I was going to perform some cursory tests in the first three places we'll be visiting, but once we get to Mosul, I'll do a more in-depth bathymetric survey. I have some fairly sophisticated equipment to get this done. What I mean by sophisticated is that I can do all the work alone. I have a modified multibeam echo sounder that is about half the size of the device we normally employ. It is specifically designed for riverine surveys, so this should be, how do you say it, a 'piece of pie?' Is that correct?"

Steve laughed and corrected Declan, "We normally say a 'piece of cake,' but whatever works for you, I got your meaning. Are you sure you don't need me to stay with you to help with your survey? I'm more than willing to stay. I blocked this entire week off."

"Thank you, Steve, but this equipment is very easy to use. Plus, I believe I mentioned this to your colleagues in Chicago; there is a strong possibility that I will meet with one of my colleagues in Mosul. He came here several months back, working with a Christian Relief Agency to coordinate food delivery for some people on the Nineveh Plain. He is on an extended vacation helping some of these groups, but he will be involved with this upcoming project if we do indeed get the bid. But thank you again. I can manage the equipment by myself, and if I can coordinate with my colleague, he can help confirm my findings."

Steve thought about this, "I guess that your modified equipment is part of your 'innovative services' that everyone is talking about. How innovative are these services? I'm a civil engineer by training and always looking for new and innovative approaches."

Declan started nodding, "Ah, yes, I see you are trying to pry trade secrets out of me. My new approaches give me a bit of a competitive advantage over the other specialty firms I work with, but I can't give away that edge at this time. Once we get the bid and our two companies enter into our agreement, you'll all get the opportunity to see my new, what do you call it, the new 'gizmo'?"

Steve shrugged his shoulders, "Yeah, that's it, gizmo. Well, my manager can't say that I didn't try." And with that, he looked at Declan and grinned sheepishly.

They drove north to the town of Al-Khalis, which, as Steve had mentioned, was right on the river. Declan asked Steve to drive for a bit longer as he kept his eyes on the river. He was looking for something, and as soon as he found what he was looking for, Steve pulled over and stopped. He got out of their truck, opened the back up, and pulled out one of his equipment cases. He also grabbed a pair of rubber boots out of another case. They walked down to the riverbank with Declan carrying his case. He put his boots on and, taking a few things out of his case, walked towards the river. He found the area he was looking for and walked into the water. There was an area in the river about five feet from the riverbank where a small waterfall had formed.

Steve could see what Declan had with him, "You going to use the bucket method to measure the flow rate?"

Declan was looking for a good area to set up his equipment. "Yes, I am. After this initial reading, I'll use a Pygmy Meter to validate it. Believe it or not, some of those old methods work fairly well, and I find that using the bucket is almost as exact as using the meter. I still like using my pencil and paper to do my initial calculations and then use my calculator to confirm them. It's just one of my little habits that I've never grown out of, but it seems to work for me. If you'd still like to help, can you time me?"

Steve had a stopwatch on his cell phone, "Let me know when you're ready."

"*Estic llest*, I'm sorry, I'm ready. I'll yell out when to

start." Declan held the bucket below the small waterfall, and as soon as he started filling the bucket, Steve started the stopwatch. He stopped it when Declan yelled out that it was full. They did this seven times and then took an average of the fill time. The flow rate was calculated by hand, and then Declan did another test using his meter to calculate the flow rate accurately. As Declan had predicted, both methods yielded similar results. They performed both tests in different areas along the river, then got in the truck and headed north to Balad. While driving, he did some initial calculations and said to Steve, "Just looking at these preliminary data, the flow rate here is very low. The average flow rate of the *Tigris* is roughly 1,000 meters cubed per second at its discharge point in Baghdad. We're nowhere close to that, and that's accounting for all of the other hydrologic and resistance factors. We have some work to do up here. Let's see how things go in Balad and then Mosul."

They performed similar tests in Balad and then caught the helicopter to Mosul; another Estuarial Engineering employee drove the company truck back to Baghdad. Once they arrived in Mosul, Steve, Declan, and the pilot had dinner at a local restaurant. Declan checked into his hotel, and Steve and the pilot headed back to Baghdad. The plan was to return to Mosul and pick Declan up in two days unless he called and changed plans.

That evening, Declan contacted Nate and discussed how events were progressing. During their call, Declan was told they had a good idea of where Toma was, and arrangements were made to provide Declan with a car and an English-speaking driver to take him north to Telskuf.

Declan was picked up at his hotel by his driver in a Land Cruiser the following day. His driver, Gurguis Audo, was a Chaldean Catholic familiar with the large city of Mosul; Mosul had a population of over a million people, and with the towns on the Nineveh Plain. They drove to Telskuf, about 20 miles or so north of Mosul. Declan had told Gurguis that he needed to get to the St. George Church in Telskuf as he was trying to find a friend. "Are you familiar with the Church, Gurguis?"

"Oh, yes, very familiar, it's my namesake. Gurguis is Aramaic for George. I know all of the Churches on the Nineveh Plain. Mar Toma, you know him as St. Thomas the Apostle, who brought the Word to all of my people two thousand years ago. We are driving on the same road Mar Toma walked with his disciples. We are some of the earliest Christians. Our Rite was founded directly by one of Our Lord's Apostles. Our Churches are of great importance to Christians throughout the world, but many of my Christian brothers and sisters have ignored our plight. About ten years ago, Archbishop Paulos Faraj Rahno was kidnapped by Islamic terrorists, and they killed him. Everyone from the Holy Father Pope Benedict to the American President Bush condemned the murder of our Archbishop, but nothing was done. Most of our people have fled their homeland to other countries throughout Europe and even to America and Australia. We used to number in the millions here in Iraq; now, we don't have many of us left."

Declan empathized with Gurguis entirely. He knew of the plight of the Christians in the Middle East. "I am so sorry for how your people have been persecuted in their own homeland. We must continue to pray for all of the Assyrian people. Have many of your family left for other countries?"

"Yes, but I will never leave. They cannot drive me out." They drove in silence for the remainder of the trip to Telskuf. Gurguis thought that he may have said too much. They arrived in Telskuf after a forty-five-minute drive, and Gurguis drove directly to the Church.

Declan exited the car and asked Gurguis if he could come with him. "Unless your priest can speak English or Spanish, I might need your help." Gurguis got out of the car, and they walked into the Church. Declan was quite surprised when he stepped inside the Church. St. George's Church celebrated a few months back their first Christmas Mass in three years since the Islamic State had overrun the area. He thought he would find a small village church, but he saw that this was no little chapel. The Church's main sanctuary was massive, with a large rib vaulted ceiling and pillars dividing the church into a main sanctuary and two side aisles. There were life-sized statues of Jesus on the right side of the altar and The Blessed Mother holding an Infant Jesus on the left. Overall, it was a very beautiful Church. Declan and Gurguis walked up to the altar, where Declan kneeled and started praying. Gurguis joined him a moment later. This was one of the moments that Declan would open himself up to be more receptive to God. He could not quite explain it, but for some reason, he felt an incredible feeling of God's presence in this place, more than he felt even at the Abbey. After a few moments, both men blessed themselves and walked towards the sacristy, hoping to find a priest.

Gurguis asked him, "It is good to see you are a believer, yes?"

"Yes, Gurguis, most of the people where I come from are Christian, and yes, I am a believer, probably more than you can imagine. Thank you for bringing me here. St. George's is a magnificent Church."

There was no priest in the sacristy, but a man was working on the overhead lights. Gurguis, speaking in Aramaic, asked the man if he knew where the priest was. The man told him that the priest was conferring the Sacrament of the Sick at a dying parishioner's home. The man got off of his ladder and asked Gurguis if there was anything that he could do to help. Declan asked, "See if he knows anything of a monk called Toma Boudagh. He is supposed to be here in Telskuf."

Gurguis asked the man, who told him they had just missed Brother Toma. He left two days ago to work at the orphanage in Alqosh, a village no more than fifteen kilometers north of Telskuf. Gurguis thanked the man, and then he and Declan walked back to the Land Cruiser. They headed north once again to the village of Alqosh. The roads were in poor condition, and between dodging flocks of sheep and goats, it took them thirty minutes to drive the eight miles to the village. Gurguis knew exactly where the orphanage was. They pulled into the gravel lot and got out of the vehicle. As soon as they got out, they could hear construction sounds, hammering and sawing, and then they could hear the workmen talking back and forth. Declan and Gurguis walked into the orphanage, and it was obvious what kind of damage the Islamic State, or as they called it here, Daesh, did to the building. The inside of the orphanage was destroyed, and the workmen were demolishing unsafe walls. Toma was on top of the scaffolding, talking away with his fellow workers in Aramaic. Declan walked over to the bottom of the scaffold and, in a lull in the workers' conversation, yelled up to Toma, "Hey, you big Gamla, what's going on?"

Toma was puzzled to hear English being spoken; "*who's calling me a big camel*," he wondered, and as he looked down to see who was talking, he was stunned to see Declan standing there. He climbed quickly down from the scaffolding and took Declan in a bear hug, "What in the world are you doing here?"

Declan whispered, "Don't call me Declan, call me Antoni. I'll explain later." Disengaging from each other, Toma looked his friend over. He could not believe that Declan was here, and he wanted to hear why he was going by a different name and faking an accent.

"It's great to see you, but what are you doing here? You were the last person I expected to see walk in here."

"It's great to see you, too, my friend, here; let me introduce you to Gurguis Audo; he is from Mosul and has helped me get here to find you. Toma greeted Gurguis, and then Declan asked, "Gurguis, let me and my friend take a walk outside so that we can visit each other. It has been a very long time since we have seen each other." They walked outside and began to walk along the road.

"Deck, talk about a shock, what's going on? I thought you were at Mepkin Abbey. Did you leave the Trappists? I have a thousand questions to ask you. What's with the accent and this 'Antoni' stuff?"

"OK, first things first. I'm here posing as a Spanish businessman trying to get contracts with the Iraqi provisional government for dredging portions of the *Tigris* River. My cover is to try and make it easier for us to travel. The purpose of my coming here is to meet with you and try to convince you to come back home. Murray and Nate—"

Toma almost screamed, "*Murray* and *Nate*? Good grief, what have they got to do with all of this? They're trying to convince me to come back home for what? What is Murray up to, Deck?"

"About three weeks ago, Nate shows up with his brother, Father Anthony, at Mepkin Abbey. Nate related his discussion with Edgeton regarding his change of heart. I can get into the details later, but the bottom line is that Murray feels open to learning about the Christian faith, and part of this is that Murray thinks that he shortchanged us regarding the outbrief that we gave the team. Nate feels as if Murray is sincere, and after I talked to him, I was skeptical but willing to hear the guy out. Right now, it looks like Murray wants to bring us back to re-present our findings to the Einstein Project Team. Murray also pointed out that instead of reading the transcript, he wants us there to be able to answer any questions. Here's what I'm thinking: If we were to go back there, give our brief again, and then maybe plead our case, we might be able to convince the team to declassify the project. Think about it, Toma; if we do this right, we might be able to let the world know that the Gospel is true; everything about Scripture is true. Think of how many people we could bring to God, Toma. This could be a once-in-a-lifetime shot to do this right. What do you think?"

"I don't know, Deck. I'm skeptical of Edgeton; I think that he has some psychological issues that need to be addressed, but that's just me. Let me think about this for a while. But I want you to think of something else. Look where you're standing. Think of your drive up here to Alqosh. Do you know where you are? Your feet are on the same ground that Mar Toma, St. Thomas the Apostle, trod as he spread Our Lord's message. Do you remember 'Doubting Thomas'? Can you recall how he said he would not believe in The Lord's Resurrection until he could put his fingers inside Our Lord's Holy Wounds? When Jesus appeared to Thomas and Thomas put his fingers in Our Lord's wounds, do you remember what Jesus said to him? He said, 'Have you come to believe because you have seen Me? Blessed are those who not seen and have believed.' Isn't our faith greater when our human minds might still have doubt? If our story is declassified and everyone learns that Jesus is the Son of the Living God, that will remove doubt, correct? We'll all be like Mar Toma; we believe because we have special knowledge. But isn't our faith more blessed and purer because we believe even though we have not seen? Am I making sense to you, Declan?"

"I never thought of it like that, Toma, but what did Our Lord tell us from His Cross? He told us to be *His witnesses* to the people of our time. Isn't that what we can do if we get the project declassified? We can witness what we know and what we saw."

Toma thought for a moment. "I don't know, Deck, I don't know. But as I said, let me think about this for a while. But do you want to know something? I think of this every day. I would do anything to be able to go back again. I belong there, Deck, and I know that I do."

"Same here, Toma. I think of it every day." They walked in silence for a while, and then Declan said, "Let me answer one of your other questions; I did not leave the Trappists. Before I left, I had a very long talk with my Abbot and told him our story. He was amazed at what I told him, but he wasn't shocked. To him, it was just another proof of God's existence. As a novice, I am free to leave at any time, but Father Abbot and I came to a quiet agreement. I will be on an academic sabbatical, and I can return when I am done with whatever we're going to be doing with Murray. At least I'm hoping that you'll come back with me."

"I need to pray about this, Deck. I am sure that you can use some prayer, too. The most important monastery in our Chaldean Rite is not too far from here, the Rabban Hormizd Monastery. Let's go." Declan and Toma returned to the orphanage, where they found Gurguis, who knew where the monastery was up in the mountains. After an hour of praying with Declan and Gurguis, Toma said, "Antoni, I was going to head back to Telskuf after work today and then head to our Archeparchy offices in Mosul tomorrow. Can you and Gurguis give me a lift instead of me having to take one of the workmen away from the orphanage?"

"We're heading back to Mosul. We can take you to Telskuf today, and if you want, we can take you to Mosul tomorrow. Will that work for you?"

Toma smiled at Declan, "Yes, that will work fine, thank you." The three men returned to Gurguis' vehicle for the ride back to Telskuf.

Chapter Seven
The Next Day

Mosul, Iraq

Gurguis dropped Declan and Toma at the Archeparchy Offices in Mosul, where Toma met with one of the priests involved in humanitarian relief for the area. They all said their goodbyes, and as Declan and Toma were walking up to the office, Toma stopped and said, "I thought quite a bit last night about what we were discussing. Two questions: first, when does Murray want to get the team back together, and secondly, how difficult will it be for us to get out of the country with all that is going on?"

"Murray is considering having the team meeting sometime late next month or early June. He needs to put a few other pieces in place and get a few more folks scheduled to come in. Regarding getting out of the country, what passport are you traveling with now?"

Toma answered, "My own, my U.S. passport. Do you think it will be a problem for me to travel out of here?"

"Don't think so. As I told you yesterday, part of what I'm here for is to try to convince you to come back and, secondly, to make it easier for us to travel out of the country. I'm traveling on a Spanish passport and have one for you. It has appropriate stamps and everything. I have to tell you, Murray has this guy back in Pasadena who has been able to get everything greased for us, everything from plane tickets to these passports. All that was asked of me was not to ask any questions.

OK, back to your cover, you are traveling as one of the team members of my new company in Catalonia. You are 'Tomas Borja' from Zaragoza in Aragon for the next few days. Don't worry. I have lots of background info for you if you decide to return with me. Your Spanish is still pretty good, isn't it?"

"It's good, but we'll speak English most of the time with everyone, won't we?"

"Yeah, no worries, I'll teach you a few Catalan phrases and then revert to Castilian if you wish, just to add to our cover. But you're right, we'll speak English most of the time. What do you think? Are you up for heading back to Pasadena with me?"

Toma said, "Yeah, let's do it, but I must get this cleared with my superiors at St. Antony's Convent in Baghdad. I've yet to profess final vows, so like you, I can leave at any time, but there is so much work that has to be done here in Iraq, especially up north on the Nineveh Plain. I'm torn, Deck; I love doing what I'm doing, but I'm also interested in seeing what Murray has to say; what if he is sincere? What could this mean? Could we declassify our mission and tell the world what we did?"

"I know what you mean about being torn between these two paths. My Abbot was incredibly understanding and if I disagree with what Murray wants to do, I'm going back to my Abbey. But to answer your question, it's my hope that we can declassify our project."

Toma continued, "Let me ask you, Deck. If I find myself in the same boat, will you get me back here? Whatever happens, I must serve God, and I'm doing God's work here."

"We'll get you back, Toma, no worries." They walked into the office of the Archeparchy of Mosul.

While Toma was in his meeting, Declan took the opportunity to contact Steve Tracy and let him know that he would be ready to be picked up at the hotel the next day. He also told Steve that his colleague, Senor Borja, would accompany him back to Baghdad. He assured Steve that his initial reconnaissance had gone exceptionally well. He then took the opportunity to go into the Chapel to pray and meditate. When Toma's meeting was over, they headed back to Declan's hotel, where he was able to get a room for Toma.

Toma balked at that, "Save your money, give it to the poor, just get me a mat and a blanket. I'll sleep on the floor; that's the way I've been sleeping for the past year."

Declan said, "In my cell back at Mepkin, I had a small twin bed, a desk, and a kneeler. I was very happy. When Nate brought me back to Pasadena, and I spent my first night in a hotel, I was in shock; I didn't know what to do with myself. The hotel here is a step up from my cell; why don't you consider it like a halfway house to help you get used to staying in a hotel again? Sound good?"

"It sounds like you're messing with me. But yeah, you're probably right. Hey, I just thought of something. What am I supposed to be if I meet these guys tomorrow?"

Declan told him, "You're supposed to be assisting me in doing a hydrographic survey. I'll give you a few items to discuss tomorrow so we don't look like fools."

"I can't look like this. Should I borrow some clothes from the priests here?" Toma asked.

"Let's go buy a pair of boots and a small duffel bag to put your gear in. I've got several pairs of work pants and a golf shirt you can wear tomorrow. We'll have you walk around the river bank this afternoon to get the boots broken in before tomorrow."

That afternoon, armed with new work boots, Toma and Declan grabbed some of Declan's equipment and walked down to the *Tigris* River. They performed a few studies in several areas along the river to add realism to their story.

The following day, Steve Tracy and a local driver picked Declan and Toma up at the hotel and then drove to the heliport. They stowed their equipment and luggage and took off for Baghdad. As soon as they were airborne, Steve asked, "How were the flow readings in Mosul? Hopefully, they were better than they were in Balad and Al-Khalis."

Declan/Antoni answered, "We were hoping they would be. Tomas, why don't you share your calculations with Steve."

"Of course. Steve, we had the opportunity to do a few

more tests besides our meter reads. The Mosul Dam and other water projects affect the discharge basin in Mosul, so we took readings in several areas. We had sounding equipment, shore signals and buoys, and angular measuring devices. Lastly, we used Antoni's modified multibeam echosounder to complete our tests. We'll have a complete report that will include all of our calculations that we'll be submitting with our proposal that your team can analyze more fully, but suffice it to say, the flow rate is severely impeded in the Mosul area, a significant amount of work needs to be done to improve the flow. Historically, the average flow rate this far north has been recorded as high as 750 meters cubed per second. We found that the flow rate in some of the areas tested is fewer than 50 meters cubed per second. We'll need to do more testing, but at this point, it appears that sea wells and backwaters need to be designed in addition to dredging to help improve the flow. I would have to defer to Antoni on what needs to be completed. *Què penses, necessitem fer més?* Excuse me, Steve, that was a bit rude of me. Antoni, do we need to do more?"

He chuckled, "For being an Aragonese, your Catalan is still pretty good. Yes, we need, as you said, more studies, but we'll discuss this with the team at Estuarial Engineering once we have all of our calculations finalized."

Steve jumped in, "Just looking at the river from up here in the helicopter, I can see how the flow is impeded, but I didn't think it was by that much. I'm looking forward to seeing the report. Tomas, your English is excellent. Did you spend a lot of time in England or the States?"

"Good pickup on your part, Steve," Toma/Tomas answered. "I went to undergraduate in Barcelona at the Polytechnic University of Catalonia, where I studied Geoscience, but I went to graduate school in Indiana, the University of Notre Dame. How about you?"

"I'm an Aggie, Texas A&M, *the* university of Texas, not that school in Austin. I hope we can all work together on this project. I'd like to learn about the differences between your dialects."

"I hope that we can all work together, too. As I discussed with your corporate team in Chicago, we should be able to have everything put together in about two weeks. We have to do some modeling, and once we can complete that, I will contact my counterpart with the Provisional Government. We plan to stay in Baghdad a bit longer for a few more planning meetings before returning to Spain. Did you have a chance to talk with your management about our trip this week and what our preliminary tests showed in Balad and Al-Khalis?"

"Yes, I did," Steve replied. "I have to say that they're interested, to say the least, in your new innovations, and they feel that developing a partnership with you would be mutually beneficial. I do hope that this all works out. Let me ask a quick question, will you gentlemen be at the Rotana Hotel again before you leave?"

Declan/Antoni said, "Yes, we'll be there for a bit longer. Is there anything that you need?"

"I was hoping to see if we could have a chance to have dinner with some of my teammates from work, just an opportunity to meet you all before you all fly out. Would you gentlemen like to meet us for a nice dinner? If you can't, we understand completely."

"Thank you, Steve, that is very kind of you and your team. Can we do this when we return with hopefully approval from the Provisional Government?"

"Absolutely," answered Steve, "That will be even better. We'll be able to toast our partnership."

Everyone smiled as they continued their way to Baghdad. The pilot announced they would land soon. Upon landing, Steve had a car ready to take Declan and Toma to their hotel. Declan thanked Steve and the pilot for their help and assistance and told them he would be in touch within a matter of weeks to let them know of their ability to move forward. With handshakes and goodbyes all around, Declan and Toma got into the car and were driven back to their hotel.

By silent agreement, they did not talk much in the car heading back to the hotel as they did not want anything untoward to get back to the Estuarial Engineering offices. They checked into their hotel rooms, and once they were settled, they went out for a nice lunch. They returned to the hotel, and Toma called for a driver to take him to St. Antony's Convent, where he would speak with his superiors of the Antonian Order of St. Ormizda of the Chaldeans. At the convent, Toma had an emotional talk with his superiors and his spiritual advisor. Like Declan, he received assurances that he could return to the order as soon as his work was done in the States. He was emotionally spent when he returned to the hotel, but he went to Declan's room, where they got ready to make their appointed call to Nate back in Pasadena. Attaching his scrambler to the phone, Declan called Nate where it was about six in the morning.

"Hi, Nate, and good morning to you. How are things back in Pasadena?"

"Thanks, all is well out here." Nate was excited to get an update from Declan on how things were progressing. "How about you? Is everything going well for you? Any problems?"

Declan put the phone on speaker, "Everything is fine here; I have someone who wants to say hello."

"Hi, Nate, how are you doing?"

"Toma, is that you?" Nate was excited and relieved to hear Toma's voice.

"Yep, one and the same," Toma was grinning at Declan when he replied. "What kind of skullduggery have you all been doing back there? Enough to get Deck to travel halfway across the world to come and fetch me. So, tell me, what's going on back there? You're on speaker with both Declan and me."

"OK, great. Declan, what have you shared with Toma to date?"

"This is Declan, Nate. So far, everyone appears to be buying our cover as two guys from Spain doing some hydrographic research on the *Tigris*. It looks like we're all set to fly out of here tomorrow unless you have an update for us. As far as I've briefed Toma, he's up to speed on everything that I know up to this point. I'll let Toma brief you on his current status."

"Hi, Nate. Deck has convinced me to come back and participate in the brief with Dr. Edgeton and the team. Do you have an update on who plans to be there and what time frame we're looking at to meet with everyone? Lastly, have you heard any rumblings of trouble for us getting out of here tomorrow?"

Nate thought for a second, "Not a thing. I have been in contact with the Estuarial Engineering team out in Chicago, and they're pleased that you and Declan have had a positive interaction with their local team in Iraq. The background work that Murray did in setting up the cover for you two has appeared to be paying off. Right now, we have not heard anything that would cause us concern. Declan, did you have any problems with your Spanish passport?"

Declan shook his head and then answered Nate, "Not a bit. That's what has me worried. Everything has gone incredibly well here, but I feel as if I am waiting for the other shoe to drop. I'm not complaining, Nate, just voicing a little concern. Understand that Toma and I are used to drafting up a lot of our own Op Plan, our operational plan, and since we didn't have any input on this, I get a bit nervous. But to go back to what you asked, no problems with the passport."

Nate continued, "Let's stick to our plan. Use your Spanish passports to get you back to the States. I have a meeting with Murray later today. I'll bring him up to speed on how things are progressing from your end. Anything else?"

Declan and Toma shook their heads, then piped up, "No, I think we're good on this end. Our flight leaves from BGW tomorrow morning to Dubai, and then we'll fly back home. With good tailwinds, we should see you all tomorrow night or the morning after. I think that once we clear BGW tomorrow, we should be good to go. OK, we're going to head down below to get Toma a carry-on and a briefcase. It's a good thing that he and I wear the same size and that you all got me enough clothes for the both of us, but I guess that was all part of the plan. Tell Murray that we'll see him soon. Thanks for everything, Nate. Keep us in your prayers."

"Of course I will. See you both soon, have a safe flight,

and may God keep and bless you both." Nate got off the phone and then called Murray at his home. "Good morning, Murray. Hey, listen, I just got off the phone with Declan and Toma. They're both in Baghdad right now and ready to fly out tomorrow. It sounds as if they're eager to get back here and find out what's going on, but we got both of them together, and to me, that's a very positive sign."

Murray was smiling, "Yes, indeed, Nate, very positive sign indeed. What do you think? Maybe we can give them a couple of days off to catch up on some sleep and get over their jet lag. Does that sound OK with you? We'll bring them in next week, meet with them, and then get the rest of the team together. Thanks for all you have done. See you this morning at the office." Hanging up, Murray said to the walls in his study, "Looks as if the third piece is in place."

*****

Declan and Toma headed downstairs and asked the concierge where a good luggage store was. They also made reservations at the Aroma Restaurant, a short walk from the hotel. They got a nice briefcase for Toma and a carry-on for the few items he had, and they continued their walk to the Aroma restaurant. There were several excellent restaurants close by the hotel, but the Aroma specialized in Italian cuisine and the more traditional Middle Eastern fare. Over dinner, Toma pressed Declan to recap his conversation with Murray and Nate. "I know that you said that Murray has had a change of heart and wants to 'give us another chance' to make our case; what was it that he said? He didn't give us a fair shake or something like that? I don't know, Deck. I've lived here among the Iraqis and have grown accustomed to their ways. They're not much different than we Chaldeans are. Still, they're very Byzantine in their dealings with people, with lots of intrigue, and their relationships with themselves and others are complicated and intricate. The bottom line is I have learned not to take anything at face value. I have to tell you, I'm optimistic because you are, and I trust your judgment, but something about what's going on doesn't pass the stink test. We'll have to figure this out once we get to LA. Speaking of which, it will be good to head down to San Diego and see my family. Do you want to head down with me?"

Declan smiled at his friend, "That would be great." He brought Toma up to speed on Murray's change of heart. "When Nate came out to Mepkin Abbey and told me of Murray's 'epiphany,' I was like you, very skeptical. Remember that one chief that we had back at BUD/S? What was his name, Niehaus or something like that? Remember that saying he used when someone was trying to make an excuse for something? He used to say, 'You're full of more shit than a pod of constipated whales,' pardon my French, but that's what I thought about Murray. And then he said something that made me stop and think. He told me that he was interested in the story of St. Paul, and then Nate's brother, Father Anthony, quipped the old saying, 'St. Paul beat and persecuted Christians before he became one,' it did make me think that maybe Murray is sincere, but I told him that I was still skeptical. Then he said something very interesting and somewhat disarming. He said that he was skeptical, too. Maybe we should give him the benefit of the doubt and listen to what he has to say with an open mind; what do you think?"

"Sure, Deck, you got me this far, didn't you? Yeah, I'm interested in what's going on. If I don't like what I hear, you guys promised me a way back here. What do I have to lose?"

The next morning, they made their way to Baghdad International. Declan checked his equipment bag at the Emirates Air counter to Los Angeles International Airport. Declan and Toma were concerned that security might be a bit tighter than usual due to the current state of affairs in Iraq. They were about to find out. Declan said to Toma, "Let's play dumb. Don't speak anything but Spanish and English. I don't want these guys to know that you speak Arabic. Let me get by with my tourist Arabic. Hopefully, they'll just consider us a couple of morons here on business." They were dressed as successful

European businessmen and walked up to the first security counter speaking to each other in Spanish. The security agent looked at them very carefully. He put his hand out and then barked, *"Guazat al-safar watthaker teiran,"* which Declan took to mean "Passports and plane tickets."

Declan answered, *"Sabah al-khayer, Seydi. Anna asfel, anna la atkalam al-arabia beshkel gade jadda. Hill tethedth al-inglizia oa al-isbaniye?"* "Good morning, sir; I am sorry, I do not speak Arabic well. Do you speak English or Spanish?"

The agent was not amused but replied, *"Al-isbaniye, lah. Al-inglizia, Kalila."* Spanish, no, English, a little.

Declan answered, *"Shukra lek, Seydi."* Thank you, sir. Then, looking at Toma and switching to Catalan, *"Tomas, lliura-li el passaport i el bitllet si us plau."* "Toma, hand him your passport and ticket, please." Toma and Declan handed over all of their documents. The agent looked at the papers sullenly and almost threw them back to Declan and Toma.

"Shukra lek, Seydi," and as they walked away, the agent smiled and said to them, *"Al-lana alik."* Declan and Toma smiled back and walked away. As soon as they got out of earshot, Toma started laughing.

"I guess that we passed the first test and that they think we're a couple of morons here on business." *"Al-lana alik"* was the big "F - U" bomb, so it appeared that security was not any tighter. Bored bureaucrats still ran it.

The same drill occurred with the customs agent, but this agent was more thorough in having Declan and Toma empty their carry-on bags and briefcases. With that completed and the obligatory *"Al-lana alik"* from the agent, they made their way to their assigned gate. Two hours later, they were airborne, and once they cleared Iraqi airspace, Declan and Toma looked at each other and smiled. Speaking very softly in Catalonian, Declan said, "Thanks be to God that's over. This went much more smoothly than I would have guessed."

"We're not out of the woods yet, but you're right; thanks be to God," Toma replied. "The UAE folks are efficient, but I'm not worried about them. We'll stay in the Emirates terminal and go on our next flight. The Emirates agent has us ticketed to LAX, so we should be good to go, but I'll feel better once we're home. It looks like Nate was right; there haven't been any problems so far. I guess that Murray did a good job with our cover, that and by the grace of God." Then, switching to English, "Tell you what, I'm going to take advantage of this quiet time, close my eyes, and get my morning prayers in."

They landed in Dubai and then walked three gates over to their connecting gate. They boarded and settled in for a sixteen-hour over-the-pole flight from Dubai to Los Angeles. Declan joked with Toma, "This is a lot better than a C-130 or a C-17, isn't it? And look at the seats that Murray got for us!"

"I hear you. Hey, listen, just like the last leg, I'm going to take advantage of the fact that Murray got us in business class. I'm going to get some shut-eye. Hit me if I snore too loud."

With Toma asleep, Declan had the chance to think. Less than three weeks ago, he was working with Brother Clement, building shelving units for their mushroom farm. Since then, he had left the life he loved, became reacquainted with his earlier life, and walked along the same paths as St. Thomas the Apostle. If this much happened in less than a month, what could the next six months or the next year bring? He thought about that until sleep overtook him. They continued winging north and back to something neither Declan nor Toma could have anticipated. But God was with them.

Chapter Eight
The First Week of May

Athens, GA

Murray contacted Jill when Declan and Toma arrived in Pasadena and asked if she could meet with him. Jill had a full teaching load and was preparing for finals, so she could not afford to take the time out of her schedule to fly to Pasadena, so Murray offered to fly to Georgia to meet with her. He was staying at the Hyatt in downtown Athens, and Jill agreed to meet with him for dinner. He stood when she approached the table, and after a friendly embrace and a polite kiss on the cheek, they sat down. Murray opened up, "You look wonderful, Jill. Academia obviously agrees with you."

"You're looking very well yourself, Murray. It is nice to see you again." Jill thought that she would be able to meet with Murray and act in a purely professional manner, but when she saw him and gave him a quick hug and a peck on the cheek, all of her memories of their time together came flooding back. She felt the fluttering in her stomach, something she had not felt for a long time. He was still so unbelievably handsome; she was having difficulty controlling her emotions as she reflected on what he once meant to her. "Murray, can you excuse me for a quick second? I'll be right back, but in the meantime, can you order me a chardonnay? Thanks."

"No problem," he said, and as Jill walked off, he thought to himself, *I have to convince her to come back. If I can persuade her to modify her position on what her hero Lorenz called the 'Butterfly Effect,' my job in getting what needs to be done will be much easier.* Their waiter came by, and Murray asked what their finest Chardonnay was.

The waiter offered, "We have a bottle of Gundlach-Bundschu from Sonoma. It is very nice on the palate, with perfect acidity to allow you to experience its subtle notes. I think that you'd enjoy it. Shall I bring a bottle over to you?"

Smiling, he replied, "Please do, and bring our menus over in about five minutes." Nodding his approval, the waiter moved off. He spied her walking across the dining room and noticed she was looking straight at him as she walked back. He smiled at her and stood when she arrived at the table. "Everything OK?"

"Yes, thanks. I had a tough day at school today and had to get my graduate assistant to deliver something to my department head. Don't get me wrong, I still enjoy teaching and have the opportunity to be involved with some research, but once in a while, I feel I would have a better time if I could open up a fruit stand. That's it. I'm going to start hawking peaches."

He kept smiling at her, "Well, you could always come back to Pasadena. I think that you may have an idea why I'm here. I told you a few weeks back that I was looking at getting a lot of the team together by late this month or early June, but things are moving quicker than we thought, so I needed to come out and talk with you. But no shop talk right now, let's catch up, oh, here's our vino."

Their waiter came over, opened the Chardonnay bottle, and gave the cork to Murray to inspect. "The wine doesn't appear to have been corked; it smells fine." The waiter then poured a small amount into Murray's glass, he sampled it, and announced, "Very nice, has a nice balanced finish," then the waiter filled Jill's glass.

She sipped her wine and said, "Very nice. I didn't know that you knew all that much about wines. Very impressive."

"I don't, actually. I read this article in the in-flight magazine on the way out here that happened to talk about the California wine industry. I just used some of the words that they mentioned in the article. The waiter probably thinks I'm a

Philistine, but the wine does taste nice, doesn't it?"

"It does, Murray. It was very nice of you to get this." Jill put her glass down and looked at him, "I was surprised when you called and asked to meet with me. What's going on?"

"Not now, Jill. Remember, I asked no shop talk." The waiter came over with their menus. "Let's look at what they have, shall we?" They had a lovely dinner.

When their dinner was over, he asked her, "Would you mind if we took a little walk to help digest our food? I'd also like to talk a little shop now. We'll have less chance for any eavesdropping if we're outside."

When they left the restaurant and walked onto Thomas Street, she asked, "Do you want to walk down by the campus? It's just down the street, or we can walk along the Oconee River. There is a nice little park along the river if you'd like."

"Let me look at the famous University of Georgia, lead on Oh Wonderous Tour Guide." And with that, they walked towards the school. Jill pointed out various landmarks: the University of Georgia School of Law, founded in 1859, which made it one of the oldest law schools in America in continuous operation, the University Library, and other buildings on the campus.

As she continued her commentary on the university, Murray said, "I do need to say something to you that is quite overdue."

"I'm listening."

He continued, "When we were in Santa Barbara, what did you call it, 'America's Riviera'? I never apologized to you for my behavior that afternoon. I was in a terrible place that day and knew you were trying your best to make it a nice weekend for us. We both needed a break by then, and I treated you abominably. I said some things to you that were mean and hurtful. I never meant to hurt you, and although I said things that are probably unforgivable, I'm asking you if you can find it in your heart to please consider forgiving me, even though I don't deserve it."

They walked on for a bit, and then Jill asked, "What has

happened to you, Murray? What has changed? When you called me a few weeks back, I didn't find you as self-assured as you normally were. You seemed a bit, how can I say it, a bit humbler, maybe? I don't know if that's the right word, but you were different. And then, at dinner, the tender side of you came out. The Murray that I fell in love with was back at the dinner table. I'm finding all of this a bit confusing—"

He stopped and turned her toward him, "I'm as confused as you, Jill, confused about a lot of things, but the one thing that I know I messed up on was how I treated you." He reached over and brushed the back of his fingers against her cheek, brushing some of her hair away from her remarkably beautiful face. She felt weak in her knees as she drew a sharp intake of breath. "I'm very sorry, Jill; hopefully, in time, you may find it in your heart to forgive me." They continued their walk, but this time, Jill slipped her arm through his.

She asked, "You haven't told me what has changed with you. Do you feel like sharing it with me? If you don't, that's fine, I understand."

"No, you're right. I have changed, and I feel you have a right to know. I went back home to Texas about two months ago. I just wanted to see how things were back in my hometown. I guess that I was going back for some closure, and then while I was back there, I met this incredible woman—"

"Oh, that's what it was. You met someone. Well, that might explain some of it, but there's still something else going on; I can feel it. We spent a year together, we've shared our lives and our bed. I know you. What's going on?"

"It's not what you think. I have had no romantic involvement with this woman, but she had an interesting impact on me. She is a devout Christian woman who did not shove religion down my throat or breathe fire and brimstone on me. She apologized for the actions of all of those people who treated me horribly for all of those years growing up. She told me that their actions were not the actions of a Christian. She asked me straight off if I were a Christian, and I told her that no, I'm an anti-theist. Do you know what she did? She told me the story of

Paul the Apostle. Do you want to know something even more surprising? I read up on Paul. It was an interesting story, but it made me stop and think. As I told Nate, I'm not a Christian, and I probably won't ever become a Christian; I don't know, but at this point in my life, I may be open to learning about the Christian faith. I think that whatever that young woman in Texas did and said has made me consider the possibility that I should at least question why a person could become a Christian. Does this answer your question?"

Jill was surprised to hear the sincerity in his voice combined with something else, possibly conviction. "That's an interesting story, Murray, and whomever this woman is, she sounds remarkable. Anyone who can have this effect on you must be special."

"She is special, and she's heading out to Southern California next week to spend a week or so out here on vacation, and I get to play tour guide; she's never been out of Texas. If you come to Pasadena, I'd like you to meet her."

"I'd like that, Murray, I really would." They continued their walk. After a few moments of silence, he asked, "I'd like to tell you why I'm out here, that bit of business about which I've been telling you. Do you remember how far along into the Einstein Project we were before you left? Where were we in the process when you left?"

"Let me see," she answered, "After you came back from Washington, D.C., where you met with the Griffith Group and the National Academy of Sciences, I was validating the numbers correlating the astrophysical activity seen in space and the unexplained aurora-like phenomena that we had seen here on Earth. Then, if I recall, I had researched archival activity going back to 650 B.C. when astronomers of antiquity had described similar phenomena in various locations throughout the ancient World. What did I do next? I have to think—"

He jumped in, "Didn't you find those records of some of Galileo's contemporaries describing a 'blink' in the Cosmos?"

"Yes, yes, yes!" she replied excitedly, "That's right, then we found that the Vatican Observatory described this as an 'accordion closing in space.' Then, by the early 1900s, astronomers had photographed this, dubbing it an 'astronomical slight contraction' or something like that. I forgot about all that until now. Then, if I recall correctly, the team ran some more numbers. They found a positive correlation between the 'contraction' and the unexplained aurorae phenomena observed worldwide. That's when we could theorize that the contraction was the closed timelike curve, the continuum folding back on itself, and that the unexplained aurorae-like activity was the Einstein-Rosen Bridge, the wormhole. That's when we said that we might have found the portal to the Space-Time Continuum."

He jumped in again, "Exactly. Then, remember that the team did additional modeling and found that the closed timelike curve and the aurorae activity were not random; they occurred with predictable regularity. Then, with further research and modeling, they found that the closed timelike curve and the associated aurorae occurred in specific geographical locations on the Earth. We coined the phrase 'Time-Launch Portal or Time-Launch Point,' the TLP, for that intersection of the three: the closed timelike curve, the aurora, and the geographical locus."

"Right. And then recall that P.K. demonstrated that the TLP behaved cyclically, what did he say, a 'delivery and return' method. He pointed out that the TLP opened in one place and point in time, transported through time to the second place and point in time, and then returned to the original point. P.K. demonstrated what Einstein, Rosen, and Flamm said. They described the 'wormhole' as a tunnel that connects two separate places in time. So, right before I left, you and the team thought that you could access the TLP and send a team back to a specific point in time and hopefully return them. That was it. That's where we were in the process when I moved on. I have not heard anything after that, so that's all I know. Hopefully, you'll give me the Paul Harvey version, the rest of the story."

"After you left, we had the opportunity to develop our mission. Based on our data and modeling, we found that we had a TLP opening on the Israeli coast, and it was going to connect via the wormhole to the first century of the Common Era, A.D.

if you prefer. To be more specific, the portal was going to deliver our team to Judea in the year 33 A.D., or so we had calculated."

"Are you telling me you sent a team to Judea in 33 A.D.? You all knew what was happening at that time, didn't you? Secondly, who did you get to go on this team? This was a one-way trip, correct?" So far, she was "blown away," and Murray had just started.

"First off, yes, we completely understood what was happening then. We identified the location and time when the TLP would open. This was our first experience in this process, and we felt confident that we could send the team back in time and return them to the present. The mission, as developed, was to test the thesis that time travel was possible and to help bolster our thesis; we wanted the team to bring back tangible evidence that they traveled back 2,000 years. We were looking for artifacts, scientific samples, and the like. One of our engineers said this was like bringing moon rocks back to Houston.

"Based upon your work in chaos theory that you had relayed to me, we had to set stringent parameters of what the team could and could not do. The bottom line was that they were to observe exclusively and not interfere with anything occurring back in time. That appeared to work because we're all here today. To answer your second question, team selection was a significant undertaking. We had a chance to listen to one of the engineers from NASA who was involved with the Mercury program, and he gave us some insights into astronaut selection. Based upon that model, we found that the candidate who would best fit our model would be someone from our military special operations teams, like the Navy SEALs, Army Delta Force, and guys like that.

"I have to be completely upfront with you and let you know that my thoughts were that the team would go back in time and observe that Jesus of Nazareth was a Jewish preacher from the boonies, and that was it; He was nothing more than that. I would be able to announce to the world that their religion was exactly what Marx said it was, opium for the masses. Those were my thoughts."

She jumped in again, "I appreciate your candor, but I have a feeling where this is going. I take it that the team found out more than you bargained for. Am I correct? That also means that the team was successful in getting back, right? Murray, is this why you're now open to learning about Christianity?"

"Yes, to your first and second questions. The team saw something much different than I had expected, and yes, they all made it back. But, to answer your third question, that's still up for debate. When the team returned with evidence that may prove who Jesus was or could be, I still denied it. But that experience, combined with what Kristin, the young woman in Texas, shared with me, has made me consider learning about Christianity. I'm still not sold."

She asked, "What kind of proof did they bring back?"

Murray continued, "They brought back some physical artifacts that were pretty convincing from an archeological perspective. But, their personal reports, their outbrief, were completely mind-boggling."

"How do you mean?"

"As I told you, I read up on Paul of Tarsus and other historical documents to better understand what the team members reported. It seems that the team had been in Jerusalem during the crucifixion of Jesus of Nazareth. As two of the team members were strong believers in Christ, they were emotionally distraught by seeing Jesus being crucified. They reported that during the crucifixion, Jesus had spoken to the team members in perfectly accented American English—"

Her mouth dropped open, "They said *what*?"

He shook his head, "That's what they claimed. They said that Jesus told them that this crucifixion *had* to occur. I'll let you read their entire transcript, but it was interesting, to say the least."

Jill was trying to take all of this in, "You said that they brought back evidence that could prove who Jesus of Nazareth was. Were the artifacts the only things that they brought back? That doesn't sound very convincing, at least to me. Did they bring anything else back?"

"As always, you pay very close attention. Yes, they brought something else back that could convince even the greatest skeptic. When Jesus was being crucified, wine was offered to Jesus on a sponge, which then fell on the ground. One of the team members brought this sponge back, which was analyzed for DNA. Nate and I brought this sample to the National Human Genome Research Institute in Bethesda. The results were remarkable. The regular chromosomes, the autosomes, indicated that the DNA was from someone of Semitic origin. But then the sex chromosomes were analyzed, and the Y-chromosome, the male chromosome, which from what I understand, is passed unchanged from a father to a son, well, what it showed was something that the geneticist at Bethesda had never seen before, the Y-chromosome was glowing."

She sat down on a park bench and was completely still, not saying anything. "As an undergrad, I took this one course in comparative religions. In one of our classes, we learned how the Catholic Church canonizes people to become saints. One of their key players is a canon lawyer assigned to argue *against* the canonization of the individual. This lawyer is called the 'Devil's Advocate'. I'm sure that you're familiar with the term. Let me take that approach right now.

"First, regarding the artifacts that were brought back, what kind of testing have they been subjected to? Have any archeologists taken a look at them? And how about that sponge sample? Was it subjected to rigorous testing or just the geneticist's observations? Has the geneticist's equipment been checked using any sophisticated tests? There have to be numerous tests out there to check on the validity of that sample. And as far as the team members and their testimony go, let's look at this from a different perspective. There was a movie a few years back about the Spanish Civil War, *Pan's Labyrinth*. Have you ever seen it?" Murray nodded his head. Jill went on, "OK, so you know what that's about? A young girl under incredible stress devises a land of make-believe to deal with the horrors of the war going on around her. Do you remember her carrying on those long conversations with that creature? In her mind, everything that she was experiencing was as real as you and me sitting here. You said that the two team members were believers in Jesus and were watching Him being crucified. Don't you think that that would have an unbelievable impact on those men?"

Murray asked her, "Are you trying to talk yourself out of what I just shared with you? I thought that you were a Christian. Do you find their testimony and the other evidence just fantasy?"

"I don't know what to think at this point. But I do know that in all of the research that we have done, we always, and I mean always, subject all of our hypotheses and data to very rigorous review and testing. Shouldn't we do the same thing here?"

Murray smiled at her, "Great points, and you're right on all counts. Let me fill you in on what has been done. The team brought back some weapons, and we sent them to the Archeological Research Facility at Cal-Berkeley. Their initial observations are that the weapons and coinage they studied appear to be the real McCoy. Secondly, we sent the sponge sample to an outside, private lab and got similar results. All indications are that what the guys brought back appears to be the real deal. After returning from Texas and meeting with Kristin, I began doing some soul-searching. I may have been precipitous in dismissing the work that the team did. I've been working with Nate on this. We have decided to bring the two main team members from our time travel group and have them re-present their findings to our group. I'd like you to come back and join our team. What do you think?"

To say that Jill was stunned by everything she heard would be an understatement. "All you have said has been difficult to believe, and it has 'blown my mind.' I'd like to see the validation studies done on everything, but I don't know what to say. This has to be one of the most important scientific advances ever, and I would like to be involved in it. What do you see me doing? It appears that all of the work has been done.

How can I help you?"

"Jill, I'd like you to bring your vast knowledge of chaos theory to bear. After the team makes their spiel again to the Einstein Project group, we'll need to consider the next steps. Before we do anything, we need to understand what kind of Pandora's Box we're opening. As I said earlier, the team's return to first-century Judea did not negatively affect the natural affairs. Were we lucky? Does this disprove chaos theory? We don't know, but we need to find out. That's why we need your help. You have an incredible mind, and I think you will find this work incredibly important and stimulating."

Jill replied, "No doubt on both accounts. OK, Murray, when do you think this will all start? If you can give me a ballpark figure, I can start the paperwork to ask for a sabbatical."

"I'm thinking at the end of this month. The first week of June at the latest. Does that help?"

"Yes, it does. I'll start my paperwork as soon as I get home tonight. Murray, thank you for an incredible evening. My mind is going a million miles an hour right now." She stood up, "Let me get going. I know you have an early flight, and I want to start my paperwork."

Again, He smiled at her, "No, thank you, Jill. Thank you for hearing me out on both things: the project, of course, and my terrible behavior toward you earlier. Let me walk you to your car."

"Oh, Murray, one last thing. You asked me earlier if I could find it in my heart to forgive you. I do forgive you."

"Thank you, Jill." They walked down to Jill's car, wishing each other good night. As she drove away, he said aloud, "There's the fourth piece of the puzzle."

Chapter Nine
Mid-May

Southern California

The Los Angeles Basin doesn't get much rain during the month of May, but when it does rain, and the winds are just right, the result is a gorgeous day where the sky is sparkling and everything is perfect. On those days when no marine layer comes in from the Pacific, the air will be as clear as crystal. Kristin was flying in from Texas on such a day, and as her flight descended into Southern California and LAX, she was awestruck by how beautiful everything was. She was in a window seat on the airplane's right side, looking at the desert below, when the pilot announced that they were coming up on the San Bernardino Mountains. The young man beside her told her that the mountain off to the right was "Big Bear," which attracts skiers and snowboarders during winter. She was amazed that a ski area would be so close to the desert. In a few moments, she was looking down and saw a spectacular view of downtown Los Angeles; her tour guide next to her pointed out the San Gabriel Mountains behind the view of downtown. Then, off to the right, he pointed out the Hollywood Hills, and she could see the Hollywood sign. He then told her to scoot down a bit and look out the window across the aisle on the left-hand side, where she could see the Pacific Ocean, and then Catalina Island came into view. She was as giddy as a child on Christmas Morning. When she was back in West Texas, one of the guests at her hotel knew of Kristin's upcoming trip, and he told her that in Los Angeles, "on a clear day, you can see your neighbor." He was wrong. Kristin could see why Los Angeles was called "The City of Angels." At least it was today; it was as if God had ordered a perfect day for her first trip out of Texas.

Murray was waiting for her right outside of Security, and he saw her walking up; she looked amazing. She was wearing a white sun dress that ended right above her knees. She was wearing a pair of sandals, and she had a nice color to her skin. She waved when she saw Murray and ran up and hugged him. Disengaging herself she began to talk non-stop about her views from the airplane, "Sure is mighty different from West Texas, I tell you *what*!"

Murray laughed so hard at how excited she was, "And it's nice to see you, too." He grabbed her bag, and she took his arm as they headed toward baggage claim. "So, I take it that the flight coming in was good."

"You have no idea. We were flying in over New Mexico and Arizona before we hit California, and everything looked just like home, then all of a sudden, there was this ski resort called Big Bend—"

"Big Bear, Big Bend is in Texas."

"Right, Big Bear, and then this entire city was below me. I saw the Hollywood sign, an island off the coast; it was amazing. I have never seen anything like this. I don't think anything can top what I just saw!"

He edged her to the right to go down an escalator to baggage claim, "Well, I might be able to show you a few more things that might change our mind. It looks as if we will have incredible weather for the next ten days. I sure hope that you have some good walking shoes."

She grinned at him impishly, "You bet, that and a new bathing suit that I think you'll like. Let me use the ladies' room; give me a second."

He stood outside the women's room and thought about how much he enjoyed Kristin's company. She had a nice mixture of a sweet young woman with a lot of country girl in her. She was fun to be with, and he enjoyed her company. Their relationship was one of two good friends, nothing more, but he hoped things between them could progress.

For her part, Kristin was thinking the same thing. She had really fallen for Murray when he was in West Texas. They kept in touch via phone and email during their time apart, but she, too, was hoping that things would move to the next stage. She thought her new bathing suit might help move the needle.

Meeting Murray outside, they retrieved her luggage from the baggage claim carousel and then headed to the parking garage, where they loaded her luggage into his BMW. Kristin settled in and asked, "You told me over the phone that you had a lot of stuff planned, but you were keeping everything a secret. Can you tell me now that I'm here what you have on our agenda?"

Murray pulled out of the parking garage and navigated his way to the freeway. "You know that Los Angeles is a huge city, and everyone here drives a car. The traffic can be incredible at times. The freeway that we'll be getting on here in a few minutes, the 405, can be a parking lot for several hours a day, so while it's early in the day and traffic is going to be light, I was going to take you up the coast to where we'll be staying for a few days. We're on our way to a beautiful city right on the ocean called Ventura. I've got you up in a vacation rental on the beach, and I'll be at a hotel right down the street. We'll stay up there for a bit to get you acclimated to Southern Cal. Then I thought we'd drive up the famous Highway 1 up to Monterey so that you can see some of Old California. After we head back down, we'll try our luck at you being in LA itself. I didn't want to bring you to LA first. You might have come down with a bad case of culture shock."

"I'm a big girl, Murray; I'll be fine. I went to school in Lubbock, right? That's a big city." He looked at her and noticed that she was smiling, "Just kidding, I know that LA is just a bit larger than Lubbock; I mean, it's Texas out there, Cowboy! Everything is bigger in Texas, right?" Murray turned and smiled at her.

They hit the 405-North and then caught the 10-West

towards Santa Monica. "You hungry, Kristin?"

"Yeah, I could eat, what's good around here?"

"I was thinking of stopping off in Malibu for lunch. It's a nice little beach community; if we're lucky, you might see some celebrities. Lots of movie stars have places out there. I don't think many of them have yet to cross the Cerebral Rubicon, but some people are in awe of them."

Kristin laughed, "I don't know what that Cerebral whatever is, but I'm not too impressed with the Hollywood group. They all make fun of the way that I talk. I don't have much use for them. If we see one of these celebrity folks, they ought to take a picture of you and ask for your autograph. You're the real star in my books."

"Don't know about that, but that was sweet of you. And you're a big star in my books, too." Kristin reached out and took his hand as they headed west toward the ocean. He made reservations for two at Duke's, a nice place on the water. As they walked in, Kristin held on to Murray for dear life, and then he softly said to her, "Look to the right. Do you recognize her without all of her makeup on?" The "her" was one of Hollywood's top draws.

Kristin was shocked, "Is that who I think it is? Good Lord, that girl is homely with a capital 'H.' She looks like she was shot at and missed and shit at and hit!"

Murray laughed so hard that people stopped what they were doing to look at him. He didn't know which was funnier, her using a bit of profanity or the fact that her West Texas accent just got about fifty percent more pronounced. It was hilarious. "What did you just say?"

"You heard me, damn, let's move on before some of that rubs off on me."

Murray reserved a nice table on the patio, where they had a beautiful view of the Pacific. The water was glassy, and there was no wind. All in all, it was an incredible day. He was here with a beautiful woman who made him laugh, and the old saw came to his mind, "It doesn't get any better than this."

Kristin was very impressed with the view and with the

restaurant, the facially challenged Hollywood star notwithstanding. Their waiter came up; it looked as if he had just got done surfing, which in all likelihood he just did, and asked if he could get them started with something. Murray asked, "What do you think? Do you want to try one of the local SoCal brews?"

She shook her head, "Normally, yes, but let me have a Mimosa for a change."

"Good choice. Let me have a Ballast Point Sculpin, please." The Surfer Boy went to place their order. "Well, Sweetie, what do you think?"

She thought *That's the first time he has used a term of endearment with me*," she liked it. "Well," as she looked out on the ocean, "I wonder how those old boys out there roughneckin' on the Permian Basin are doing right now." They both laughed at that. "Murray, I was talking with my folks about coming out here to visit you, and you know what? My mom and dad are good people. They told me that they both remembered your mother from the restaurant. Remember I told you that we used to go there after Church on Sundays? Well, they remember her very well. They said she was so nice and friendly, and then my dad said they didn't make them any prettier. They were very friendly with your mom and were saddened by her death."

He was wistful for a second, "That was very nice of your folks to tell you that. Please let your parents know that I appreciate their kind words about my mother." Surfer Boy showed up with Kristin's mimosa and Murray's IPA and asked if they were ready to order; Murray said they would be ready in about fifteen minutes.

When their waiter left, Kristin looked out at the Pacific and smiled. "I could get used to this; it is so beautiful out here." She then lifted her glass in salute and toasted Murray, "How about you? Do you spend your weekends in places like this?"

"Actually, no," he replied, "I've been out here several times, but I prefer heading up the coast a ways. I think that you'll like Ventura."

"As long as you're there to show me around, I'm sure I will."

After a nice lunch, they headed back up Highway 1, passing through several beach parks, past Point Mugu, where she was stunned by the beauty of the coast and Mugu Rock, and then up to Ventura. Murray helped Kristin settle into the rental and then headed out the door.

"Where you goin', Cowboy?" Kristin asked. "You're not bailin' out on me, are you?"

"No, just getting a few things from the trunk that I picked up for you. I had the place stocked with some food and other supplies, but I've got a few bottles of wine from the Central Coast that we can enjoy while you're out here. We can't sit on the lanai without some California wine, can we?"

"Of course not, but hold on, Sweetie, before you go out, I need to give you something. That was such a wonderful lunch, thank you." She put her arms around his waist, pulled him to her, and kissed him softly. Murray kissed her back as he enveloped her in his arms. Coming up for air, she said to him, "I know that this must be costing you a mint, and I appreciate it more than you'll know, but I'm worried about this spending—"

He interrupted her, "It's nothing, I have been—"

She put her index finger to his lips, "Let me finish, Sweetie. I was trying to say, why don't you save a little money on little old me? Do you think that you need to stay in that hotel? This place here looks as if it has more than enough room."

"I'd like that, Kristin. I'd like that a lot."

"OK, that settles it, go out and get your toothbrush and stay here with me." He brought his bag into the condo and didn't make it back out the door for quite a while.

They spent the next few days in Ventura. They had a chance to go on a fishing excursion, and then they took a boat out to the Channel Islands off the coast. Later, they drove up Highway 1 to Monterey, where they spent the day enjoying the peninsula. Kristin enjoyed learning the area's history, and Murray told her that the early white settlers in Monterey were like "Texans with an ocean nearby." After two days in Monterey and Big Sur, they drove back down the coast to Ventura. By this time, a serious romance had begun.

Kristin decided that she would rather stay in Ventura during her first visit to California, and they planned to take in all of the sights in Los Angeles on her next visit. At the end of the ten days, it was time for Kristin to return to West Texas. "This has been the most memorable time in my life, Murray. I cannot thank you enough for being the perfect host and guide."

"It has been my pleasure. I have enjoyed myself so much with you, but I need to ask you something, when can I see you again?"

"I've been thinking about that since lunch at Duke's," she answered. "I don't know, would tomorrow be soon enough?" They both laughed.

"No, that's not soon enough. I wish that you could stay; I mean that. I don't want you to go, but I know you must. When can you get some more time off? Could we take a long weekend, like around the Fourth of July? Is that too soon? If you can't get the time off, do you want me to head out to West Texas?" Murray was surprised at how fast he had fallen for Kristin, but it happened.

She looked over at him, reached over, and touched his right cheek, "I'd like that a lot, Sweetie, but let me check and see if I can get a long weekend in July. If I can't get the time off, let's plan on you heading out. Does that sound fair?"

"Sounds fair. Tell you what. If you can get out here for the Fourth, let's head down to San Diego. There is a little town I'd like to take you to, Coronado Island. A very patriotic town with a great parade, we'd have a blast."

Kristin answered, "That sounds good, too. You're spoiling me, Murray, you know that, don't you? I like that you're spoiling me, but I'm a simple girl from West Texas, and going out with you for tacos and a pitcher of beer would be perfect also. I'm not high maintenance, but I think you know that."

"That's just one of the many reasons, Kristin," he answered with a big smile.

"Many reasons for what, Cowboy? You gonna leave a Country Girl just hangin' like that?" He continued smiling, so she spoke the unanswered words they knew were there. "Don't worry, your secret's safe with me. And oh, if you haven't figured it out yet, I'm completely in love with you and have been for a while. Just get me to the airport on time so that I can start planning the next trip."

"Yes, ma'am, we're almost there, and Kristin? I love you, too," he admitted.

She smiled at him, "I know."

*****

Declan and Toma spent the last few weeks working with Nate and other members of the Einstein Project Team to review everything related to their mission two years ago. In addition to this review, Nate also brought Declan and Toma up to speed on several of the Einstein Project Team's advances since the initial mission. Nate told Declan and Toma that Murray would be discussing this more at length with the two of them prior to re-engaging the entire team.

Nate let Declan and Toma know that the team composition was firming up and that the latest person to join the team was Jill. Nate was hoping that the two former SEALs would have the opportunity to spend some time with her; the three of them had never met, so she could have the chance to discuss her thoughts on chaos theory with them. The team was scheduled to meet the first week of June to have Declan and Toma re-present their findings, and by the time Murray returned from vacation, everything was set to move forward.

Murray was meeting Nate in his office. "It looks like great progress to date. Thanks for putting everything together. I couldn't have done any of this without you. All right, give me a rundown on who will be here next week."

"Right now, we have from our initial candidate selection group and our engineering design team, Lead Engineer Arne Johansson and Psychiatrist Stephen Oliphant. From Astronomy and Astrophysics, we have Drs. Morris Kimber, Jay Agrawal, and P.K. Chakraborty. Jill McAllister is here, still acting as an ad hoc member of our team. Lastly, we have renowned ethicist and philosopher Professor John Barkley from Harvard's Safra Center for Ethics. Then we have you, Declan, and Toma, so our group is small enough to keep the leak potential down to a minimum, but it's large enough to give us a robust cross-section of the disciplines that we need to be involved with this. I think that we have a good representation of people involved right now. I have two hours set aside for this afternoon for you to meet with Declan and Toma to review the advances we have made over the past two years and give them a preview of what you are planning. I have to tell you, after you tell them what your plans are and what it is that you are trying to accomplish, I think that Declan and Toma will jump at what it is you're proposing. I wish I were younger and in as good physical condition as Declan and Toma. I want to go, but I think that my wife would have something to say about that."

"Yeah, this is still somewhat dangerous, but we've learned quite a bit in the past two years. I think that our safety cushion has increased quite a bit. But I hear you; how exciting would it be to do what Declan and Toma have done? Incredible."

Later that afternoon, Declan and Toma met Murray and Nate in Murray's office. After the greetings were out of the way, Murray said, "I believe that congratulations are in order for your ability to get out of Iraq without any major problems. Good job to both of you. I take it that your cover as Spanish businessmen was successful?"

Declan and Toma nodded yes, and then Declan said, "Our hat is off to your director of security. Everything was set up well, and our cover went off without a hitch. It seemed to us that everyone at Estuarial Engineering was expecting us and rolled out the red carpets for us."

Murray nodded knowingly, "Yes, our Security team had everything set for you. I wanted to let both of you know that it will be communicated to the Estuarial Engineering team that Senores Coixet and Borja were killed in a tragic car accident in Barcelona, so those gentlemen and their corporate plans will be no more. But let me get back to you regarding what I need to discuss with you gentlemen.

"I wanted to give the two of you a personal review of our team's advances following your mission of two years ago. You recall how we gained access to the Space-Time Continuum through the Einstein–Rosen Bridge, or wormholes, correct? We were able to identify that the wormholes connected two points in time at a specific location. Our research pinpointed where the wormhole would open and to what time it would connect; so far, so good. Additionally, as you all demonstrated, the wormhole behaves in a 'back and forth' manner in that what goes back in time can return. So, let me discuss what we have discovered since your return. Initially, we found that our Time-Launch Point, or Time-Launch Portal, if you prefer, our TLPs, were isolated in the eastern Mediterranean area and around present-day Israel, and the TLPs could connect us to first-century Judea. We have uncovered much more TLP activity in other parts of the world, and these TLPs are associated with different time periods. Let me illustrate this: We were able to send your team back to first-century Jerusalem in the year 33 A.D. What if we told you we could send you to Jerusalem in 33 A.D. and then transfer you to Rome in 60 A.D. and then to India in 72 A.D.? What if we could pinpoint where to send you and when?"

Toma jumped in, "What are you saying, Murray?"

Murray looked at Toma and Declan, "How would you two like to go back?"

Chapter Ten
Early June

Pasadena, CA

Dr. Murray Edgeton opened the team meeting at 8:00 AM sharp in the Einstein Project Team's conference room. Due to the highly classified nature of their work, the room was afforded similar security as a conference room in the Pentagon. The team members attending this meeting had the opportunity to meet Declan and Toma at their initial debrief two years ago, but most of them did not know either SEAL's background. He wanted to hold his own little "dog and pony" show with Declan and Toma, so he pulled out all the stops. He had a PowerPoint presentation chronicling the careers of both former Naval Officers, which he would show during his talk. He also had their official Navy portraits of them in their full-dress uniforms included with the presentation materials.

"Colleagues," Murray said, "Thank you for taking the time out of your hectic schedules to attend this meeting this morning. I assure you that you will find today's meeting both thought-provoking and intellectually stimulating. We will revisit former Navy SEAL Lieutenants Declan O'Sullivan's and Ashur Toma Boudagh's mission debrief, which we all heard about two years ago. Several factors have resulted in my decision to reengage our team to allow these gentlemen to 'make their case' with us again.

"Before we hear their presentation, I wanted to take this opportunity to introduce these American heroes to you all and

111

to attempt to offer you all a biographical sketch of their backgrounds and highlight some of their professional accomplishments. I should point out that some of their exploits are so highly classified that even we here in this secure facility cannot discuss them, so we will be discussing those events that have been declassified." Murray started his PowerPoint presentation by showing several pictures of both officers in various settings, for example, at their respective colleges, at SEAL training in San Diego, and in different combat zones.

"Lieutenant Toma Boudagh comes to us as a living example of 'The American Dream.' He and his family are Assyrian Christians, Chaldean Rite Catholics to be exact, from the Nineveh Plain in Northern Iraq. Like many who follow this ancient Christian Rite, their Rite was founded by St. Thomas the Apostle; Toma and his family fled Iraq following the First Gulf War and settled in the United States. Toma became interested in the Navy SEALs as a young lad, and becoming a SEAL was his life's goal. He attended the University of Notre Dame on a Navy Scholarship, where he majored in the Classics with special emphases in Classical Latin and Ancient Greek; Toma also speaks Aramaic, Arabic, Modern Greek, and Spanish. Toma was an All-American Water Polo player at Notre Dame, excellent training for a Navy SEAL.

"Lieutenant Declan O'Sullivan became a Naval Officer in the more traditional manner. His father, grandfather, and several uncles are all former United States Marines. Declan was exposed to the Navy and the Marine Corps at a very young age. He was appointed to the United States Naval Academy, where he received his degree in Physics. He was also an Olympian representing the United States in the 2008 Olympics as a gymnast. It appears that Declan was planning on being commissioned as a Marine Lieutenant upon graduating from Annapolis, but he, too, was bitten by the bug to become a SEAL. Like Toma, Declan also speaks several languages. He is fluent in Spanish and Catalonian, and during his training for this project, he attended immersion courses in Aramaic and Greek. Recently, Declan has become fluent in Classical Latin.

"As you can see, both of these gentlemen have very impressive academic and personal backgrounds, but as seen in this presentation, they are also highly decorated combat veterans, as you can also see by the accouterments on their uniforms."

Murray gave an overview of the various operations that they participated in both Iraq and Afghanistan. To say that the audience was impressed was an understatement. Still, he accomplished what he needed to do: He painted a picture of two very courageous, resourceful, and intelligent men who would do what needed to be done, no matter what the level of danger might be. Following his introduction of Declan and Toma, they again presented their mission outbrief to the team.

Declan and Toma gave their presentation in a "tag-team" fashion, where Declan discussed one aspect of their mission, and then Toma followed up. They discussed the initial transit and their experience at Bethany, where they came upon the family of Lazarus and his sisters as they recounted Lazarus' resurrection from the dead. They gave a detailed narrative, even stressing what some villagers had noticed in the sky at dawn, the "dancing lights," which were the aurora-like activity associated with the portal being opened. Jill was the only team member who did not hear the initial brief. She was reared as a Southern Baptist, and as a practicing Christian, she was amazed at what she heard. But when the two former SEALs began to discuss the Passion of Jesus, Jill became emotionally overcome. When Declan and Toma related what they experienced at the foot of the Cross and then when they discussed Christ's death on the Cross, she was emotionally drained. At the end of the presentation, she was in her seat with her forearms resting on her thighs, her hands dangling, and she was leaning over with her head hanging almost to her knees. She was happy that Murray announced a break at this point, giving her a chance to compose herself in the women's room.

When the presentation resumed, Nate went to the lectern and began to discuss what had occurred after the time travel team's return to California. He discussed his and Murray's experience at the National Human Genome Research Institute and what the geneticist had found on the sponge. Even though everyone in the meeting, including Jill, had heard this information before, to an individual, they were stunned. At this time, Declan and Toma opened the meeting up to questions.

Jill had composed herself reasonably well. "Gentlemen, I must tell you that I am impressed beyond words with what you have presented today. I know we were trying to get some time before today to discuss a few things, but as we couldn't, I'll raise some of my questions to you all this morning. First off, I must say that I admire your courage and your willingness to undertake this project. Secondly, from a personal perspective, I wished I could have been there with you." A few other team members began to indicate that they agreed with her. "I do need to ask a few questions regarding your report, and let me point out that I am not attacking either of you or saying that I don't believe you, but I do need to get this clear in my head what you experienced. First, when the Man you identified as Jesus of Nazareth was on the Cross, you said He spoke to you. Dr. Edgeton mentioned earlier that both of you can speak Aramaic, the language of Judea at that time, correct?" Both Declan and Toma nodded their heads, indicating yes. "Could it have been that what you heard was Aramaic, not English, and that due to the stress that you were both under, you both *thought* that the Man on the Cross was speaking English?"

Toma picked this one up. "Dr. McAllister, that's a great question. It's one that we have been asking ourselves since it happened. Please understand that my first language is Aramaic, and I had been speaking it to the people in the crowd. I know the language when I hear it, and I know English when I hear it. However, when I spoke Aramaic to the crowd, they understood me perfectly. But when Jesus looked down on Deck and me, and spoke not only English but English with a perfect modern American accent. I knew that it was English, definitely not Aramaic. The other teammates at the foot of the Cross also heard our exchange and were completely stunned."

Jill asked, "Do you mean to say that other team

114

members heard Jesus speaking English to you?"

"Yes, but not only that, the other people at the foot of the Cross heard it. For example, the Roman centurion Crispinus asked us what language we were speaking. As the centurion spoke Latin and Aramaic, he would have understood Aramaic if it were spoken. But the centurion did not understand what was being said. He then told us that he thought we were Angels sent to save Jesus. He must have thought that English was some celestial language, and we all know that that is not true; Italian is." That got a few chuckles from the group. "No, ma'am, there is no doubt in my military mind that what was spoken from the Cross was most definitely English."

She thought about this momentarily and then began to nod as if she were accepting that what Toma said was true. "Thank you, Lieutenant. I guess I can still call you that, correct?"

Declan chimed in, "We both resigned our commissions. It might be easier to refer to us by our first names."

Jill continued, "Thank you, Declan. So, Toma, let's go back and talk about the sponge that you brought back."

Toma answered promptly, "You bet."

"OK, can you tell me how you came to be in possession of it, and then can you tell me about its chain of custody?"

"We mentioned the centurion earlier, Gaius Valerius Crispinus, the centurion mentioned in the Gospels. As Jesus was on the Cross, He yelled out that He was thirsty. Crispinus got a sponge from one of his soldiers and plunged it into an earthen jug of wine. He put the sponge on the end of a pilum, a spear, and then lifted it up for Jesus to drink. When He was done drinking, the sponge fell to the ground. Without thinking, I picked the sponge up and put it in my bag. My bag stayed with me until we arrived back home. One of the things that we learned as SEALs is to keep your gear with you. You are responsible for your gear, so the bag was treated as part of my equipment; it was never separated from me. The chain of custody of that sponge? As I said, I had it the entire time until I gave it to Dr. Joseph."

Jill had another thought, "Was the sponge checked for

any other DNA? You said that one of the soldiers picked the sponge up and soaked it in the wine. Shouldn't we expect to see at least a fragment of someone else's DNA on that sample?"

Nate answered, "Let me address this, Jill. Great question; you should have studied law back in school. You'd be a great prosecutor. Bethesda's geneticist said she found two distinct cell samples on the sponge. The first sample was determined to be from oral mucosa, and a considerable amount of this sample was available. The other sample consisted of fragments of some epithelial cells that were on the sponge. She sent the sample to the histology lab at the center, that's the tissue lab. These epithelial cells were determined to be skin cells that may have sloughed off someone's hands. This sample was subjected to the same tests as the oral mucosa sample. Still, it contained entirely different DNA, and the DNA, specifically the Y-chromosome, did not exhibit the same behavior as the oral mucosa sample. So, yes, to answer your question, there were two samples on the sponge, one from skin cells and one from cells in the mouth."

"Thank you, Nate. But Toma, can you see how I might be skeptical of this sample? If this were a court of law, the question would be, 'Could this sample have been altered?' Did someone modify this sample?"

Considering the question, Toma looked like he was saying "hmmm" to himself. "All I can tell you is that the sponge was placed up to Jesus' mouth. He drank the wine on the sponge, and then the sponge fell. I placed it in my bag and brought it back here. What could I use to alter that sample? A better question would be, why would I alter it? I didn't even know the sponge was there until we returned home. As I said earlier, I wasn't even thinking when I picked it up, I just did. If this were a court of law, what would I do? I would swear or affirm, on my honor, what had occurred. I must tell you that military officers have a code, 'we neither lie, cheat, or steal nor tolerate those who do.' As officers, people's lives depend on what we say. We have to be truthful in everything we do, even if it means we're fired. I also mentioned that I would swear or affirm on my honor if this were a court of law. Dr. McAllister, I am an Assyrian, a Chaldean. The blood of an ancient Mesopotamian civilization runs through my veins, the same civilization that gave us the Code of Hammurabi. This code gave rise to reciprocal justice, an eye for an eye, a tooth for a tooth. This law's basis was to limit retribution; the retribution of a wrong could be no worse than the crime. So, if I cause you to lose your tooth, your retribution could not compel me to lose a limb. Your retribution will have to be commensurate with your loss. The Romans called this concept *lex talionis,* the law of retribution. You know, I just knew that Classics degree from Notre Dame would come in handy." The group smiled at that. "But as I was saying, living a *just* and *civilized* life, living with *honor*, these are the hallmarks of what it means to be an Assyrian. When I tell you *on my honor* what happened, then, as the old movies would say, you can take it to the bank."

Jill put both hands out in front of her, palms out, indicating that she did not mean any harm, "I'm sorry if I came across as doubting your word. I don't, as a matter of fact, as a fellow Christian, I believe in everything that you have said. I want to ensure that if and when your mission is made public, and the proverbial knives come out because they will, and you can definitely take *that* to the bank, I want to ensure you're prepared to counter their arguments."

"Thank you, Dr. McAllister, but believe me, no need to apologize as no offense was taken."

She continued, questioning, "Gentlemen, as you both know, my background is in chaos theory, and I have been focusing a lot of my research on what is known as the 'Butterfly Effect.' Are you gentlemen familiar with this theory?"

Declan answered, "I've heard of it but couldn't spout it off for you. How about you, Toma?" Toma shook his head, "No."

She continued, "It's something that we study in chaos theory, and the short answer is, a small change in one condition; we call this the 'initial condition,' can have a significant impact on a much larger and complex system and could result in vastly different outcomes. The example used is that a butterfly flapping its wings in one part of the world could result in a typhoon in the western Pacific. Think of the old Ben Franklin poem, 'For want of a nail…' My question to you, gentlemen, is that you may have moved something out of place or interrupted someone doing something. This could result in significant changes to the future state of affairs."

Declan again said, "We were very careful to observe events only. We did not interfere or participate in anything back in Judea; we just watched things unfold. But how I see it is that we must have done something right because we're all here today, and the world is operating the same way it was when we left. Does that make sense?"

She thought about this, "Chaos theory is just that, it's a theory, but it's a theory that a lot of people put credence into, but you're right in saying that you must not have left much of a footprint at all because as you said, everything appears to be normal. I don't know. Does anyone else have any thoughts on all of this?"

Everyone started talking at once. It was a spirited session.

Later in the day, Toma approached Declan and said, "You didn't disclose what we did back there; you almost interfered, Deck. Even that small change could have had a serious impact."

Declan replied, "Well then, maybe that chaos theory isn't all it's cracked up to be. Maybe we can go back into the past, and as long as we don't make any overt changes, it will not affect the future state; as Jill said, 'I don't know.' We'll have to see what happens if and when we get there. Think about it. Did we do anything overtly disruptive when we were there? Yes, we did stop the crowd from attempting to tear Jesus down from the Cross, but He stopped us—"

"That's because He knew that we would be upsetting what was to be," Toma's emotions were up. "I think that we got lucky back there, Deck; if we go back, we have to make sure that we do not do anything to interfere, but I don't know why we're even discussing this; I still don't have any idea what Murray's planning. If he wants us to go back into the portal, why? What's his reason for doing it? The first time made sense. He wanted to see if time travel was possible. We proved that it is possible, chalk one up for science, but I can't think of any reason to go back now. What do you think?"

"I don't know, Toma, I honestly do not know. But I have another question. What do you think about Murray's conversion? Do you have any different feelings now that we've been back here and seen him in action?"

Toma screwed his face up as he thought about this, "He seems sincere, and he seems to be a bit more human, so maybe he's just searching for The Way. We'll see. In the meantime, let's go out for a run. I need to clear the cobwebs out of my head."

At the same time that Declan and Toma were out on a run, Murray was in his office thinking back on the meeting. He thought to himself, *looks as if everything is falling into place.* He then called Kristin. He was still amazed at the effect she had on him. He had not been with anyone since his breakup with Jill two years ago, but in the short time he had been with Kristin, he knew he had found a soul mate. Two years earlier, he did enjoy Jill's company, and they did have some wonderful times together, but it was very different with Kristin. He felt that his life had taken on new meaning with Kristin, something other than his work, and another feeling came over him. He thought that he could make a life with her. What was it? Was it because she was from the same town as him? Was it because she understood what he had gone through as a child and how it affected him? He didn't know, but what he did know was that he thought of her all the time. What was that old Garth Brooks song, "What's she doing now?" That's what he thought about all day; he could see her going to work and then heading home at night, grabbing a cold beer from the fridge; he had to see her again. They talked on the phone and visited on their computers daily, but it wasn't enough. He had to be with her. When they spoke last week, he had the opportunity to chat with her parents.

He even liked them! All these thoughts were running through his mind as he dialed the phone.

She picked it up on the first ring, "I've been waiting for your call! Hi, Baby, how are you?"

He was touched by the warmth in her voice, "I'm doing fine, Sweetie. I just wanted to hear your voice. Listen, I know this is last minute, but do you have any slack time at work coming up? I know we plan to get back together again on the Fourth of July weekend, but I need to see you, and I can't wait until July; it's driving me crazy! So...do you know if your schedule will allow it? Can I come out for a weekend?"

"Oh, Baby, that would be wonderful. My schedule is out, and I have the weekend after next off, starting at 2 P.M. on Friday, and I don't have to be back to work until 1:00 Monday afternoon. Will that work?"

He smiled into the phone, "That'll work, Sweetie. Let me get my flights to Midland-Odessa locked on, and we'll go from there. Now tell me, what else has been going on?" They talked for an hour, and then Murray got back to work. He started to look over a few reports from one of the modeling teams when his phone rang. It was a call from Richard Hollander, one of the scientists from the astrophysics team, asking for a few moments of his time. Murray asked him to drop by at 5 PM. Richard was one of the original members of the Einstein Project Team. During their work together, they discovered they shared similar perspectives on religion and held the same anti-theistic views. Richard had become an ally of Murray and discussed that Murray's goal was to prove that Jesus was simply a rabbi from the backwaters of Nazareth and nothing more. Richard could not agree more.

Richard arrived at the appointed time, and without preamble, he asked, "Murray, I'm hearing some strange vibes; what's going on?"

Chapter Eleven
Early June – the same day

Pasadena, CA

Murray sat back down at his desk and looked at Richard. "Close the door and grab a seat." Richard closed the door and sat down. "OK, let me know what you're hearing and what the buzz is all about."

"Sorry to just barge in like this," Richard began, "I heard some of the guys in the team talking about the meeting you all had today, but before that, I heard that two of the SEALs from the time travel team were back and were doing their brief again to the team. Some guys were joking around the shop that it looked like Murray got religion. Needless to say, that gave me a reason to pause; I was thinking, 'That doesn't sound like Murray,' then, after today's meeting, I heard similar rumblings, so I decided just to be upfront and ask you, what's going on?"

"Richard, do you have time to go out for a beer? I don't want to talk in here." They headed to a brew pub near the JPL in Murray's BMW. The place was deserted, and they decided to sit outside on the patio. They grabbed a table and ordered a couple of beers. Murray opened up, "What's on your mind?"

"Just a bit confused. We chatted at length before the team entered the portal about your real reasons for going back in time. I wholeheartedly agree with everything that you said. We agree when it comes to this. The world would be a much better place if we didn't have this superstitious mindset of the deluded masses. How much death, destruction, and suffering has been caused because of religion? It's all bullshit, we both know that.

We've discussed this many, many times. Again, I'm just a bit confused. Have you come across any new empirical data that show that there was something to what those SEALs said happened back there? Have you changed your way of thinking about all of this? Level with me, Murray. I have never betrayed your confidence and don't plan on starting."

Murray sat back and began to chuckle a bit. "Man, this is some good beer. Who was it that first brewed beer, the Sumerians? Whoever it was, my hat's off to them. I'm glad to hear that there is a bit of rumbling with the team on what's happening. Good. It sounds as if people are buying it."

"Buying what, Murray?"

"Why, this whole masquerade. It sounds to me as if you have even bought into it. Do you honestly think I would suddenly become a believer after all we have discussed? Maybe I should consider heading over to Hollywood. My acting appears to be worthy of an Oscar. No, you and I are still on the same wavelength. I've just tweaked my goals a bit here. In the meantime, I need to present a new side of me, a side that appears to be searching for something. That's why I have been acting the way I have. If you take the time to talk with either of the SEALs, Nate, or even Jill, they'll tell you that I have not come to their particular fold. I keep telling them I am *open* to hearing about the Christian message. I can be honest with them, but they all think I am open to learning about their faith. But nothing could be further from the truth. Listen, you were there when the time travel team came back to the present, and they gave their out brief; those of us in the room who heard them were split on how we should proceed. Recall that some of the group thought that we should declassify those findings and let the scientific community in on what we did. The other part of the team echoed what Jill was asking about today. She asked if the samples could have been altered; were the SEALs overcome with emotion, and that's why they thought they heard English spoken by the man on the cross? Jill unintentionally did a better job of dissuading people than I. So, here is where I am at this point: If I am unable to demonstrate that Jesus of Nazareth was just some backwoods preacher, then the next best thing that I can do is stop His message from ever gaining a foothold on civilization."

Richard asked, "How are you going to do that?"

Murray continued, "It will be relatively simple—chaos theory. Jill and I went round and round on this. She is convinced by what Lorenz said: A minor change in the initial condition can significantly impact the future state. For some odd reason, when the time travel team went back, they were cautious not to do anything that would interfere with the state of affairs. But you should have heard the exchange in the meeting today. Jill went over her discussion of chaos theory and Lorenz's Butterfly Effect. Still, the two SEALs pointed out that they were cautious, and it must have worked because everything back here in the twenty-first century is fine, no harm, no foul. Then Jill said something very telling. She said that chaos theory is just that, a theory. But it's a theory that many people will bet the farm on. She left the door wide open to interpretation. I was trying to think of a way to dilute, if not completely discount, chaos theory. Jill did it for me. She cast doubt on it. So here is what I'm thinking: I want to send the team back in time, and my reason for re-engaging the project is to demonstrate that what we have discovered about these 'intersecting portals' is workable, and the team will prove it. But if we can let the team know that whatever they do back in time will not have the negative effect on the future that Jill keeps harping about, they will not have any impact at all. Let those clowns run around back in time with their Christian friends. I'm telling you, Richard, the only impact they will have is to alter the course of their religion; it will not take off. They're unknowingly going to alter the past. Does this make sense to you?"

Richard took another sip of beer, "Let me think about this. If you want to, how did you say it, stop the Christian message from taking a foothold, you may want to stop the people who spread it. We have to find a way to ensure the team members interact closely with the key players from that time. Who was their big guy, Peter? Is that right? They have to work closely with guys like him to screw things up."

Murray was nodding his head, "You're onto something. Keep thinking about this, and let me know what you come up with, OK?"

"I will. My brain is racing right now. Let me research this. Give me about a week to put something together."

"Sounds good, Richard. I know this goes without saying, but all of this is for our knowledge only, just as we did two years ago. How about another beer?"

Chapter Twelve
Mid-June

Pasadena, CA

Murray returned that Monday after spending the weekend with Kristin in West Texas. The meeting was planned for Wednesday morning with the entire team to discuss Murray's proposal. Dr. P.K. Chakraborty, who initially uncovered the cyclical behavior of the TLPs, was going to present the results of his most recent research. Jill would discuss chaos theory again, and Murray would take it from there.

Dr. Chakraborty greeted the group and opened the meeting, "We have a number of you here with our group this morning who were not involved with our team when we discussed the research that was done regarding our work with the Time Launch Point, or Time Launch Portal if you prefer, our TLP. For those of you who were here when I made our initial presentation a few years back, I beg your indulgence as I review this again for our other team members, and actually, a quick review of how we got to where we are now might be somewhat helpful.

"You may all recall that it was Dr. McAllister's work that demonstrated the relationship between what had been called the 'accordion fold' in the Cosmos, which we identified as the Space-Time Continuum folding back on itself, the Einstein-Rosen 'wormhole,' and the associated geographical location here on the Earth. We coined the term TLP for the intersection of those three elements. Dr. McAllister, your work was groundbreaking." The group recognized Jill, and it could be seen that the recognition of her peers touched her. Dr. Chakraborty continued, "Armed with Jill's data, we performed even more sophisticated modeling and discovered that the portal behaved cyclically. I don't wish to go too in-depth at this point, but what we found was that the wormhole would 'open' at a specific geographical and chronological point, it would then 'connect' for lack of a better term at the same geographical point in the past, but at a different chronological location. What I am saying is what Einstein and Rosen predicted: This wormhole would connect disparate points, both chronologic and geographic, in the Space-Time Continuum. To illustrate this, the wormhole will connect at a specific geographic location in the present day, then connect to that same geographic location at a different time, and then reconnect with the present time. The entire phenomenon behaved cyclically. What we hypothesized, we demonstrated with our time travel team to include Messrs. O'Sullivan and Boudagh. We were able to access the portal at a specific geographical point, in our case, in the desert north of present-day Ashdod, Israel. We transported the team back to the same location, but in the year 33 A.D. We were then able to transport them back to our current time."

This was the first time Jill and several other attendees heard of the completed work. They all had a basic idea of what the team accomplished, but to hear it described was mind-boggling. For Declan and Toma, this was the first time they had heard any of this background on how the team uncovered the secrets of the Space-Time Continuum, and they were fascinated by what they were hearing. During earlier briefings prior to their mission, they were given some background on what the Einstein Project Team did, but the proverbial nuts and bolts of how the discoveries occurred were never shared with them.

"Since completing that first mission, our team has continued researching what we had discovered earlier. Due to the exponential advances in computing technology over the past few years, we have uncovered additional 'secrets,' as it were, of the Space-Time Continuum. Initially, we found that the intersectionality of our three discrete factors, our TLPs, was confined to the geographical region of the present-day Middle East. The historical data we analyzed and the modeling we carried out three years ago indicated that we had geographical locations in the Middle East connecting to chronological points in the first century A.D. Since then, we have discovered that we can now identify the Time Launch Portal, TLP, and its activity in numerous areas worldwide. What we also discovered, which is all theoretical at this point, is that there is the possibility of additional, and I need to use this word again, *intersectionality,* between various TLPs. For lack of better terminology, let me try and describe this. It may be possible to 'jump' between TLPs if our modeling data are correct. Again, in theory, we could send a team to Jerusalem in 33 A.D. and then transport them to Rome in 60 A.D. We could then send the team to India in 70 A.D. Think of this as transferring airplane flights from Jerusalem, Rome, and then to Mumbai, but this time, our flights will be transporting someone not only to a different geographical location but to a different point in time. We're calling this discovery 'portal jumping.' Before we continue, do we have any questions at this time?"

As expected, the conference room erupted, with everyone talking at once. Murray stood up and asked for quiet, "Seems that we got everyone's attention. OK, let's start off. I think it's only right that the first question goes to someone intimately involved in this. Declan, please take it from here."

"Thank you, Dr. Edgeton," Declan began. "I can speak for Toma and me regarding this; this is important as we both have skin in the game. This is the first time Toma and I have heard of any background on how we got here. Although I majored in physics at the Boat School, I am at a complete loss as to how you all accomplished all of this. My brain hurts just thinking about it.

"When our team undertook our mission, we were briefed on what our purpose was. We were to demonstrate that time travel was possible. We accomplished that. We've demonstrated that time travel is possible. So, what is the reason for us to undertake this new mission, this 'portal jumping?'"

Murray said, "Fair question. Let me ask you something, Declan. Why do we undertake any scientific endeavor?"

"I would imagine it's because, as a species, we question things: What's across that mountain range? What awaits us in outer space? I believe that we humans have a natural curiosity; we need to know unknown things; this is something that we have done throughout our entire history as a species. It's in our DNA. But let me pose my question again. We've shown that time travel is possible, so what is the reason to return? We run the risk of altering the past. Jill said she is unsure if chaos theory applies, but why risk it? We're entering into some pretty shaky territory."

Murray replied to Declan, "You bring up the critical point. We as humans have a natural curiosity; we need to know things that are unknown; this is something that we have done throughout our entire history as a species. As you said, it's in our DNA. So yes, the main reason for attempting this mission is to continue unlocking the secrets of the Universe. Can we access different times and places along the Space-Time Continuum? That's part of our human condition, to explore the unknown.

"But there is another reason that we should consider this mission, which I have been discussing with Dr. Joseph and Professor John Barkley from Harvard's Safra Center for Ethics. Even though we think we live in an enlightened age, aren't we still experiencing significant hate and unbridled greed among various nations and peoples? Aren't we seeing significant cultural and class warfare throughout various societies? Let me ask you all a question. What is the single biggest threat to us as a species at this moment?" There were a number of answers shouted out from the group, including climate change, a plague, worldwide famine, and then one member said nuclear holocaust. Murray continued, "All those are huge threats against us as a species and other species on our planet. Absolutely. But if you think about nuclear holocaust, in addition to the overwhelming death and destruction that would occur, wouldn't the follow on to that holocaust be climactic change, famine, droughts, all of the curses known to us if that particular Pandora's Box were opened? So here is what we were thinking: Consider the Apostolic evangelizations that took place in the early days of Christianity. In a few short years, with no such thing as mass communication or mass transportation, these early Evangelists spread the message of Jesus of Nazareth to the entire known world. How did they do that? What could we learn from their success?

"Is it possible that one of the areas that we can study is the success that they enjoyed? Here is why this might be considered: What if the unthinkable happens, the world's Superpowers lose control, and the doctrine of Mutually Assured Destruction takes place? Those people who survive will have to have the ability to communicate what knowledge exists in the world. The possibility exists that mass communications will be non-existent. Would the knowledge of how the early Christian Evangelists communicated their message successfully to the known world be of import?"

Once again, a robust discussion took place, and Murray thought, *Oh, yes, coming together nicely indeed!*

*****

Declan and Toma were in the middle of their morning five-mile run, talking about the meeting of the day before. Toma said, "I thought about what Murray said all night. Some of what he said made a lot of sense. You have to admit that the early Evangelists successfully spread the Gospel; if you think about it, they did it all by preaching from village to village, from town to town. Word of mouth, and look how successful they were. Then, if you take what Murray is saying, could we use that 'model' to spread knowledge if the unthinkable were to happen? It is an interesting question."

"Yeah, I guess. But we discussed this earlier. I think we're both being drawn back. What do you think?"

Toma laughed, "You wouldn't even have to offer me a reason to go back. I'd go back right now just to hold St. Paul's books and writing materials. Remember when we first met with

Murray after returning from Iraq? He was talking with us about the TLP and then began talking about multiple TLPs and how they can access them. Remember, he asked us both point blank, 'How would you two like to go back'? I would have gone right then."

"I'm with you, Toma, so what do you want to do? Should we tell Murray that we're a go for whatever mission he's planning?"

"Yeah, I'm game. Let's do it." They continued their run for another two miles and then went to call Nate. Nate agreed to meet with them at nine o'clock that morning.

They met Nate in the dining room, where he was the only person in the room enjoying a cup of tea. "Good morning, Declan. Good morning, Toma. Please, might I get you both some tea?"

Toma answered, "No, thanks, we're set. But thanks for meeting us here this morning. Deck and I discussed what we heard yesterday, and looking back on what Murray told us when we first got back, it sounds like he wants to put a mission on. Is that the way you see it?"

Nate smiled at both men, "Yes, it does appear to be where he's going. I think the scientist in him wants to prove that he can unlock this mystery of the Space-Time Continuum. Still, his discussion on learning how the early Evangelists were able to spread the Word does have practical applications. Why? What are you two thinking?"

Declan picked it up from here, "I'll just cut to the chase. If he wants someone to take this one on, Toma and I want to go. Who is better qualified for us to do this? No one is. The only thing that we want to do is be in the planning phase from the outset. Do you think that that is doable?"

"I will ask him this morning. Murray was very upbeat after yesterday's meeting. It looks like he has significant buy-in from the team, but you know how he operates; he'll bust through walls if he wants something bad enough."

Toma asked, "Do you know what kind of time frame we're looking at for this project? What's driving the timeline?"

Nate said, "As you heard in our meeting yesterday, the team is working on determining the cycle of the various TLPs. It might be six months from now, or it might be next year. It depends on what the Astronomy team and the modeling team can come up with. Besides that, I understand that Jill is doing quite a bit of work on chaos theory. She is trying to ensure that whoever is sent back will be fully prepared to react to various scenarios. She's doing a lot of sensitivity analysis right now, some very esoteric stuff."

Declan added, "Let us know if there is anything that we can do to convince Murray to get us suited up for game time. We're both pretty antsy about getting this show on the road."

Nate laughed, "I can tell. As I told you two years ago, I wish I could have gone with you on your mission. Now, with the possibility of going to India in 70 A.D., I can't even begin to tell you how much I want to go. Mar Toma, St. Thomas the Apostle, landed in Kerala around that time and brought the Gospel to my home. I could enjoy being on the beach and watching Mar Toma arrive with the Word of God in his mind, lips, and heart. What a gift God has given you. I can't envy you as that is a sin, but you know what I mean!"

Toma said, "Declan and I walked the same paths as Mar Toma when Deck came to get me in Iraq. We know exactly what you mean."

"Declan and Toma, God has touched you both, He has something planned for you, of that I am certain." At that time, they could not envision what was in store for them.

131

Chapter Thirteen
Early July

Pasadena, CA

Dr. P.K. Chakraborty was reviewing the modeling reports of the latest work completed by the Einstein Project Team with Declan and Toma, specifically the recent discovery of being able to transport a team between various time periods.

"Gentlemen," Dr. Chakraborty began, "during the initial work that we did before your mission, we had found, and you all confirmed, that the TLP being opened was associated with a *specific event* occurring on Earth; recall that we only found evidence of TLP activity in the area of modern-day Israel in the period of the early first century. You all confirmed this premise when you discovered that the portal opened during the incident with the man called Lazarus. You further validated our premise of the association of the portal opening with a significant event when you confirmed that the portal reopened on the third day after the crucifixion of your Christ. Before I continue, let me apologize in advance for something. Please excuse my ignorance of some of these religious matters, as I am not a Christian, I am not familiar with much of your history. If I am speaking something a bit incorrectly, it is not intended to discount your Christian history; it's just, as I said, my ignorance of it."

Declan and Toma let him know they were not offended by what he presented.

Dr. Chakraborty continued, "But we found in our latest research that possible TLP activity with a subsequent opening of the portal has been found to exist in many other areas, as we mentioned, Rome, India, Mesopotamia, and such. We are examining archival data from numerous sources. There appear to be several significant events on the Earth that have not made it into many Western history texts; these events may be associated with the portal opening. Be that as it may, what is of main interest to us is that we have some potential portal openings to insert a team back through the Space-Time Continuum. What is of concern to our team at this point is the intersectionality of the various TLPs. We don't know exactly how that intersection may behave. To illustrate this, we are hypothesizing that a team could be in Jerusalem in the year 33, intersect with another TLP that is theoretically going to connect with Rome in the year 60, but for all we know, instead of being transported to Rome in the year 60, you may be transported to Southern India in the year 72, that is what we are attempting to analyze at this time. Any questions so far?"

Declan asked, "How will we be able to find these intersecting TLPs? When we went back the first time, the portal opened on both occasions, for our arrival from the present and our return to the present in a remote area in the desert north of Ashdod. We were all dialed in to go to one specific location for 'recovery.' Let me see if I have this right. We will be transported back to Ashdod in 33 A.D. Would the intersecting TLP 'responsible' for getting us to Rome be in the same Ashdod point, or another geographical location? And if it is, how will we know where to go? The same question would pertain to the TLP for the transfer to India."

Dr. Chakraborty replied, "When you all went back to Judea for your first mission, you were given several modern-day tools, for example, stand-alone pre-loaded hand-held computers for navigation that could be used without GPS satellites. You were also equipped with short-range person-to-person communication devices. We have been working on developing similar devices to take back with you. In addition to navigation devices, we are looking at a hand-held computer that will be pre-loaded with all the information you need relative to TLP activity.

But right now, our main concern deals with the TLP intersection. We need to ensure that if your computer tells you that this portal will take you to Rome, Rome will be your destination, not another location. We're working on it. We will focus considerable energy and computing power on this question when Dr. Edgeton returns from his long weekend in San Diego."

Murray, for his part, had been enjoying San Diego with Kristin for the Fourth of July holiday. They had reservations at the famous Hotel del Coronado and spent most of their day on the beach and enjoying Coronado Island's many shops. The highlight of their weekend was the Fourth of July Parade, the largest Fourth of July Parade west of the Mississippi River. They enjoyed their weekend together, and on Monday, Kristin returned to Texas with a promise that they would see each other the following month. Their romance had taken a serious turn, and Murray was still amazed at how hard he had fallen for Kristin. Earlier that weekend, as they walked along the shops at Coronado's Ferry Landing, watching the families enjoying the Independence Day holiday, he thought he and Kristin could have a future together. "Why not," he thought to himself. He began to give serious thought about asking Kristin if he could fly out to West Texas the following month and meet with her family.

On a whim, they caught the ferry and crossed the bay to San Diego's Embarcadero, where they spent time playing tourist and seeing the sights along the waterfront. They caught a pedicab that took them a few blocks up to San Diego's Little Italy, where they enjoyed a nice lunch and then walked around the open-air farmers' market. They walked past a beautiful fountain at the end of the marketplace, then turned right at the following street and found themselves in front of a stately-looking white church. There was a plaque inscribed in Italian with an English translation. Towards the bottom of the plaque, it read that the church was built in 1925. Kristin grabbed Murray's hand as she read aloud, "Chiesa Cattolica dedicata alla Madonna del Santo Rosario." Then, in English, she read, "Our

Lady of the Rosary Catholic Church. Wow. Let's take a look. If it's as beautiful inside as outside, it must be fairly remarkable." Reluctantly, Murray joined her.

Walking inside the church, they were both struck by how simple yet unbelievably beautiful the sanctuary was. There was an altar at the front of the church flanked by life-sized statues of Jesus and the Madonna, the paintings on the ceilings were reminiscent of pictures Kristin had seen of churches in Europe, and the church walls offered more statues to view in addition to breathtaking stained-glass windows. Murray, as jaded as he was, was duly impressed.

As they continued walking around the church, they saw a priest carrying a box into the church. Kristin smiled at him, "Good afternoon, Reverend."

"Good afternoon," the priest smiled at them, "Please, 'Reverend' is too formal. Please call me Father Sal. Welcome to Our Lady of the Rosary. Are you both visiting?"

"Yes, Father Sal, I'm Kristin, coming from West Texas," and looking at Murray, he answered, "And I'm Murray, coming down from Pasadena, but originally from West Texas."

Father Sal put the box on a table in the church's vestibule. "Well, welcome once again. Will you be joining us for the Vigil Mass this afternoon?"

Kristin looked at Murray questioningly, "Don't think so, Father. Neither of us is Catholic. We were enjoying the beauty of your church. But if I might ask a question, your church is called 'Our Lady of the Rosary,' what is the significance of that name?"

"Let's head over to the rectory. I have to get something, and I think it might be time for an espresso." They walked over to the rectory, where Father Sal offered them each a cup of espresso. "OK, the name of our Church. As you may have noticed, this neighborhood was made up of nothing but Italian immigrants, hence our neighborhood name, 'Little Italy.' This parish is comprised of Italian immigrants, and Our Lady of the Rosary is particularly important to many Italians. Are you familiar with the Battle of Lepanto?"

Murray said, "Wasn't that something to do with Muslim expansion in the Mediterranean?"

"Full marks for you, Murray, yes, it was. In the 16th century, the Ottoman Empire was terrifying Christian Europe. Their great Sultan, Suleiman the Magnificent, had captured Belgrade, the island of Rhodes, and had defeated the Hungarian Army. His sacking of Christian European cities was stopped at the Siege of Vienna. Years later, the Ottoman Navy attempted to attack Christian Europe again when they met a combined fleet of The Holy League led by Don Juan of Austria. The Holy League, a coalition of Catholic States including Spain, Italy, the Papal States, and others, prayed for the intercession of Our Blessed Mother by praying the Rosary. They credit her intercession for the victory over the Ottoman Fleet. This victory's historical significance is that it stopped Muslim westward expansion and denied them access to the Atlantic and potentially the New World. As Italy and other southern European nations were spared this onslaught, the Italian people have had a special devotion to Our Lady of the Rosary, hence the name of our Church, so there you go. How is the espresso?"

Kristin put her cup down, "It's wonderful, Father, thank you. So, how long have you been here at this church and in San Diego?"

"I've been here at this Church for three years, but San Diego is home. I'm from right across the bay; Point Loma is where my family is from; that's another community full of Italian and Portuguese immigrants. My family was in the commercial fishing industry, as were most of the Italian and Portuguese families out in this neck of the woods, and it was anticipated that I would be in the fishing business, too. But I followed Our Lord's admonition to be a fisher of men instead."

Kristin smiled at his story, "Well, this is a beautiful city and a beautiful church, Father, and we enjoyed your hospitality and your sharing with us the background of Our Lady of the Rosary. Can we make a donation to your church before we leave?"

"That's very kind of you, but here is what I would ask

you to do. When you see one of our many homeless out there on the street, see if you can give one of them something to eat and share with all of them your smile; that would be a wonderful gift to God."

"We will, Father; visiting with you has been a blessing. Thank you, Father Sal, and we hope to see you the next time we're out here."

"You're both always welcome here, and it's always nice to visit friends from the Lone Star Republic. May God bless you both, and may He watch over you in all you do."

As they walked back through Little Italy, Kristin looked at Murray, "What a nice visit. That was an interesting story about how God's intervention preserved Christian Europe, don't you think, Sweetie?"

Murray paused briefly, "Before I met you, I would have said something like, 'No, it's more of a story of how religion led to lots of bloodshed', but not now. I'm not a believer, but as I told you, I'm open to learning about what else might be out there." He thought to himself that he meant what he said. Even though he talked with his colleague Richard not long ago about his goal in his new proposal, when he was with Kristin, something about what she said made him look at things differently. It was a very confusing time for him.

Murray returned to Pasadena that Tuesday after his long weekend. The plan for that week was to take all of their preliminary data and run their calculations through the Blue Gene/P Supercomputer at the Lawrence Livermore National Laboratory up north in Livermore, California; he and Nate were scheduled to fly up to Livermore in a couple of weeks. But that evening at home, he called Kristin.

Kristin was jazzed as usual to hear his voice, "Hi, Sweetie, how are you doing?"

Murray, as usual, was touched by how happy she was to talk to him, "Hey, I'm doing great, thanks. How are things on your end?"

"All things considered, Baby, doing well, just wish you were here."

"Same here," he smiled, "That's what I'm calling about. Remember how you told me about how your folks had mentioned that they knew my Mamma?"

"Of course I do. They said that she was a very nice person and they enjoyed seeing her. Why do you ask?"

"Well, as you recall, when we were talking about that, I said that I appreciated what they said about my Mamma, and I asked you to please pass my regards on to them. Do you think it might be a bit more appropriate if I thanked them myself, you know, in person? Would your parents mind meeting me so I can thank them?"

"Sweetie, are you telling me you'd like to meet my parents?"

"Yeah, I guess I am. What do you think?"

Kristin was grinning from ear to ear, and her excitement was welling up. "You coming out here to meet my parents would be wonderful. I told them about everything we had done, and they somewhat hinted at me when I would bring my 'beau' home to meet them. Baby, I am so happy. You have no idea what this means to me." She started tearing up at this. "Is there anything else you wanted to talk to my folks about while you're out here? Did you want to talk about your mother to them?"

Murray thought about how to answer this. He was thinking with his heart and not his head. "You know, that's very kind of you to ask me that. I want to talk with your folks about that. Most people back in town would never talk with me about my Mamma, and you saw how Randall treated me; that's how it has been my whole life with those people. Your folks had nice things to say about my mother. I'd like to hear them. I could talk to your folks, especially your dad, about some other things."

Kristin felt her heart racing in her chest. If he asked her to marry him, she would tell him yes. "What kind of 'other things' would you want to talk with my dad about?" She held her breath.

"Your dad works in the insurance field, correct?"

She was slightly puzzled by his question, "Yes, Dad has been a broker for years. What kind of questions would you have?

If you let me know, I can talk with him about it earlier so he would know what kind of information he could get you."

"Well, I was wondering if he had some actuarial data on what type of health and life insurance a thirty-something married man might need to have in this day and age, especially one living in Southern California. I know there might be some geographical price differences, and I was wondering if your dad might know what they might be. Do you think that he would?"

She was puzzled at the direction this was going, "I'm sure that Dad would. Are you looking for one of your colleagues for this information? It might be easier for them to see a local agent or broker."

"No, I was looking for this information for myself."

"Murray, what are you talking about? You're not married—" She was hit with a horrible thought, and she asked, "Are you?"

"No, but that was something else I wanted to discuss with your dad. I wondered if he would mind if I asked for his daughter's hand in marriage."

There was dead silence on the phone, and the only thing that Kristin could hear was the rapid beating of her heart in her chest. "Murray, are you asking me to marry you?"

He smiled into the phone, "I sure am, Sweetie. Do you think that you could spend the rest of your life with me? I hope you'll say yes because I can't imagine spending another day without you. We'd be perfect together, so what do you think? Do you want to start having some real fun?"

Kristin was crying and could not stop; between her sobs, she answered, "Yes, my love, I will be your wife. I will answer you a thousand times and gladly be your wife; I cannot spend another day without you. I love you, Sweetie. I fell in love with you when we had dinner the first night you were here."

He continued to smile into the phone. "The only problem is, I don't know if I can wait another couple of months to see you. Do you think that we can hold out that long?"

This made Kristin laugh, "I tell you *what,* if I have to wait two more months to see you, I can tell you that when I do see you, the second thing I'm going to do is put my suitcase down! No, we can wait if we have to. The problem is that I don't want to wait any longer. What do you want to do?"

"I have a weeklong meeting in the Bay Area in a couple of weeks. We'll be done by that Friday. How about the first part of August? Can we shoot for then?"

"Yes, Baby, let's shoot for then. I'll ask my manager to rearrange my schedule if needed, but yes, let's plan on it. Honey, you have made me the happiest woman in the whole world! I can't wait to see you; I love you and am so happy for us! And I know my parents will be thrilled, they enjoyed talking to you on the phone the other day. Oh, I am so happy!"

"Same here, my love. I can't wait to see you."

*****

Murray and Nate flew up to Livermore on a Monday morning, and as they were close, Murray decided that the first person he would talk to about his engagement would be Nate. Murray waited until they were in their rental car driving from the San Jose Airport to Livermore.

"I'm glad we have this time by ourselves as I wanted to discuss something with you. You know that I have been dating Kristin for several months, and as I have told you before, she has had a significant impact on me."

Nate looked at his friend, "I can tell you, she has been good for you. You've changed quite a bit in the last several months. As we discussed a while ago, the young woman who could convince you to even talk about religion must be an amazing person. Declan, Toma, and I have been discussing your interest in learning about the faith. While we were initially skeptical, you have convinced us of your sincerity in at least wanting to learn about the faith. I take it that a lot of that is due to Kristin. Am I right?"

Murray nodded his head "yes" while watching the traffic. "Not only has she made me open to learning about the faith, she has shown me that the goodness that comes out of her is due to her faith as a Christian person. I have to ask myself, what makes her tick? It all comes down to the faith that she learned as a child. The scientist in me has to say that it's fascinating, at the least. So, you think she is good for me and that, as you said, she must be an amazing person. Is that how you feel?"

"Yes, it is. I think she has had a very good influence on you. I can tell that you must care for her quite a bit."

Murray continued to nod his head. "You're right in all that you say. There's me, Kristin, and now there's you."

"You, Kristin, and me, what?"

Murray smiled at his friend, "There's me, there's Kristin, and you. The three of us know I have asked Kristin to marry me, and she accepted."

Nate was surprised but very pleased, "That's wonderful, Murray. I take it that congratulations are in order, my friend, so congratulations! Have you all set a date?"

"Not yet; I will be flying out next weekend. I need to talk with you about that as this has happened at the last minute. I'll head to Texas next weekend to ask Kristin's father for her hand in marriage. There might be some movement on the project, and I'll need to ask you to cover for me if anything pressing arises. Are you OK with that?"

"Of course, no worries at all. This is a wonderful surprise; will you announce it to the group when we return?"

Murray thought, "Don't know right yet. Let me think about that for a bit. OK, I thought about it. No, I think that at this point, I will let my best friend know for now, and that's it. After I return from Texas, I'll let the team know; that way, it will be more official. Damn, Nate, who would have thought that I'd be doing something like this? I'm still not certain that I am."

The work at the Lawrence Livermore National Laboratory took all week, but the computer run of their data indicated they were on the right track.

Chapter Fourteen
Early August

Pasadena, CA

"But you see, Declan, that is the main difference between classical physics and chaos theory. Physicists, chemists, biologists, and those involved with the other, how shall I say, the 'traditional sciences,' focus on linear, predictable, deterministic phenomena, not so with chaos theory." Jill acted very much like the professor she was in her meeting with Declan and Toma. "Do you both recall when you were able to represent your findings to the team, and at that meeting, I discussed chaos theory?" Both Declan and Toma slowly nodded their heads. "Remember how I said that a slight change in the 'initial condition' can result in vastly different outcomes? That is still my concern."

Toma jumped into her discussion, "Yes, Jill, we understand that. But recall that Declan had mentioned in that meeting that we were careful not to interfere, and it must have worked because nothing has changed. We're all still here, right? We were at the 'initial condition' and could not see any discernible difference in the outcome. But let me back up because, unlike Deck, I did not study physics at Notre Dame. You mentioned that the traditional sciences focus on what you say, deterministic phenomena. What does that mean? You lost me there, Doc."

"Sorry, Toma. Most of the sciences deal with linear, predictable problems. Let me illustrate this. You can ask an astronomer where Jupiter will be next week. They can run calculations based on Jupiter's planetary motion, point to a specific spot in the sky, and tell you where Jupiter will be. They can calculate further, tell you where Jupiter will be in one hundred years, and they'll be pretty close. The planet's motion in the cosmos is predictable. The final outcome, its location in a hundred years, can be predicted from its initial condition; we mathematicians call it 'deterministic.' But let's look at something like human behavior, the stock market, the number of patients going to an emergency room, and turbulence in flight; these are all examples of a non-linear, unpredictable phenomenon. That's what we deal with in chaos theory. We attempt to address phenomena that are impossible to predict or control. We deal with incredibly complex systems, compounded by the fact that their initial condition is extremely sensitive to even the slightest change. These changes can result in incredibly different outcomes." Jill took a sip of water. "Let's look at this from what you all experienced, and this was the same argument that I had with Murray a few years back. What if, during your time back there, one of your teammates inadvertently moved a small rock from the side of a path to the middle of the path? That's part of the initial condition. Then, later that week, in the middle of the night, an individual walks down that path, the same path that they have taken for the last ten years; the path has been unchanged this entire time. But this time, this individual is walking down the path and stumbles on the rock your team member moved. That person falls, breaks his neck, and dies. But here is the problem: That individual was destined to marry and father a son. That son was destined to be a great statesman or a general, destined to bring peace to the region. However, the outcome will change significantly due to a change in the initial condition. The peace that was supposed to be in that region will not come to fruition because of that minor, seemingly insignificant change in the initial condition."

Declan looked at Toma and then at Jill, "But how can we explain what happened? We were there. Shouldn't the fact that we were there have been in and of itself a change in the initial condition? I'm not talking about moving rocks or anything. I'm just saying that we interacted with people back there. People heard us talking to Jesus of Nazareth; people saw our weapons, and an entire group of them followed us into the desert. We had to have some impact on the initial condition. That leads me to believe that chaos theory may not be correct in all of its assumptions. Think about it. By definition, you say that the initial condition is extremely sensitive to even the slightest change. Yes, we were careful and attempted to be invisible and hidden, but Jill, as I said before, we interacted with those people. One of our team members went to the market and bought a knife from one of the merchants. Now, using the logic of this theory, what if that knife was supposed to have been purchased by a revolutionary who was planning on assassinating one of the Roman officials? Well then, I guess we changed the course of history. But our history did not change; everything was the same as when we left; what are we to make of this?"

Jill thought about this for a moment. "I don't know, Declan, I honestly don't, but didn't you say in your brief that Our Lord told the two of you that He would get you back home safely? Could it be that He might have had something to do with everything staying the same? Could He have had a kind of insulating effect on the presence of your team back there?"

Declan and Toma were both taken by surprise. Toma answered, "We never thought about that, but that is possible. But let me ask you to consider this: Deck, we went back to Jerusalem two thousand years ago, correct?"

Declan nodded, "Yes, we were there."

Toma continued, "OK, so we were there at the crucifixion of Jesus, so what happened two thousand years ago actually *occurred*, correct?"

"I see where you're going with this. Yes, what happened when we were there actually occurred."

Toma was warming up to what he was thinking and saying, "Right. So, what if our being there actually altered history and we irrevocably changed the future? What if what we're experiencing today results from our going back in time and changing things? What if what we are experiencing today is based on something we did two thousand years ago?"

Declan asked, "Do you think that everything we have done with our lives, everything we did, was based upon something we did two thousand years ago? Let me ask you this: We went through BUD/S and deployed with the teams. The Einstein Project then selected us to go on our mission. If we decided not to sign on with the Einstein Project, does that mean we did not go through BUD/S eight or nine years ago? Is that what you're saying? If we had not gone on our time travel mission, everything that we did in our lives up to that point would have changed?"

Toma answered, "Yes, I think I'm saying something like that."

Declan continued, "Then what that means is that there is no concept of free will. Our lives have been predetermined. Nothing we could do or say would affect our lives."

"As I said, Deck, I'm just asking you to consider this. I don't know, what do you think, Jill?"

Jill thought about that possibility, "So what you're saying is that all of the world's history from the time of Jesus is based upon the time travel that you all did? You know, that is not out of the realm of possibility. The only thing that it is doing is making my brain hurt by just thinking about it."

*****

Jill met with Murray and Nate and related everything regarding her meeting with Declan and Toma. "I'm still of the mind that what chaos theory predicted about how subtle changes in the initial condition will significantly affect the outcome. All of the evidence points to that. However, what may be different at this point is how *sensitive* the initial condition will be to those subtle changes. There is the possibility that the initial condition may offer us a bit of 'wiggle room,' now, there's a scientific term if I ever heard one. That wiggle room may be able to absorb some of the subtle changes in the initial condition. I don't know at this point."

Murray sat back in his chair, "Chaos theory might allow for some wiggle room; I think that term is very descriptive. I like it, Jill. Our having some wiggle room might explain how the team went back there, interacted with people of that time, returned to the present, and found that the world just kept chugging along as if nothing happened. That lets me know that we can send a team back in time, and if they follow the ground rules, they won't impact the initial condition; what do you think, Nate?"

Nate leaned forward towards Jill and Murray, "What Toma postulated is fascinating. What if all we are experiencing today has been altered by what we did two years ago?"

Jill looked up, almost as if searching for an answer, "I've been thinking about this since I talked with Declan and Toma. Let's look at this historically: What happened before Jesus of Nazareth was born? The Romans occupied Judea. Zealots attempted to overthrow their Roman occupiers; everything led to the Romans destroying the Temple in 70 A.D. The march of history, as outlined in the Jewish Scriptures and by the historian Josephus, did not appear to be affected. I think that history progressed as we know it, the Einstein Project notwithstanding. I don't think that our time travel team did anything to alter history. It's an interesting premise, but I don't think they did anything overt that modified the initial condition. At least that's how I see it, but thinking about this still hurts my brain."

Murray jumped up, "I have an idea. Why don't we bring John Barkley into this discussion? He's a philosopher and might have a different perspective on this that the three of us might overlook. Let me get a hold of John and ask him to meet with us via conference call."

Murray's call with Professor Barkley was productive and enlightening, resulting in several other calls. Based upon their meetings, it was decided that the time travel team did not have any discernible impact on the future and that any subsequent ventures through the portal would have to follow the same strict guidelines as the initial mission. This guidance, the team felt, would help to ensure that the initial condition, that is, the occurrences from the past, would not be affected.

But Murray was conflicted. He was sitting at his desk reviewing a report and thought about the influence Kristin, Nate, and the others had on him. He then thought about his earlier discussion with his colleague, Richard Hollander. Murray still harbored thoughts that religion may have played a negative role in the world's history. Still, his earlier anti-theistic and atheistic stances were not as pronounced as they were, and he began reevaluating his discussion with Richard. Did he still want to interrupt the evangelization of Christianity? Did he believe that the world would be a better place without the Christian religion playing a pivotal role in the progress of Western Civilization? He was not so sure; he was beginning to have serious doubts about how he viewed the existence of a Supreme Being. Recently, he found himself impressed with the deeply held religious beliefs of Nate, Jill, Declan, Toma, and, most importantly, Kristin.

He wondered once again how Kristin had made such a significant impact on him. If Christianity played a major role in her life, he had to respect it. He put his report down on the desk and sat there. He and Kristin would have their nightly phone call in a couple of hours, and he thought about what he would tell her. He had to level with her. He was going to tell her about his earlier hatred of her religion, how deep it was, but how she had opened his heart to not only a deep and abiding love, but how she soothed his anger with his past. For the first time in his life, he was beginning to experience inner peace. He had to talk to her. He had to hear her voice.

He called her at their usual time, seven in the evening, but his call went to her voice mail. She called back within fifteen minutes, "Sorry, I couldn't pick up. I'm having a big problem here, and I'm trying to get things resolved. I'll be out of here about nine your time. Can I give you a call when I get home? It will be nice to unwind at home with a glass of wine and talk with my baby. Does that sound good?"

"You bet there's lots to talk about tonight. I have

something to share with you, OK? Be talking in a bit, Baby, love you."

"Sorry, sweetie, I have to run; talk in a couple of hours."

He thought she must be distracted; she always told him she loved him at the end of every call. Oh well, he smiled to himself; she'd make it up to him when they chatted later that evening.

But it didn't work out that way.

Chapter Fifteen
That night

West Texas

Randall met his old buddy, Johnny, at one of their favorite watering holes, The Broken Spoke, right outside of town. Randall hadn't seen Johnny for a few years, but they ran into each other out on a rig up north, and they made plans to meet for a few beers later that afternoon once Johnny had a chance to come back to town. By ten o'clock that evening, they both had a belly full of beer and several shots of whiskey.

"Well, let me tell you one of the other reasons why I was hoping to get together with you," Randall told Johnny. You ain't ever gonna guess who I ran into at that new pub in town."

Johnny looked over his beer mug at Randall, "All right, how many guesses do I get?"

"You only get one, but as I said, you'll never guess," Randall taunted.

"Oh, hell, I don't know, OK, I got it, you ran into George Bush."

"George Bush? Now that's a laugher, no, sir, I ran into somebody you'd never guess who. Johnny, I ran into that bastard boy of yours. If you ask me, he's all grown up and a real educated, snooty type. Hard to believe that I'm blood to that uppity bastard. No, I ran into him, and he had some hot little number with him, I tell you what. He may have gotten himself all educated and such, but he didn't learn much. He still acted like the little boy I used to needle all the time. And just like when he was a young 'un, he had to hide behind the woman he was with. I felt like hoppin' off that bar stool and opening up a big ole can of whoop ass on him. You should have seen him, Johnny, one minute he was—"

"What's he look like, Randall?"

"What's he look like? What's he *look* like?" Randall repeated. "Well, I guess that women would find him all nice and handsome like, but I don't swing that way, Johnny. He did have a lot of RaeAnn in him, I'll tell you that much. And I still don't know what in the hell he came out here for, but I ain't seen hide nor hair of him since. I have my feelers out with a lot of the old group that still live out there, ain't nobody seen him."

Johnny sat there and mused about what he just heard. "So, he's good lookin', and he's all educated up; well, how about that? I guess that I did all right."

Randall laughed at that, "You did all right? Are you shittin' me? Do you think you had anything to do with that boy growin' up? Now that's a funny one right there, folks. Let me tell you, Johnny, I know that you sweet-talked my sister and all to get into her pants, but listen up, son, in case you forgot, you left her high and dry and on her own with a little surprise that you left her. You didn't do jack shit for that boy except make his life a livin' hell." With that, he threw his head back and unleashed a volley of laughter. "Well, maybe me and my kin might a had somethin' to do with that."

"OK, Randall, I get it, no reason to keep throwin' that shit in my face. But what did he say to you?"

"Not much. I think that he was just scared of me, acting like a little whinin' maggot. You didn't miss much, but I tell you what, that little split tail he was with was somethin'. Damn, boy, that's somethin' that a man could enjoy comin' home to every night. Maybe I shouldn't have treated him so poorly that night. Hell, I could have had a chance to get friendly with those two; I could have seen a lot more of that little thing. What the hell is wrong with me?"

"Damn near everything as far as I can see," Johnny replied, they both broke out in laughter. "Hey, listen, Randall, I got to get up early tomorrow, and I know for damn sure that I can't drive. Can you give me a lift back into town? The company has a bunch of us stayin' at that old hotel out by where you used to live. Can you drop me off over there, and I can have one of my crew bring me back here tomorrow to pick up my truck? You OK with that?"

"Sure, Johnny, no big deal. Let's finish this pitcher and then we'll hit the road, but I gotta tell ya, I'm half in the bag my own self, but it's only a couple of miles, drink up."

*****

At the same time that Johnny and Randall were pouring themselves into Randall's pick-up, Kristin was finishing up at work. She could be home in ten minutes and then call Murray. She was on the rural highway heading north when Randall and Johnny got on the same road heading south. There was a bit of a tricky turn in the highway where the southbound lane had to climb a bit of a rise, take a sharp S-curve to the right, then back to the left, and then continue south. The northbound lane continued straight, and where the southbound lane climbed the slight rise, the northbound lane continued on flat ground and was ten feet below the rising southbound lane.

Randall and Johnny had a country station playing loud on the radio while driving back to town. They came up on the rise, and Randall was moving too fast for the curve. He was supposed to take the curve at thirty-five miles per hour, but he was going closer to sixty. Randall took his eyes off the road for a second as he looked at Johnny when Johnny mentioned something, and when Randall looked back at the road, the S-curve was already upon him. He missed the turn and went flying straight through the guardrail.

Kristin was approaching the rise when she noticed something that puzzled her; for a split second, what she saw couldn't be real. Her brain could not make sense of what was coming her way. She saw a truck flying down from the other side of the highway, aiming right at her windshield. She had no time to react, but her last conscious thought was of Murray—then everything went black.

*****

The Texas State trooper pulled into Graham's driveway and walked to the door; it was almost midnight. Ringing the doorbell, the trooper thought to himself, "How many of these calls have I had to make in the past twenty years?" Mr. Graham, Kristin's father, answered the door, and when he saw the Trooper standing there, he knew something was terribly wrong.

Mr. Graham stood there with his heart in his throat. "Yes, Officer, may I help you?"

"Yes, sir, Mr. Graham. Sir, do you have a daughter named Kristin Graham?"

"Yes, sir, I do. Is anything wrong?"

The trooper paused for a brief second, "Yes, sir, there has been a terrible accident out on Rural-Route-4, and your daughter has been severely injured. She was life-flighted to the West Texas Medical Center, and that's where she is right now. If y'all can be ready in a few moments, I can escort you to the medical center. If you follow me, we can get there much quicker."

Mr. Graham asked, "Is my little girl dead, Officer?"

"No, sir, she has been gravely injured, and her condition is very critical, but she appears to be hanging in there. Do you want to please follow me, sir?"

"Yes, sir, let me get my wife. We'll be right with you."

Forty minutes later, the Grahams arrived at the medical center. Mr. Graham was wearing his pajama shirt, bedroom slippers, and an old pair of work pants to punctuate the suddenness of how quickly this happened and how unprepared the Grahams were for it. Mrs. Graham was in her nightgown and robe; she was holding her Bible and was praying Psalm 34:

When the just cry out, the LORD hears them, and from all their distress, He rescues them. The LORD is close to the brokenhearted, and those who are crushed in spirit, He saves.

A little after two in the morning, an exhausted-looking surgeon appeared in the lobby where the Grahams were seated. The doctor looked around the lobby and saw the couple seated there. By their appearance, he knew exactly who they were. "Mr. and Mrs. Graham, I'm Dr. Wiekowski, and I'm taking care of your daughter right now. She has made it through surgery and is now in the Intensive Care Unit. I must be very upfront and let you know it is touch-and-go right with Kristin. She is in very grave condition. I need to ask you to please be strong and prepare yourself for what may happen."

Mrs. Graham looked at the doctor, "Is my daughter going to die, Doctor?"

He looked down and saw her Bible open to the Psalms. "That's in the hands of Our Heavenly Father. Let's go see your daughter."

Mrs. Graham began to pray the Psalms aloud, "The Lord is kind and merciful!"

Dr. Wiekowski responded, "He is slow to anger and rich in compassion. Shall we pray together before we go in?"

Mr. Graham was strengthened by the knowledge that the physician was a believer, "You are praying with us now, Doctor Wiekowski. Praise be to God that He, in His mercy, sent you to be with us."

They walked into the Intensive Care Unit where Kristin was and were horrified at what they saw. Kristin's head was covered in bandages, but they could see that she had sustained severe head trauma. Her skull appeared to have been crushed, and her entire body looked to be broken and bruised. Tubes were going down her throat, and there were several infusion devices and vital sign monitors hooked up to her. Mrs. Graham began to weep, and Mr. Graham had to turn and walk away. He looked at the doctor and asked, "I know you're trying to be upfront with us. What do you think her chances are?" The two men walked a few feet away to talk.

"Mr. Graham, as I said, she is in very grave condition. She has sustained significant cranial damage, and she had tremendous trauma to her chest, which resulted in massive internal bleeding. We have stabilized her and are hoping to transfer her to the Level I trauma center in Lubbock. In the meantime, you all can stay close to Kristin, but please prepare yourselves for what may come at any time. That is as upfront as I can be. I recommend talking and praying with your daughter. That is the best that we can do for her right now."

"Thank you for your honesty, Dr. Wiekowski. As you said, all of this is in the hands of Our Heavenly Father. I have one last question, what happened?"

"I'll have the nurse who took the initial report from Trooper Watkins; I believe you already met him; come by and share with you what she received from the Highway Patrol. If I can get a hold of Trooper Watkins, he might be able to give you more information. Do you have any other questions for me at this time?"

"No, sir, you have been most helpful. Thank you, Dr. Wiekowski." Mr. Graham could not hold back any longer and broke down completely. Dr. Wiekowski stood there with his hand on Mr. Graham's shoulder, his head bowed in prayer. Mr. Graham composed himself, "If you'll please excuse me, Doctor, I have a few calls to make." Mr. Graham approached his wife, seated beside Kristin's bed. He sat with his wife and daughter and said, "I have to make some calls. Let me borrow your cell phone for a second." As he walked back to the lobby, a young nurse approached him.

"Mr. Graham, I'm Monica Alvarez, the nurse who took the trauma call a few hours back. Can we go sit down and talk? Dr. Wiekowski told me you asked what happened with your daughter, Kristin. If you're up for it, I have all of the information with me."

"Sure. I need to hear what happened to her." They walked over to a small consultation room where Nurse Alvarez explained everything.

"Do you know that spot on Rural- Route-4 north of

town where the southbound lane goes up that small rise and the northbound lane skirts alongside the bottom of it?"

"Yes, ma'am, I know it. Is that where this happened? That's only a few minutes from her place."

"Yes, sir, that's where it happened. A few Good Samaritans who witnessed the accident were on the scene. They called 9-1-1 and helped Kristin. From what we can gather from the eyewitness statements, there was a GMC truck heading southbound that was traveling over the speed limit, but it also appeared as if the driver was impaired. Actually, it looked as if the driver was really drunk. The driver took that S-curve too fast and smashed right through the guardrail down onto the incoming northbound lane. The folks driving about three or four car lengths from Kristin witnessed the accident. They were able to stop in time. They called 9-1-1, and they were the first people on the scene. The husband tried to pull Kristin out of the car. She was unconscious at the time, but the damage was too great, and she was trapped in the car."

Mr. Graham asked, "That gentleman stayed by my daughter's car?"

"Yes, sir, he stayed there and tried to stop the bleeding. She was injured very badly, but the witness, his name is Mr. De La Torre, is a retired U.S. Marine, and he said that he felt it was his duty to stay there and render aid until the First Responders arrived."

Mr. Graham was amazed by Mr. De La Torre's courage. "The car could have blown; he could have been killed. I do not know what to say."

Nurse Alvarez continued, "I know, he said that he did not smell any gasoline or anything, but you never know. His wife, Mrs. De La Torre, said they had a fire extinguisher in the car she gave to her husband. I guess the Marines teach their people to be prepared for any emergency. The first rig arrived within twenty minutes, and they relieved Mr. De La Torre. It appears that the De La Torres were holding Kristin's hand and praying the Rosary when the rig got there. The second rig arrived shortly after that, and they had the jaws of life with them, which they had to use to get Kristin out of the car. The Life Flight helicopter was on the scene, and they transported Kristin to us. She was here at around eleven-thirty that night, and she was immediately prepped for surgery. Dr. Wiekowski finished around two o'clock this morning, and then she was transferred to the Unit."

"Thank you, Miss Alvarez. Can you let me know about the people in the truck? What happened to them?"

"Both of them were declared dead at the scene. Neither one wore their seat belt, and they were ejected from the cab. It looks as if their vehicle rolled over and crushed the two of them. Trooper Watkins reported that it was a fairly gruesome scene where they found the two victims."

"I'm very sorry to hear that. One last thing, is there a way that I can meet the De La Torres? I want to meet them; they were both very brave in what they did, and I need to thank them."

"Of course, Mr. Graham, we'll arrange this for you. Their names are Dave and Barbara De La Torre; we'll get you their contact information directly. In the meantime, do you have any other questions?"

"No, ma'am, thank you for your help. I need to find a place to make some calls. I need to call my family and Kristin's fiancé. Can you excuse me, please?"

Nurse Alvarez told him, "Mr. Graham, you can use this consultation room if you wish. Just close the door and make your calls. Please let me know if you need anything, OK?"

"Yes, ma'am. I will."

*****

It was about one-thirty in the morning in Pasadena. Murray was sound asleep, dreaming that he heard the phone ringing, but it kept ringing. He realized that it wasn't a dream. He reached for his phone and thought about who in the world would be calling him at that time. He noticed on his screen that the area code was from West Texas. This puzzled him for a second, and then he remembered that he hadn't gotten a hold of Kristin the previous night. He sat straight up in bed and answered the phone. He thought he heard a familiar voice on the phone talking with him, but he couldn't be sure. "I'm sorry, I just woke up. Who is this again?"

"This is Bert Graham, Kristin's father. Can you hear me, OK?"

Murray was fully awake now. "Yes, Mr. Graham, I can hear you." He looked at his watch and realized it was three-thirty in the morning in West Texas. What *was going on*? "Mr. Graham, what's happening? Is something wrong?"

"Yes, Murray, there has been a horrible car accident out here—"

"Is Kristin all right, sir?"

"No, son, she's not. She's in very grave condition right now. She survived the surgery, and they're trying to get her stable enough to transfer her to the big trauma center up in Lubbock. I've talked with the surgeon who operated on her, and he was very upfront with me. He said it's touch and go with Kristin right now and that we should prepare ourselves for the worst." There was a long silence on the phone. "Murray, are you still there, son? Can you hear me?"

"Yes, sir, I can hear you. Mr. Graham, please let Kristin know that I love her and am on my way out there. I can get a flight out first thing this morning. Can you do that for me, please?"

"Of course I will, Murray. Please get out here as soon as possible. Be safe, and may God bless you."

"Thank you, sir and Mr. Graham," Murray surprised himself as he uttered this without thinking, "May God bless you, too. "

He called Nate right after that. "Nate, I'm sorry to awaken you, but I just got some bad news. It looks as if Kristin was involved in a serious car accident, and it doesn't look good for her. I will try to catch a flight out of LAX this morning. Can you cover for me for the next few days?"

"Murray, I am so sorry. Why don't you contact the airlines and get a flight out, get yourself packed up, and I'll be there in the next forty-five minutes. I'll get you to the airport. Are you going to try both LAX and Burbank?"

"Damn, Nate, I didn't even think of Burbank, good call. Yeah, I'll get on the horn and get this going. See you when you get here. Thanks, Buddy."

"No worries, I'll get everyone praying for Kristin. See you within the hour."

After Nate hung up, Murray went into a flurry of activity to get things packed up. As he was looking in his closet, he was hit with a very sobering thought: She may not make it. He looked in his closet and cursed himself for having to do this; he took a dark suit out of his closet to pack up, just in case.

Nate showed up a little after three to drive Murray to LAX. Murray was lucky to catch a flight to West Texas at seven that morning. When Nate arrived, Murray had a set of notes he wanted to discuss with him, but Nate gently took the notes from him. "Murray, I've got this. I can have our team continue our research and prep; this is the least of your worries. If you're up for it, can you tell me what's going on as you finish getting ready?"

Murray related everything Mr. Graham told him, including the doctor telling them to prepare for the worst. Nate listened and didn't say a word. Murray called Mr. Graham back, but the cell phone was off. "I guess I'll hear from them if there are any changes. OK, Nate, ready to head out? I can get a hold of a hotel out there and get a room, but right now, I need to get out there." The drive to the airport was very subdued.

Murray arrived in West Texas and got a rental car. He got an update from Mr. Graham right before he boarded in Los Angeles; there was no change in Kristin's status. He drove straight out to the West Texas Medical Center. When he arrived, he walked into the waiting area outside the ICU, where he saw Mr. and Mrs. Graham and two other people he had yet to meet. As soon as he walked in, he knew that bad news awaited him. Mr. and Mrs. Graham were seated at a bench seat; Mrs. Graham was crying inconsolably, with Mr. Graham rocking her in his arms. The man and woman standing there were also crying. Murray just stood there, stunned. Mr. Graham finally noticed him standing there. He walked over to him and said, "You must be Murray. Son, you just missed her; she slipped away about ten minutes ago. I am so sorry." Mr. Graham crumpled in grief and went back to sit with his wife.

The young man walked up to Murray and extended his hand. "I'm Robert Graham, Kristin's brother." The young woman walked up to them. "This is my sister, Sheila." Sheila just stood there with tears coursing down her cheeks.

Murray continued to stand there. Finally, he looked at Robert and Sheila and said, "I am so very sorry for your loss. Your sister Kristin is an amazing person; I'm sorry, she was an amazing person. I can only imagine what you and your parents are going through. I need to offer your parents my condolences." He walked over to Mr. and Mrs. Graham but stood apart from them. Mr. Graham looked up and motioned Murray, Robert, and Sheila over. "Mr. Graham, Mrs. Graham, I am so sorry for the loss of your daughter."

Mrs. Graham stood up and embraced Murray, "She loved you so much. All she could talk about was how happy she was and looking forward to being your wife. She let the cat out of the bag that you would be coming out here to ask for her hand. We are all sorry for you, too."

"Thank you, Mrs. Graham. She always told me what a great family she had." Then, looking at Mr. Graham, "Thank you, sir, for calling me. Is there a chance that I can say goodbye to Kristin?"

Mr. Graham grabbed Murray by the arm and steered him towards the nurses' station, "Let's go see." They walked to the nurses' station, where Mr. Graham found the charge nurse. He asked if they had already transferred Kristin off the Unit, and the charge nurse told him that patient transport had yet to move her. "Can Dr. Edgeton see her, please? They are engaged to be married, and he just flew in from California."

The nurse led the two of them to Kristin's room. Mr.

Graham said to Murray, "Be strong, son, she was injured very badly, and it shows. I'll let you see your betrothed by yourself."

"Thank you, Mr. Graham." Murray walked into Kristin's room, and his heart broke when he saw her covered with a sheet. He walked over and pulled the sheet down to see her face. He was stunned beyond words by what he saw. No one should have been violated in such a manner; no one needed to suffer this much, and no one needed to be mangled and tortured the way that Kristin was. The monitors, IV leads, and tubes were all removed from her, but she was still a terrible sight to see. Murray took her cold, stiff hands in his and looked where her engagement ring was supposed to go. "Oh, Baby, what did they do to you? I am so sorry it's you, not me, on this table. Oh, my dear and precious love, I love you; I love you with all of my heart and soul. With every ounce of my being, I love you." He could not maintain his composure any longer, and he collapsed in grief and shed tears that had been held back for thirty years.

Finally composing himself, he bid goodbye to Kristin and walked back into the waiting room, where he found the Graham family waiting for him. Mr. Graham told the family, "Let's head home so we can make some plans. Murray, can you join us, please?"

"Thank you, sir. I'll follow you all to your place."

They arrived at Graham's house, where a group of people was already waiting for them. Interestingly enough, a Texas Highway Patrol cruiser parked outside the house with a State Trooper waiting outside with the rest of the group. The Grahams and Murray walked inside the house with their family friends, and the State Trooper followed the family. Mrs. Graham and Sheila began to greet the crowd; most of them must have been ladies from the church as they all had platters of food with them; the word traveled fast. The trooper approached Mr. Graham and said, "Sir, I don't think this is a good time to bring this up with you, but you left a message to give you any information about the accident as soon as we got it. I've got additional information for you if you want to hear it. If not, I can come by another time; it's up to you."

"Thank you, Trooper Watkins. Here, let's all go into my office. This is my son, Robert, and my daughter Kristin's fiancé, Murray Edgeton. They're going to join me if you don't mind."

"No, not at all, Mr. Graham, thank you." They all entered Mr. Graham's office, where they sat down. Trooper Watkins took out his notebook. "Mr. Graham, we all heard that your daughter just passed; please accept the condolences of our entire department; it was a tragic accident that didn't need to happen. I am so sorry, sir, and to you, gentlemen. Please accept our condolences on your loss." All three men nodded their heads in appreciation. "Ok, let me see here, yes, sir, we got the toxicology report from the lab, and it looked like the two other victims had blood alcohol levels of 0.21 and 0.24, respectively. That's three times the legal limit in the state. They were both very intoxicated and should have never been behind the wheel of their truck." Something then struck the officer. He looked at Murray and asked, "Murray, what was your last name again, please?"

"It's Edgeton," Murray replied.

"Well, ain't that a coincidence, and where are you coming from, Mr. Edgeton?"

Mr. Graham said, "That's Dr. Edgeton, and he's from California. He just flew in no more than an hour ago."

The trooper shuffled through his notes, "I'm just saying that it's a coincidence. One of the victims in the crash was also named 'Edgeton,' let me see here, yep, here it is. We had two oil workers from the Basin in the truck that caused the accident: one 'Randall James Edgeton' who is from right here in town, and another worker, 'Johnny Ray Chapman' from Lawton, Oklahoma. Do those names mean anything to you, Dr. Edgeton?"

All eyes were on Murray as he answered, "No, sir, I can't say they do."

Chapter Sixteen
Early September

Pasadena, CA

Murray returned to work in late August after he and the Graham family laid Kristin to rest. The demons from his past that Kristin had worked so hard to help him face and defeat had reared their collective head and attacked him with a vengeance. Any hope of a conversion of his soul was gone; dead and gone would be a better way of putting it. The hate that he felt toward God and religion had multiplied a hundred-fold from his early days growing up in West Texas and his time at MIT. He held God accountable for Kristin's death and for allowing Randall Edgeton and Johnny Ray Chapman to draw breath. He declared war on God and vowed to himself that whatever it took, he would win.

The project team in Pasadena was very somber upon his return. Nate had asked him to take as much time off as needed before returning to work, but Murray was adamant that he would return on time. When he returned to work, he looked like a man possessed, attacking his work with an unbelievable release of energy. People were polite and respectful to him, but it could be seen that they would go out of their way to avoid him. Murray saw this and couldn't care, but he did set aside a considerable block of time on his calendar to meet with Richard Hollander.

Richard met Murray in his office, and as soon as he arrived, Murray told him that they were going out for a drive and then lunch. "I need to be able to speak freely and not worry about someone walking in or overhearing anything I'm going to discuss with you. I take it that you cleared this afternoon on your calendar?"

Richard replied, "Yeah, cleared the entire afternoon off. Nothing like a hot day in SoCal driving around with the top down."

They left Pasadena, caught the Ventura Freeway, and headed west toward Ventura County. "I wanted to take a drive out towards Simi Valley. On a day like today, having the top down out there will be a nice change from what we have out here," Murray said as he navigated through the traffic. "I just had to get out of the office with all of those prying eyes and everyone offering me 'their heartfelt condolences.' I appreciate it, don't get me wrong, but I don't need to be reminded fifty times a day that Kristin is dead. I am acutely aware of that." He was quiet for a while as he enjoyed the performance of his BMW Z-4. Richard, for his part, had not uttered a word since they left the office. He wanted Murray to talk about whatever it was on his mind. They caught Interstate 5 North until they caught the 118 West towards Simi Valley. They slowed down on this stretch of highway and could talk to each other without yelling. "OK, Richard, how are you progressing with that research we discussed? Who were the main evangelists in the early days of Christianity? You mentioned that 'Peter was their big guy.' Have you had a chance to research any of the other main players?"

"Sure did, Murray. Peter was one of their main evangelists and looked like he took a strong leadership role in the early movement, but their main evangelist was Paul, or, originally, Saul of Tarsus. He has a fascinating history and is responsible for more than half of the writings in the Christian Testament. There were other people involved with the evangelization of the Christian message. For example, all of the Apostles, except Judas Iscariot, were actively involved in spreading their message, but Paul, Peter, Thomas, Andrew, Bartholomew, and others were all key players. I had a chance to do some contemporary research on these evangelists, and you have to hand it to them; they were unbelievable in spreading the word."

"Yes, I know that," answered Murray. "That's what we have to work on. We need to find out which of these evangelists had the most impact and where. Then I'd like to see if we can run a program and see how Christianity would be impacted if these evangelists were removed from the playing field, to coin a sports metaphor."

"I'm a bit confused, Murray. Earlier, you had mentioned that a time travel team could be inserted back into the portal, and simply by their presence in the past, it would have wide-ranging effects on the spread of Christianity. Now you're mentioning removing some of these historical figures. Did I get that right?"

Murray looked at Richard and laughed, "Yep, that's about it. Why send a team back into the past just hoping for the chance that they might get it right and throw a monkey wrench into the annals of history? No, I have a better idea, a bit of insurance, as it were."

"What are you thinking of doing, Murray?"

Murray sat back in his seat and relaxed, "If we can send two guys back through the portal, we can very easily send a third one later, right?"

Richard thought about this briefly, "Yeah, sure, I guess we could. As long as everything lines up right, that shouldn't be a problem. Do you want me to start doing some modeling for this?"

"No, not yet. I'm still formulating this in my mind. When the team returned to Judea in the year 33, they were careful not to do anything back there that could impact the future state. As I told you earlier, Jill left the door open that their past actions might be open to interpretation, so the next time we send those guys through the portal, they might get sloppy. For example, consider what you said earlier. What if they could get close to one of their big guys, like Peter? What if the team could alter things in the past so that Peter does not evangelize at all? Any little thing they could do would affect the 'initial condition,' as Jill says. My gut tells me that those guys will affect the work of the evangelists, which will impact the subsequent spread of Christianity. But here is the insurance that I was talking with you about. How about we send another team member back there? We could say that this guy will go back to help Declan and Toma; whatever, we can make up some scenarios. But my real goal is to send a highly trained operative back through the portal, and this guy's job is to push things along. I want this third guy to go back with the mission of assassinating the major evangelists and ensure that those two hot shots, Declan and Toma, don't make it back through the portal. For those two clowns, this will be a one-way trip."

"Damn, Murray, that's pretty drastic. But don't you think those actions back there will impact the present as we know it?"

Murray scoffed at this, "Nah, the only thing that will happen is that Christianity won't be a major influence in the world. It might end up being a minor cult localized in the Middle East, but it won't take root elsewhere. In the meantime, try to develop a model to see what would happen if people like Paul and Peter were removed from history, and see what kind of effect that would have."

Richard answered, "You bet, Murray, I'll get on it as soon as we get back to Pasadena." But Richard thought to himself that Murray might be going mad.

They had a nice lunch in Moorpark and then had a leisurely drive back to Pasadena.

Murray was alone with his thoughts later that afternoon when he got home. On too many occasions these past few weeks, he would want to pick up the phone and call Kristin, but then the ugly reality would hit him square in the face. He couldn't believe it. That evil cretin Randall and that atavistic sperm donor Johnny were the ones who killed his Kristin. Talk about a horrible irony. He hoped that they had a slow and agonizing death. But their actions caused him to embark on the path that he was pursuing. He would show God, frustrate His plan, and make sure that God would know all about him.

He was a bit pissed at himself, though. He had put all of the pieces into play. He got Nate, Declan, Toma, and Jill on board with his plan to go back through the portal. He got buy-in from the entire Einstein Project Team to send the time travelers back through the portal to learn how the early evangelists were so successful in spreading the Christian message. He put all those pieces into place only to have it potentially jeopardized by his weakness and lack of resolve. He looked up to the ceiling and yelled, "You think you almost won, don't you, Big Guy?" Nope, you can't count Murray Edgeton out just yet. Not yet, Old Man, not yet.

His next piece of the puzzle was to try and find the ideal candidate to follow Declan and Toma through the portal. He sat down and began to write on a notepad: Who would the perfect candidate be for a job like this? How could he find this candidate? Where would he even begin to look? He sat at his desk in his home office for an hour, and the answer finally came. He laid his pen down and said aloud, "Of course."

*****

The following day, he went through an old address book and found the name of the person he was looking for, Henri Comeau. Henri was an international student at MIT's Sloan School of Business studying for his Master of Finance. Murray met Henri while doing his post-Ph.D. research, and they built a solid personal relationship. Henri was from France and worked in his father's "export" business. Henri's father had a very shady background, and the word was that he was involved in moving large amounts of illegal drugs, including heroin, through Marseille to different parts of the world. Murray had gathered from Henri's many trips to Thailand, Laos, and Burma that Henri's father had a significant operation in that part of the world, the Golden Triangle. Through many a night of drinking, he also learned that Henri had connections with people with special talents. He sent his old friend an email, and by early afternoon, he received a very warm reply. Henri asked Murray to call him as soon as possible and not worry about the hour. He looked at his watch; it was almost two in the afternoon in California; with the eight-hour difference to Paris, it would be ten that evening, not too late. Murray picked up his phone to call Henri; he picked up on the third ring, "Allo?"

Murray smiled into the phone, "*Bonsoir, mon ami, comment vas-tu?* And don't ask me to say anything else. That's the extent of my *Francais*."

"Hello, Murray, so nice to hear from you. How are you doing out there in California?"

"Doing well, Henri, how are you? How is business? I know that the business is a big part of everything for you. How is it going?"

"Oh, you know, *comme ci, comme ca*, so so, as you say. I have been working exclusively here in France for the past year, but my *Papa* wants me to visit some of our outlying businesses. I will be, how do you say it over there, back on the road, *non?* Yes, I will be traveling again soon, and you, how is your research coming along? I know how excited you were to work for the Propulsion Laboratory, you got your dream job, *non?*"

"Yes, my friend, I got the job of a lifetime, for a physicist at least. The research has proven to be very important. I am fortunate to work with some of the best minds in the world out here; very stimulating. I think you would enjoy talking with some of my colleagues."

Henri enjoyed the ongoing pleasantries, but he was curious about why Murray called; they had not talked for several years, "So tell me, Murray, I was happy and surprised to receive your email. It's always nice to hear from you; what's going on?"

"Henri, you said that you might be traveling again soon. Is there any chance that you might be coming out to California? Or anywhere here in the States, for that matter. I need to run something by you; it has something to do with our time back in Cambridge. But it's a very personal matter, and I'd prefer to talk with you in person about it. If you're not coming out this way anytime soon, I can get some time off and take a trip to Paris. Do you think that you might have some time for me?"

Henri was looking at his calendar, "Murray, your timing is quite good. One of my first site visits will be to the Society Islands in French Polynesia. I will be leaving within the next two weeks, and my flight will have a stop at LAX. If you wish, I can reschedule a few things, stay in Los Angeles for a day, and then fly out to Papeete. Would that work for you, *mon ami*?"

"Yes, it does, and thank you, Henri. It will be nice to see you again, my friend. There will be lots of catching up to do. Shoot me your itinerary when you have a chance. If you're going to stay here for a day, I can put you up at my place; that's the least I can do."

"That sounds fine, Murray, and yes, it will be nice to see you. We do have lots to talk about, *c'est bon*?"

"Yes, my friend, that is good. See you soon, and have a safe trip."

Murray met Henri at LAX twelve days later. They drove out to Pasadena, where they enjoyed a nice meal at an upscale restaurant, and then they went to Murray's house to talk.

Murray gave Henri a tulip-shaped glass of Armagnac that he had poured fifteen minutes earlier, and he began to talk, "Henri, let me preface this by saying that what I am going to tell you is something that will never come back to you or to me for that matter. There is no way that any of this will be attributed to us; nothing can be linked to us, but it is a very personal matter for me. I need to ask if you can provide some information and point me in the right direction."

Henri was swirling the Armagnac in the glass, enjoying the aroma, "Go ahead, I'm listening."

Murray continued, "During one of our nights talking, you mentioned that your father had connections with people with a particular skill set. Do you recall discussing that?"

"Oh, Murray, now you have my interest. Yes, I recall that conversation very clearly. That was quite indiscreet of me, wasn't it?"

"I have never mentioned that conversation until this evening, so your indiscretion was safe with me. But back to my question, does your father still know of these individuals with that specific skill set?"

Henri looked over his glass at Murray, "*Non, mon ami*, my father is not involved with that aspect of our business anymore, and he does not need to maintain those connections any longer."

"Oh, I see."

Henri leaned in towards Murray, "My *Papa* doesn't. But *I* do. Why do you ask, *mon ami?*"

Murray was a bit surprised, "Henri, I need to have someone who can help me prevent a problem from occurring. I need to have several people, how shall I say it, neutralized so that they will not become part of a conspiracy that will have far-reaching effects on our society."

Henri kept swirling his glass and inhaling the fragrance of the Armagnac, "Will this neutralization affect any of my business enterprises, either in Europe or elsewhere? And you are positively certain that there will be no attribution?"

"To answer your first question, this will not affect any of your businesses anywhere; there is no effect whatsoever. Secondly, I am one hundred percent certain that there will be no connection to you, to me, to anyone we know, none, zero, nada."

"Murray, I have always known you to be very forthright with your dealings. I take it that you have not changed in that aspect. So how may I be of assistance in this matter?"

"Henri, although there will be no attribution, I would prefer that I do all of this alone and not involve you. I want to protect you from any involvement. I need to ask you, if I were to look for someone with this special talent, how would I do it? Secondly, how will I be able to determine if this person is the right one for this undertaking?"

"I do appreciate your desire to go this alone and not to involve me, but I am already involved, *non?* If you are completely sure that there is no attribution, I will gladly help, as you say, point you in the right direction. I can give you the names of some people who can assist you. I will make, how shall we say, introductions for you so that you can make these queries with a

169

bit more credibility. Now, Murray, tell me, what kind of person are you looking for?"

"Thank you, Henri. I am looking for someone who can adapt to a very different environment, culture, and language. Ideally, I would like to have someone who speaks classical Latin and Classical Greek and appears as someone from the Mediterranean area. Lastly, I need someone who is experienced in performing an assassination."

"Now you most certainly have my interest. This sounds fascinating, especially the part about ancient languages. I take it that you cannot tell me what the job is?"

"That, my friend, I cannot do at this time; however, if the job is successful and when it is done, I will be more than happy to tell you about it."

Henri gave the classic Gallic shrug, "*C'est la vie*. I have a contact in Strasbourg, an Alsatian colleague of mine, who will be able to give you considerable guidance in these matters. Let me contact him this week, and once I get this coordinated, I will send you his contact information. But I need to let you know that his services are expensive. You certainly have my interest and curiosity aroused. Are you absolutely certain you cannot share more information with me?"

Murray relaxed and smiled, "Not at this time, but tell me, how are you enjoying the Armagnac?" They both laughed. They continued talking through the night; Murray shared with Henri what happened with Kristin. Henri began to think he understood his friend's motives, but he was not even close to understanding.

*****

As Henri had promised, within a week, Murray had contact information for Henri's colleague in Alsace and with Henri's assurances that his colleague, Herr Fischer, was expecting his call and that Henri had given Herr Fischer some preliminary information regarding Murray's request. Murray contacted Herr Fischer via email the following week and arranged to meet by telephone. Herr Fischer forwarded a link to Murray that, when installed on his cell phone, allowed them to speak on a secure phone line.

They had the opportunity to talk the next day; Murray explicitly outlined what was needed. Herr Fischer listened attentively and then told Murray how he could deposit into Herr Fischer's Swiss bank account. It appeared that the Gnomes of Zurich had worked several transactions with Herr Fischer through the years. Once the deposit was made, Herr Fischer could line up several potential candidates that met the criteria as established by Murray.

*****

Murray met with Herr Fischer's recommended candidate, Qemal, an ethnic Albanian, at an Armenian restaurant in Glendale. He did not appear very imposing. He was average height, possibly five feet, eight inches tall, and looked to weigh about one hundred fifty pounds, but Herr Fischer assured Murray that he was very formidable and extremely good at his craft.

Murray looked at Qemal, who was enjoying the shish-kebabs and the rice pilaf, and asked him, "Our mutual friend tells me that you have a facility in several languages. Might I ask which languages you can speak?"

Qemal moved the food on his plate around, mixing the pilaf with pieces of lamb. "I am fluent in Greek and Italian, and my English is fairly good, but I have also studied Classical Greek and Latin, which are helpful languages. Of course, I am fluent in my native tongue, Shqipetar, which you may know as 'Albanian.' I speak the Tosk dialect of our language." He picked up his wine glass and took a sip of wine. "This is a very nice wine, by the way."

Murray observed Qemal a bit more closely. He looked as if he could pass for an Italian, a Greek, or someone from North Africa. He had dark eyes and hair and a somewhat dark Mediterranean complexion. Murray thought that he looked perfect for the role. "I don't know how much our friend told you about our project, but I think you might find it interesting."

Qemal put his wine glass down, "Why would you think I might find it interesting?"

Murray smiled at him, "Our friend told me that you enjoy 'living on the edge' and that the possibility of danger excites you. If that is the case, you will find this most interesting."

Chapter Seventeen
Mid-November

Pasadena, CA

The decision was made to formally "kick-off" the new mission to the entire team. Dr. P.K. Chakraborty was addressing the assembly, "As you can see from the attached summary, our modeling does demonstrate that although there is some intersectionality between the various TLPs, they do behave in the 'delivery and return' method that we confirmed through our earlier research and the mission to the first century. Additionally, the modeling predicts with significant confidence that each TLP is associated with its chronologic and geographical locus. In other words, if Declan and Toma enter a portal that predicts they will go to Rome in the year 60 A.D., that is where they will go. The TLPs behave exactly as predicted." Dr. Chakraborty looked through his notes again. "Therefore, we will be able to transport our team back through the portal with a high degree of confidence. Our model shows that we are at a higher level of confidence than when the team entered the portal two years ago, which is most heartening. Any questions at this point?" Several questions were asked, and Murray began to address the team.

"Thank you, P.K., and the entire Astronomy team, for confirming the model. For the remainder of our meeting, I would like to summarize our mission and discuss briefly how our continuing research into various technological advances may impact the mission as it is ongoing. As we have discussed for several months, we are highly confident based on our research, experience, and modeling. As P.K. said earlier, our confidence level is much higher than our initial mission; the new mission will demonstrate our ability to take advantage of the intersectionality of the recently identified 'Time-Launch Portals.'

"Our mission has a two-part objective; the first objective is to demonstrate the ability to travel through multiple portals and multiple times. The second objective is to learn how the early Christian Evangelists were so successful in spreading their message throughout the known world of that time. We can use that knowledge in our present time as a template for spreading information in a 'manual' method versus using our current methods of disseminating information. Think snail mail vice email.

"I wanted to thank Drs. Chakraborty and McAllister for the work they completed identifying the TLP correlations. For example, our initial TLP is right on the heels of the TLP that we used almost three years ago. This one is correlated to the year 33 A.D., and its geographical location is Jerusalem. Secondly, we have a TLP correlation for the year 46 A.D. the geographical locus is on the island of Cyprus. We have a TLP for 52 A.D. in Southwest India, a TLP for 60 A.D. in Rome, and numerous others. Another interesting piece of research that was completed was regarding how the 'intersectionality' between the different loci would be accomplished. Again, thanks to P.K. and Jill for all your work on that. It looks like they could work all of the bugs out and that our team should have minimal difficulty entering and traveling through the various portals. At this point, an 'itinerary' for lack of a better term has been developed for our team. As you may recall from our first mission, the team had a strict timeline that they had to follow to reenter the portal following the completion of their mission. With the advances that we have made, using our new technology, the team will have instruments with them that will allow them to identify where and when a new portal will open. Lastly, our two team members, Declan and Toma, have been intimately involved in developing the operational plan for this mission. That is a bit of a departure from our initial mission in which we developed our plan without significant input from those who, as Declan said, 'have skin in the game.' Let me turn this part of our presentation over to Declan and Toma so they can give you all an outline of our mission. Gentlemen, you have the floor."

Declan arranged his notes and then looked at the audience, "Thank you, Dr. Edgeton. Our 'order of march,' to coin an old military phrase, will be to follow in the historical paths of the early Christian Evangelists, for example, the travels of St. Peter to include his initial work in Jerusalem followed by his journeys to Antioch, Asia Minor, Greece and then Rome; St. Paul to Cyprus, Asia Minor, Greece, Malta, and Rome; St. Thomas through Mesopotamia and India and other routes taken by other evangelists. Our tentative plan right now is to be transported through various portals. Toma and I will initially travel together. Then, Toma will head north towards Mesopotamia and east to India, following the paths of St. Thomas, St. Bartholomew, and St. Jude Thaddeus. I will travel west to Egypt, Ethiopia, and Libya, following the paths of St. Simon, St. Matthew, and St. Mark the Evangelist. Following this initial transit, Toma and I will rendezvous in Jerusalem, reenter the portal, and travel to the year 46 A.D. in Cyprus to join St. Paul on his first missionary journey. We will travel through parts of Asia Minor with St. Paul and then reenter the portal to the year 60 A.D. to join St. Peter and St. Paul in Rome. We will then return to the present. But please note that Toma and I will have to adapt to the situation on the ground. Our routes may change. This is typical in any military operation: Situation and terrain dictate. Any questions at this point?"

Nate asked, "How long do you anticipate being gone?"

Toma fielded this question, "Declan and I worked out our timeline. We anticipate being in our first segment, where we'll be together initially in Judea for one chronological year. We will then separate and will be separated for two years. We will reunite in Cyprus and travel with St. Paul for two years. We will then travel to 60 A.D. and will be in Rome for four chronological years. We will then return home to the present time. To you here, we will have been gone for possibly a year; if the calculations are correct, that is when our TLP is scheduled to return to the present as we know it. We have examined several historical documents and feel that our living and traveling with these teams for nine years should provide us with more than enough information on how the message of a rabbi from Nazareth could be transmitted throughout the known world simply by word of mouth and from preaching in town squares. Any other questions?"

One of the astrophysicists asked, "Murray had mentioned that when you all went back the first time, you had a rigorous schedule to follow to reenter the portal and go back to the present. You knew when and where to be at a specific time, correct?"

Declan answered, "That's correct. If we were to miss that 'rally point,' we would not have been able to return home.

The scientist continued, "That's what I recall. Now, this mission is different, and the technology has advanced. How will you all be able to know where and when to go to catch the correct portal to either be 'transferred' or to return home?"

Murray jumped in, "I'd like to answer this one. We have worked with various science, technology, and engineering subgroups for two to three years. When we had our first mission almost three years ago, the team had stand-alone navigation and communication equipment that could work without modern-day GPS technology. Our science and technology team has been working in concert with what is now available in the private sector, and what they have been able to provide our team is much more highly advanced. We've seen how commercial communication equipment has seen quantum leaps in technological advances over the past five to ten years. Our team has made those commercial leaps look like baby steps. When they return to the past, Declan and Toma will have solar-powered hand-held devices that can be used for several purposes. They have one that they will use to determine where they are geographically and chronologically and another to use to enable them to communicate with each other over a limited range. They'll have a chronometer that will keep local and present times for them, and they'll know exactly what time and day it is here in Pasadena.

"One of their hand-held devices, the SQQ-38, Declan and Toma have dubbed this specific one the 'peripheral brain'; will also be preprogrammed with their entire 'itinerary' so that they'll know where and when they have to be. This program will also tell them how long it will take them to walk at a normal pace to get from point A to point B. This system will also be self-modified if they travel via waterborne craft or by a camel caravan. You can see how this technology will play a vital role in this mission. We have redundancy. Declan and Toma will each have two completely functioning units. They are very robust and would pass military-grade specifications. These devices are what is called 'battle-hardened' in the military and are difficult to destroy. We feel confident that our team should have no difficulties during their mission using these devices. Does that answer your question?"

"Yes, Dr. Edgeton, it does, thank you."

Murray continued, "Which brings me to another point, and this is something that several of us have been working on, including Declan and Toma. We may be on the cusp of developing some new technology that will surpass what we are sending out with the team. Depending on how revolutionary and advanced this technology will be and how it will help the team on the ground, we may have to consider sending a follow-on team to rendezvous with Declan and Toma to provide them with this new technology. We may consider this to be another objective of our mission. If a team is operating within the portal, is it possible to provide them a 'lifeline' to assist or even rescue the team? This 'mini-mission' will help answer this additional question. Are there any questions at this time?

"If that is the case, our next presenter will be Dr. Jill McAllister, who will update us on what her team has found relative to chaos theory and what our team needs to be concerned with, Dr. McAllister."

"Thank you, Dr. Edgeton. My comments today will be

brief. I have discussed chaos theory with you before, so I won't bore you all with the same background again. One of the main areas that I have been discussing with Declan and Toma has been relative to the *initial condition*. Specifically, how sensitive that condition is and how much potential interference the condition might be able to tolerate. As we said in our meetings, how much 'wiggle room' do we have with our initial condition?

"What we found through our research and then augmented by information from Harvard's Safra Center is that when our team embarked on their mission almost three years ago, they had interacted with people of that time. Those interactions could be considered significant. The team went back in time, interacted with people on the ground, and then returned. We have seen that there has been no discernible effect on the present. So, what does this mean? It means that our team can go back into the past and interact with people in everyday activities, but they must exercise caution, as they did with their first mission. The initial condition should be able to absorb or tolerate a small amount of interference.

"Our guidance to the team is to observe the same precautions as they did before, but to act naturally. The thinking is that natural events should flow naturally. If the team were to do something untoward or unnatural, those perturbations might be amplified in the initial condition, resulting in significant changes to the current state. Their method of operation during their first mission was to be 'observers.' If we follow that same approach, we should generate similar results. Any questions?"

Richard Hollander asked, "Dr. McAllister, doesn't this fly in the face of everything you have been saying since 2014?"

Jill looked over at Murray, "That's a great question. Yes, it does fly in the face of everything that we said. But why is there a seismic change in our thinking? As we would say in Southern Georgia, 'the proof of the pudding is in the tasting.' We had our major 'taste' almost three years ago. The team went back in time and did not seem to interfere with the present state. Remember, chaos theory is just that, a theory. We have demonstrated some tolerance in that theory, returning to my scientific descriptor, some wiggle room. Does that answer your question?"

Richard knew Murray would wonder what he was up to, "Somewhat, Jill. I'm concerned about unintended consequences. We might risk interfering with what was meant to be, just my two cents worth." Richard didn't care what Murray thought. Richard began to have serious questions about Murray's state of mind, and he wanted the others in this group to consider what was happening. Richard had been an atheist for the majority of his life, but his past was catching up to him lately. He began to have second thoughts about the existence of God. That notwithstanding, he believed in fate and felt that Murray was tempting it. He looked over at Murray and saw that Murray was staring at him with a blank look on his face. He looked very strange, almost scary.

*****

After the meeting, Murray called Richard into his office. Richard knew that the summons would be coming. Murray was still standing but asked Richard to sit down. He then asked, "I can't figure out what side you are on, Richard. I thought we talked about what I was doing. What in the hell has gotten into you?"

"Murray, remember you telling me that Jill was taking the 'Devil's Advocate's' position at one of your meetings? That's all that I was doing. I was hoping to get Jill to state that the team's presence in the past would not have a significant impact if they were cautious. She said as much during her presentation. That's why I did that; why is something wrong?"

Murray looked skeptical, "No, nothing's wrong. It sounded like you were saying something to counter what Jill said."

"No, on the contrary, and if it came across that way, that was not my intent," Richard answered, wondering if his voice betrayed his nervousness.

"Well, whatever." Murray sat down and went through some papers on his desk, "Just watch what you're doing,

Richard, just watch what you're doing. All right, I've got some work to do."

Richard got up from his chair and stood there momentarily while Murray ignored him. Richard turned on his heel and walked out the door. As he was walking back to his office, he was certain that Murray was going mad. He made up his mind that he wasn't going to get in Murray's way. He thought he should consider looking for another position; he felt that Murray could resort to violence to get what he wanted. Richard did not want any part of that.

Chapter Eighteen
Spring, 33 A.D.

Jerusalem

Early in the morning on the third day after the crucifixion of Jesus of Nazareth, the women who had prepared His body for burial three days before returned to His tomb to complete their work. Mary of Magdala, Mary the mother of James, and Joanna were walking with others to His tomb. They were still suffering and were overwhelmingly saddened by the events of the past few days. Mary of Magdala was hurrying to the tomb when Joanna called out to her, "Mary, please slow down. My legs can't carry me as fast as they used to. We will get to the Master in due time."

The Magdalene slowed so her friend could catch up with her, "I am just so sad by all that has happened. My sadness is making me lash out at everyone. When I talked with Simon Peter this morning before I left, I asked if he and some of the brothers could come with us to help move the stone away. He said that they had to stay inside for fear of the Jews. I yelled at him and told him that they fled when the Master was being crucified, and who stayed behind? We did, and the men all fled, well, John stayed, but the rest of them all cowered in fear. I yelled at him again and told him they were all still hiding in fear. What is there to be afraid of? They had already killed the Master. And then I thought of Him; He would not act as I did. He would not humiliate Peter in front of the rest. I mumbled an apology to Peter and left him with his head hanging down. I know that he loved the Master. He is just grief-stricken. I should not have acted like that to him."

"We will need him later; he'll be fine; just let him think about what you said. You might have forced him into being stronger," Joanna replied. "It might be that the brothers might be confused as to why our Master always included us. You know how our leaders are; they never include us, but the Master did. I think that just confused the brothers."

Mary of Magdala thought about what Joanna said, "He always included us in everything. No one has given us a thought of doing anything, but He did. Look what He did for me, do you remember Joanna? Remember how long the demons tormented me and how the Master forced them out? He has done so much for me; I miss Him so. Look, we're almost there."

They all hurried to the tomb. Mary, the mother of James, asked, "Why couldn't the brothers come with us? Who will help us to move the stone out of the way of the tomb entrance? We can't move it ourselves."

Joanna answered, "We will if we have to. Don't worry, Mary, what did King David tell us? *'Baruch ha Shem*, Blessed be The Lord, for He has heard the sound of my pleading. The Lord is my strength and my shield. In Him my heart trusts, and I find help.'"

Mary continued, "'Then my heart exults, and with my song, I give Him thanks.' You're right, Joanna, He will provide."

But when they arrived at the tomb, they were puzzled: The large stone at its entrance had been rolled back. They all ran into the tomb to look for the body of Jesus, and their puzzlement changed into their being mystified, which quickly changed into shock. Jesus' body was not in the tomb, and on the stone upon which they had laid His body, there was now a young man dressed in a white robe; he looked as if he were bathed in light. The women saw him and fell to their knees with their faces to the ground; they were terrified. The young man looked at them and began to speak, "Why do you seek the Living One, Jesus, here among the dead? Look around you. Do you see Him here? He has risen as He said He would. Can you not recall what

He said while He was with you in Galilee? Do you not remember? He told you all that the Son of Man had to be turned over to the sinful ones, He would be crucified, and on the third day, His Father would raise Him. Get up and tell the brothers and Peter what He told you before, 'He is now going to Galilee before you. You will see Him there.'"

The women ran back to tell the disciples what they had seen, but Mary of Magdala stayed outside the tomb and wept. While still weeping, she went back inside the tomb where she saw two men, not one, one standing near the front of where they had laid Jesus three days ago, and the other man stood at the foot of the stone where they had laid Jesus. One of the young men asked her why she was weeping. The Magdalene replied, "They have taken the body of my Lord, and I don't know where they have taken Him." She turned to walk out of the tomb and saw a man standing there, but she could not recognize that the man in front of her was Jesus.

Jesus asked her, **"Why are you weeping? Who are you looking for in the tomb?"**

She replied, "They have taken away my Lord. If it was you, Sir, who took Him, could you please let me know where He is, and I will go to take Him."

Jesus looked at her with love and compassion, **"Mary!"**

Her eyes were opened, and she saw that it was the Lord. "Rabbouni!" And she attempted to take hold of His feet as is the custom.

"Mary! Stop, take your hands off of Me. I have yet to ascend to my Heavenly Father. Listen to Me. I want you to go back to the brothers and tell them that I am going back to My Father, who is your Father, My God, who is your God. Now go, go to tell them what I have told you."

Mary Magdalene ran back to the house where the disciples were staying. As she walked in, she saw the women who had accompanied her to the tomb arguing with the disciples. Peter approached her and said, "Mary, talk some sense into these women. They told us that they had gone to the tomb of the Master and that they had seen an angel who had told them that the Master had risen from the dead. Are they all crazed? No wonder our leaders do not put stock in the testimony of women. That's why you can't testify in court. How do they expect us to believe them? Tell them to quit making up stories."

Mary, the mother of James, and Joanna were talking at once, pleading with Mary Magdalene to tell them what they all saw. The disciples and all the others began to speak at once, clamoring to be heard. Peter roared at the top of his voice, the same voice he used to yell at the other boats to drop their nets while fishing. "SILENCE!!" Everyone stopped talking, and the women looked down at the ground. "Let's hear what Mary Magdalene has to say."

Mary looked up to the ceiling and then raised her arms in an attitude of praise, "I have seen the Master. He is alive!" She then related to everyone what Jesus had told her. Peter could not believe what he heard. He stormed out of the house and ran to the tomb; he noticed that the stone was rolled away, as the women had said. He walked tentatively into the tomb, looked around in the faint light, and saw that Jesus was not there. His eyes adjusted to the darkness in the tomb and noticed that the burial cloths were lying on the stone slab on which Jesus had been laid. He could not believe what he saw and ran back to the house to report what he had seen to the others.

"There is no one in the tomb. All that I saw were His burial linens. He's gone." They were terrified and did not leave the house for the rest of the day.

That evening, as they were sitting by the fire, they felt, more than heard, a sudden gust of wind. They wondered how that could happen as the door and windows were closed. Then, out of the darkness, they watched as someone approached them. Peter stood up and screamed, "It is the Master!"

Jesus walked up to them, stood in their midst, and said, **"Shlama, my Peace be with you."** The disciples were terrified and thought they were seeing a ghost. Then Jesus said to them, **"Why are you afraid? Why do your hearts question that which you see before you? Look, it is I."** He then showed them His hands, which bore the nail marks from His crucifixion and the large wound on His side.

Everyone in the room stood and started praising, "*Hoshiya na! Hoshiya na! Hoshiya na* to the Son of David! *Hoshiya na in the highest!*"

Jesus stayed with His disciples for another forty days and then had them meet Him at the mountain He told them of earlier. The disciples continued to praise Him; they were overjoyed to be in His presence, but Jesus stopped them for a moment. "**Do you recall how when I appeared to you, your hearts were still hardened and you could not believe that it was I who was in your presence? How hard were your hearts then and before? When the sisters came to you and told you what they had seen, how hard were your hearts then? What do the Psalms tell us, 'If today you hear His voice, harden not your hearts.' Enough, no more. You will be my witnesses to everything I have taught you. I will send to you all the promise of My Father, the Holy Spirit, but stay in the city until you are clothed with His power. All power on Heaven and Earth will be given to you. Therefore, go and make disciples of all nations, beginning in Jerusalem, baptizing them in the name of The Father, Son, and Holy Spirit. Proclaim to them all the Good News and teach them all that I have commanded you. Whoever is baptized and believes will be saved. Whoever does not believe will be condemned. And behold, know that I am with you until the end of the age.**"

As they were looking at Him, Jesus ascended into Heaven, and a cloud took Him from their sight.

Chapter Nineteen
Late November

Pasadena, CA

Richard Hollander had a meeting scheduled with Murray for that afternoon. Walking into Murray's office, he was surprised to see him so upbeat and friendly. Murray offered Richard a seat, and Richard pulled a report out of his binder. "Thanks, Murray, for the time this afternoon. I was able to finalize my model last week and have the numbers all validated. It looks pretty interesting. Based on what we discussed last September, I developed a model to simulate what would happen if the actions of the two Christian evangelists, Peter of Galilee and Saul of Tarsus, were removed from history.

"The model demonstrated that if the fisherman, Peter, were removed, there would be a significant void in leadership and decision-making in the early Christian Church. According to the Christian Scriptures, Peter played a key role among the Apostles, often acting as their spokesman. Interestingly enough, Peter was the Apostle who denied Jesus of Nazareth during the crucifixion, but following the death of Jesus and the supposed resurrection, the first Apostle Jesus appeared to was Peter; supposedly, that was to symbolize forgiveness and something to do with being redeemed from your mistakes. Peter became the example of a forgiven sinner, and the story of his forgiveness played a central role in restoring Peter's position. Peter was a major player in several theological arguments, and his leadership was crucial to establishing the Christian Church. He became the

Bishop of Rome, the first Pope, and the snappers still consider his successors as the 'Pope', a direct line back to Peter—"

Murray interrupted, "What was that you said, the snappers? What are snappers?"

"Oh, I'm sorry, Murray. I'm using a slang word for Catholics that my parents used to use when I was a kid growing up. 'Mackerel Snappers, Herring Chokers'. When my parents were younger, the Catholics used to have to eat fish on Fridays. That's where we get these restaurants and clubs having Friday Fish Frys. The nicknames that the non-Catholic kids had for the Catholic kids were mackerel snappers and herring chokers. That nickname just popped into my head."

Murray was laughing, "That's hilarious, mackerel snappers. Too funny."

Richard continued, "So removing the role of Peter from history would, as I said, leave a leadership void and would also affect some of their theological decisions, something about converting the Gentiles, non-Jews. Peter played a major role in holding the various factions of early Christians together, so he was of significant importance to the development of the early Christian Church. Peter also wrote two major letters, or epistles, in the Christian Scriptures. Peter played a major role in the Church, and removing his place in history would significantly impact the development of the Christian Church. Any questions so far?"

"No, Richard, not yet, this is interesting history."

"Saul of Tarsus, later known as Paul, played a different role. Whereas Peter may be considered an operational manager, Paul was a marketing manager. He played a considerable role in the spreading of the Christian message. Now, he has a fascinating history. Born as a Roman citizen, he was a devout Jew, a member of the Pharisees, a school of Judaic thought during the time of the Second Temple Judaism, which lasted roughly from the fifth century before the Common Era to the first century of the Common Era. This belief system became the foundation for Rabbinic Judaism, so he was a devoutly religious Jew. While he was a young man, he was sent to the holy city of

Jerusalem to study under the noted scholar of Jewish Law, the Rabbi Gamaliel.

"Saul originally persecuted the early Christian Church in Jerusalem, even being involved with the execution of a young Christian deacon called 'Stephen' who is recognized in the Christian tradition as being their 'Protomartyr.' Saul was recognized in Jerusalem as persecuting the early Christians 'beyond measure', and he received permission from the authorities in Jerusalem to travel to Damascus to 'round up' more Christians. As the story goes, he encountered the Ascended Christ on the road to Damascus and was converted to be one of Jesus' Apostles. After his conversion, he became a zealous evangelist for the Christian movement and was responsible for founding many Christian communities throughout Asia Minor and Europe. His writings make up roughly one-half of the Christian Scriptures. As you can see, this man played an integral role in the spread of Christianity; if his role were removed, it would have an unbelievable impact on the spread of Christianity.

"The model suggests that by removing these two men from the equation, Christianity will not be successful in spreading at all, and the most optimistic fate that it will have is that it will become a small Jewish sect confined to the Levant. However, the model also demonstrated that if there were even a minor interference with the missionary activities of either Peter or Paul, Christianity would not take root outside of the Levant, and it would never enjoy the success seen today."

Murray thought about this for a moment, "What do you mean by a 'minor interference,' and what is the probability of that happening?"

"Good question. The model factored in variables such as travel, weather, the political environment, etc. Let's look at the variable 'travel.' If Paul is scheduled to leave Cyprus, one of his initial journeys, on, let's say, a Monday, and for whatever reason he is delayed for even an hour, a minor interference, the model projects with a 95% probability that he would not be able to establish churches in Pisidia, Antioch, Iconium, and Derbe; if this were to occur, all of his other missionary activities would be affected negatively. The initial condition is extremely sensitive. This is not what Jill and her team predicted."

Murray nodded his head in approval, "Fascinating. How about the impact of Peter? How could a minor interference affect his role in spreading Christianity?"

"Similar effect. Remember the important leadership role that he played. For example, he held together that 'fragile coalition' of early Christian communities and took a decisive role in appointing new leaders in the community. He was also one of the primary evangelists in Jerusalem, and his preaching there resulted in many new converts. The model mapped out the old city of Jerusalem and laid out the paths where people in the old city would walk. If Peter were preaching at the Judgment Gate and was supposed to preach next at the Sheep Gate, what if he were delayed or took a wrong turn and instead of going to the Sheep Gate, he goes to the Golden Gate or the Royal Portico, he could miss his intended converts by an hour or so, what would the result be? The model predicts that he would not make any converts. How would this play out? It's like the old pebble in the stream and the ripple effect. People who were supposed to convert others would be affected. The model predicts an overall failure of Peter's preaching if he were to miss any of his 'preaching on the corner' appointments. You can see how that would affect his success.

"But let me bring something else up. In doing this research I read about something right after the Christ Child was born. The local king, Herod, attempted to have this Child murdered before His 'reign' could begin. He ordered that all male children in the province under a certain age be killed. This plot didn't work as Jesus' family learned of it and escaped. Why don't we consider doing something like that, a 'preemptive strike.' This way, we wouldn't have to worry about rounding up a bunch of Apostles wandering around the countryside. We're risking some of these Apostles succeeding in spreading the word of Jesus."

Murray couldn't help but smile, "You bring up a good

point, but that will screw up my plans. I want to prove to God that Murray Edgeton from Texas can beat Him at this game."

Richard began to think that Murray really was insane. When they had lunch in Moorpark a few months back, he thought Murray might be going mad. Now, he had no doubt.

Murray continued, "Great job, Richard. I appreciate all you have done and am glad we're working this together. I have a meeting with the planning team. We're looking at moving forward with the mission sometime next year, no later than mid-to-late spring, so I will keep this information in my hip pocket. One last question: Where are the software programs and the documentation for your model?"

"As we discussed, I kept this very close to the vest. I worked with several of the guys from the modeling team, but they only worked on certain fragments of the model. They had no idea what the overall program was designed to model or what the other guys were working on. I have erased the program and all of the docs from the system and kept everything else on an external drive under lock and key. Did you want me to go ahead and dump everything? I've run multiple scenarios and various algorithms and shown you everything that was programmed, so if I dump everything, even my copies, you have all of the info you need for planning. Let me know, and I'll dump everything, no traces back to what I did. Sound good?"

Murray replied in a low voice, "Yeah, go ahead, dump it all. Let me go with you, and we can wipe it together. What do you use to wipe everything off?"

"I've been using BleachBit, and it works perfectly every time. Let's head over and knock this out." Richard handed his report packet over to Murray. "Here, do you want to keep the hard copies of everything? I don't need them, and you may want to review them later."

Murray shook his head, "I'm not going to keep them; you gave me all the info I need. We'll shred them over at your office."

They headed over to Richard's office, but Richard anticipated that Murray would do this. He kept a copy of his work on a storage medium he had already taken home. He no longer trusted Murray and wanted to keep this information with him, just in case.

Chapter Twenty
Late February – April the next year

Pasadena, CA

Working their way into the new year, the planning team solved several issues with the various computer runs and modeling programs. It appeared as if they were ready to move forward with the new mission; in the parlance of NASA, all systems were "go" for launch. Declan and Toma had been intimately involved with the development process for the operational plan, and working in tandem with the Science and Technology Team, they felt they were more than adequately prepared for this mission.

Declan provided an overview of the project status to the Einstein Project Team, "At this time, we feel that we can embark on this mission right now. That is how prepared our team is. As you all may recall, our insertion point for our initial mission, and it's hard to believe, was almost three years ago, north of the Israeli city of Ashdod." The JPL, working with NASA, had an agreement with the ISA, the Israeli Space Agency, and had a small station established in an uninhabited area on the coast north of Ashdod. "The JPL has been working with the ISA again in reestablishing our station, and due to the advances that we have made since our first mission, combined with the fact that we are sending a much smaller team through the portal, our footprint will be considerably smaller than it was for the first mission. We are happy to report that the station is operational.

"Dr. Chakraborty and Dr. McAllister have been working on the predictions of our Time-Launch Points, or portals, and they have completed fine-tuning their projections. Our portal is scheduled to open on the twenty-ninth of April, and P.K. and Jill tell us that from their review of archival information, this TLP appears to be associated with the First Christian Pentecost in the year 33 A.D. and will be again located at our initial insertion point north of Ashdod. We will discuss the other TLPs and the events that will precipitate their openings at a later meeting, but for now, we'd like to focus on the upcoming portal opening that will be coming up in about eight weeks.

"The overall objectives of this mission have been discussed, in addition to the various journeys we will be taking and the technological support we will have. The possibility of a concurrent mission running parallel to our mission has also been discussed, so at this time, we would like to outline briefly how this mission will proceed. We will use our station in Ashdod to 'launch' our team into the portal, and we will 'land' in Jerusalem in the year 33 A.D. Our landing will coincide with the Pentecost celebrations occurring at that time. Toma and I will be joining the Jewish pilgrims celebrating Pentecost. Our goal is to be part of the crowd listening to the various gates of the old city of Jerusalem when Peter is beginning to preach." Declan looked down at his notes to check something.

Jill asked, "Declan, may I ask something, please? I'm a bit confused about something. You mentioned that there were Jewish pilgrims in Jerusalem celebrating Pentecost. I thought that Pentecost was a Christian holiday. Are you saying that these pilgrims coming into Jerusalem are newly converted Christians?

Toma jumped in, "Let me take this one, Deck. That's a great question. Actually, it's both Jewish and Christian. In Jewish tradition, this is a significant feast, but the Jews call this holy day 'Shavuot,' and it commemorates two significant events. First, it celebrates when the Lord gave the Torah, the Law, to Moses and the Israelites at Mt. Sinai, and it also marks the wheat harvest; this festival was also known as the 'Festival of the First Fruits.'

This holy day is to be commemorated fifty days following Passover. Hellenized Jews called this holy day 'Pentecost,' Greek for 'fiftieth,' to denote the fifty days between Passover and Shavuot. Shavuot is one of three special feasts when each adult male is required to be in Jerusalem. So, when the disciples of Jesus were in their house in Jerusalem awaiting the coming of the Holy Spirit, the city was full of pilgrims celebrating Shavuot, or Pentecost. Does that answer your question?"

"Yes, it does, Toma, thank you," answered Jill.

Declan then continued with his briefing, "We have had an interesting development in our operational plan. You may recall that we gave our initial brief last fall where we discussed our 'order of march.' Due to some additional modeling that has been completed, we can modify our plan. As discussed before, we will enter the portal and be in Jerusalem in the Spring of 33 A.D. We will be there for the first Christian Pentecost. To test one of our theories, there is projected to be a return portal opening up approximately six months after we arrive. Drs. Edgeton, Chakraborty, Joseph, and others have found that there appears to be significant portal activity in the first century. We aim to test these openings to see how easily they can be utilized. We plan to 'catch' for lack of a better term, the return portal within six months. Projections then show that another portal will be projected to open that will take us back to Jerusalem in the year 43 A.D. We will then continue with our earlier mission as planned. This includes our concurrent, parallel mission of sending an additional team back through the portal to rendezvous with Toma and me. We have a very robust and complex operation planned, but all modeling and calculations point to a successful mission. Do you have any questions?"

*****

On 29 April at 0400 local time, there were two teams on the Israeli coast north of the city of Ashdod: the Time Travel Team, Declan and Toma, who were in their predetermined location, and the local monitoring station team located several thousand meters from Declan's and Toma's position. The regional monitoring station acted as the local control team and would broadcast real-time information to the Central Control team in Pasadena. Like their first mission, Declan and Toma were outfitted to appear as Jewish pilgrims of that era; their cover was that they were Greek Jews making their required pilgrimage to Jerusalem. Both men could speak Classical Latin and Greek, while Declan had a working knowledge of Aramaic, the language of the Jews in first-century Palestine; Toma was fluent. They were also equipped with the technological devices required for their mission; this included their 'peripheral brain' device. Lastly, as they had with their first mission, they had a cart designed as a replica of carts used at that time and a European donkey; this added authenticity to their cover as pilgrims. In their cart, they had water, food, and a tent in addition to other supplies, typical of how pilgrims of that time traveled. Before transport, the donkey was anesthetized and strapped in a large wooden container; the animal was due to come out of anesthesia within two hours. According to their calculations and schedule, the portal was scheduled to open within the next twenty minutes, and their mission would be underway.

Declan and Toma sat in their cart with all their equipment and prepared for transport, and as the clock counted down, all personnel completed their final checks. Declan's and Toma's vital signs, as were the donkey's, were monitored. All indications were that they were on schedule and ready for portal opening. During the countdown, they anticipated that this transport would be similar to their initial transport through the portal, and as the countdown continued, things appeared to be the same. The same low-frequency hum they had heard before could now be heard throughout the area, and the local control team reported back to the Central Control Team in Pasadena that the sound was identical to what they had experienced during the first mission. The vital sign monitors reported that Declan, Toma, and the donkey were within normal limits. Looking eastward over the desert, a greenish, blue haze appeared in what looked like a false dawn, and then what seemed to be a borealis-type of wavering light appeared on the western horizon, again, just like it happened before. The countdown reached "0," and things changed rapidly as the time travel team "launched" into the portal. The first thing that Declan and Toma noticed was that they were encased in a translucent blue bubble as they entered a long tunnel. The low-intensity hum they heard before launch intensified, and then they heard what sounded like a "rip in the Earth" and the massive "whooshing" sound as they felt themselves accelerate into the tunnel. Then, the shaking began. This was much worse than they had experienced before, and then the walls of their bubble began to look as if they were rippling in wavelike forms. The greenish, blue haze they had seen initially in the east had changed rapidly to a deep purple, and then, incredibly, it changed to a deep red. The sky lit up in a way that he could only describe as light twinkling on the waves over the ocean. The light to the east and west began to shimmer like the Borealis light they had seen off to the west a few moments before. They accelerated into the tunnel like before, and light streaks appeared. The light streaks began to waver, and amazingly, they were dissected into individual, discrete particles of light. It seemed to Declan and Toma that they were seeing individual photons. Then, they began to experience a sensory warp in which they saw trailing images of themselves and each other on the walls of the blue bubble. The acceleration continued, and they felt pressed against the side of the cart and could not move. After a few seconds of this acceleration, both men lost consciousness. As rapidly as this had started, it ended.

After a few moments, Declan and Toma awoke. They noticed that the transmitting tower close to their launch position was no longer visible. During their first mission, they used the fact that the transmitting tower was not there as their first indication that they were no longer in the present time. Toma keyed his communication device, and all that he received was static. This was their second indication that they were transported back in time. They needed to determine their location to confirm that they were transported. Both men, as

Naval Officers and Navy SEALs, were well qualified in celestial and land navigation, and like their first mission, they had equipment that would allow them to fix their position. As they had used earlier, Declan and Toma had their modified TI-Star Pilot 89T navigation device that contained loaded into its software the necessary Nautical Almanac and Sight Reduction Tables required for navigation in addition to their chronometer set to Greenwich Mean Time. This solar-powered device was used in concert with a sextant that would be used to fix their geographical position manually. The team used the coordinates of their launch position north of Ashdod as a reference point, their "assumed" dead reckoning position. Declan waited for the appropriate time before sunrise, then used his sextant and navigation device to calculate their current position. He found they were at their original "Lat and Lon" in an uninhabited section of the desert on the Israeli coast north of Ashdod. All indications were that they made it through the portal and were now in Judea in the first century A.D.

Declan and Toma organized their equipment and supplies while waiting for the anesthetic to wear off on their donkey and for the animal to wake up. They had one other task to accomplish before they headed towards the central mountains. They were instructed to bury a small metal canister in the ground at a predetermined location. Approximately two hours after they entered the portal, the beast awakened, and after the animal appeared stable, they fed and watered him. Satisfied that the donkey was ready to proceed, they harnessed him to the cart, began walking away from the coast, and headed east toward Jerusalem. They were roughly forty-five miles away from the city and estimated that they could travel fifteen miles each day. Their progress depended upon the donkey, who traveled at his own pace. They were planning a three-day hike to Jerusalem.

Toma led the donkey for the first segment of their day's walk, "We should be in Jerusalem as the Pentecost events are in full swing. What do you think, we should arrive by Sunday, or as the Jews would say, yom rishon, the first day of the week, sound good?"

"Yeah," Declan replied. "Looking at the Peripheral Brain, it estimates that walking with Mr. Donkey on this rough terrain we should be there by Sunday. Tell you what, the guys back at the Science and Tech group loaded this thing with all kinds of stuff. Based on archival data, it even tells us where St. Peter is supposed to be preaching. The SciTech guys even loaded into the Brain that right after the Holy Spirit descended on the Apostles and the Community on Pentecost Sunday, over three thousand people converted. We should fall into that crowd and work to become part of the community of believers. That should work perfectly for us."

"And since the project team got us those replica obels and drachmas again, we can exchange these for shekels and make a contribution to the community to help them get things started. That should help. Recall in Acts of the Apostles how they pooled all of their resources together for the good of the group. We can be seen as believers who are serious and willing to put their money where their mouth is." They walked silently, alone with their thoughts as they walked towards the rising sun. Then Toma continued, "Have to tell you, Deck, I am happy to be back here. Something keeps telling me that I am where God needs me to be."

"I hear you. Let's go ahead and start praying the Divine Office. In the Name of The Father, and of The Son and of The Holy Spirit, Amen…" They walked through the desert, watching the sunrise on a new day, and prayed, giving Praise to the Lord.

At the same time that Declan and Toma were praying, Murray was meeting Qemal by phone. "The team has made it through the portal. Everything is progressing as planned. We should be able to get you up and running and ready to enter the next portal within the next year. Any questions at this time?"

Qemal answered in a low voice, "None at this time, but I did want to let you know that your first payment installment was deposited into my Swiss account. Thank you for being so timely. I'm getting excited about matching wits with your two SEALs. It should be very interesting."

Chapter Twenty-One
33 A.D.

Jerusalem – The Feast of Shavuot

Declan, Toma, and Mr. Donkey had traveled well from the coast, hiking through hills and valleys, when they came out of a set of hills and looked across the valley to see the city of Jerusalem in the distance. Jerusalem is built on seven hills and sits approximately two-thousand-five hundred feet above sea level. They had not seen the city from this vantage point, and they were both stunned by the view. Toma said, "Now I can see what Our Lord meant when he talked about a city set on a mountain that cannot be hidden. Look at it; it's spectacular."

Early that morning, as they approached Jerusalem, Declan quoted the Psalms, "Remember how King David said, 'If I forget thee, Jerusalem, may my right hand be forgotten.' You could see how this was God's city." They passed majestic oak trees, stately sycamores, towering cedars, and countless pines as they made their way to Jerusalem. They entered the city through the Judgment Gate, where they were halted by Roman Legionnaires who guarded the gate. The young *milites gregarious,* a Roman foot soldier, eyed Declan and Toma as they approached the gate. He yelled out in rudimentary Aramaic, "Halt," and Toma answered him in flawless Latin, "Yes, sir, please let us know what you need from us."

The soldier was surprised and relieved that this pilgrim could speak Latin so well, "What is your business here?"

Toma replied politely, "Sir, my brother and I are pilgrims from Thessaloniki here to fulfill our obligation as men

199

of the God of our Fathers and participate in the Feast of Shavuot."

The young soldier looked over both shoulders before he replied, "Save your 'sir' for that dung heap of an officer of mine." He began to do a cursory inspection of their cart. "What are you bringing into the city with you?"

This time, Declan answered, "Just our supplies, water, and food. We may have a few other items in there, but it's what we need for our travels."

The Roman pulled out a container and examined it, "How do you two Thessalonicans know how to speak our language so well, and what is this?"

Declan smiled at him, "That's what we do. We're wine merchants and have significant dealings with our Roman business partners; we travel to the Roman provinces several times a year. That is an amphora filled with our newest wine from the Boeotia region. It is a light white wine that goes very well with cheeses, garlic, onions, and stuffed grape leaves. Smell the amphora. Can you smell the pine resin? We use Aleppo pine resin to seal the bottles so the wine will not turn." The guard smelled the bottle and looked at it from different angles. He began to turn the bottle a bit to hear the sound of the wine in the container.

As if on cue, Toma jumped in, "We can't open it now because once it is opened, the wine must be enjoyed, but if it is acceptable to you and your officer, we will gladly leave this for your enjoyment after your duty is over. We have several samples of our wares, and we use our samples for potential buyers to try. We will gladly leave this with you, but only if you and your friends enjoy it and tell others of its wonderful taste; it's good for our business. Please, take this with our thanks for your telling your comrades."

The soldier was intrigued with the amphora and the thought of a new type of wine, "What do you call this wine so I can tell my comrades what this is?"

Declan told him, "One of our Roman partners calls it 'resina', but that's the Latin word. We call it 'retsina,' the word from our province. Let us know how you like it." The guard was too absorbed in admiring the amphora and thinking of how the wine would taste. He didn't even notice Declan begin to pull Mr. Donkey through the gate, but with a quick look at them and a desultory wave, he let them pass.

Once out of earshot, Toma started laughing, "What did that kid say, 'my dung heap of an officer?' It's good to know that troops are always the same."

Once they got into the city, they walked over to one of the numerous marketplaces set up for the many pilgrims. People were everywhere, and Declan and Toma were assaulted by the overwhelming smell of many people and animals in one area. But it was incredible. Stalls were jammed into each other, merchants were jostling for space, and every spare inch of the marketplace was occupied. And the *noise*. People were screaming at each other. They were shoving others out of the way, everyone hawking for customers and threatening other merchants who dared to infringe even a hair's width into their staked-out area. It was hard to believe that there was a religious festival with all the insults and curses being hurled back and forth between merchants.

You could purchase anything at the market. Tools, household implements, pots and pans, and even weapons were being sold. Animals to be used for sacrifices in the Temple, along with animals to be used for other purposes, were being sold, and their clucking, screeching, cooing, bleating, barking, lowing, and other plaintive cries added to the cacophony of noise. And the food that was being sold! Eggs, bread, all types of produce, food being cooked on small charcoal braziers, all kinds of fish, meats of all stripes, bread basted with olive oil, and cheese melted on the top of the bread. On the other side of the small walkway, wines and medicinal herbs were available for purchase. Statues, cheap jewelry, sandals, fishing nets, water jugs, combs for ladies' hair, and fruits from all over the region were being sold. Toma told Declan that if you couldn't find it here, you didn't need it. When they got to the other side of the marketplace, closer to the temple, they found what they were looking for, the moneychangers. If people thought that the noise of the merchants was loud, it was deafening with the money changers. There were rows of tables set up with moneychangers doing the essential task of exchanging foreign coins. During the festivals of Passover, Shavuot, and Sukkot, large numbers of Jews from, as Scripture records, "out of every nation under Heaven" poured into Jerusalem, and they brought their native currency with them. The pilgrims had to use money to pay for lodging and food and to purchase gifts, so currency had to be exchanged. During their pilgrimage to the Holy City, they were also required to pay their annual tribute to the Temple with a "half-shekel" of the local currency. The moneychangers' role in exchanging currency was vital.

Declan asked, "OK, who do we go to to get our money exchanged? Listen to these guys. They're amazing. I expect a big fight to break out any second with all the threats and screaming." The moneychangers were all yelling that they had the best exchange rate and that their fees were the fairest. It was all quite amusing. "Toma, what do you call these guys?"

Toma was taking this all in. "There are several different names for the moneychangers. The most common one is the local term, *shulhani,* and they performed several services. They changed currency, but they also changed large denominations into smaller coinage in addition to acting as a banker, taking funds in for deposits, loaning money out, and then charging interest for loans and interest for deposits. Also, recall that the Law prohibited them from charging pilgrims usurious rates for exchange, so they had to make it up in volume; that's why they're all yelling at each other. They want lots of customers, and you're right; it looks as if things could get heated pretty quickly. Oh yeah, another one of the names used for the moneychangers was 'trapezites', from the Greek word, 'trapeza' meaning 'table', the moneychangers always worked at a table. Let's keep walking until we find a guy who suits our fancy."

They walked as Toma recommended until they found a *shulhani* who did appear to offer a reasonable rate. With their Greek obels and drachmas exchanged for shekels, they moved away from the Temple and headed to the southern part of the Old City, looking for the room where the Apostles, the mother of Jesus, and the others were staying. Archival records indicated that the Apostles and the others were staying in an upper room at a house outside of the city walls close to the Essenes Gate in the southern part of the Upper City. During their first mission, they had patrolled this area, so they had a general idea of where they were staying. The place they were looking for was not too far from the house of Caiaphas. As they were moving through the city, they had the opportunity to find lodging, and they were able to get their animal boarded.

By mid-morning, they were close to the city's outer walls by the Essenes Gate, which led out of the city to Mt. Zion. Many pilgrims in this part of the city were still shopping in various marketplaces held throughout Jerusalem, and some were leaving the city to view the mountains. As they cleared the city walls, they heard a massive wind funneling through a mountain pass. They walked in that direction, anticipating what was happening. As they turned onto the street where the house was, they noticed that a large group of pilgrims were also attracted to the noise and were all standing outside.

Coming from the house were numerous voices, all speaking different languages. The people gathered outside were surprised to hear their own language being spoken and then confused as to why. One of the pilgrims, a Jew from Rome, told the man next to him, "I'm in the same building as these men. I know them; they're all from the north, from Galilee. I have only heard them speak their language; when did they learn how to speak mine?"

Then, others began to echo the same question. Greek could be heard from the house, as well as Arab, Egyptian, Thracian, Pisidian, and other languages from Anatolia. Languages from farther east could be heard: Parthian, Elamite, the language of the Medes, and those from Mesopotamia. They were all amazed, and then some of the younger ones in the group began to yell, "They're drunk; just listen to them!" And then they laughed as they walked off.

But Simon Peter, the big fisherman, had heard that remark, and in a commanding voice, he silenced the group standing in the street below, "Drunk? Do you dare call us drunk? How can we be drunk? It's only nine o'clock in the morning. No, we're not drunk. You who are Jews, you children of *Yisra'el*, all of you here in Jerusalem, listen to my words. What did you learn from the Prophet Joel? Didn't he tell us that in the last days, the Lord, and blessed be His holy name, would pour out a portion of His Spirit upon all of us?" Simon Peter continued to quote the Prophet Joel, pointing out that everyone who calls upon the name of the Lord will be saved. He then preached about Jesus of Nazareth. "You Sons of *Yisra'el*, hear my words. *Yeshua* the Nazorean was a man commended to you by God with mighty deeds, wonders, and signs, which God worked through Him in your midst. This man, you killed, using lawless men to crucify Him, but God raised Him up, releasing Him from the throes of death because death could not hold Him!" Simon Peter preached in this way for some time; he spoke eloquently and convincingly, and in the end, he convicted them. "God the Father raised *Yeshua* from death. Of this, we are all witnesses. *Yeshua* received the promise of the Holy Spirit from the Father and poured it forth as you have seen and heard. Therefore, let the house of *Yisra'el* know that God has made *Yeshua* both Lord and Messiah, *Yeshua*, whom YOU crucified!"

With that, many of them began screaming to Simon Peter and the other disciples there, "What are we to do?" Simon Peter told them they needed to repent and be baptized, and they would receive the gift of the Holy Spirit. He stayed there, encouraging the crowd. He testified to the message of Jesus, argued with them, and convinced many to become followers of Jesus. Shouts of *"Hoshiya na!"* were heard as the other ten disciples and Simon Peter led everyone east to the Pool of Siloam outside the city wall. Three thousand pilgrims were baptized that day, and the nascent seeds of the Christian Church were sown.

Later in the day, when the crowd had finally dispersed, two pilgrims remained, and they made their way to the upper room. They knocked on the door and were greeted warmly by those in the house. Simon Peter introduced himself and welcomed them in Aramaic, "Welcome, brothers, please join us." It was dusk, and the only light in the room came from the small fire in the hearth. Declan and Toma noticed a young man and a woman, probably in her late forties or possibly as old as fifty, seated at the table. The young man and the woman were looking intently at Declan and Toma. The woman told the young man, "Fetch those two here, please."

The young man approached Declan and Toma and said, "How do we know you? Please come sit by me and our Mother." They walked up to the table, and the woman looked at Declan. No one else in the room was speaking; they were all silent, observing the interaction between the Mother and the two pilgrims.

"Please come closer, my son." She looked at his face very closely. "Yes, you are the one. You were there when they crucified my Son, weren't you?" Then she looked at Toma, "And you, too, were at the Place of the Skulls. Yes, I saw you there."

Toma looked at her. The beauty of her youth had not abandoned her. She had delicate features and piercing yellowish-brown hazel eyes with flecks of gold and green in the center. Her dark hair, covered by her headcloth but still visible, had streaks of gray but was still full and flowing. "Yes, *Yimma*," using the Aramaic for 'Mother,' "we were there. We were there when they crucified your Son, *Yeshua*, whom we know now to be the Christ, the anointed one of God the Father. It is He who has come to save His people."

Peter and the rest began to shout, "*Hoshiya na!*" while Declan and Toma stood facing the Mother. Then the young man beside her said, "Yes, but we saw you in Bethany when The Master raised Lazarus from the dead. You were there, too."

Declan answered, "Yes, we were. We were traveling to Jerusalem for Passover when we stopped in Bethany. How are you called, Brother?"

"I am called John," he said. Then, indicating with his

head another man standing to the side. "My brother, James, and I are the sons of Zebedee."

Then the Mother spoke, "Yes, but who are you? I can tell from your accent that you are not from here," then looking at Toma, "But your accent is familiar. You sound like one of us. When John and I saw you at the Place of the Skulls, we heard you both speaking a language we had never heard. We saw you using weapons that we had never seen. We all saw you protecting my Son. I heard one of my kinswomen say you were the Angels sent to save my Son. Who are you? Are you angels sent to us by God most high? Blessed be His name."

Toma picked up from here, "Yes, *Yimma*, we were speaking a different language and using what may be considered strange weapons, but no, we are not angels. *Yimma,* we are from a province far to the east of here. Years ago, three of our Magi who studied the stars and their movements identified a star that heralded the birth of your Son, and they traveled to this land to pay Him homage. These Magi returned to our province telling of the birth of He who would become the King of the Jews. Magi, such as those who came to worship your Son and other scholars from our province, have developed different tools used in our cities for various tasks and in our outer provinces for agriculture and other purposes. All we had at the Place of the Skulls were just some of our tools."

"Yes, but who are you, and why did you try to save my Son?"

Declan answered her, "Mother, according to our records, when our Magi came back after honoring your Son, they told their community of astrologers that your Son would be falsely accused and put to death for something that He did not do. As we saw this testimony unfolding before us, we decided to act to save this innocent Man."

The Mother thought, "Why didn't you save Him?"

Declan looked at Toma and told the Mother, "*Yimma*, I was talking directly to Him. He knew what we were trying to do. He looked at us and told us to stop; He said that what He had to do was for the atonement of all of us, and it was the will of

His Father. He was right, wasn't He? If we interfered, then He could not be raised." Then, looking at Peter, Declan asked, "Am I right?"

Everyone was quiet. No one dared to speak, then the Mother broke the silence, "Yes, my son, you are right. Without my Son, *Yeshua*, accepting this physical death, He could not fulfill the will of His Father, Blessed be His name. But your courage in trying to defend Him and your faith in who He is should not be forgotten, nor shall they go without the thanks of those of us who are here. How are you called, my sons?"

Declan used his middle name, "I am called Antoni, Mother, and my brother is Toma. Today, we have accepted Simon Peter's exhortation and have been baptized. We ask to follow you all in spreading the Good News that *Yeshua* has commanded you to spread to all the nations. We will forsake all that we have to follow you." Declan/Antoni took out his money bag, which was full of Tyrenian shekels. "My brother and I must keep enough money for our return trip home. We plan to leave after the Feast of Shavuot. We will settle our business accounts and sell what we have." Antoni took enough money from the bag for their return home. "Here, please take this. All we have is yours," he handed Peter the money bag.

Peter took the bag and said, "You are both welcome to be with us. We can use men who are brave and willing to do the work of the Master. Will you stay with us this night?"

"Not for tonight, thank you, Simon Peter. We have lodgings in the lower city, and our beast is boarded close by. We will return there to gather our belongings and return in the morning." Then, looking at The Mother and the others, Antoni and Toma wished them all a good night and went out the door.

They were quiet as they made their way to their lodgings for the night. Tomorrow they would return to stay with the Believers and await the portal's opening to return to the present.

Chapter Twenty-Two
44 A.D.

Jerusalem – Early Spring

"And before Our Lord ascended into the clouds, He told us exactly what He expected of us." John, the son of Zebedee, was walking towards Jerusalem on a road north of Bethany, talking with Declan, known by the Community as Antoni, and Toma. The three of them had become very close during the past year. Declan and Toma had returned through the portal a year earlier, telling the community of Believers that they had to go "home" to sell their business. They then returned to the community in Jerusalem in what seemed like years. They donated all of the proceeds to the fledgling Christian Church, which provided them with funds to continue their work in Jerusalem and the outer provinces. "Some of the brothers and others in the community wanted to focus on the Resurrection of the Lord and how He is the Messiah promised by God the Father, but Peter pointed out that The Master wanted us to also focus on His message and what He taught us. If you could have heard Him when He preached to a huge crowd when we were in Galilee, it was incredible. Yes, He is the Son of God. Yes, He is the Messiah. And yes, salvation comes through Him, but we must focus on what He taught us when He preached on that mountain. What He taught us was a message of how we should live with each other, how we should treat each other, and how we should act in the face of adversity. He taught us that we should focus on love and compassion, and He also taught us how much Our Father in Heaven loves us. He told us before He went back to His Father that He wanted us to go and teach all of the nations and make disciples of all peoples starting in Jerusalem, throughout Judea, Samaria, and to the ends of the Earth. That is our life's work, and that's what we'll continue to do."

Toma pointed out, "You've been able to make many converts. In Jerusalem and throughout Judea and Samaria, look at how successful you and the other brothers were in Lydda and Joppa. How do you think you have been able to accomplish this in such a short time?"

As he kept walking, John thought about this. "The Master told us that He would send His Holy Spirit upon us and that we would have 'all power on Heaven and Earth' given to us. Plus, He said that He would be with us. But look at the role that Peter has taken since Our Lord ascended. Recall the morning when you two first came to us. Do you remember his speech to the pilgrims outside of our house? He convinced three thousand people to become followers that day alone. Then, look at the miracles that he performed. Do you remember the crippled beggar he healed at the Temple? That he had healed that man silenced the Sadducees and the Temple authorities. But I think that when the High Priest and the Sadducees threw Peter and some of the brothers in jail under a strict guard, that may have helped us spread the Word. Remember that the Angel of the Lord released them, and the brothers returned to the Temple and began to preach; the priests had the brothers flogged because of this. They went back to the Temple and continued to preach. People saw that the brothers rejoiced that they could suffer for the sake of the Holy Name of *Yeshua*, that made people wonder. Many things have helped us in spreading God's Word."

Then Antoni asked him, "What about Paul? He has made many converts; what has led to his success? Paul isn't even one of the original community of brothers. How could he have so much success in converting people?"

John looked at Toma and Antoni, "Ah, now there's a

good question. When Peter went first before the Sanhedrin, the priests were confused about what to do with the brothers. A very learned Pharisee named Gamaliel, a scholar of the Law who was respected by all, spoke to the Temple authorities. He reminded them how many times in our history, people have always stood up and claimed to be this or that, and many would follow this person. He recalled two in particular, Theudas and Judas the Galilean. Both of these men had numerous followers, but they both died, and when they did, their followers scattered to the wind. Gamaliel convinced the Sanhedrin that the same thing would happen to us: *Yeshua* would die, and His followers would scatter. Gamaliel presented a logical argument, and the Sanhedrin listened to him. Gamaliel was able to turn a dangerous situation into something that could be dealt with appropriately by using logic and a convincing argument. In most situations, Gamaliel would be correct; he didn't realize that, in this case, he was not dealing with a Theudas or a Judas from Galilee; he was dealing with the Messiah. He did not factor that into his argument."

Antoni was puzzled, "What does that have to do with how successful and convincing Paul could be?"

John just smiled at them, "Gamaliel was Paul's teacher."

Then Toma got into the discussion, "Are you saying that Paul could just use logic, and that is what made him so successful in gaining converts?"

"No, Toma, not exactly. I'm saying that Gamaliel could teach his students to speak persuasively and to know their facts. Paul can do both, but you must understand that The Lord Himself converted Paul and chose him to be His instrument. There can be no more powerful combination than being chosen by The Lord and having the ability to speak so eloquently. The Lord chose His instrument well, didn't he?"

Antoni nodded his head, "It would appear so. I have heard among the brothers that the Word of The Lord has spread as far north as Phoenicia and Syria. How did The Word spread so far so quickly?"

"Remember, Antoni, that we lost one of our younger

brothers, Stephen, several years ago and that it was Paul, who was then known as Saul, who had approved of his being stoned to death. Many of our new converts who witnessed that fled Jerusalem in fear and traveled to the north. They are the ones who brought The Word there. But for now, let us pray for our brothers in Jerusalem and get there quickly. You both heard what was told to us earlier. Herod is causing problems yet again, and we need to be able to support our brothers in their time of need."

Toma asked, "Why is Herod doing this? No one is challenging him or his reign."

"It is because this is his way. No one can understand the mind of Herod, Toma. He is full of evil and greed and jealousy." They picked up their pace. "One thing that I have never asked either of you before. Do you remember years back after the Holy Spirit descended on us in Jerusalem, when you first came to our Community?"

Toma looked at Antoni, "Yes, that day was seared into our memories. Yes, we both remember it well."

John continued, "Do you recall how *Yimma* questioned the two of you? She was asking you who you were as she recognized you when The Master was being crucified. She mentioned that you were speaking a different language and using tools she had never seen before. She even mentioned that one of her kinswomen said you were angels sent by the Lord on high. Since that day, we have accepted you both as Believers as we know that you are; your faith is true; we know this. But things make me wonder, are you angels sent from the Lord? Look at the two of you. You left here what, ten years ago, to go back home. You return here to be back with us, but you look the same. You have not aged ten years, maybe a few years, but you look the same. Here is the question I have never asked you: How can this be? Are you angels? Tell me."

Antoni looked at Toma with a knowing look. When they returned to Pasadena, they worked with a group of make-up artists from Hollywood to address the issue they would face upon returning to the past: How to appear to have aged appropriately during their ten-year "absence." The artists taught Declan and Toma how to apply latex around their eyes and mouths to make wrinkles and lines appear. They were also given silicone and gels to add some "sagging" to their faces, but this was to be used during later transports through the portal. Lastly, they had hair coloring and thinning shears to simulate hair thinning and greying.

Antoni answered, "My brother John, do you recall how we told *Yimma* that we have philosophers and astrologers from where we came? These brilliant men have created many tools we use in our country. We also have some very learned physicians in our country who have developed balms and lotions that we use to keep our skin supple and youthful looking. During our time back home, we used much of our balms to help replenish our skin following our journey. As you can see, it is most effective, is it not?"

As they were walking, John thought of this for a moment, "Thank you, Antoni, that answers my question, but it gives rise to another question, do you have more of this balm?" They all laughed with each other and then continued their journey south.

*****

They arrived in Jerusalem before noon and went immediately to the house where they were all staying. One of their community members caught them as they approached the house, "John, you must go to Herod's Palace and find Peter. King Herod is arresting a number of the faithful, and your brother, James, is arguing with Herod; your brother will not back down."

John, Antoni, and Toma ran to Herod's Palace; when they arrived, John said, "My brother has such a temper. Our Lord called James and me *Boanerges,* the sons of thunder. I think that's because of James' quick temper and his love of argument. Let's see if we can find Peter." They searched the grounds outside Herod's Palace, asking anyone if they had seen Peter.

They were told that he was inside. The three of them walked up to the Palace Gate, and when they told the guards who they were, the guards sneered and said they were more than welcome to go inside and see the proceedings.

They could hear James conversing with the king when they entered the atrium leading to the courtyard where Herod held his daily court. "Our people have done nothing to offend you, Majesty, nor have they done anything against the Roman Procurator. We have done nothing but preach in the public square and the Temple. We have not talked sedition nor fomented any rebellion against your rule. All that we ask is that we be allowed to preach the Good News to the people of Jerusalem." Looking around the atrium, John, Antoni, and Toma saw several of the Faithful standing against the far wall guarded by armed soldiers. They also noticed members of the Sanhedrin standing next to Herod's throne, whispering to him.

Herod stroked his beard and then fixed his eyes on James, "Do you not think that I know who you are and what it is you are trying to do in my kingdom? You and the rest of this," he waved his hand in a dismissive gesture toward the believers that were under guard against the far wall, "the rest of this, this, offal. Don't you think I know you are trying to subvert my authority?"

James spoke again, "We have done nothing of the sort, Majesty."

Herod sat back on his throne, "Are you calling me a liar, you miserable insect? Don't you know that I have the authority over your life and the lives of your disgusting rabble? How dare you insult me."

John was saying under his breath, "Don't do it, Brother, he is just baiting you. Don't do it."

James spoke in a very low voice, "We have been a faithful and law-abiding people and have never disrespected Your Majesty." His voice began to rise, "But please know that your authority has been granted to you by Almighty God; Blessed be His holy name. It is He who has granted me the authority to speak in the name of His Son, *Yeshua* of Nazareth, whom you put to death by hanging Him on a tree," by this time James was roaring like a lion, "and you have the audacity to say that you can command me not to preach in His Holy Name? How dare *you* to presume that you can dictate the will of The Father!"

Herod jumped up, screaming unintelligibly. Then, he looked at his Captain of the Guard and gave him a prearranged sign. In a flash, the officer unsheathed his sword and beheaded James, dropping him where he stood. John screamed as if he, too, were wounded. Toma and Antoni grabbed John and took him outside before any of the palace officials recognized who he was.

Herod sat down on his throne, very calm, as if nothing had happened. The priests from the Temple standing off to his side all had satisfied looks on their faces. When Herod saw that his actions pleased the priests, he ordered his guards to bring him Peter, but first to put him in chains.

Chapter Twenty-Three
Spring

Pasadena, CA

The project team had completed all of the calculations required for the next portal opening, scheduled to occur the following week. Qemal had been introduced to the team nine months ago as "Mr. Vasilios Pananas," a retired Greek Marine of the Thirty-second Marine Brigade, the Hellenic Naval Infantry trained as an elite special forces unit. Like other countries' Marine units, the Thirty-second Marine Brigade operated on naval vessels. Unlike other Marine units, this Marine branch is a specialized unit of the Hellenic Army. Mr. Pananas had specialized training and language skills similar to Declan's and Toma's. According to Murray, Mr. Pananas was uniquely qualified and personally selected by Murray to bring the recently released advanced technology to Declan and Toma to help facilitate their mission. The plan was to send Mr. Pananas through the portal, rendezvous with Declan and Toma in Jerusalem, and then return to the present time via another portal. This portal was scheduled to open within six months after Mr. Pananas' arrival in Jerusalem. At least, that was the plan that Murray presented to the Project team.

But Richard Hollander knew better. Earlier, when he had been in Murray's confidence, an ally of sorts, he knew what Murray was planning; Murray called it his "masquerade." Richard knew Murray's objective was to eliminate the major Christian evangelists and to ensure that Declan and Toma would not survive this mission. Richard knew, as an atheist, that religious implications notwithstanding, Western Civilization was inextricably tied to Christianity. He understood that Murray's plan to thwart the spread of Christianity would have a significant impact on Western Civilization. He knew that Murray was tempting fate and had to be stopped.

And that was the problem. Richard knew that Murray was following his every move and that Murray did not trust him anymore. He knew that Murray might do something to get back at Richard. He was convinced that Murray was insane. But how to warn the others? Richard had to put some thought into this.

Murray was also thinking about Qemal's upcoming mission to Jerusalem. Upon passing through the portal, Qemal would confirm his position with the homing beacon that Declan and Toma had buried in the desert east of Ashdod. The beacon was programmed to start transmitting at the time that Qemal was scheduled to arrive at the portal in 44 A.D. Qemal would be traveling with equipment similar to Declan and Toma, and his "Peripheral Brain" had programmed all of the information that he would require to complete his mission. Unlike what was presented to the Project team, he was not scheduled to return to the present in six months. The plan devised by Murray was that Qemal would follow Declan and Toma into the portals going to Cyprus, Asia Minor, Mesopotamia, and other sites and eliminate the evangelists as the opportunities became available. Murray felt that his plan was progressing very well. He had the Project team ready to do his bidding, and they all bought into his "masquerade." Oh yes, things were progressing quite well. The only source of concern for him was Richard. It appeared to Murray that Richard was having second thoughts about this plan. He thought he should not have brought him into his confidence, but what was done was done. In the meantime, he had eyes on Richard as he did deem watching. In reality, it was Murray who needed watching as he was very rapidly losing his mind. He became so obsessed with destroying Christianity that he lost all sense of perspective. He had no remorse for things he was planning on doing, and his drive to complete his mission blinded him to all reason. Richard knew Murray was becoming insane, but Nate and Jill had also noticed a change in Murray and were questioning some of his decisions.

The following week, Qemal's transport through the portal was flawless. Later that week, a meeting was held with various project team members to review the portal activity's final projections. Murray had Richard attend the meeting. It was as if he wanted to keep Richard close by to monitor his activities. The meeting was uneventful, and at the close, Murray was talking with one of the engineers. Richard realized that he had a chance, probably the only chance, to speak with Nate and Jill. Richard got up to sit next to Nate and Jill, and he noticed that Murray was watching him. He sat beside them with uncharacteristic friendliness, trying to appear calm. Richard asked, "Jill, I was hoping to follow up with you and Nate about a question regarding chaos theory."

Jill looked at Nate, "Sure, how can I help you?"

"I was recalling one of the briefs that Declan and Toma gave. They were talking about what they experienced on Mt. Calvary during the crucifixion of Christ. From a chaos theory perspective, I was just wondering what would happen if only the two thieves were crucified on that hill. What do you think would happen, Jill?"

Jill was a bit perplexed at this question, "I don't think that I'm following, Richard; what if only the two thieves were crucified? Is that what you're asking?"

"Yes, that's it exactly. Maybe I'm saying this wrong, but instead of asking *what* would happen, why don't you and Nate think about this: Can you envision how it would look on the hill if only the two thieves were crucified? Just think about it, but keep visualizing it, OK? Thanks, and catch up at the next meeting." He walked away with a pleasant smile, but as he looked at Murray, he saw that Murray was glaring at him; Richard just smiled back at him.

Nate and Jill were walking back to their offices when Jill said, "That was a bizarre conversation. I have not had many conversations with Richard, but he came over to where we were sitting and acted as if we were best friends, very unusual. But the question he asked, were you able to follow that?"

"Not really, but he said something interesting. He asked us to 'keep visualizing' what he was talking about. What does that have to do with chaos theory? Did you notice how he made a point of wanting to know something from a chaos theory perspective? Maybe I'm tired or dense, but I couldn't figure out what he wanted to discuss, most unusual."

Jill thought about this more. "I don't know. I wonder if he was trying to tell us something. Just come out and say what's on your mind, good grief. Oh, well, I'm not going to worry about it."

But they would find that there was something to worry about. They just didn't know at the time.

Murray called Richard and asked him to come to his office. Richard had expected this to happen, but he dreaded meeting with him. Without preamble, Murray asked Richard, "What were you talking to Nate and Jill about after the meeting? I thought that you would head right back to your office to read the latest telemetry data."

Richard appeared calm but felt like reaching over the desk and throttling Murray. "I didn't know I had to answer to you regarding my daily schedule and my comings and goings. Is that what you expect of me? If that is the case, please accept my resignation."

Murray's jaw muscles were working overtime, and it appeared he might lose it at any moment, "No, Richard, I like it right where you are. I just don't want you conversing with Nate and Jill behind my back."

Richard looked at Murray in a new light, and he knew that Murray had clearly gone over the edge. "No worries, Murray, no worries at all. Is that it? Is there anything else that you need to talk with me about?"

"No, you're free to leave." Richard got up and walked out the door.

Later that evening, as Richard was driving home, he

thought about how things had stood at that point in time. He knew Murray had to be stopped, but his subtle defiance of him in front of others put him at significant risk. He felt that Murray would do something rash. Richard knew that his path could very well cost him his life, but with a sense of fatalism, he accepted this, strengthening his resolve to stop him. He laughed to himself as he thought about the irony of his situation. Richard was a World War II history buff. As a grandchild of Dutch Jews, he took a keen interest in how the Nazis could overrun Europe so quickly at the beginning of the war. While he despised the German people in general and the Nazis in particular, he knew that there were many German Christians who had a strong sense of justice and Christian morality. These people did what they could to save Jews and stop Hitler. One of these men, General Dietrich von Choltitz, the "Savior of Paris," openly defied Hitler as the general thought that he was insane. That is precisely how Richard felt about Murray. Then there were the two Wehrmacht officers, Claus von Stauffenberg and Henning von Tresckow. They attempted to assassinate Hitler in July 1944. Both of these men thought that the treatment of Jews and others was "a personal humiliation and a degradation of civilization." What steeled Richard to pursue his course of action was what von Tresckow said before the assassination attempt. He said what was of the highest consequence was that "men of the resistance dared to take the decisive step." It was hard for him to believe, but Richard would emulate them. He was determined to be that man of resistance.

Murray, for his part, began to plan to get rid of Richard. He did not want him to get any ideas.

A month later, on a Monday morning, Murray announced to the team that Richard Hollander had died in a horrible car accident as he was driving to Antelope Valley for the weekend. The Highway Patrol was investigating the accident, but the car that Richard was in was severely burned. It was barely recognizable. His vehicle was identified by one of his license plates that had blown clear of the car, and he was identified through dental records. Richard did not have any close friends at work, but it was still a shock to the Project team. Murray had scheduled grief counselors to be available for anyone who needed to talk about this tragic incident.

Nate sent a text to Jill asking her to meet him after work. He had thought about Richard's conversation with him and Jill and did not want to discuss it at work. Jill agreed to meet him at a restaurant in Arcadia, a city not too far from Pasadena. She, too, had some concerns, but she was glad that she would be meeting Nate.

Jill pulled into the restaurant parking lot and was happy to see Nate's car there. After what she had learned today, she was looking forward to a glass of wine. Nate had a table for them in the lounge and stood for her when she walked in. She gave him a quick hug and a peck on the cheek, and they sat down. Nate had a glass of Chardonnay waiting for her.

Nate leaned in closer to her, "Jill, I have a bad feeling about things. I have been playing over what Richard said to us several weeks ago, may God have mercy on his soul. As soon as I heard this morning that he was killed in a car accident, it dawned on me what he was trying to tell us. Think about it. Two thieves being crucified on Calvary versus the two thieves and Our Lord. What would we have if Our Lord were not crucified and it was only the two thieves? Two crosses on Calvary. But Richard kept telling us something. I've been trying to reconstruct his conversation with us, and he said something like, 'How would that look?' and 'Try to visualize it' or something like that. Jill, what would you see on the hill if you tried to visualize it?"

"You would see two crosses on the hill, so?"

"He was trying to tell us something. You felt it, and I felt it. How strange his behavior was, that false attempt at being our friend, that phony smile of his. He was trying to tell us something. Think, Jill, two crosses, a *double* cross."

Jill almost came out of her seat as it dawned on her, "Of course! Something is a double cross. But what?"

"Have you noticed a change in Murray at all since

Kristin died? Grief is one thing, but have you noticed something else? Anything out of the ordinary? Then, think of his relationship with Richard. But how about Murray? Does anything strike you as unusual about his behavior?"

"Yes, several things. When Kristin was still alive, he always asked us questions about our faith. Then, after she passed away, he never brought it up again. His relationship with Richard was odd. I saw them together talking all the time, and then it was as if Murray was angry with him. He was rude to him, and I caught him looking at Richard in meetings; it was as if Murray was always glaring at him. Is that what you're asking, stuff like that?"

"Yes, that's part of it, but there's something else. I was the closest thing to a best friend that Murray had. He and I did get along quite well despite our differences. He told me in no uncertain terms what his goal was for the first mission; he wanted to prove to the world that Jesus was nothing more than a preacher from the backwaters of Galilee. That was it. He told me many times that he not only denied the existence of God but that he despised even those who were religious. I guess that he made exceptions for you and me. Then, when the team returned with incontrovertible proof that Jesus was the Son of God and that God truly existed, he could not be persuaded.

"And then a couple of years later, all of a sudden, he is now open to the possibility of the existence of God? But he kept telling us that he was not part of the fold; he would always say that he was on the outside looking in, correct? He never said he was a believer, but he would keep questioning us about our faith, remember?" Jill nodded yes. "And then Kristin died. Normally speaking, and I have seen a lot of death and a lot of mourning, I could see sadness and then acceptance and then moving on with your life. But how did you see Murray after that initial stage of grief?"

Jill thought about this. "I would say that I saw Murray much more driven in his work, especially with this latest mission, not the one that Declan and Toma went on a year ago, but this latest one with Mr. Pananas going through the portal. I found him incredibly driven to get buy-in from all of us and then for Mr. Pananas' mission to deliver the new technology to the team. He wanted to demonstrate that we could send a 'rescue team' into the portal. That's the way that I saw it."

Nate was becoming more animated, "OK, few questions here. How about this Mr. Pananas? What do we know about him except that he was 'personally selected' by Murray? You weren't here when we were going through team selection for the first mission, but it was a deliberate and methodical process for candidate selection. But this Mr. Pananas shows up, and no one says a word. Why is that? Secondly, what about the new technology that the Science and Tech team developed? Do you know much about it? What did we develop? Looking back on things, it looks like we, as the project team, rubber-stamped anything that Murray, and for that matter, Richard, brought up to us. I remember working with Richard on the first mission. He was a bright guy, but I got the impression that he was like Murray; I mean, he had strong anti-theistic beliefs. You could pick up little things that he would say that would let you know that he thought religion was a charade. Murray and Richard became very close right after Declan and Toma gave their joint presentation to the team, and you gave your initial overview of chaos theory. And then later, last fall, I believe, when you gave your updated presentation on chaos theory. You discussed that the possibility of the team going back in time would not cause any problems for the future state, especially if they were as careful as they were the first time. Do you remember that?"

"Yes, Nate, I do. But looking back on that, I feel that what I was saying was misinterpreted. It feels as if what I said played right into what Murray *wanted* me to say. Nate, I feel as if I were played."

"I think that we all were. We got so wrapped up in this new mission that we rested on our laurels about what we accomplished with the first mission—but going back to what I was saying. Do you remember who spoke up in that meeting and asked if what you were presenting then flew in the face of everything you said before? Do you remember that?"

"Yes, I do. It was Richard, which makes me feel even stronger that I've been played. Dammit, Nate, this whole thing was a setup, but to what end?"

"Think, Jill. Murray still harbors a very anti-theistic attitude, no matter how he has tried to smooth it over. Then this latest mission, which, looking at it now, part of it sounds phony, this 'trying to find out how the evangelists were so successful in spreading the Gospel' and how that can help us in the event of a nuclear holocaust. It was an attractive proposition then, but something was wrong with this. Then, Mr. Pananas took innovative technology to Declan and Toma, and we never vetted him. Who is he? Lastly, Richard's message to us, a *double* cross, what do you think it means, Jill?"

"I think it means that we screwed up. Declan and Toma are in danger, aren't they?"

He replied, "I think they might be. I think Murray is trying to interfere with their mission and make them fail; to what end, I don't know quite yet. But first things first. Let's start looking into a few things, but we must be cautious. I have a funny feeling that Murray is not who we think he is. Let me run a few things down, like who this Mr. Pananas is. Secondly, do you think that you can get a feel for what the Science and Technology Group developed? This might let us know that some of our suspicions are correct."

"Nate, I have to share something with you. I need to tell you why Murray and I broke up. He and I were together in Santa Barbara for a weekend as we had no time together before that. But when we were there, I saw an ugly side of Murray, a mean and hurtful side to him. I don't know if that means anything to you, but at one point that weekend, I felt that he could have become violent with me."

Nate patted her hand as she shook. "It answers a few of my questions. I also need to share something with you. I have a very frightening feeling in my soul that Richard's death was not an accident, and I have a feeling that Murray is somehow involved. You might think I'm overreacting, but I have a friend who can help me check my house and phone for listening devices. I'm that nervous about Murray. If you want, he can get your place, too."

They decided to start taking measures to protect themselves against what they felt was Murray's becoming increasingly unstable.

Chapter Twenty-Four
44 A.D.

Jerusalem – Mid-Spring

Qemal was fascinated by his passage through the portal, but he went to work immediately after the effects of the transit wore off. He organized all his equipment and supplies and searched for the homing beacon using his "peripheral brain." His device was able to establish a connection with the beacon, so he knew that he had made it through the portal and was now in Judea in the first century A.D. Using the Brain again, he was able to determine his route to Jerusalem, he expected that he could make his way through the Central Mountains and arrive in Jerusalem in a day and a half, he did not see a reason to push himself, plus, he was enjoying the solitude and the fact that there was no civilization for as far as he could see, he found a semblance of peace in this part of his journey.

As he expected, he made it to Jerusalem on the morning of his second day of travel. Walking through the city gate, he was stopped by the Roman guards, but unlike Declan and Toma, he had no wine to share. After a brief inspection and finding nothing of interest, the guards let him pass. He walked through the gate and entered the city of Jerusalem. He reconnoitered Fortress Antonia, the Temple Area, and other parts of the Upper City until he arrived at Herod's Palace. Following the instructions programmed into his peripheral brain device, he arrived at the location he was directed to go to. He did not have to wait long for what he was expecting. An armed group of ten soldiers was marching out of the palace gate. In the center of this small formation was a large man chained and led out of the palace.

Qemal noticed a Roman officer walking out of the Palace with an officer of King Herod's guards. He approached the Roman and asked him in Latin who was being led off in chains. The Roman replied, "What? Have you been living under a rock? That is Peter, the lead follower of an executed revolutionary."

He answered the Roman, "Forgive me, sir, I am a Greek pilgrim here for Passover. I am unaware of this, Peter; is he a revolutionary also?"

"No, he is just stupid. Maybe some time in the dungeon will clear his mind; that's where they're taking him. He is on his way to the Hasmonean Palace; they have a larger prison there. It should be filled tonight with all of these malcontents."

Qemal thought, *Their leader is right here. That makes my first job easier. I must find a way to get into that cell with him by tonight.*

Outside the city walls at their house, the faithful heard word of Peter's imprisonment and James' execution by Herod. Antoni and Toma had carried John back to the house as he was distraught after seeing the death of his brother, James. But John regained his composure and addressed the group, "My brother was killed as he was doing his best to protect the faithful from Herod's wrath. Herod wanted to imprison all of the brothers, and you know what occurs if Herod imprisons you. James defended the brothers and proclaimed to Herod that the only authority he may have comes from God the Father, blessed be His name. James died with the name of Our Lord on his lips and the love of the Lord in his heart. He is rejoicing in Heaven with Our Lord, but Peter is languishing in prison. Herod is happy to please his masters in the Sanhedrin, so we know what fate awaits Peter. Come, let us all pray for our brother, Peter, and brothers who may feel Herod's wrath this day." The entire community began to pray for Peter.

Qemal made his way to the Hasmonean Palace, where he noticed one of Herod's Palace Guards standing sentry watch at the gate. He approached the guard and tried to speak with him in Greek, but the guard just shook his head. Qemal asked him, "Do you speak Latin?"

The guard looked at him, "I can speak their language. What do you want?"

He answered, "That brute, Peter, whom they brought in earlier, how can I see him?"

"You can't. He's under an armed guard, doubled in force. He is the only prisoner we have tonight, as the King wants to make an example of Peter. He'll be brought to trial tomorrow, but the decision has already been made." At this, he scoffed. "So why do you want to see him?"

Qemal leaned in close to the guard, "Listen, this Peter claims to be a fisherman, but he is nothing more than a murderer. He killed my brother over a disagreement about some stupid nets. I know His Majesty wants to have his diversion with Peter, but I promised my brother that I would make Peter suffer. Can you get me into his cell for maybe a short time? I don't need long; I just need to inflict some injury on him."

"Are you out of your mind? I can't let you in there. You might be one of them. You may want to help him escape. Get out of here. You're bothering me and distracting me from my duty. Get out of here before I call one of my officers. They'll make an exception and throw you in with Peter."

"Wait. Didn't you say that Peter is under double guard?"

The guard looked back at Qemal, "Yes, so?"

"Well, if he's under a double guard, how do you expect me to free him? Check my bag. I have no weapons at all. I'm unarmed, and all I want to do is punch him in the face and maybe break his nose. He murdered my brother; I just need to make him suffer for what he did. I know that your king will have him executed tomorrow, and I won't deny him that, but please, I have to avenge my brother. Look, how many guards do you have guarding this prisoner, four, eight? Are there any officers here with you tonight?"

The guard was growing weary of this, "No, no officers,

but Peter is double-chained under a double guard, that means two guards in the cell and two outside the cell."

"Then let me make this worth your time. I will make an offering to each of you; just give me a short time in his cell. I'll let him know who I am and whose brother he killed. I will make him suffer and then be gone."

The money got the guard's attention, "How much for each of us?"

Qemal knew a guard's wages were a half shekel every two days. Thirty shekels each would be more than three to four months' wages, but he was willing to go as high as fifty shekels for each man. "I will give each of you thirty shekels."

"The guard could almost see the money in his belt, but he had to barter with this Greek, "No, forty-five shekels each. We could lose our positions!"

He almost laughed aloud, "Done. Forty-five for each of you. Shall I give everything to you right now, or do you want to talk with your comrades first?"

"No, these fools are all from the country. They'll be more than happy to take it. It's only one prisoner. All that you're going to do is beat him, correct?"

"Yes, yes, that's all. I might pull off an ear, but I will definitely break his nose. Here, I will give you two hundred fifty shekels, more than you bargained for. You can keep the extra if you wish; just let me get in there."

The guard congratulated himself on driving such a bargain. This Greek was a fool, but he took the money gladly. "Follow me." He led Qemal through a side sally port into the lower dungeon. It was dark inside, with light coming from two torches by the door. Two guards were sitting outside the cell on the floor, and two were on the inside. The guards inside were dozing. Peter was sitting on the ground, wrapped in heavy chains between the two inside guards. He was wide awake, and he appeared to be praying. The guard walked up to his comrades and shouted, "Get up. We have an important visitor here to see the prisoner."

All four guards got up with a great noise of chains

shaking. The lead guard approached the guard who came in from outside. "We've had no word of a visitor for this prisoner. Where is your authorization?"

The outside guard offered a greedy smile, "Is this authorization enough?" as he showed them the bag of shekels.

The guards inside the cell jumped over Peter to look at the bag through the bars, and the two other guards couldn't take their eyes off the bag. Peter remained seated, closed his eyes, and continued to pray. Qemal moved towards the cell, analyzing how he could kill Peter and then disable all five guards with the least amount of noise. It was unnecessary to kill the guards. He'd sweep through all five of them without working up a sweat; he had the moves already planned out in his mind. He walked up to the cell door and asked the lead guard to please open the door so that he could visit Peter for a moment. The guard opened the door, and Qemal walked in. The first thing he noticed was that it was slightly darker inside the cell. Becoming adjusted to the darkness, he felt that his eyes were playing tricks on him as he thought he saw a huge man standing at the rear of the cell. As he took another step deeper inside the cell, he realized too late that the large man at the back of the cell was not a vision. The man moved towards Qemal, touched Peter on his shoulder, and the chains fell off him; Peter was now unshackled. The man told Peter, "Get up quickly, put on your sandals and cloak, and come with me." The guards were shocked at what they saw but recovered quickly and charged the man. All at once, there was a brilliant light that blinded Qemal and the five guards, and immediately after the light blinded them, a deafening noise louder than a thunderstorm exploded within the cell, knocking the six men to the floor in agonizing pain. The last conscious thought that Qemal had as he felt, more than saw, Peter and the huge man exit the cell was, "I can't believe it, whoever that was used a flash-bang on us," and then he passed out.

Peter was walking as if he were in a dream. He thought, *What happened back there?* He had no idea that an angel freed him, but as he walked out of the prison, he looked over at the man walking next to him. He noticed that a soft glow surrounded the man. It was then that Peter realized that it was an angel. Suddenly, the angel disappeared, but by then, he was almost at the house where the brothers were. He walked up to the gate and began to knock on the door. One of the servants in the house heard the knock and went to answer it. When she saw it was Peter, she ran back into the house to tell everyone that Peter was at the door. Everyone told her to be quiet. Peter couldn't be at the gate as he was in prison, but she insisted he was waiting to get in. One of the brothers joked, "It's not Peter; it's his angel coming to visit us," but the servant, her name was Rhoda, kept telling them to go check for themselves. They got up and went to the door, amazed to see Peter at the gate. They began praising God loudly until Peter told them to be quiet and for everyone to go inside. Once inside, Peter told them, "Inside my cell, I was chained between two guards, and outside of the cell, Herod's captain had posted two more. The two guards inside were sleeping until the guard from outside came in, leading a stranger into the cell. The outside guard identified the stranger as an important visitor who wanted to see me, but I had never seen this man; he had a strange accent and behaved in an unusual way. The lead guard inside the jail asked the outside guard where his authorization was as they were not told to allow entry to any visitors. The outside guard showed them a bag of shekels that the stranger paid him to come in and see me. The stranger then walked towards my cell and had a look of pure evil, a look of bad intent on his face.

"As soon as the stranger was in my cell, out of the shadows came an angel. I thought at first that it was just a man, another guard perhaps, who was posted at the back of the cell, but the angel touched me on my shoulder, and all of the chains fell off of me. The angel then told me to get dressed and follow him. I was in no position to argue with him, but then the four guards, the sentry, and the stranger attacked the angel. As soon as they moved towards him, the cell was bathed in a very intense light that blinded the six men, but the light did not bother the angel or me. The next thing that I saw was all of the men putting their hands over their ears and screaming in pain, then they became as still as the dead, but I could see that they were still breathing. The angel and I walked out of the cell and out onto the street. I looked up at the angel, and he said, 'Continue straight up this street; your house is ahead.' As I looked at him, he disappeared right in front of me. And here I am, standing before you as the Lord, blessed be His holy name, sent one of his angels to rescue me from the clutches of Herod Agrippa."

Toma asked Peter, "Brother, can you describe the stranger? What did he look like? What did he say?"

Peter replied, "As I said, he had a strange accent but spoke Latin. His clothes were like ours, but they did not look as if they were worn or old. His clothes looked new. He did not look like a Jew or like anyone from our province, but he didn't look Roman either. I do remember the look on his face; he had the look of someone who would hurt me, and it looked as if he would enjoy it. He was full of evil. I am wondering if he could have been one of Satan's minions, if not Satan himself, but the Angel of the Lord was able to overpower him."

Toma looked at Antoni. A knowing nod between them indicated that they would discuss this later, but they were both thinking, who could this stranger have been?

Inside the cell, Qemal had awoken, and the five guards were still unconscious. As he woke, he looked around and noticed that Peter and the colossal man were no longer there. Looking inside the cell, he saw the chains lying on the ground, which had not been cut or broken. They were just there, undisturbed. Qemal stood up and left the cell as quickly as he could. He knew what would happen when the alarm was raised that the prisoner had escaped. As he was walking away from the palace, he replayed everything that happened inside the cell. He wasn't able to do what he intended to do, to kill Peter, and he needed to analyze what happened inside the cell so that he would not make that mistake again. He said aloud, "Who was that huge man inside the cell? How did he get in there? Was he a member of the palace Guard who had been bribed to release

Peter? And what weapon did he use? I have seen my share of flash-bang grenades in my time, and whatever the huge man used had all the characteristics of a flash-bang. But I had my eyes on him the entire time. He did not reach or throw anything; the flash-bang just happened. And how could that man have access to a flash-bang? There was no such thing at this time. What is happening?"

He kept walking and talking to the empty alleyway, intrigued by what he had seen and what was transpiring. "Something else, I noticed that the huge man in the cell. It may have been the low light, but something about that man; it looked like a soft light surrounded him. Fascinating. OK, Peter, you may have eluded me this time, but I will get you sooner or later." He walked on.

The following day, Herod sent for the prisoner to be delivered to him. The Captain of the Guard reported to the king that the prisoner had escaped. Herod flew into a rage and had the five guards brought to him.

"What happened to my prisoner? Where is he?" Herod was screaming. "Answer quickly, as your lives depend upon your answer."

The lead guard looked at his fellow guards, who stood before the king with their heads bowed. "Majesty, I opened the door to check on the prisoner's chains, and he overpowered all of us, threw off his chains, and escaped. There was nothing we could do, Majesty; he was like a man possessed and had the strength of ten men."

Herod sneered at his guards with a look of complete disgust, "Then how do you explain the fact that his irons are completely intact, there are no breaks, it does not appear as if a hammer had broken them, it looks as if his irons were not even attached, could it be that you did not restrain my prisoner as you were instructed?"

"No, Sire, they were completely locked as you commanded, but the prisoner did break through his chains as we reported. His gods must have been with him, and his magic must have been powerful."

"You first report that he had the strength of ten men and overpowered five of my Palace Guards. Then you report that it must have been his gods or magic. Which is it? How can I decide if I have two conflicting answers?" Herod was deep in thought. "Well, it does not matter what the answer is; my decision has been made. The five of you have failed in your duty to your king. Captain, take these worms out of my presence. At dusk, I want them tied at stakes and covered with pitch. As soon as it is completely dark, I want these five to be put to the torch and have them provide light to the outside of my Palace."

The five guards began to scream for mercy, but as Herod had said, his decision was made. That night, the palace was illuminated and could be seen from miles away.

Chapter Twenty-Five
44 A.D.

Jerusalem – Late Spring

Antoni and Toma spent the next few months preaching with the Apostles in various parts of Judea and Samaria but spent much of their time in Jerusalem. One afternoon, while they were in Jerusalem, they had the opportunity to be alone, giving them time to discuss their mission. Antoni said, "I know that we were to stay here in Jerusalem and other parts of the provinces, and then in 46 A.D., we were going to join up with St. Paul on his first missionary journey. But things are changing. What do you think? Should we change our original plan?"

Toma said, "We told the team back in Pasadena that the situation here on the ground would dictate how we proceed. I agree with you; things have changed. The plan is to go to Rome around 62 A.D. to meet with St. Peter and St. Paul. Until then, why don't we spend some time working with the other Apostles? We could split up now. You could go with St. Paul to Cyprus, and I could catch the portal that will take me to Mesopotamia and Armenia in 61 A.D. Then we could coordinate using the appropriate portals to meet and go together to Rome. How does that sound?"

"I was thinking along similar lines. I could follow Paul to Greece on his third mission around 53 A.D. St. Paul established a number of these churches on his first and second missions, but by the time he was on his third missionary journey, problems began to happen in some of the communities. St. Paul wrote some of his letters to the established communities, like Corinth. I want to learn how he united some of the fractured communities and brought them all back into the fold. After this trip, we can meet up in Rome. As you said, we can coordinate our devices to know when to meet. We can cover a lot more ground and get insights from differing perspectives. Plus, this will allow us to demonstrate that the theory our project team in Pasadena hypothesized would work holds water. How did PK explain this? It's like going to an airport and transferring from one aircraft to another to take you to a different destination. What did he call intersectionality? Well, I, for one, hope that it works."

Toma added, "True enough, I hope so, too. But going back to what we were saying, I would also like to visit Assyria and other parts of Mesopotamia. It would be like going home for me. St. Thomas, St. Bartholomew, and St. Jude all evangelized in that part of the world. I'd like to work with them. Let's check our peripheral brain and see how we can access both portals."

Someone else considered his plans in another part of Jerusalem through the portal. Since Qemal had pictures and bios of Antoni and Toma, he knew who they were and their capabilities; neither Antoni nor Toma knew who Qemal was, putting them at a distinct disadvantage. Qemal could shadow the two former SEALs, so he had an idea of their movements and activities. Qemal also had another piece of information that Antoni and Toma didn't have. Qemal, through his meetings with Murray, knew that the Einstein Project Team had discovered that once the portal opened, it remained open for at least six hours after a transit. What this meant was that Qemal could follow Antoni and Toma and could follow them into the portal. As Qemal's peripheral brain device was programmed with the same information as Antoni's and Toma's, he would be able to know where they were attempting to go. A distinct advantage indeed.

Using his device, Qemal considered the possible paths that they could take. Paul would take them to Asia Minor,

Greece, and eventually Rome. Peter would take them to Syria, Babylon, and Rome. Simon and Matthew would take them to North Africa, Iraq, and Persia. He looked at all of the possibilities. Following Peter and Paul would be a primary consideration due to their importance in establishing the Church. Still, there were other routes that they could follow that were of equal importance. But who should Qemal follow? He had already failed to assassinate Peter, so he would later make Peter a target. He was also going to follow Paul, and the fact that those two would be in the same area, namely Rome, at the same time made that city a target-rich environment. No, he thought, let me go to Rome later. In the meantime, Bartholomew, Jude Thaddeus, and Thomas were going to Mesopotamia, Armenia, Persia, and then the big prize, the subcontinent of India. Historically speaking, Armenia was the world's first Christian country, and disrupting their activities would impact the spread of Christianity. And then India. If Christianity took hold in India, that would lead to a massive increase in the number of Christians. Then, there was India's scholastic tradition. If those gigantic intellects in India became Christian, there would be no telling how powerful Christianity would become in a brief period of time.

After studying Antoni's and Toma's bios, he knew what route they would take. Antoni was of Western European descent, and Qemal assumed he would follow Paul through Greece and Italy. Toma was an Assyrian. The thought was that he would follow Bartholomew, Jude Thaddeus, and Thomas to Mesopotamia, Armenia, and India. Qemal flipped a mental coin and decided to follow Toma.

*****

Antoni and Toma coordinated their devices and programmed where and when they would meet. Antoni's portal to link up with St. Paul's group would open in the desert east of the city of Caesarea, about a four-day journey from Jerusalem, and transport him to the city of Ephesus in Asia Minor in the year 52 A.D. Antoni had the time and the coordinates locked into his device. He would be transported twenty-nine days before Toma's portal would open, and he planned to meet with St. Paul's team in Ephesus and travel with them.

Toma's portal was also scheduled to open in Caesarea. It was projected to transport him to the ancient city of Nineveh in Mesopotamia on the eastern bank of the *Tigris River* in the year 61 A.D. When they were ready to go, they said their goodbyes to their community, telling them they would preach in the north. They bid each other an emotional goodbye and then embarked on their journey.

Closely watching all of this was Qemal. He, too, made all of his preparations for following Toma to the north. He planned to enter the portal four hours after Toma was transported, and then he would track his movements. He had another advantage over Toma. Toma's peripheral brain contained a small tracking device that could transmit a ten-mile signal. Qemal's device had an embedded receiver that could track Toma's signal, so he would have no difficulty following him. He had planned a violent end for Toma and the disciples traveling with him. Things looked quite good for Qemal. He smiled to himself. This would more than compensate for his failure to eliminate Peter, but that, too, would come, all in good time.

Antoni had planned on entering the portal east of Caesarea and being transported to Ephesus in 52 A.D. to meet with St. Paul as he preached in Asia Minor. Using his SQQ-38, his peripheral brain, he accessed the portal that would transport him to Ephesus. But right before the portal began transporting him, he felt uneasy. It felt as if he and Toma were being followed.

237

Chapter Twenty-Six
Late Spring

Pasadena, CA

It had been a couple of months since the death of Richard Hollander, and the events surrounding his death were still a mystery. His car, which was found up in the high desert, had been completely burned, as was Richard's body. Two months later, there was still no report on what could have caused the accident. At least no one on the team had any information they could share. If Murray had any information about what happened, he didn't share it with anyone.

Richard had been single with no family to speak of. His parents died years ago, but there was an older sister. She had yet to be found by either the authorities or the insurance companies attempting to pay out Richard's insurance benefits. Richard's immediate supervisor, Dr. Jay Agrawal, employed a private investigations agency to try to locate Richard's sister. As Nate was on friendly terms with him, he asked Jay to update him on whether he had successfully found Richard's sister. He also stressed to keep this confidential between the two of them.

Within several weeks, Richard's sister was located. She was an artist living in San Francisco. Jay was in the process of contacting the sister when he experienced a family emergency in India and had to return to Mumbai. Jay turned everything over to Nate to coordinate until he could return to California. Nate jumped at this opportunity. This might shed some light on what happened to Richard. He met with Murray that afternoon and, at the end of their meeting, very casually told him, "One other thing, Jay asked me to take over his work with the disposition of Richard's property until he returns from India. Just to keep you in the loop."

Murray was preoccupied with a printout, "Yeah, sure, Nate, no problem. Let me know if there is anything that you might need from me, but I think that Jay has all of the particulars on Richard's background. Whatever works."

That evening, Nate successfully contacted Richard's sister. Her name was Regan, and she first learned of her brother's death when the private investigator contacted her. Nate informed her that he was working with the team at the JPL to help with Richard's assets as his estate was going to go through the Probate Court. Regan was designated as the sole beneficiary and as his executrix, but the address in Richard's will was no longer accurate. It took some time to locate her.

Regan sighed and then started to talk, "Richard and I were not very close. He was ten years younger than me, and I left home to go to college when he was still a little kid. I think he was in third grade when I left. I saw him throughout the years, you know, at family events, holidays, and at our parents' funerals. But I never really knew him. I mourn his passing, of course, and now that he's gone, I have no family left. I should have at least tried to reach out to him more. I took it for granted that I would always have some semblance of a family; now, I don't. Please don't think that I'm being callous. I'm not. It's just that this is a bit to process right now. I'm sorry, Dr. Joseph. How can I be of assistance to you?"

Nate replied, "Thank you, Ms. Hollander, and once again, please accept the condolences of your brother's colleagues. He was a very bright and dedicated scientist who contributed significantly to our team's work. I need to ask if you could take a leave of absence from your work to help settle your brother's estate. I realize this is short notice, but can you come down here to the Los Angeles area?"

Regan laughed a bit, "Leave of absence from work? Dr. Joseph—"

Nate interrupted her gently, "Please call me Nate."

"Yes, thank you, Nate, please call me Regan. Well, I exemplify the stereotype of the 'starving artist.' I sell some of my work at a local gallery, but for me, it's pretty much a hand-to-mouth existence. I went through what little my parents left me years ago, and I live in a loft that doubles as my studio. I don't need to worry about a leave of absence. I can be down there as long as you need me. I think that my VW can get me down there safely enough, but I need to ask you something. Can you see if you can help me find some 'reasonable' lodging down there? I'll be very frank and let you know that my financial situation is not what it once was."

"Well, we should be able to help you with that. Your brother was very organized and had an attorney who drafted his will and other legal documents. Richard had a savings and checking account at a local bank, so you should be able to access those funds. Let's contact his attorney when you're down here. As far as a place for you to stay, we'll cross that bridge when we get to it. In the meantime, please let me know when you'll be down here, and we'll take care of this. Does that sound satisfactory to you?"

"Yes, it does. I'll let you know as soon as I'm ready to come down, but I think I can be down in LA by this weekend. Thank you for all you have done to help, and I look forward to meeting you."

As soon as he hung up with Regan, he called Jill on his secure line to update her on his call with Regan. "She's willing to come down and help get things taken care of with Richard's estate. From what I can gather, she is on a very tight budget and asked me to help her find reasonable accommodations while she is down here. I'll be working on that with Richard's attorney to get her access to Richard's bank accounts, but this might help us out. If we could get inside Richard's home, we could see if he left any information or leads on what's happening. This would help us get to the bottom of what is happening. I still feel that Murray is behind Richard's accident, and the situation with Mr. Pananas is very concerning to me."

Jill asked, "What was Regan like? How did she sound to you?"

He thought for a moment, "She seemed to be honest and open about her relationship with her brother. But she seemed quite sad, as if things didn't work out for her as she had hoped. She and Richard were not very close. There was a large age difference between them. She has some regrets right now and feels that she should have made a better attempt at being a sister to Richard. Why do you ask?"

"I was just thinking, wouldn't it be a good idea if we had a good and trusting relationship with Regan? We need to get into Richard's home and see if we can find any notes or anything related to whatever may have led to his death, correct? Well, what if we, or more precisely, what if I were able to help Regan organize Richard's personal effects? Can you see where I'm going with this?"

Nate was getting excited about this, "That's brilliant! Yes, that would give you definite access to his home and wouldn't raise any suspicions. How do you think you can do this?"

"She's essentially broke with no place to stay, correct? You're going to try to get her access to her brother's money, which, by law, is hers. It might take some time to get those funds, right? And if she has no money, where can she stay? I've got two spare bedrooms in my condo. She can stay with me. Listen, when she gets down here, why don't we meet her at a restaurant for lunch, and I can offer her my place? How does this sound?"

He was smiling into the phone, "As I said, brilliant! She said she would be down by this weekend, so I'll have her at my house for lunch or dinner. Amala will be able to prepare a nice Indian meal for her. She sounds like a very artsy Bohemian type, and I think she'd like an exotic meal. Plus, we can speak freely at my house and make her comfortable."

"Sounds great. I have a good feeling about this. But to go back a bit, I'm still working with Arne Johannson on the equipment the Science and Technology group was working on.

241

Arne and I are meeting tomorrow, so I'll give you a heads-up on what I find."

She hung up the phone, went to her fridge, and pulled out a bottle of Chardonnay. She was thinking about her call with Nate when her phone rang. She looked at the screen and noticed that it was a Georgia area code. She first thought that something was wrong with her parents, but when she answered the phone, she heard her brother's voice. "Fraser, what a surprise. How are you, Big Brother?"

"I'm fine, Baby Sister, how about you? How are things in Pasadena?" he answered.

"Things are great, lots going on. Where are you right now? Are you at home?" She hadn't seen her brother since she left Georgia over a year ago.

"No, not at home, didn't Mom tell you? OK, let me see where I am. I just passed some waterpark a few exits ago and am gassing up. OK, let's see, oh yeah, I'm in San Dimas. Hey, is that the same San Dimas from Bill and Ted?"

Jill was puzzled, "Yes, it is, but what are you doing in San Dimas?"

"Didn't Mom tell you? Oh, I think I just asked that. Yeah, I'm in San Dimas heading to your place. I've been working with some of Ravi Shankar's students in San Diego. You remember Ravi Shankar, right? Since he passed away a few years back, some of his students have opened up a master's studio in Encinitas dedicated to teaching sitar and Hindustani music to select musicians. I've been living with these guys for the past six weeks and have learned an unbelievable amount of music theory and history from some of them. It's incredible. Mom said I should stay with you for a bit before heading up to San Francisco. I have a teaching gig up there starting in a few weeks; at least, that's the plan right now. So, what do you think? Are you up for a bit of company?"

"Sure, be great to see you."

*****

242

Regan arrived in Pasadena late on Saturday afternoon and called Nate to tell him she was in town. He asked her to meet him at his house to discuss her stay in Southern California. He let her know that his wife, Amala, had planned a nice dinner for them and that another one of Richard's colleagues would be over to meet with them. Jill and her brother Fraser would be joining them for dinner, and they were visiting with Nate and Amala when Regan arrived.

Nate met Regan at the front door and invited her in. She came into the kitchen where Jill and Fraser were visiting with Amala as she was preparing dinner. Jill expected to meet the stereotypical starving artist who would look, as Nate described her, very Bohemian. They were all surprised, Regan was beautiful. She was about five and a half feet tall and very lithe, and although Nate knew that she was about forty-five years old, she appeared to be in her early thirties. She had long, curly black hair with just a few hints of grey, piercing blue eyes and wore very little makeup. She was wearing an off-white sheer cotton dress with tiny straps over her shoulders. With the sunlight streaming in behind her, you could see the contours of her athletic body and the fact that she wasn't wearing very much underneath her dress. Fraser, being the dog he was, thought about how long it would take to get her out of her dress—he then mentally slapped himself.

Regan was introduced to everyone, and she volunteered to help Amala in the kitchen. Amala insisted that she relax and visit everyone. With their drinks refreshed and sitting outside on the patio, they all sat down to visit. Nate had mentioned to Regan that he had just met Jill's brother, Fraser, so he asked Regan and Fraser to tell everyone about themselves. Regan told everyone what she had discussed with Nate, and when she began to discuss her work, Fraser began to ask her some very pointed and incisive questions about her art. Regan appreciated that Fraser knew quite a bit about painting. When he mentioned that he had a degree in music from Vanderbilt and minored in music history, she realized he had a strong background in the arts. As an artist, she was pleased that someone could appreciate her

243

work, so she and Fraser had a good conversation regarding fine art. Fraser asked if she had any examples of her work with her. She had a few paintings in her car and offered to show them whenever he wanted. Fraser then began to share a bit of his background in music. When he mentioned that he was in San Diego studying Hindustani music under some of Ravi Shankar's students, Nate and Amala perked up. He pointed out that his main focus of study was classical guitar, and Regan asked him if he would play for them that evening.

Jill laughed and said, "Be careful what you ask for. Fraser will take you around the world with his guitar music."

Regan asked, "What kind of music do you appreciate the most, Fraser?"

He answered, "The guitar is an incredibly versatile and beautiful instrument that lends itself to so many different styles of music, but I enjoy playing the classical Spanish pieces. For example, the Albeniz piece, *Leyenda* transcribed by Segovia is most romantic. I like that piece quite a bit. Or the lute pieces written by Vincenzo Galilee, which Segovia also transcribed. Oh, Nate, you may remember Vincenzo Galilee's son, Galileo Galilee." Nate smiled at that. "But the lute pieces are amazing. I think that you'd like them."

Regan looked at Fraser and said, "I'd love to hear them. Hopefully, you can play them for us." The way that she looked at Fraser made his heart skip a beat.

At that point, Nate told Regan what he had accomplished in the past week. "I contacted Richard's attorney regarding your being down here and ready to start settling Richard's estate. He was very pleased to hear that. He will begin on Monday to prepare documents for your signature that will give you access to Richard's financial accounts. The attorney, whose name is Rory Hughes, understands that you will need access to funds to do the work you need to do. Getting you access to your money is his first priority."

A concerned look clouded Regan's face, "Thanks, Nate. Were you able to find me any accommodations?"

Jill jumped in, "Regan, both Nate and I worked with

your brother for several years and, like you, were very saddened by his sudden death. We realize how difficult of a time this might be for you, and we would like to try to help you get through it. Until you can get access to your funds, I'd like to invite you to stay with me. I have a large condo centrally located here in town. I have a spare bedroom that would be a bit nicer than going to a motel in Pasadena. You can have full access to my condo, the kitchen, the gym, whatever you need. As soon as Attorney Hughes can get you access to what you need, please consider my home your home, too. You have your own vehicle, so you can come and go as you please. We know you have a lot to do, so worrying about a place to stay should not be something to worry about. Does this sound OK with you?"

Regan was delighted and touched by Jill's hospitality. "Yes, Jill, that sounds wonderful, and it takes some of the anxiety off my plate. Thank you, I am most grateful."

Then Fraser added, "And think of all the music I'll be able to play for you and how much of your artwork you can share with me. This is going to be great!"

Now, it was Regan's turn to be surprised. Looking at Fraser, she said, "You're staying there, too?" She thought to herself, *Please say yes.* She found herself very attracted to Fraser.

"Yeah, Sis is putting me up until I head to San Francisco for a teaching position. I'll be leaving in a week or so."

Regan asked him, "You're going up to San Francisco? For how long?"

"Yes, I will be a guest professor at the San Francisco Conservatory of Music for several special workshops lasting about four weeks. I'll be lecturing on a wide array of subjects, for example, Segovia's transcription of several pieces by Bach, including his Prelude to the Cello Suite No. 1 in G major, which is incredible music. Why do you ask?"

Regan looked at Jill and Nate and then at Fraser, "The Conservatory is on Oak Street. My loft is no more than two blocks away. If I will be down here for the next few months, why don't you stay at my place?"

Fraser replied, "I'll gladly take you up on your offer."

Amala excused herself, grabbed Nate to help her, and in a few moments, she asked everyone to come inside for supper. The spread on the table looked amazing, and the oak dining room table was groaning under the weight of all the food. "I have made some traditional dishes from various parts of India. Here is our traditional appetizer, samosas, which are fried pastries stuffed with various savory fillings. This evening, I used a filling of potatoes, peas, and onions, and on the side, I have our traditional chutney and green chilis. Here, we have roasted chicken with spices and yogurt, which I roast in our traditional tandoor oven. Here we have something from the state of Goa, vindaloo, the Indian pronunciation of, help me with this Ignatius, *carne de vinha d'alhos,* Portuguese for meat marinated in a garlic sauce. This is a traditional Portuguese dish that we have adopted. Then, here from our home state of Kerala, which is on the Malabar coast, we have roasted prawns, curried red snapper, and curried duck. I think that you'll all like this. Oh, and of course, Basmati rice." Amala sat down and said, "In our home, we always start every meal with grace, In the name of The Father, and of The Son, and of the Holy Spirit." Amala said a beautiful prayer followed by the traditional blessing of the food, and then they began to eat. It was an incredible experience. Regan was pleased to have been invited to this gathering.

After dinner, Fraser got up, went out to Jill's car, and returned carrying an instrument in what looked like a large trombone case, but it didn't carry a trombone. Fraser sat back at the table while Nate and Jill cleared off the table, "Amala, I have not eaten anything like this ever; that was a most amazing meal; thank you for having me. In honor of you and Nate, I would like to play for my supper as the old nursery rhyme goes, but with a twist." He opened up the case and brought out a magnificent sitar. "I would like to play something for you if that is all right."

Nate came out of the kitchen and said, "Where would be the best place for you to play?"

"Anywhere I can sit on the floor and play would be fine, but do you have a cushion or blanket I can use?"

"Of course. Let's go into the living room so we can all

sit together. Let me get you a traditional Indian cushion you can sit on."

Properly seated, Fraser said, "I would like to play a traditional *Raga* for you. A *Raga* is a, how can I say it, is like a model, no, more like a framework, that allows the musicians to improvise an array of musical structures that will help to affect your emotions. There is nothing like this in the traditional European music that we associate with music here in the West. Just relax and let the music soothe you."

He played for fifteen minutes, and it was the end to a most memorable evening. Regan did not know it yet, but she would play a crucial part in unraveling the mystery of what Murray was trying to do.

Chapter Twenty-Seven
The following week

Pasadena, CA

"So, at this time, you have access to your brother's house to do whatever it is you need to get done. I can get the keys to you by tomorrow morning," Attorney Rory Hughes was in his office reviewing various documents with Regan; she had invited Jill and Fraser to accompany her to this meeting. "One other thing, did you experience any difficulty at the bank regarding your brother's accounts?"

"No trouble at all. It looks as if your letter did the trick," Regan replied. "And as per the judge's order, I can start packing up his personal belongings and organizing some of his other things once I get inside. At this time, Mr. Hughes, I have no idea what I will do with his estate after this is all probated. I'm still trying to take all of this in. But do you know how long it might take for his estate to be probated?"

"Two things. Your brother was very organized, and his legal documents, including his Last Will and Testament, appear to be in order. To use a sports metaphor, this should be a slam dunk. I don't see any problems with the probate, and this should all be done in about six months, possibly shorter than that. As you are the only beneficiary, that simplifies things, but what has helped is that your brother named you as his beneficiary for his life insurance policies, and as you saw on my documents to the bank, he named all of his accounts 'payable upon death' to you, so he set things up pretty well."

Regan was quiet, and after a few seconds, she said, "My brother knew that I was struggling financially, and every time he saw me, he always asked if I needed anything. Richard tried to keep in contact with me, but I always found a way to delay meeting him. I always thought he would be there, and I always had a family connection. I can't believe how I behaved towards my flesh and blood." She began to sob uncontrollably.

Rory waited for her to regain her composure while Jill held onto her. He experienced this on many occasions. "Ms. Hollander, if it is any consolation, you must know that your brother felt very strongly for you as he trusted you to take care of things for him, which brings me to another point. Not that long ago, your brother had me add a codicil to his will, an amendment of sorts, which he wanted me to discuss with you." He turned the document towards her so that she could read it. "Since you and your brother have no male relatives, your brother designated a specific amount of money, a donation, to be given to the Pasadena Jewish Temple and Center to pray Kaddish for him. He has designated an appropriate remuneration for ten men to offer this prayer for him for the specified time. He asked that you be present for this if at all possible. As we discussed earlier, your brother was buried at Mt. Sinai Memorial Park a day after his body was released from the Los Angeles County Medical Examiner's office in accordance with Jewish Law. Everything was taken care of through the codicil in your brother's will, so there is nothing for you to take care of at this time. According to the Rabbi with whom I spoke at the Center, Richard had been very observant for the past six months, participating in Torah studies and being involved with a Jewish Meditation Group exploring Jewish Spirituality. From what I can gather, Richard had become somewhat of a fixture at the Center."

Regan was stunned, "We were brought up as Jews, but after my *Bat Mitzvah*, I didn't practice my faith or attend services with any regularity, but it appears that Richard may have returned. I wonder what prompted him to do that." She then looked at Jill, "I'll talk with you about this later, but this is a bit puzzling, Mr. Hughes. Is that all for now? I want to be by myself for a bit, and I have to do something according to our traditions. Might I ask what time we can get together tomorrow for the keys to my brother's home?"

"I'll call you, but I think you can plan for some time in the mid-morning. Again, Ms. Hollander, I mourn your loss. Your brother was a very nice man to work with, and he and I got along very well."

Offering her hand, "Thank you, Mr. Hughes, I will await your call."

Regan, Jill, and Fraser walked out to Jill's car and drove back to Jill's home. Regan was very subdued on the ride back, and when they were inside Jill's condo, Regan opened up, "As I told Mr. Hughes, Richard and I were reared as Jews but were not very observant. I think the last time I walked into a *Shul* was for Richard's *Bar Mitzvah*. After that, I can't recall ever going back. My parents were both cremated when they died, so they cut their ties with the Jewish community when they did that. At the time when my parents died, cremation was still not permitted for Jews. But Richard's returning to our faith is very surprising to me. I don't know how close you were to Richard, but ever since college, he shunned all things religious, and I believe he began to hold some extreme atheistic views. I may not have been the best Jew, but I have never abandoned my belief in The King of the Universe. I have no idea what prompted Richard to go back. Do you have any idea? You worked with him for a long time. Did you see any change in his behavior?"

"Richard was a very private man, but recently, Nate and I have noticed how he had tried to be a bit friendlier to us. He was always very polite and a consummate professional in all of our dealings with him, and he would always be available and willing to help us at any time. Still, we did notice how he was trying to reach out to his colleagues more. Does that help?"

Regan said, "My brother was always a bit of a loner, but how you described his recent behavior was out of character for him. I was wondering if something was going on with him. I can't do anything about it now, but can I ask you a question?"

"Of course, please do."

"Thanks. I don't know what I'm looking for, but I think there might be something in his house among his personal possessions that might shed some light on this. Do you think that I could ask you to help me look through his stuff once I get access to his house? If that is too much of an imposition, I understand, but you knew Richard, maybe there is something that that you could figure out more easily than I could."

Fraser jumped in, "If you need someone to move stuff around for you, I'd be happy to help. Here, feel these guns."

Regan laughed, "I'm not touching any part of you, but I will gladly use your help and your big guns."

Jill was laughing, too. Fraser seemed to have broken the somber mood, "And I will gladly help you in any way I can. I'll be at work, but I'll come right over to see what I can do as soon as I get off work. Now, what do you all want to do for supper?"

*****

The next day, Regan was given the keys to Richard's house, and she and Fraser finally got inside. They went from room to room, opening up windows to get some fresh air in, and then Fraser took what little trash was in the house and threw it into the trash cans on the side of the house. Richard's home was in excellent condition and hardly looked lived in, but Regan explained to Fraser that Richard was meticulous about keeping a clean house. "As my brother used to say, there is a place for everything, and everything should be in its place. He was a committed bachelor, and I can see why; he'd probably drive any normal girl out of her mind. He was too neat."

Fraser added, "Well, if it's a slob you're after, I'm your guy. Well, I am not a slob, but my idea of putting clothes away after I do laundry is to throw all the clothes out of the dryer into the laundry basket and take them out as needed. Regan was laughing, making her feel good, "Oh, Fraser, I am fond of you, dear boy, and you do make me laugh, but tell me, and I wanted to ask you this the other evening. What made you want to study

251

the sitar? You played it well, and it sounded so exotic, but why the sitar?"

"Great question. The music from Asia is entirely different from what we're used to in the West, not just how it sounds but from a technical and theoretical perspective, it's different. It's difficult to explain as I don't want to discuss Mixolydian modes, pentatonics, or heptatonics, but let me just put it this way. Have you ever seen sheet music and noticed how the bars of music are written linearly? You know, you read the music the same way we read a book, do you know what I'm saying?"

"Sure, you just follow the notes from left to right across the page, got it."

"OK, now imagine this, instead of the music being laid out linearly, the music is laid out in a circle. Can you see that?"

Regan looked puzzled, "Yeah, I guess I can see it; that's an interesting departure from what I'm used to. So, is that what interested you in the sitar?"

"Partly, but just think about how women swoon when they hear me playing this ethereal music. It worked on you, didn't it?" Fraser smiled at her when he said this to let her know he was joking.

"So first, you asked me to feel your muscles, and now you're telling me you made me swoon. Good grief, what an imagination you have!"

"All right, all right, you done shot me out of the saddle, girl. OK, so where do you want me to start working?" They went out and purchased some cardboard storage boxes to start packing up some of Richard's belongings.

Later, as they were packing things, Regan asked, "I was thinking, what if I decide to stay here? Packing up all of his kitchen items and household effects wouldn't do any good. Maybe we should concentrate on his personal items like clothes and such. Why don't we go through that stuff first?"

They walked into Richard's guest bedroom, where Regan opened the closet and went through several coats and sweaters. "These must be Richard's; they're his size, and I recall him wearing this London Fog when he visited me in San Francisco years ago. Look at this coat. They certainly don't make them like this anymore." She looked over her shoulder at Fraser, who was close behind her. Neither one of them said anything; they just looked at each other. She turned and faced Fraser, who put his hand up to the side of her face, and then his hand slid behind her head, and he gently pulled her to him; she offered no resistance as he leaned forward to kiss her lips softly. He pulled her closer, and she responded by wrapping her arms around him. They didn't get much work done after that.

Jill made it to Richard's house after work and was surprised to see Regan and Fraser sitting at the breakfast bar, looking at a small notebook. "Hi, guys. How is the pack-up coming along?"

Regan looked at Jill and said, "Jill, I found something that might interest you. It doesn't make much sense to me or Fraser, but it has some bizarre things in it. I also found this thumb drive. Now that you're here, I'd like to see if we can look at this drive with you." She handed the notebook and thumb drive to Jill.

Jill opened the notebook, and after reading for about two minutes, she gasped in shock and continued reading. After some time, she asked Regan and Fraser, "Where did you find these things? Were they in a safe or something like that?"

Regan was concerned as she could hear the anxiety in Jill's voice, "There is a safe in his closet, but I don't have the combo, so I couldn't open it. We were going to start packing Richard's clothes and going through the closet in his guest bedroom." Jill noticed Fraser and Regan locked eyes right then, "I found several of his old coats in there. There was this one old work coat that he's had since he was in college. I was folding it up when I felt something in one of the inside pockets; I found this notebook and thumb drive. Do you know what he's talking about? Portals and first-century Palestine? As I said, some of this stuff is very weird."

Jill said, "Regan and Fraser, please don't discuss this with anyone until I tell you. Fraser, you trust me, right?"

"Of course, Sis, but what's going on?"

"I can't say right now as I don't know the whole story. I need to get a hold of Nate to run this by him. In the meantime, is there any way that I can ask you two to please get out of town for a few days until we can get this sorted out? I will tell you everything in time, but please believe me, you must leave town."

Fraser took his sister's hand, "Jill, are you and Nate in trouble? I'm not too keen on leaving you like this. What's going on?"

"Fraser, I love you for your concern. I am not in danger, but I don't want you two even remotely involved in what is happening. Let's head back to my place so that you two can grab your stuff, and then please go; I'll let you know everything, well, most of everything within the next few days." Regan and Fraser locked the house up and drove back to Jill's.

Jill called Nate on the phone as she was driving, "Nate, I think I know what's going on with Murray, and I don't think that Richard's death was an accident."

Nate grabbed his phone harder, "Where are you right now?"

"I'm driving home. Regan and Fraser found some materials at Richard's house. It looks like he kept a diary of everything going on, and what I've read so far is pretty damning. Richard was careful not to record anything to do with the nature of our work; you and I would understand what he was saying, but to someone not involved with the project, by reading the notebook, they wouldn't know what we were doing. First things first, I told Regan and Fraser to get out of town for a while—"

Nate interrupted her, "Why did you do that? Are you afraid that you're being watched or something?"

"In a word, yes, wouldn't you be?"

"If you're being watched, don't you think that something as drastic as Regan and Fraser leaving would tip off whoever might be watching that something is amiss? Don't you think it might be better if everyone kept things normal?"

"I never thought of that; you're probably right; I just don't know. I'm so scared right now. I can't think straight."

"Listen, you may not remember this, but Amala's nephew who lives here is an attorney. Let me call him and ask him for some advice. He'll do as I ask; it's a cultural thing, OK?"

"Sure, Nate, just please call me as soon as possible. We need to talk immediately. Oh, one last thing, I was supposed to meet with Arne Johansson to discuss the Science and Technology issue, but he had to cancel. I'm backed up with some other project-related tasks that Murray wants me to do. Do you think that you can contact Arne?"

"Of course. Keep working with Murray as if everything is normal, but I'll get that info from Arne."

Jill went home and sat down with Regan and Fraser, who were both anxious but more about Jill than themselves. "I think that I owe you both a bit of an explanation. Some things have been happening at the Lab that are causing many of us to be concerned. Regan, your brother, Richard, was very concerned about what was happening, and that may have had something to do with why he may have returned to his religious roots. I don't know, but it may have. I had a call to Nate, who was checking a few things, but he told me that I may have overreacted back at Richard's house. Let's wait until I talk with Nate. He has calmed me down quite a bit and recommends that we all stay put. There is no reason to head for the hills."

Fraser looked over at Regan, who appeared more relaxed, "What's going on, Sis? You had us both freaked out back at Richard's house. Can you let us know what is happening?"

"I can't right now, Fraser. This concerns some work we're doing for the government, but I misread what Richard wrote. That's the wrong word; I misinterpreted what Richard wrote, and Nate explained things. In the meantime, as tomorrow is Saturday, we can all head over to Richard's in the morning and continue getting his personal effects boxed up." Looking at Regan, she asked, "Any idea what you plan on doing with all of his stuff?"

"I'm going to go through everything to look for things that may have sentimental value. I will probably donate things to charity for most of his clothes and such. The Pasadena Temple might be a good place to start." Regan looked at Jill and realized that she had become very fond of her and, most definitely, her brother. She knew something was bothering Jill, "When I go through everything at Richard's house, I'll double-check everything as there may be some more items there that may be of import to you. We'll figure everything out, OK? If Fraser says he trusts you, know I do, too."

"Thanks, Regan." She reached over and gave her a quick hug. "Well, let's get some dinner going." They had a nice and relaxed dinner. Afterward, Jill and Regan listened to Fraser play classical guitar.

In between pieces, Regan asked him, "I know you are very well-versed in classical music, but I'm a rock and roll kind of girl. Do you know if classical music influenced rock music at all?"

Fraser smiled at her, "You'd be surprised. Just off the top of my head, there was a song from the late 60s, 'A Whiter Shade of Pale' by a British group called 'Procol Harem' that used very liberally parts of Bach's 'Air on a G-string'. Then Robby Krieger of 'The Doors' used Isaac Albeniz's piece 'Asturias' on their song 'Spanish Caravan'. Billy Joel used Beethoven's 'Sonata Pathetique' in his song 'This Night'. But my favorite adaptation of classical music by a rock group was 'Knife Edge' by an amazing group, 'Emerson, Lake, and Palmer.' They incorporated music by Janáček and Bach into this piece. Those three guys were incredible, especially their drummer, Carl Palmer, who was easily the best drummer on the rock music scene. Palmer could easily hold his own with jazz drummers, who are a million times better than rock drummers. Yeah, classical music influenced a lot of rock music. But be careful; rock music will ruin your ears."

Fraser played for a bit longer, and then they all said goodnight and turned in. Jill called Nate, and he answered on the first ring, "I'm glad that you called. I just got off the phone with my nephew to let him know that I might need some help from him very soon. What did you find at Richard's?"

Before Jill could answer, she heard one of the bedroom doors open and close and someone padding down the hall. She heard a soft knock farther down the hall and then another door open and close. She thought, *I don't believe they'll be discussing music,* and then she answered Nate's question. "Regan was going through some of Richard's belongings, some old jackets, and she found a notebook and a thumb drive in one of the pockets. I thought it strange that he would hide something like that in a jacket. Why not his safe? When I looked at his safe in the closet, I understood why. His safe was a small floor safe. It looks well constructed, fire and waterproof, but it weighs no more than fifty pounds. It could be easily carried out of the bedroom. But he hid the notebook and the thumb drive in an old coat in another bedroom, that makes sense. He probably thought that if someone broke into his house, they would take the safe, thinking everything important would be there and not look through old clothes. However, be that as it may, what I have read so far is pretty scary. As we thought, Declan and Toma might be in danger, but that's not the worst of it. Murray may be involved in an attempt to alter the past. That can have unbelievable repercussions. I need to share this with you as soon as possible, but something else: Richard was afraid that he was being watched. As I said earlier, I don't think that his death was an accident. I'm a bit spooked, Nate, that we might be next."

"OK, listen to me. Your home has a security system, correct?"

"Yes, it does, pretty much state of the art."

"Good. OK, you know the PI firm I told you about that Jay Agrawal retained to find Regan? Their lead investigator has worked with my nephew in several cases. I found this out when Jay turned Regan's search over to me. My nephew mentioned that this investigator has contacts who are pretty good at providing private security. I will work something out with them to get us some protection until we figure this out. In the meantime, do you have anything to protect yourself at home?"

"I'm from Georgia, Nate. I've been plinking targets with firearms since I was a kid. I have a nice Sig Sauer nine-millimeter in my safe, and believe me, Nate, I know how to use it."

"OK, that's good, and remind me never to get on your bad side. Just be vigilant. I'll be on this right away."

Chapter Twenty-Eight
The next day

Pasadena, CA

Nate and Amala met Jill, Regan, and Fraser at Richard's house, and Amala jumped right in to help Regan and Fraser sort through clothes. Nate and Jill went into the kitchen with a laptop, the notebook, and the thumb drive. They spent the next three hours going through everything, and they were convinced, as was Richard, that Murray was planning on silencing Richard because of what he knew.

Jill asked, "What should we do, Nate? All of this looks pretty convincing to me."

Nate thought for a moment. "Let's run a few things down first. All of what Richard has said here might be the ramblings of a disgruntled employee for all we know. We cannot act precipitously. Let me contact one of my classmates from university. I want to check Mr. Pananas' background. Secondly, I will also see if I can work with Arne Johansson to learn anything about the new equipment that the Science and Technology team developed. Lastly, I'm going to see if my nephew or some of his contacts can try and run down what happened with Richard on the night that he was killed. I have never figured out what he was doing in the high desert. It never made sense to me. OK, let's see if we can help with any packing. If not, maybe we should call it a day and go out and grab some lunch."

*****

Nate and Jill had breakfast at the JPL cafeteria that Friday. They had a chance to greet several of their colleagues, and all appeared to be a typical day at work. Nate said, "I have some interesting info to share with you. Let's get a chance to chat as soon as we can."

That evening, they were working late validating a computer run when Murray walked into Nate's office. "What are you two doing here?" he demanded.

Nate looked at Jill with a look that said, "Here we go again." "Hi Murray, we're validating these numbers from our latest run relative to portal stability. Is there anything that we can share with you regarding these numbers? Everything looks good, just as the model predicted."

Murray appeared to calm down, but he had the air of someone suspicious of people around him, "No, just heard you all down here, and I didn't know that anyone was still here."

Jill said, "Nate and I were going to go out for a drink afterward; we'll be meeting Amala at a restaurant about fifteen minutes from here. Would you care to join us? Since Nate's meeting his wife there, you can come as my date." She smiled at him as she said this.

"Thanks, but I have some things I'm working on right now. Rain check?"

"You bet." Murray stepped away and headed for the door when Jill stopped him. "Murray, the three of us have worked as a team for a long time and have all gone through a lot together. We know that you have a lot going on right now, and I just wanted to say," she hesitated for a second, "just wanted to let you know that the offer always stands if you want to go out and grab a beer anytime, OK?"

Murray looked at her with a somewhat puzzled look on his face, "Sure, whatever you say. Yeah, going out for a beer sounds nice. I need to get out. OK, I'll leave you all to it." He walked out and back down to his office.

"OK, Jill, let's validate this run." Nate and Jill finished

260

up and then headed out to the restaurant. Jill walked in and saw Nate waiting for her in the bar. It was early Friday evening, and the bar was only about half full.

Nate stood as Jill took a seat, and then he sat back down. "It was very nice of you to invite Murray to meet with us. He is still acting very aloof from everyone."

She almost shivered, "I have to tell you, I am very nervous around him. I feel as if I am looking at a wild beast in a cage, but the only problem is I don't know how strong the cage is; it feels as if he is ready to spring out and attack me. It's a very weird feeling. I don't even know him anymore. To think we shared the same bed for a year. I think you figured out that I invited him to make him think all is well. I'm finding him to be increasingly suspicious of everything that we do. You saw how he walked in on us and demanded to know what we were doing. It was a bit scary, don't you think?"

"I am very concerned for his mental health. I think that he has gone over the edge. Do you think he suspects we have seen Richard's notes?"

She shook her head, "I don't know, but tell me, what was it that you found out."

"Right, OK, this is regarding the mysterious Mr. Pananas. As I told you earlier, one of my old classmates from university is with Interpol. He has been with them for over twenty years, and I had a chance to run a few things by him on Monday. I discussed Mr. Pananas, formerly a Greek Marine. I gave him an in-depth summary of what we read in Richard's notebook and forwarded him a copy of Richard's photograph of Mr. Pananas and Murray, the one we found on the thumb drive. You could tell from the photograph that neither Murray nor Mr. Pananas knew their picture was being taken. Richard was not taking any chances; he wanted some documentation about this gentleman. After discussing what Richard's notes had, my classmate said that he could look into this on an informal basis. He got back to me last night and said he found something very interesting. He thanked me for running this by him. What started as an informal investigation involved not only Interpol but also several European intelligence services. First, there is no 'Vasilios Pananas' on record for serving with the Thirty-second Marine Brigade of the Greek military, none whatsoever. Then, the picture I provided to my colleague identified the gentleman as Qemal Taxsani, who is not Greek but an ethnic Albanian. Interpol wants this Taxsani character in several countries as he appears to be a contracted assassin, a hitman. I guess that explains why there was no vetting with this individual."

"But what does this mean for Declan and Toma?" Jill asked, "What can we do?"

"Let's get a few more things lined up first. I've got a meeting with Arne Johansson next Monday to chat about a project-related issue. Then, I'm going to talk with him offline. I have a good relationship with Arne and trust him, but I'm having a problem getting any info from the California Highway Patrol on Richard's accident. My private investigator is looking into it, but he's not had any luck getting any inside information, so no luck."

"Nate, let me run with this and see what I can scare up. It couldn't hurt, right? One other thing, you mentioned that your investigator would look into helping us with some private security. Is there any word on that? I'm concerned about Regan and Fraser as they have been in and out of Richard's house quite a bit. I don't want them being followed and possibly harmed."

Nate smiled at her, "It looks as if the investigator is as good as he said he would be. He told me that we are all being surveilled by his team and that we wouldn't even know it."

"Thanks, Nate, that is very good to know. OK, let me get going on that CHP issue, but first, I think I could use a glass of wine."

*****

Jill called Nate late Sunday morning as she knew that he went to early Mass on Sundays. "Nate, I have some information that I think you may find very interesting. I have a colleague of mine back in Georgia. Well, I shouldn't go too deep into this, but this friend of mine gave us the information we needed regarding Richard's accident. He told me not to ask how he got this information, but he is a computer genius. He was able to get into the CHP mainframe and he went into the accident investigation section and looked at any accidents on the date that Richard was killed. There was an accident on the Pear Blossom Highway up by Littlerock, that's up in the high desert in the northernmost part of the county, heading out towards the Lancaster and Palmdale area. It's pretty desolate out where the accident happened. According to the CHP report, Richard's car was heading westbound on Highway 138, and they found skid marks behind his car and another set of skid marks left by a vehicle heading east. According to the report, these marks indicated that these vehicles impacted at a high rate of speed. There was a lot of debris at the scene, and Richard's car was found smoldering on the side of the road at two in the morning by some residents in a truck driving home to Antelope Valley.

"According to the CHP's Multidisciplinary Accident Investigation Team report they left the investigation open as they thought it very unusual that the amount of debris found at the scene was not indicative of a crash at that speed, plus, they never found the other car. If the other car that was involved in the accident fled the scene, there would have been a trail of debris heading east, but nothing was found. They found something unusual, a lot of wood chips were mixed in with the debris. Something else that is of interest, the report stated that Richard's charred remains were transported to the County Medical Examiner's office, and my friend tracked that report. It appears that the pathologist who did the autopsy had performed a significant number of autopsies that week, it looked like a busy week down there. My friend asked, could the doctor who did Richard's autopsy breeze through his postmortem exam due to the volume that week? He said that since this was a horrible motor vehicle accident, the cause of death was apparent and Richard was burned beyond recognition. Remember, he was identified through dental records. My friend thinks that something doesn't add up when looking at the CHP report and the Medical Examiner's report. Then you and I know from Richard's notes that he was concerned that Murray wanted to silence him. What do you think we can do?"

Nate thought about this moment, "We can't do anything, but Regan can. If she thinks that there might be more to her brother's death, she might be able to get him exhumed and have a more thorough autopsy performed. Do you think that you might be able to convince her to consider this?"

"Let me see what I can do. I can tell you that Regan and my brother, Fraser, have become quite; how can I say this—"

"They've become close?" offered Nate.

Laughing, she answered, "As a matter of fact, they have, and she and I have developed a very close friendship. Let me talk to the two of them. I won't discuss anything about our project, of course, but I can let them know that there may have been something with his work that could have led to his death. I'll handle this, Nate, no worries."

"Thanks, Jill, we'll catch up soon."

She went to the kitchen where Regan and Fraser were having coffee and laughing about something Fraser said. After a few moments, she touched Regan's arm, "Regan, I need to talk with you about something important. It's something that I alluded to earlier, but after talking with my colleague, I need to discuss this with you this morning, OK?"

Regan was suddenly serious, "Yes, of course. Can we discuss this right here, or do we need to go into the front room?" The three of them were all seated at the breakfast bar.

"No, no, right here is fine." Jill adjusted herself on her breakfast stool and opened up, "As I mentioned before, we are doing some important work for the federal government, some significant scientific work. Your brother was intimately involved in this work and was a very dedicated scientist. It appears that someone may have been taking some shortcuts. Some shortcuts may jeopardize the project and, more importantly, endanger some individuals involved in this research. I cannot go into much detail, but your brother may have uncovered some of this fraudulent work. I believe that he was ready to go to the authorities. I need to come right out and tell you this. I mentioned to you earlier that there is a possibility that Richard's death was not an accident. It appears now to be a very strong possibility."

"But the autopsy came back and said that he died due to burns caused by a motor vehicle accident, isn't that correct?"

"Yes, that's what the report reads. But it may have been possible that the County Medical Examiner's Office was swamped that week. Since the cause of Richard's death *appeared* to be caused by the accident, the staff may have done a cursory autopsy on Richard and not a thorough one. They may have assumed that he was killed in the accident and with this new information, a forensic autopsy may be required. We may have to get a court order to have his body exhumed."

Regan was shocked by this news, "I have to think. I need to talk to someone about this. If I remember correctly, the Talmud prohibits the exhumation of the dead. There may be some exceptions, but I need to check. I have to respect Richard's faith. Let's go back to what you were saying, who could be so evil as to kill someone like this? Do you have any idea?"

"Not right now, but we're looking into it."

Fraser asked, "Have you all gone to the authorities? I mean, if there is a chance that Richard's death was not an accident, a murderer is walking around right now."

Jill replied, "That's a great point. I talked with Nate, and he will be going to the authorities, but this might get tricky because of the nature of our work. I will let Nate handle this, but to answer your question, yes, the authorities will be notified. Regarding your brother's exhumation, we need to contact your attorney for some guidance. We'll need to get something like a court order to do this, but can we let this go for a day or two so that Nate can take the necessary steps to preserve the classified nature of our work?"

Regan said, "Of course, Jill, but I do have to say that this entire thing is so surreal. It's hard for me to process everything. I have cried for my brother and have done what I think is an appropriate *shiva*, but now that you're telling me that he may have been *murdered,* this is too much." Regan got up and walked to her room.

Jill looked at her brother, "Do you want to go say something to her, or should I?"

"Is it that obvious?"

"Fraser, I could see that you two connected when she walked into Nate's house. Why don't you go to her?"

"I will, Sis. Let me give her a few minutes, and then I'll go to her. She is an amazing woman."

"Yes, she is, Big Brother. Now go to her."

Fraser went to comfort Regan, and when he did, Jill called Nate. "I just had a good talk with Regan. I told her that her brother may have uncovered evidence of someone taking shortcuts in our research that may impact the project. I said that Richard was probably ready to go to the authorities and that his death was not an accident. We discussed that because of what happened, they may have to do a forensic autopsy, and that will require exhumation. I recommended that she contact her attorney for some guidance and asked that she give us a couple of days so that we could sort things out. She knows we're working on highly classified work for the government and must do some work in the background before we call the police."

"Good job, Jill. Let me meet with Arne to get one last piece of information. Once we get that done, I'll put something together. I have been discussing some things with my nephew, who has been thinking about how best to approach this. He does not know what our work is except that it is highly classified. He has a colleague who has dealt with something like this before. It was a whistleblower incident on a classified military project. My nephew said that this man knows how to handle this. We'll chat tomorrow after I meet with Arne, sound good?"

"Yes, it does, Nate. I do not know what I would have done without you being here. Thank you again." She hung up, and it felt as if a huge weight had been lifted off of her. But she had this nagging feeling in her belly that Murray was up to something. She didn't know what it was, but there was something evil behind that very handsome façade of his.

Chapter Twenty-Nine
The first week of summer - Monday

Pasadena, CA

Nate finally scheduled a meeting with Arne, and they met that afternoon in Arne's office. Arne was an engineer who had been involved with the Einstein Project since the inception of the team and he had a very good relationship with Nate. "So good to see you, Arne, and thanks for taking the time to meet with me, I know how busy you have been."

"Always good to see you, Nate, so what's going on?"

Nate knew that there was no love lost between Arne and Murray, but he had to be careful as to how this discussion was going to proceed, "I know that you were involved in some of the equipment upgrades that Declan and Toma took with them through the portal, just have a couple of questions regarding these upgrades."

"Sure, Nate, shoot."

"OK, when we had our initial planning meetings for our new mission, one of the potential operations we discussed was sending an additional team through the portal to bring advanced equipment to Declan and Toma."

Arne didn't wait for Nate to finish, "That always bugged me, Nate. I mean, we all listened to Dr. Edgeton as if he were supposed to be some wunderkind, right? I figured that he knew what he was doing, but the 'major equipment advances' that he told the group about, what advances? The tech guys added new solar converters and a better battery. That was it."

Nate looked puzzled for a second, "That was it? Why didn't anyone raise this issue with the group?"

"Nate, as I said, no one says anything to Edgeton. As I said, he's lightyears ahead of the rest of us. Sorry for my sarcasm, but I tell you what, and we discussed this before, I think that Edgeton is a nut case. Especially lately, haven't you noticed how bizarre he has become? I can sympathize with him in that he lost his fiancée, but his behavior is not of someone sad and blue. His behavior is of someone who is on the verge of flipping out. I don't think you knew this, but I worked with Richard Hollander on several ad hoc projects. We never got close by any stretch of the imagination, but he occasionally met with some of the guys, and we'd go out and slam some brewskis down. He used to joke that when Watson and Crick were unraveling the double helix they would do more work in the pub than in the lab. But back to what I was saying, there was a time when Richard got a bit in his cups, and he said to me something like, 'Murray is out to get me,' and I just gaffed it off. But then I noticed how Edgeton would treat Richard in meetings; something was creepy. When Richard died, I chalked it up to a bad accident, but then his words came back to me. It felt like The Grim Reaper snuck up behind me, and the hair on the back of my neck all stood up. It was a weird feeling, but I'm avoiding Edgeton at all costs. Something is not right with that guy."

Nate looked at Arne, "Arne, what if I told you that there are others who feel the same way that you do?"

"That wouldn't surprise me, Nate, but I have to tell you, be careful around Edgeton. As I said, something is not right with him. What was that expression I read once, 'People are barbarians beneath the thin veneer of civilization' or something like that? I can't even remember who wrote it, but to me, that's how I feel about our illustrious Dr. Edgeton. I can't say it enough; he's a nut case, and I'll tell him to his face."

Nate said, "But going back to the equipment sent through the portal, were there any other upgrades that would make a big difference to our team?"

"Now that you mention it, I thought something else

was weird. When Declan and Toma went through, small beacons like a transmitting device were installed. I thought nothing of it until that Pananas guy went through it. He had a receiving device installed in his, not a transmitter, but a receiver. I guess that was to be used to catch up to Declan and Toma, but why not install transmitters *and* receivers in all of the equipment? Now that I think back on that, it makes less sense to me now."

"Yeah, that is a bit strange. Listen, Arne, if you can think of anything else, please let me know. Let's keep this under our collective hat for now."

"No worries again. Just keep me in the loop, OK?"

"You bet; thanks again for your time. We'll chat soon.

That evening, Nate called Jill on his secure line, "Hi, Jill. I had an interesting talk with Arne today and he is convinced that Murray is, as he said, 'A nut case.' He shared with me two interesting little tidbits. First, the 'highly advanced equipment' that Mr. Pananas, or should I say Taxsani, brought through the portal to Declan and Toma had a tracking device on it. To be more specific, Declan and Toma had small transmitters installed on their devices, and Mr. Taxsani had a receiver installed on his. I think this Qemal character was sent through the portal to track down our two guys. With all that we have now, Richard's book and thumb drive, Arne's info, the CHP and ME info, and what we learned from Interpol, I think we need to contact my nephew's colleague and bring all this to light."

"Sounds good. How soon will it take to make an appointment to meet with this attorney?" Jill asked.

"My nephew, Pranji, said he could arrange an appointment for us as soon as needed. He just needs to give him a couple of days' notice. I'm concerned that we would both be out of the office to visit with this attorney. Would you mind if we made this appointment late afternoon or possibly on a Saturday?"

"That's a great point. I'll make myself available whenever we get in."

Nate called Jill on Wednesday evening, "Jill, my nephew, Pranji, called regarding our appointment. His colleague, Aaron Paulson, will meet with us tomorrow after we get off work. Does six tomorrow evening work for you?"

"Absolutely, where is his office?"

"Pranji told Attorney Paulson that this is an incredibly sensitive issue and that our absence would cause some problems. His office is in Westwood, but he can head out this way tomorrow as he is doing some work in Burbank at a colleague's office. How does that sound?"

Jill was scrolling through her calendar, "I actually have a light day tomorrow, and I can get out of the office early. Maybe if we leave at different times, that would look better, what do you think?"

"I actually took a few days off, so I will just see you there, let me give you the address…"

The next evening, Jill met Nate at the attorney's office in Burbank. They walked into the office lobby and were ushered into a conference room. Attorney Paulson walked in, handshakes were exchanged, and introductions were made. Mr. Paulson opened up the dialogue, "Dr. Joseph, Dr. McAllister, talking with my colleague Pranji, it appears that you have a case that needs to be handled with an extremely high level of confidentiality. Is that a fair assumption?"

Nate and Jill both nodded their heads as Nate answered, "Yes, it is. But I'm a bit concerned about how much I can disclose to you before you decide to take our case."

Mr. Paulson replied, "I understand and appreciate your dilemma. I can tell you that whatever you say to me in this preliminary discussion will also be treated with the same confidentiality accorded to any of my clients. And please, from here on out, please call me Aaron."

"Thank you, Aaron, and it is Nate and Jill. Let me try to summarize this situation for you. We are part of a team involved in a highly classified project with the federal government and certain entities in the private sector. I can tell you that we completed our initial project three years ago and are currently in the midst of our follow-up project. I can also tell you that in our initial and present missions, we have 'deployed' certain team members to work in another part of the world, namely, the Middle East. We believe that one of our team leaders has been involved in sabotaging our efforts by interfering with the natural progression of events and one of our team scientists, Dr. Richard Hollander, came upon these subversive activities and was killed because of his knowledge of what was happening.

"I mentioned Dr. Hollander; let's use his first name, Richard. The heir of his estate is his sister and she is concerned that he may have been murdered. He received a Jewish burial which dictates that the deceased must be buried within twenty-four hours. He was identified through dental records, and upon identification, his attorney was notified and alerted the authorities of his religious request. The County Medical Examiner's office was swamped that week. As Richard's remains were burned beyond recognition following the motor vehicle accident, it appears that the medical examiner staff determined that the cause of death was evident. The case was closed. Since then, it has come to light that before his death, Richard felt that his life was in danger, and then an unexplained car accident occurred, an accident that the CHP has yet to close. At least no one has been notified of it being closed. Do I have your interest so far?"

Aaron stood and walked to the window to look outside, "Yes, you certainly do. I need to have one of you give me a dollar." Nate handed Aaron a five-dollar bill. "Thank you, you have retained my services. OK, how would you like to proceed?"

Jill said, "Nate, let me address this one. Regan, Richard's sister, wants to know if her brother was murdered. We think that the murderer is our boss, the team leader, and we're afraid that any snooping around might tip him off. How do *you* propose that we proceed? We've never been involved in anything like this before."

Aaron answered, "How much can you tell me without compromising national security? I'm going to need to have something to take to a judge, and I have to let you know that with his being a Jew, I have to get a rabbi to give me approval also. The Talmud has strict laws about disturbing the dead."

Nate brought out the notebook, and he and Jill began to tell the entire story of how they came to their conclusions. About an hour later, Aaron shook his head and said, "Although much of this is circumstantial and conjecture, it is still very compelling. The key would be to determine how Richard died. Let me get working on this. I'll need to meet with Regan, so I'll need you to coordinate her meeting. At first glance, I think that Regan, being a third party and not involved with anything to do with your work, will help keep some of your boss's suspicions to a minimum. As Richard's heir and executrix, she is within her rights to ask for Richard to be reexamined. Let me think of how to make this work."

Jill and Nate walked out the door, and Jill said, "I'm going to get Regan to see Aaron as soon as possible. That's a good move, having Regan involved. I think that it will keep the heat off of us."

That evening, Jill brought Regan and Fraser up to speed on what took place at Aaron's office. She summarized the information she and Nate disclosed to their attorney. The following day, Regan was able to schedule an appointment with Aaron for that Friday morning.

Two weeks later, Aaron was able to obtain a judicial order to exhume Richard's body. A forensic autopsy was scheduled for that week, and following this new autopsy, it was determined that Richard had been shot in the back of the head, and his death was ruled a homicide. Homicide detectives of the Los Angeles County Sheriff's Department opened a case to investigate Richard's murder.

Chapter Thirty
Late Spring, 61 A.D.

The Nineveh Plain

It was approaching dusk as Toma sat on the banks of the *Tigris River* humming an old Bob Dylan song. Several days earlier, he transited through the portal to this part of ancient Mesopotamia. He made the trek from his portal entry point to the banks of the river, where he was waiting for three of the Apostles, Bartholomew, Jude Thaddeus, and Thomas, to arrive. Toma had visited several local temples, but there was no sign of them. He rose and walked up the riverbank. He heard a screeching call and looked up into the brilliant blue sky and saw what could be either a kite or a small eagle hunting for prey. He watched the raptor hunt and was then distracted by a noise from the south. He looked to his left and noticed a group of people walking in his direction. As the group approached, he saw that the Apostles he was waiting for had finally arrived.

It looked as if Bartholomew was having a spirited discussion with one of the local men as they were walking, and when they got closer, Bartholomew stopped short and caught sight of Toma. "Toma!" he yelled as he ran over to hug him. He asked in Aramaic, "What are you doing here? Here, let me look at you." He held him at arm's length so that he could see him better. "Brothers, come look at Toma!" Jude Thaddeus and Thomas ran over to see Toma, and when they saw him, they both gave him bear hugs. It was getting dark, and Bartholomew looked at Toma again, this time more closely, and exclaimed,

"Look at him, brothers. He has barely aged. Look at him!"

Jude Thaddeus and Thomas looked at Toma again, and Jude said, "Bartholomew is right. The years have been good to you. Your hair is grey, and your face shows the wearing of the years, but you haven't gained the belly we all have, and you're not bent!"

Then Thomas added, "I remember once when John asked you the same question, that was what, fifteen or so years ago? You look maybe ten to fifteen years older since you first joined us, and that was almost thirty years ago when the Holy Spirit descended on us. How can this be?"

Toma laughed, "Do you remember what I told you all back then? We had great physicians in my province; they used balms on us to keep our skin supple and our joints young; that's all that it is, but you should not have to wonder anymore; I have no more balm, so I will appear as I should as our time together grows. Does that satisfy your curiosity, my brothers?" They all laughed, and then they continued to walk north along the road by the river. "Where have your journeys taken you since I saw you last in Jerusalem? Tell me how many you have brought to the Way of Our Lord. And where are you planning to journey next?"

Thomas told him of their travels, "We brought many to the Way when we were preaching throughout Anatolia. Everywhere we went, people wanted to hear of Our Lord. Other brothers will preach in Anatolia and head west to Greece and Rome, but we will head east. There is a huge empire east of here, starting on what we have heard travelers call the Malabar Coast, where we will go to preach. These merchants who traveled various routes to this huge empire have told us that the people there are the most learned in the world. We will travel first to the north to a country called 'Hayk,' which we call Arminiya, and then to the Malabar Coast. You will come with us, won't you, Toma?"

"Yes, I will. I want to travel with you and spread the Way of Our Lord if you will have me." So began Toma's journey with the Apostles, which started in his ancestral home. They were traveling with a group of about forty believers. Blending in with this group was a newcomer, a man who appeared to be a Roman or possibly a northern Greek, and although pleasant enough, he kept to himself for the most part.

Chapter Thirty-One
Early Summer

Pasadena, CA

Detective Anthony Pangelinan of the Los Angeles County Sheriff's Department Detective Division, Homicide Bureau, was meeting with Regan Hollander and her attorney, Aaron Paulson, regarding the murder of her brother, Richard. Jill and Nate were also in attendance. As his exhumation order was at the behest of his sister, it was hoped that this interview would shed some light on what happened to Richard. Aaron had Regan's notebook and summarized the contents for Detective Pangelinan and the background information provided by Nate and Jill. Afterward, the detective pointed out, "We'll probably need a copy of the notebook for our records, and the District Attorney will need the notebook itself and the thumb drive as the People's evidence if this case does indeed move forward."

Aaron replied, "Of course. At this point, please let us know if there is anything else that we can provide for you."

Detective Pangelinan met with his bureau captain, Captain Mulvaney, to discuss his interview with Regan, "I think that we have enough to meet with this Dr. Edgeton as a person of interest. Their argument was fairly convincing that something was going on in that lab, and much circumstantial evidence pointed toward Edgeton. The work they're doing in Pasadena appears to be pretty sensitive. Do you want to bring in anyone from the DA's office to get this on their radar? I think this might involve some stuff with a slight smell of national security on it.

If it does, I'm sure the Feds will be crawling all over this. Giving the DA's team a heads-up might be a good idea."

Captain Mulvaney sat back in his chair. "Yeah, good idea, Tony. Even though it's early in the game and we have no suspects, *per se*, it would be good to have this on their radar, as you said. Yeah, let me run this by our liaison in the DA's office as a courtesy. Keep me in the loop on how this plays out."

"You bet. I'll pop over to the Jet Propulsion Lab and see if I can meet with this Dr. Edgeton. From what I can gather, he is supposed to be some super genius. We'll see what it's like when he and I cross swords." He drove out to the JPL that afternoon, and when he flashed his detective's badge to the guard at the gate, he gained immediate access to the site. He entered the building, where a receptionist met him at the desk and asked if he had an appointment to meet with someone at the Lab.

"Yes, I do. Here is my appointment confirmation," he said, showing the receptionist his badge. "Can you please tell me how I can get to Dr. Murray Edgeton's office?"

The receptionist didn't know exactly how to respond as the policy in the lab was for visitors to be escorted to wherever they were visiting, "If you can wait a moment, Detective, I can have someone from Dr. Edgeton's branch come down and escort you to his office." She reached for the phone, and Detective Pangelinan looked at her name tag and told her, "Hold on a second, Della, is there someone here in reception who can walk me down to his office? I don't want to bother anyone up there. I know that they're plenty busy right now."

The receptionist slowly put the phone down, "Yes, sir, if you can give me a moment, I can have someone come over and watch the desk. I'll gladly escort you to his office."

"That would be great, thanks."

A young man took over the desk within five minutes while Della collected Tony. They walked down the wide hallway to Dr. Edgeton's office. When they arrived, Della told his secretary that Dr. Edgeton had a visitor. She then excused herself and walked hurriedly back down the hallway.

The administrative assistant, whose nameplate read "Ms. Meyer," asked Tony, "Do you have an appointment, sir? I don't see any appointments listed here in Dr. Edgeton's calendar for this afternoon."

"No, Ms. Meyer. I didn't mean to barge in unannounced like this. I have a few questions for Dr. Edgeton regarding one of his staff members." He showed her his detective's badge.

She looked closely at his badge, "Oh, I see. Well, Dr. Edgeton is in a meeting right now."

He pulled out his cell phone, "That's OK; I have a few notes to go through. I'll wait for him."

Ms. Meyer made a big show of going over her boss's calendar, "I'm sorry, it looks like he might be gone for at least another hour."

Tony looked up and smiled at her, "I'll wait at least another hour." He went back to his cell phone.

She must have hit the snippy button under her desk, "He might be gone for two hours," as she gave Tony a smile that said, "I dare you to say something to me now."

Tony played the game long enough with this one. "Hmm, I see. I'll tell you what, I'm investigating a homicide and have a few questions I need Dr. Edgeton to answer. Why don't you help us all out and get a hold of Dr. Edgeton? Please let him know that the Los Angeles County Sheriff's Department Homicide Bureau has some questions they need him to clear up. Can you do that for us?"

Ms. Meyer stiffened noticeably as she thought, *how dare this guy come in here and make demands of me?* Tony just kept smiling at her. "Well, if you insist, I'll call Dr. Edgeton out of his important meeting."

"Oh, that would be wonderful. Thank you, Ms. Meyers."

She made her call. "It appears that he is back from the meeting. I'll see you in." She got up and walked into the inner sanctum that was Murray's office, "Dr. Edgeton, you have a Detective here to see you."

Murray got up and offered his hand to Tony, "Yes, thank you, Ms. Meyers. Please, Detective, have a seat. May I offer you a cup of coffee?"

"No, thank you, Dr. Edgeton. I have a couple of questions I need to clear up regarding one of your scientists," he said as he handed his card to Murray.

Murray read the card, "Of course, how can I help the Los Angeles County Sheriff's Office, Detective, um, you might have to help me with your last name, sorry."

"No worries, I get that a lot, it's Pangelinan, Pang-ga-*lee*-nan. My parents are from the island of Guam in the Western Pacific."

"The American Territory of Guam. If I remember my World War II history correctly, they have an interesting story. Yes, Detective Pangelinan, which of our staff scientists can I help you with, please?"

Tony took his notepad out, "Yes, sir, I need to ask a couple of questions regarding one of your physicists, Dr. Richard Hollander."

"Oh, yes, of course, what happened to my poor friend was terrible. To be killed like that in a horrific car accident, it's just terrible."

"So, you were a friend of Dr. Hollander?"

Murray looked at Tony and cocked his head to the side a bit, "Well, yes, of course. I was probably Richard's best friend here at the Lab."

Tony continued with his questions, "So it must have come as quite a shock to you when your friend died. How did the rest of the staff take it?"

Murray looked down and then shook his head. It was almost as if he were trying to recall the emotions from that day. "The staff members were all shocked; Richard was a valued colleague here and contributed a tremendous amount to the work that we were involved with; his absence has been felt, even after all this time."

"I'm sorry for the loss of your colleague and your friend. Did you socialize with Dr. Hollander?"

Murray smiled as if reminiscing about all the good times he had with Richard, "On occasion, we would go out for dinner, and then we would meet for beers at a number of the local pubs. Richard and I were both bachelors and enjoyed each other's company professionally and socially."

Tony knew that Richard did not socialize with Murray. He tucked that back into a small compartment in his brain. "I know this is difficult, but when did you last see Richard?"

"Well, it's been a while. Richard died in what, the first part of April, I believe, so three months ago. I saw him the Friday before he was killed. I saw him here at work before the weekend."

"All right, that's all my questions. I appreciate your time; we're just completing the report before closing the case."

Murray stood to shake Tony's hand, "Of course, anything that I can do to help. Do you all think you'll be able to close this out soon? I mean, for some closure for his friends and such. I also understand that Richard had a sister, so maybe closing this out would help her, too."

Tony nodded his head, "Yes, I'm sure that will help his family and friends, some finality to a tragic death." Tony shook Murray's hand and headed towards the door. Murray thought to himself, *he didn't answer my question.*

Tony reached for the door handle and turned back to Murray, "Oh, I almost forgot. We did get a final report back from the County Medical Examiner. There appears to be a slight discrepancy in their initial findings. It appears that there might be a question as to the actual cause of Dr. Hollander's death. It's weird the way these forensics play out. But then again, you can understand and appreciate that as a scientist, right?" Tony spoke casually, but he observed Murray's reaction. When Tony mentioned that the cause of Richard's death was being questioned, Murray's eyes widened as he felt a slight catch in his throat. Tony noticed Murray swallow hard. *Gotcha, Dr. Edgeton.* "Thanks again, Doc."

Murray just stood there and watched him walk down the hallway.

*****

Tony was briefing Captain Mulvaney, "He's involved, Captain, I know he is. I will follow up on my interview with Ms. Hollander and the two scientists from the JPL. I'll get some statements from the people there and see if this gets a rise out of Edgeton. He might be as smart as they come, but you can't stop the human body's reactions."

Captain Mulvaney asked, "Did you sweat anything out of him?"

"Yeah, you should have seen him when I mentioned that the cause of death is being questioned. He had the proverbial deer in the headlights look, and then when his brain processed what I said to him, he gulped like he was swallowing an oyster shooter. Yeah, he's involved, Cap'n, I know he is."

"Oh, one other thing, the DA's office is apprised of this case. They're asking us to keep them in the loop, too, so let me know what you find out in your other interviews. We'll summarize this for the DA. Good job, Tony."

Tony contacted Aaron Paulson and told him he wanted to clarify a quick question regarding the information that Jill and Nate shared with him earlier. "I want to see if I can make Dr. Edgeton start calling about why I'm back at the JPL. He's still a person of interest, but I want to see if my presence at the JPL shakes things up a bit. Can you let your clients know that I'm coming in? Please ask them to act as if this is the first time they're meeting me. I don't want Edgeton to know that I've already met with his colleagues." He returned the next day to the JPL, and this time, he asked to meet with Drs. Joseph and McAllister. Unlike yesterday, one of the staff members from Jill's and Nate's group came down to escort Tony to their offices. The word that a homicide detective was back at the JPL spread like wildfire throughout the office. People were gathering and talking in whispers in the hallways. Tony approached Jill's office first, noticing three people talking in the outer office. All three looked at Tony as he walked up. A young man asked, "May I help you, sir?"

Tony flashed his detective's badge, "Yes, thank you. I'm Detective Pangelinan from the LA County Sheriff's Department, and I need to speak with Dr. Jill McAllister for a moment." The young man walked into Jill's office and returned with Jill in tow.

Jill came out of her office, "Good morning, Detective, how may I help you?"

"Yes, Dr. McAllister, is there a place where I can ask you a few questions regarding the death of one of your colleagues?"

"Can we chat out here, or do you need something more private?"

Tony answered her, "Ma'am, I need to speak with you privately if that's OK with you. I need some background information regarding Dr. Richard Hollander. I understand that you worked with him on various projects?"

"Yes, I did. Let's go into my office for a moment." They talked about the background information that Jill gave to Tony earlier, and Tony asked if he could be escorted to Dr. Joseph's office. Tony spoke with Nate for fifteen minutes and then left the lab. Within ten minutes of Tony leaving Nate's office, Murray knocked on Nate's door.

"Hi, Nate. Do you have a minute?" Nate invited Murray to have a seat. "I heard that some detective was in to see you this morning. I had a detective interview me yesterday about Richard's accident. Tell me what he was here to see you about."

Nate said, "Yes, he just wanted to know the extent of the work that I was doing with Richard. He was only here for about ten minutes or so."

"He didn't mention anything else about the accident?"

Nate looked at Murray, "No, just about my work with Richard, nothing else. Why, what's going on?"

"Nothing, Nate." Murray walked out the door and hurried down the hallway toward Jill's office.

*****

That evening, Jill called Nate about Murray's visit to her office. Nate told her that Murray was in his office and asked the same question. "Jill, let's contact Mr. Paulson and tell him what happened. He'll know what we should do, if anything, at this time, sound good?"

"Sure does, talk soon."

Nate called Aaron the following day and told him Murray had come to his and Jill's office within ten minutes of Detective Pangelinan leaving. Aaron thanked Nate for this info and said he would handle it from his end.

Aaron contacted Detective Pangelinan and let him know that Dr. Edgeton was very concerned that Tony was back at the JPL asking questions of other staff members. He relayed to Tony that Murray was asking what Tony was doing back there and what he was asking. According to Jill and Nate, Murray appeared to be very concerned about the questions being asked. Detective Pangelinan thanked Aaron for this information and called his captain to tell him he'd be right down.

"I told you that he's involved. And after I popped by to get clarification on a comment that was made, he ran down to find out what was going on. He's beginning to sweat; a little push might push him over the edge, and he might make a mistake. Let me push him a bit more. Are you OK with that?" Tony asked Captain Mulvaney.

"At this point, here is what the DA will tell us: All that we have to go on is that he might simply be a concerned citizen and he's asking why a detective is asking questions in his place of employment. Secondly, the sworn statements of the two staff members from JPL might be professional jealousy. We need something tangible to go on. Then, the other pieces will fall into place. But listen up, I got some info this morning that you might find interesting. I got a call from one of my buddies out at the Antelope Valley CHP Office up in Lancaster. It seems that the CHP received a call from a local yesterday regarding Dr. Hollander's accident."

Tony jumped in, "They got a call about this accident yesterday? This accident happened three months ago!"

Captain Mulvaney continued, "Exactly. It appears that these locals saw something weird on the highway the night that Dr. Hollander was killed, but they never thought anything of it. These folks just got back from their annual vacation. They drove the ALCAN highway from British Columbia to Alaska, vacationed in Alaska, and then returned home. They were talking with one of their neighbors about the goings on up there while they were gone, and as things are normally pretty quiet, Hollander's death was a big deal, especially since it was never solved. The husband and wife put two and two together and contacted the CHP to let them know what they saw. According to my buddy up in Antelope Valley, this couple was heading home late in the evening, and they noticed a truck on the eastbound side of Highway 138. Directly across from it on the westbound side of the highway, they saw what they thought was a 'nice car' on the side of the road. But there was one thing that stood out in the husband's mind. He said that there was something unusual about the truck. It had a large wooden block attached to the front. It was like what some tow companies used to push disabled vehicles out of the roadway or some farmers and ranchers used as a makeshift bulldozer to push vegetation out of the way. You don't see a set-up like that used that much anymore. But that made me think. I looked at the CHP accident investigation, and they mentioned in their report that they did not see the amount of debris at the crash site that you would expect to find at an accident like that one, but what was interesting is that they found wood chips mixed in with the debris found at the crash site. Now, we hear that a makeshift bulldozer was seen on the side of the road that evening. Interesting, don't you think?

"Yeah, go see if you can rattle his cage some more, but we need to get some proof before we can pick this guy up. Right now, I have forensics going over the car for anything, and the bullet that the ME was able to get out of the decedent's skull is being analyzed. Let's see what we can get out of those folks. In the meantime, see what you can do to make him sweat."

That evening, Tony showed up, unannounced, at

Murray's home accompanied by another detective from the Homicide Bureau. When Murray answered the door, he was startled to see Detective Pangelinan there with another man, obviously another police officer, but he recovered nicely, "Good evening, Detective, um, a, what a surprise. Is there something that I can help you with this evening?"

"Thanks, Dr. Edgeton. I have a follow-up question from our meeting a couple of days back. Do you have a moment?"

"Well, I was busy getting something done for a meeting tomorrow. Is there a chance we can do this at my office sometime next week? I can have my admin assistant get something on the calendar for us. Would that be acceptable?"

Tony looked at his partner, "This will just take a minute, Doc. We're trying to tie up a few loose ends to wrap this case up. Why wait another week to close this out?"

Murray felt trapped. He knew that if he put things off, the detectives might get suspicious, but he didn't have anything incriminating here at his house, so why not answer their questions? "Sure, come on in, gents."

The detectives went inside, and Tony introduced his partner, "Dr. Edgeton, this is my partner, Detective Derrick Sykes; he will be taking over for me as I might be transferred out in a month." Murray nodded at Detective Sykes; he was an African-American who looked like a serious powerlifter; he could have been a starting defensive lineman for any NFL team. "Thanks for your time, Dr. Edgeton. I only had to clear up one question regarding the night that your colleague was killed, but before we get into that, I wanted to share with you a breakthrough that we have had in the case."

"Oh? I hope this breakthrough will help you solve and close this out."

"Yes, so are we, hoping that is." Tony consulted his notes briefly while Detective Sykes sat on the couch, staring a hole into Murray's skull. This seemed to agitate Murray, precisely what Tony wanted. "When we talked a few days back, you mentioned that the last time you saw Dr. Hollander was the

Friday before he died, correct?"

Murray slowly nodded his head, "Yes, that's correct, that was the last time that I saw him."

"OK, good, that answers that. Thanks, Doc. One last question, I never asked this one when we talked, but can you recall where you were on the night that Dr. Hollander was killed?"

Murray asked, "Do I need a lawyer present for this? I have never dealt with the police before, and I'm unsure what the procedures are."

"Having an attorney is your right, of course, but I just need to ask you a couple of quick questions to close this out, and I have to cross all my "T's" and dot all my "I's" to do that."

"Well, as I said, I'm not sure what your protocols are, and I don't know if I should answer your questions without my attorney." Murray was beginning to squirm in his seat; he thought, stay calm; you *can outthink these two Neandertals.*

"I realize that you might have to check your calendar and such. We can check back with you when you retain counsel, but that will delay our closing this out. I hoped to have this done as soon as possible, but if you want to drag this out unnecessarily, that's your right."

Murray calmed down a bit. He thought he had the upper hand now, "Do you think you can close this out soon?"

"As I said, I was hoping to close this out as the whole thing just looks like a horrible accident, but I have to tie up my loose ends, like where you were on the night that Dr. Hollander died."

"Well, I can tell you that I was nowhere near where Richard was killed."

Tony offered a smile of resignation, "That's not what I asked, Dr. Edgeton. I just wanted to know where you were on the night that your friend was killed. But if you can't remember, that's fine. We'll follow up later." Tony made a great show of reviewing his notes again, "Well, I think that's about it. I'll write this up. Derrick, do you have any questions?" Detective Sykes kept his eyes fixed on Murray and then slowly shook his head.

"OK, I guess that's it." Tony and Detective Sykes got up to leave.

"Detective, you told me you had a breakthrough in the case and would share it with me. Might I ask if you could let me know what you all found?"

"Oh, that's right, I'm glad you reminded me of that. That's one of my loose ends you can help me tie up. We heard from the CHP that the vehicle that may have been involved in causing the accident appears to be a large pickup truck. From the impact of Dr. Hollander's vehicle, that makes sense. I need to ask you, Dr. Edgeton, do you drive a pick-up truck?"

This time he genuinely smiled, "No, Detective, I drive a BMW, would you care to see it? My vehicle is in my garage; you're welcome to look. Let's go."

"That would be great, Doc. My captain is a real ball-buster; I need to rule this out. I appreciate your cooperation; this will help close this case."

Murray walked the detectives out to his garage, opened the door, and let the detectives see that he indeed had a BMW. "Please, detectives, please inspect the car if you wish. As you can see, it's not a pick-up truck." Tony and Derrick walked around, took a slow and deliberate look at the car, and walked back into the driveway.

"Thanks, Dr. Edgeton. I'll write this up and get it finalized. We appreciate your level of cooperation. That will help stop my captain from busting my balls again."

"You're welcome, Detectives, and please don't think of me as being rude, but I hope we do not have to meet again." Murray walked back into his house and closed the door.

Tony looked at Derrick, "Let's get a hold of the captain. We need to get a warrant. Did you see what I saw in the garage?"

"No, what was I supposed to see?"

Tony was pulling his cell phone out. "On the side of the garage was a large canvas tarp covering something. I could see a large wooden object, about the size of a standard shipping pallet, but it was solid. I think that might be the front of our modified bulldozer." He dialed a number, "Hey, Captain, Dee and I are just leaving the doc's house. We need a warrant; I may have found our first piece of hard evidence."

*****

The next evening, a group of forensics specialists and Detectives Pangelinan and Sykes showed up at Murray's house armed with a warrant. Murray demanded to see the warrant and threatened to call his attorney. Tony invited him to please do so, but they would search his home and garage in the meantime. Tony went out to the garage with one of the techs. Pulling the tarp off the wooden block, he yelled to Detective Sykes, "Yo, Dee, look what I found out here!" Murray called his attorney as the techs bagged up the wooden block. Tony checked with the techs and Derrick and told Dr. Edgeton, "Thanks again for your cooperation. We'll be in touch, and if I were you, I'd stay close by."

Murray was shocked by this turn of events. With his friend Henri's help, he had orchestrated Richard's death, and while he had no direct involvement with his murder, he wanted to keep something as a reminder that you just didn't fuck around with Murray. He laughed at himself, realizing his hubris in keeping the pallet as his trophy could be his undoing. The room around him began spinning, and then he realized he didn't care anymore. He put the phone down and went into his bedroom to go to sleep

The next day, the forensics lab analyzed the wooden block and debris from the crash site. The lead technician called Captain Mulvaney and informed him that the wooden chips found at the accident scene were identical material to the block and that there were fragments of paint on the block that matched the paint collected from Richard's late model Lexus; there was a small section of the back of the car that was not destroyed. Additionally, some plastic fragments from a signal light were consistent with the signal light lenses found in Lexus models.

Captain Mulvaney, joined by one of the Assistant

District Attorneys, was briefing Tony and Derrick, "Look, guys, while all of this is not completely conclusive, the physical evidence combined with the victim's notebook and the statements of Drs. Joseph and McAllister, all of this looks pretty strong. What do you think, Counselor?"

The ADA, Gus Stavros, answered, "I think we have enough. Bring him in."

It was a Friday afternoon at the lab, and the senior staff members were holding a roundtable discussion in Murray's office when Detectives Pangelinan and Sykes, along with a group of uniformed officers from the Pasadena Police Department, showed up at Ms. Meyer's desk. Tony asked Ms. Meyer where Dr. Edgeton was. "He's holding a very important meeting with the senior scientists. He can't be disturbed!"

Derrick grinned and said, "Oh, he'll make an exception for us." The two detectives walked into the room. Everyone was shocked by their entrance, but Murray wasn't; it was as if he was expecting them to arrive. "On your feet, Doc." Murray stood up while Derrick handcuffed him. Derrick addressed the group, "You all can continue your discussion without this guy; he'll be holding another meeting elsewhere, but with a different group. Have a nice weekend!"

Once outside his office, Murray said to Ms. Meyer over his shoulder while being led away, "Call my attorney, Joseph Raymer; his number is in my cell. Call him now!"

The senior staff members decided to adjourn their meeting.

Chapter Thirty-Two
Late Fall

Pasadena, CA

The evidence against Murray was somewhat shaky at first, but more pieces started falling together once the detectives' investigation got into high gear. By the time November rolled around, it had become apparent that the brilliant Dr. Edgeton had suffered major psychotic trauma. He was being treated as an inpatient at a locked psychiatric facility in the western section of Los Angeles. Charges were filed against him, but he collapsed at his bail hearing and was in a severe catatonic state. The charges were essentially on hold until he was able to stand trial. The District Attorney likened this situation to Murray being out on bail. He wasn't going anywhere. In the interim, Dr. Jay Agrawal was in charge of the Einstein Project, and the main subject of discussion was what to do now that the role of Murray's efforts to sabotage their mission and assassinate Declan and Toma had come to light.

Jay had been working with Nate and Jill exclusively on this issue. "What do you think, Nate? Should we attempt to enter the portal and warn Declan and Toma about what has occurred?"

"Can I talk to this real briefly?" Jill asked. Nate motioned her to proceed. "Thanks. I was talking with Nate about this earlier. I know that the work that has been done relative to chaos theory is good, solid work, and that the theory still pertains, my earlier comments notwithstanding. I feel as if I was 'played' by Murray, for lack of a better term, to make it sound like the team entering the portal would have minimal effects on affecting the future state. We had a good protocol during the first mission, and my earlier recommendation was that we continue to follow that protocol. What I said earlier about the team not having much impact on the future was wrong. Dead wrong. The potential for altering the future state is a real possibility. I know that when I was talking offline with both Declan and Toma, they stated that based upon their experience in the first mission, they were going to proceed with caution, as Toma said, 'regardless of whatever Murray says.'

"Based on that, I think Declan and Toma will proceed cautiously. The wild card is Qemal. If his goal is to assassinate the Evangelists and eliminate Declan and Toma, we have a major problem. Secondly, if we attempt to send more people back into the portal, the chances of affecting the future state will increase exponentially."

"But, Jill," Nate said, "Since Christianity is the world's largest single religion, doesn't that demonstrate that nothing happened back in the past?"

"We don't know that, Nate. Qemal has only recently entered the portal. We don't know what effect he will have. But what about Declan and Toma? If Qemal does assassinate them, how will that affect the future, meaning the present, right now?"

Jay got into the discussion, "This is an interesting question. Maybe we should bring a philosopher or a logician into this discussion. Nate, let me ask you, if you were to go back in time and not come back, what would happen to your children?"

Nate was surprised by the question, "My son and daughter would not be born. But I did not go back into the portal so my children would not be affected. If I were to go back, that would be a different story."

It looked like a light bulb went off in Jill's mind, "Yes, but Declan and Toma *are* back there right now. If they make it back, they will continue their lives. But if they don't return, there are no offspring to worry about. Declan and Toma are celibate monks; they have no children and no wives. You know what that means; Declan and Toma may not make it back; there is nothing here at present that would be affected adversely if they do not make it home. I hate to sound so detached, but that's the reality of it. Oh, those poor boys, what can we do?"

Nate replied in a very resigned tone, "They are both skillful warriors. We will have to leave them to their wits and their training. And I agree with you, Jill. The more people we send back, people who may not be as disciplined as Declan and Toma, the more we may have a significant negative impact on the future state. I hate to sound so detached and cold, but Declan and Toma are on their own. We can't send a rescue party to warn them."

Jay added, "We don't know what Murray arranged with Qemal, but if the portal opens and he is transported back, we need to ensure that Security is made aware of his arrival and that he is detained on the spot until the authorities can be onsite. Even if we have no idea what he may have done back in Jerusalem or wherever, I am sure that Interpol would be happy to know that we are holding him. Are we in agreement with this?"

Jill and Nate nodded their assent. Then Jill brought up another point, "I am just a bit concerned about this project. We have demonstrated all that we set out to do and have demonstrated that Einstein's theories are correct. As we have seen from what Murray has attempted to do, there is too much of a danger in being able to be transported by the portal. We are dealing with a huge Pandora's Box and need to address this. Can we call a meeting with our team and the National Academy to see if we can close this project out?"

Nate looked over at Jay, "I agree with Jill. I recall something Arne Johansson told me several years back when we were involved with the first mission. He was very concerned with where we were going with this project. He asked me if I remembered what J. Robert Oppenheimer said after he witnessed the Trinity test in New Mexico, the first detonation of an atomic weapon. Oppenheimer quoted from the *Bhagavad Gita:* 'Now I am become Death, the destroyer of Worlds.' Arne asked me if I was scared about what we were doing. He said that we were playing with fire. Arne was right back then, and Jill is right in her thinking. We need to shut this down."

Jay was very thoughtful, "Good points. Yeah, let's have a meeting with our group. We need to be able to think this through and come to a good decision. We need to ask how long we should wait. Declan and Toma said they would be back in Pasadena by the middle of next Spring; we can't close the portal until we let the schedule play out. Do you have any thoughts on that?"

Nate answered, "This is a good subject for us to discuss. Let me go back over my notes. If I recall correctly, Declan and Toma anticipated being gone for *nine* years, but remember that they said it would seem like one chronological year for us. They said they calculated that the portal would return them here next Spring, as Jay said. But here is what I am thinking. First, we need to go over the calculations again. Did Murray perform these calculations? If he did, they might be suspect. Secondly, for them, they would be gone for nine years, but only one of ours. If we "keep" the portal open for an additional year, two years total, that would be similar to eighteen years to them. As a starting point, we should monitor the portal for at least two years."

Jay said, "That's something we should discuss as a group. That's good thinking. OK, let's get going and start planning this out. Thanks, Jill and Nate. Great thoughts, but I have to tell you, I am still shocked at what Murray did. It's unbelievable."

Jill just shook her head, "Yes, unbelievable. But I am so worried for Declan and Toma; there has to be a way for us to warn them. I guess they're both in God's hands now."

Chapter Thirty-Three
Late Fall, 62 A.D.

Ancient *Arminiya*

Bar Tolomai, commonly called Bartholomew, was teaching the royal household of the King of *Arminiya*, Polymius. As promised by Jesus, the Holy Spirit, working through Bartholomew, converted the king. Several other members of the Royal Household were listening to Bartholomew's preaching to them and asking him questions. As the Kingdom of Armenia had been a Roman Protectorate for over one hundred years, they spoke in Latin.

A young woman from the upper class of nobility, the *Nakharars,* was debating Bartholomew. "Bar Tolomai, I have two questions for you; first, you claimed that when your Master had risen from the dead, He appeared to you and your brothers and performed what you called 'miracles.' Then you said that when your Holy Spirit came to you all when you were supposedly able to speak different languages, some of the people said that you and your brothers had all been drinking all day and that you were all drunk. Could it have been that you all *were* drinking when you witnessed these miracles and supposedly saw your Master? That might be a better explanation, as all philosophers have repeatedly pointed out that a dead body cannot be reanimated. Secondly, could it have been that you, as drunkards, were speaking gibberish?"

"These are great questions, Lady Ashkhan. But have you ever seen someone who has been drinking all day?"

"Of course, my brothers consider themselves devotees of *Bacchus* and enjoy their daily sessions with him. Singlehandedly, they keep the wine merchants in business."

Bartholomew looked at her two brothers and saw they were enjoying their wine. "When your brothers are drinking, I mean *really* drinking, how is their speech?"

"*Really* drinking? Do you mean like now? Look at them. They can barely stand. As far as their speech, they are unintelligible. Their words come out as if they are speaking with a mouthful of sheep dung."

"And would that be their mother tongue, or are they speaking another language?"

The Lady Ashkhan laughed, "They tell me they are speaking with *Bacchus*. Therefore, I would be unable to understand them as they are in communion with their god of wine." She laughed again, "No, they were trying to speak the language we were born to. In the condition that they were in, they wouldn't even attempt to speak another language."

Bartholomew continued, "But you and your brothers are learned nobles, and you have been taught to speak different languages. Am I correct in saying that?"

Others listened intently to this conversation, and His Majesty Arqa Polymius was entertained by this back and forth. Ashkhan replied cautiously, "Yes, we have had the privilege of learning from the scholars."

Bartholomew nodded, "My brothers and I did not have the privilege of learning from scholars. We are all simple men, fishermen, tax collectors, nothing more than that, and we speak only our language and Latin. But how could we, simple unschooled fishermen, be able to speak every language of the Roman provinces? Not just Latin, but all of them? How could that be if we were all drunk?"

"Maybe all those in the crowd were drunk, I don't know."

"That's possible but not likely. Everyone in the crowd heard us speaking their language, so it was obviously not gibberish. But going back to your first question, *Yeshua,* our

Master, told us that He would rise on the third day. When He did rise, He appeared to all of the brothers, He appeared to the sisters who were with us, and He appeared to over five hundred of the brothers and sisters throughout Jerusalem. He appeared to brothers walking on the road. He appeared to us as we were putting our boats on shore. Now, how can this be explained? Were we all drunk, all of us, all the time? Is that why we all claimed to have seen Our Master? That doesn't seem likely. Within our Community of Believers, only a few drink, much less get drunk. All that I am asking you, Lady Ashkhan, is for you to consider what I am saying. Yes, *Yeshua* performed many miracles when He was with us. We needed to see that because, in our lack of faith, we needed something to show us that He was the Messiah, the Promised One who would bring us salvation. He told us to spread His Gospel to all nations so that whoever is baptized will be saved."

One of the young noblemen, Hamazasp, who had listened intently to this discussion, asked Bartholomew, "Bar Tolomai, what was it that your Master taught you? What can I do to believe in Him?"

And so it began. Bartholomew and his Brother Apostle, Jude Thaddeus, began to share the moral teachings of the Gospel. However, one traveler with their group of believers was from a city in Italia south of Rome called Neopolis. He did not participate with the rest of the brothers in sharing the Gospel. He was called Quintous and seemed content to be with the group and listen to the discussions. After Bartholomew and Jude had finished talking with the group of young nobles, Quintous approached Lady Ashkhan. "You didn't seem too impressed with what Bar Tolomai and Jude were preaching today. Am I correct in saying that?"

She was annoyed that this stranger had the audacity to approach her. She had the grace of one trained at Court to reply, but she had the arrogant attitude of the wealthy to dismiss him with a curt answer. "You might be, but I do not see how what I may think of something would be any of your concern. Now, if you will excuse me." As she walked away, she thought to herself,

He was correct. I was not very impressed with what Bar Tolomai was saying. Whoever heard of loving your enemies, what good would that do? But how could that stranger know that? That is interesting. I'll need to watch that one.

During the next several months, Bartholomew, Jude, and the brothers made many converts. Many members of the royal family and the nobility were baptized, and their community grew. However, not everyone in the royal family or among the *Nakharars* was enamored with this new group of missionaries. The King's brother, Prince Astyages, felt that the followers of *Yeshua* were distracting his brother from overseeing his kingdom. But Prince Astyages' feelings were not reason enough to halt this Community of Believers from Jerusalem. While Prince Astyages tolerated the Community, he deeply resented Bartholomew, for he made the first conversions within the Royal Family, including their *Arqa* Polymius. The prince needed to find a way to dissuade his brother from listening to Bartholomew. Prince Astyages voiced his feelings about Bartholomew and the others whenever he was in Court or when he had his brother's ear, but Polymius would look at his brother and smile, telling him that all was well.

Early one evening, Lady Ashkhan approached the Prince and told him that one amongst Bartholomew's group was not of the same mind as the rest. "His name is Quintous and I do not believe he is one of them. He travels with them and is with the group when they preach, but I have been watching him; he does not actively preach or discuss the teachings of their Gospel. He might be able to share some insights about the group with you."

The Prince asked, "Do you know this Quintous? Can you set up a meeting for him to speak with me?"

Askhan laughed, "He's a presumptuous sort, but I can set up a meeting with him. Men normally do what I ask of them."

"Well, then do it, but don't let other members of the Court or the Royal Family know, do you understand?"

"I can play the game as well as anyone at Court."

"No, Your Highness, I am traveling with this group as I find some of their beliefs to be 'interesting,' but I am not a believer as they are." Quintous was explaining to Prince Astyages. "They are Jews from Judea. I am not from their country."

The Prince asked, "But with your name, 'Quintous,' you are a Roman, correct?"

"I am from a city south of Rome, Neopolis, but I come from the tribal lands east of there. Yes, my Roman name is Quintous, but the name I was born with is Qemal. I am nothing like the rest of the travelers. But I did need to let you know that I have heard that Rome is not in favor of this new cult, these followers of *Yeshua;* I have heard that some of the Roman Provinces and Protectorates that are tolerant of this cult are facing a backlash from Rome. If you desire to break free from Rome, that is your business, but if you wish to continue your alliance with Rome, then you should relate to your brother, the Arqa, that associating with these cult members is something with a certain amount of risk. Is this not something that you should consider discussing with your brother?"

"Don't presume what I should discuss with *my* king; I have been told that you are presumptuous, and your insolent tongue is proving that point. You are excused from my presence."

"Of course, Your Highness, no disrespect was intended." Qemal walked away from the Prince, smiling as he did so and thinking to himself, he*'ll talk with his brother, the* Arqa.

That evening, Prince Astyages approached his brother, *Arqa* Polymius. "Brother, as I have said to you on many occasions, you must be careful of dealing with these Israelites. I know that you find their new religion to your liking, but you must be concerned about your Kingdom, my *Arqa,*"

The king replied, "I am concerned about the Kingdom, but more importantly, I am concerned about my subjects. *Yeshua* is the Son of the Living God, the God of Abraham, Isaac, and

Jacob. It is He who has brought salvation to the world, and it is He who will bring salvation to our people. Should not an *Arqa* be more concerned with that for his people?"

"I understand, my Brother, but I have a more immediate concern, and that is about Rome. I have heard reports that Rome disapproves of this new cult and that some of the Roman Provinces that are embracing this new cult are facing a significant backlash from Rome. Should we invite Roman anger to our front door?" asked Prince Astyages.

"Interesting, my Brother, that you heard of this, but I have not. I wonder who keeps important state secrets like this from their *Arqa*. Might I ask if you know who might be keeping these secrets from me?"

"I heard it directly from one of them, one of the Israelites. And when I heard of this, I immediately brought it to your attention. That should demonstrate my loyalty, my brother, and my *Arqa*." Prince Astyages offered a slight bow when he said this.

King Polymius sat there rubbing his chin through his beard, "Thank you for relating this information to me, Astyages. We will discuss this again after returning from my royal visit to the north. You have my leave to depart."

Astyages left his brother's chamber and began developing a plan to eliminate the leader of this group of Israelites, "I'm not going to risk being on the wrong side of Rome over this cult. When Polymius is gone, I'll take care of this problem."

The king and his entourage left the capital city the next day, and upon his departure, Astyages ordered Bartholomew to be brought to him for questioning. Bartholomew was surprised to see that one of the men on the dais with Astyages was the man from their group called Quintous. He wondered what Quintous was doing up there. Astyages asked Bartholomew, "Is it true that the Romans do not approve of your cult and have tried to persuade the governments in some provinces to prohibit your groups from preaching your religion?"

Bartholomew could not understand what Quintous was

doing on the dais with the Prince. Was he trying to prevent us from spreading the Gospel? "Yes, Highness, I have heard of some reluctance on the part of Rome to accept the teachings of *Yeshua*, but they have not prohibited it. Our reports from provinces west of here indicate our message is well received. Is there a problem with our preaching here among your people, Highness?"

"I don't want you to preach here in the City anymore, and I want you and your group to prepare to leave our country. Now, leave my presence." Bartholomew opened his mouth to say something and then thought better of it. He left the palace and returned to the brothers.

When he returned to where they were staying, Toma noticed a difference in Bartholomew. He asked him, "What is the matter? Is something wrong?"

Bartholomew answered, "The king has left the city, and his brother is in charge. He has commanded me to stop teaching and to make all preparations to leave the country. It's at times like these that I wish Thomas were still here. I know that he needed to travel south to the Malabar Coast and make preparations for all of us to start our work there, but he knew how to deal with some of these officials. I wish that I had Thomas' ability to deal with people." Toma let Bartholomew keep talking. "There are times that my faith is weak, but then I recall how Simon Peter's faith was weak at times, and the Master told him that upon him He would build His Church, but my weakness sometimes overpowers me, and I lose my will to go on." Bartholomew then looked over at Toma. "Toma, is your faith in the Master so absolute, is it unshakable? If it is, do you have any words at this time to help get me through this dark night? I am overcome with doubt in my weakness. Am I doing the right thing? Is the Master who He says He is? Will I successfully spread His message if He is indeed the Messiah? My faith may sometimes weaken, but my wits have yet to leave me. I look at you and know that you are not who you say you are; you must be one of the angels; I know that you must be. How can a mortal man barely age in thirty years? Can't you tell me

300

what I need to know? If I only knew for certain that what I was doing was right, I would be able to withstand any trial, any torture, and I could emulate the Master. Tell me, my Brother."

Toma had developed such a strong affection for this man. He also knew that except for John the Evangelist, all of the Apostles would die a martyr's death. What would it hurt to help reinforce this holy man's faith and tell him his work is not in vain? "No, Bartholomew, I am not an angel, but I am from a land far from here and know many things. I can tell you that *Yeshua* is exactly as you say. He is the Messiah who has brought salvation to us all, and the message that you and the others are spreading of His Gospel will be heard in every corner of the world. All you are doing is for the Glory of God, Blessed be His Holy Name."

Bartholomew closed his eyes and echoed Toma, "Yes, Blessed be His Holy Name. Thank you, Toma. I know that the Master has sent you to be with us and help us on our mission, but I also know He sent you to help me overcome my moment of weakness. Thank you again, Toma. The Master said that He would always be with us. I should have never doubted Him, but He knew of our weakness and said He would send His Spirit to guide us. I am thankful for that, but I am thankful that He sent you to be with us, too."

The door burst open as soon as Bartholomew finished, and a group of soldiers charged into the room. Their leader grabbed Bartholomew and announced, "Bar Tolomai, you have been commanded to appear before His Highness, Prince Astyages, and answer to the charge of inciting a rebellion against Our Sovereign Majesty, the *Arqa* Polymius. Let's go." And with that, they dragged Bartholomew out.

Toma yelled, "Take heart, Bartholomew, I will tell the brothers, we will petition the Prince for you." He then ran out of the house to find Jude Thaddeus and the brothers. He found them and explained what happened. They all ran to the Royal Palace to appeal to Prince Astyages to release Bartholomew, as the charge was ridiculous. Jude and Toma were admitted to the Court and began to plead their case. They were both shocked to see Quintous standing behind the prince, but they quickly regained their composure and petitioned Prince Astyages. Toma began, "Your Highness, you were present when Bar Tolomai was preaching to the Royal Household and members of the Nakharar, and you know that he has done nothing to foment rebellion against your rightful king. His Majesty, the *Arqa,* has accepted the Word of God— "

Astyages interrupted Toma, "How dare you presume to know my mind. And yes, I know that Bar Tolomai has preached against our ancient gods. Our gods are as important to this kingdom as the Arqa himself, so when you preach against our gods, you preach against our entire way of life, including the life of His Majesty himself. Your precious Bar Tolomai has proven himself guilty by his own tongue, and now he will have to answer to *our* gods for his crime. Now get out of my presence. Your stench is filling my nostrils. Get out before I change my mind and have my executioners work their dark arts on you also. They're busy enough with Bar Tolomai; do not try my patience."

Toma moved forward to say something, but Jude grabbed his arm and dragged him away. They passed Lady Ashkhan on their way out of the Palace, and they began to plead with her to intercede for Bartholomew; she turned and walked away from them. Jude said, "Let us return to the brothers and pray for Bartholomew." They ran back to the house where they were staying.

Astyages was walking to the dungeon when he saw Lady Ashkhan. "Ashkhan, come with me." They both walked quickly to the dungeon, where they found Bartholomew chained to the wall and the executioner and his assistants preparing their equipment. Astyages looked through the bars into the torture chamber and began to taunt Bartholomew. The executioner looked to the prince, who nodded, signaling to proceed.

The executioner selected from the tray proffered to him by one of his assistants a long-bladed flaying knife. He examined it and then made parallel incisions from Bartholomew's shoulder to his wrist. Bartholomew shut his eyes tightly and gritted his teeth, stifling a scream deep in his throat. Unable to stand the pain, he began to pray the Psalms aloud,

> Do me justice, Oh Lord, because I am just and because
> of the innocence that is mine,
> Oh searcher of heart and soul, Oh just God,
> A Shield before me is God, who saves the upright of
> heart!

The executioner then reached for a pair of tongs and began to strip off the skin from Bartholomew's arms in long swaths. Bartholomew continued to pray the Psalms, yelling out to his torturer, "A SHIELD BEFORE ME IS GOD!" with his eyes to Heaven and his mouth open, he heard himself speaking in his mind, *I see you, my Master, I see you coming for me. I feel nothing else as my heart bursts for you,* Mari w Alahi, *my Lord and my God. I can but reach out to You as I know that You will take me home to be with You and the Father, but it is not yet time. I can hear screaming as this poor man is doing his terrible deed to my other self*

The executioner looked down at his victim; he could hear the screaming in his ears, but as he looked at Bartholomew, it was like nothing he had seen before. In between the screams, he heard Bartholomew praying the same words repeatedly; Bartholomew's eyes were transfixed on a spot above them. The executioner turned to look over his right shoulder, and he was stunned to see flashes of light coming through the rock ceiling. For a moment, the executioner began to doubt the justification of this execution, but he continued for what seemed an eternity.

For his part, Bartholomew continued to stare intently at Jesus coming to him in the light; as Bartholomew's other self continued to endure the agony of this torture, his inner self prayed with Jesus as Jesus beckoned Bartholomew home. With almost all of his skin flayed, Bartholomew's inner self and his other self merged momentarily. Bartholomew looked at his executioner and said loudly so that all could hear, "I forgive you for what you have been forced to do." Then, looking back into the light, he repeated the thirty-first Psalm, as Jesus had at His crucifixion: "Father, into Your hands, I commend my spirit."

And in one final conscious moment, he smiled as he screamed an exultation of joy, "*Mari w Alahi!* My Lord and my God!" and with that, Bartholomew rejoined Jesus in the home of the Father.

*****

Astyages and Ashkhan watched as Bartholomew left this vale of tears for his eternal home. Astyages seemed to enjoy watching Bartholomew's agony. Turning towards Lady Ashkhan, he said, "I'll get to enjoy this again and again as I get rid of the rest of those parasites." He began to walk away and beckoned her to join him. As they entered the main palace, she told the prince, "I beg your leave, Highness. I need to return home now as I promised my mother I would assist her with a matter at home."

"Very well, you have my permission to leave."

She raced away from the palace and found the house where Jude Thaddeus, Toma, and the brothers were staying. Knocking upon the door, she found herself face to face with Jude and Toma. Jude was surprised to see her, "Lady Ashkhan, please, come in."

"No, I can't. I must get to my home as quickly as I can, but I came to warn you that the prince will be sending soldiers for you. He plans on doing to you what he has done to your friend, Bar Tolomai."

Toma asked, "Where is Bar Tolomai? What has happened to him?"

She shivered at the question. "I am telling you to make haste. You must leave immediately or suffer the same fate as him."

Jude looked to Toma and then the lady, "Is he alive?" She shook her head, her eyes brimming with unshed tears. "Why are you telling us this?"

She looked at them, "I was angry with Bar Tolomai as I thought he was trying to have one over us. It was like he was mocking us and our gods. But I just witnessed a horrible execution. Bar Tolomai was in the most incredible agony that a human can suffer, but right before he died, he looked at his executioner, his torturer, and he forgave him for what he had done to him. Bar Tolomai is right. His God teaches love, something that is missing in this world. Now go, please go, before Astyages learns that I am here."

*****

The brothers packed everything they had and started leaving in groups of three with instructions to meet several miles outside the city. Later, once all the brothers had gathered together, Toma took over. "Which of you is the fastest runner?"

One of the younger brothers, Barsabbas, stood up and said, "I am as swift as the wind, Brother Toma. What do you need of me?"

"Come up here with me. Who of you has the best eyesight?" Another young brother, Ananias, stepped forward and stood with Toma and Barsabbas. "Good, I need one more who can see like an eagle." Youel stepped forward. Now, I need two of you who have worked plowing fields." Two more brothers, Addai and Japheth, joined Toma. "Let me tell you what we are going to do. We have to head south by southwest out of this country back towards the Plain of Nineveh and back to our community. We will travel together as a group, but in several small groups so as not to make too much dust. Barsabbas will stay in the rear with Ananias. They are going to act as our rear guard. When Ananias can detect we are being followed, Barsabbas will act as our messenger and alert the rest of the brothers. Youel will act as our advance guard. He will scout ahead of us and return to the group if he senses danger. Addai and Japheth will work with me. We will separate from the main group and cause a diversion. Now let's continue south by southwest to Nineveh." The brothers began their journey away from *Arminiya* and Prince Astyages.

Chapter Thirty-Four
Late Fall, 62 A.D.

Fleeing Ancient *Arminiya*

The journey from *Arminiya* to the Nineveh Plain would be difficult this time of year as the winter would begin to set in as they traveled. Their route would take them west of the capital city through a dry plateau and then south through the *Arminiyan* Highlands in the shadow of Mt. Ararat. Traveling through the mountains of eastern Anatolia would be difficult, but Toma knew that the narrow mountain passes would offer them a strategic advantage.

The land was arid leading up to the foothills, and after several hours into their escape, they stopped to discuss their plan. Jude Thaddeus and the leading group continued their southerly trek towards Nineveh while Toma, Addai, and Japheth headed towards the east. When they were a reasonable distance away from the leading group, they turned towards the south. Toma and his companions broke branches off of a scrub tree, and as they jogged towards the foothills, dragging the tree branches behind them, they left a cloud of dust in their wake. Ananias, trailing the leading group, looked to the east and saw what Toma was doing as his "diversion." He realized that if the group were followed, the trackers would more than likely follow the dust cloud.

It was later in the afternoon back in the capital city when Prince Astyages sent his Captain of the Guard to take a detachment of soldiers, go to the house where the brothers were staying, and bring them all back to the Royal Court. The captain reported that the house was empty and that there was no word of the brothers' whereabouts. The prince flew into a rage and demanded that his guards find out when the Israelites left the city. The guards found one of the residents, who said he had seen them leaving in small groups before midday. When the captain had his forces ready to pursue the brothers, they had at least a four-hour head start. Further interrogation of the residents revealed that the group had exited the city through various gates. The captain sent riders in all directions to see if they could find any trace of where the group may have gone. One of the riders returned and reported a large dust cloud southeast of the city that a group of almost forty men would make running toward the mountains. A group of riders and a troop of soldiers formed up and headed off in pursuit. By this time, the brothers had almost a six-hour head start.

Qemal, a part of this pursuit team, approached the captain and told him, "Although most of the Israelites are fishermen or laborers, one of them is a warrior and will know how to set up a diversion and utilize hit-and-run tactics. Be cautious how you proceed, Captain."

The Captain of the Guard replied, "They are no match for our men and our horses. We'll have them in chains in no time."

Qemal thought, we *shall see.*

Toma, Addai, and Japheth continued their climb through the mountain paths. After a couple of hours into their climb, they looked back, and from this elevation, they had a clear view back to the capital city, which was far off in the distance. They climbed for another hour and then took their first break. They looked back toward the capital city and saw a large plume of dust caused by a group of riders heading in their direction. Farther back, they were able to see a smaller cloud of dust. Toma thought Prince Astyages had sent an advance team of riders, followed by foot soldiers, to search for them. He then looked up towards even higher ground and picked out his spot. He stood up and said to Addai and Japheth, "Let's go. We have work to do." The three of them made their way up the mountain to the spot he picked. Toma had some equipment in his pack that he had collected from the rest of the brothers, and the three of them went to work. Two hours later, they looked back toward the plateau and saw the riders continuing toward the mountains. Toma finished what he was doing and told his companions, "We're done with this one. Let's head up to our next pass."

The captain and Qemal, with their riders, had stopped to give the horses a break after running them hard for several miles. The captain knew that over this terrain, the horses would need to walk and canter for short distances; they could travel maybe five miles in an hour, and at this speed, he estimated that it would take them another three hours until they would start their climb up the mountain paths. There was still no sign of their prey, but they did leave them a large trail to follow. Looking at the tracks, the captain called Qemal over to him, "Look at these drag marks here. Do you know if they had any equipment with them that they were pulling, or are they trying to disguise their movements?"

Qemal looked at the marks, "It looks as if they may have been trying to hide their tracks, between that and the wind, to help cover these marks. Looking at this trail's width, it looks like they have a large group moving. I don't know. I'm not much of a tracker."

"Hmph. I agree with you. It looks like they may have been trying to cover their tracks. This poor attempt at doing this lets me know they're not as smart as they think." Confident they were getting close, the captain pressed on. "We should be at the foothills in a few hours. While we wait for the others to catch up with us, I'll send a few riders ahead to fan out and see which direction your Israelites took." Farther up the mountain, Toma could see that the riders had stopped but were now back on the move. He estimated that it would take the riders over three hours to get to the foothills, and then they would begin their climb up the mountain. He looked at Addai and Japheth, "I think our odds have increased. Let's see how well our surprises work for them, but after we reach our next point, I need you both to go and meet up with the brothers. I can continue to even our odds against them more easily by myself." Addai and Japheth did not argue. They could see that Toma was a warrior who knew precisely what he was doing. They continued to the next pass, where Toma told them where to meet with the brothers. He wished them a safe journey, "I will see you both on the road to Nineveh. God's blessings on you both, now go!"

Toma worked his way back down the mountain. After an hour, he had a good vantage point to watch for the captain's and his men's approach. Safely concealed in his hiding place, he bundled himself in his cloak and slept.

Rising before dawn the next morning, he could hear the soldiers working their way up the mountain. "They have no noise discipline whatsoever," he said aloud. They were still maybe two miles down the mountain, but they did not care that they were making so much noise, "They're very confident that they're going to catch us, well we shall see, now, won't we?" Toma settled in, waiting for the soldiers to approach the first pass.

An hour later, he watched as the soldiers on foot and the riders leading the horses approached the first pass. Toma watched as they maneuvered through the small boulders and ditches that he, Addai, and Japheth put in their way to slow them down and funnel them into a narrow passage. When the majority of the men and horses were in the passage, Toma pulled on the line that he had connected to a thick tree branch, and an avalanche of rocks fell on them, killing and injuring a number of the soldiers and horses. In the noise and confusion, Toma left his "hidey hole" and ran to his next position.

The captain and Qemal counted the dead and wounded. They found that they had lost almost all of their riders and a number of their other soldiers. To add insult to injury, a number of their horses were killed or injured. The captain cursed his luck. He had heard of many of these avalanches in the mountains, but Qemal was not so sure that this was an avalanche. But he didn't care. He operated better working alone, so as far as he was concerned, all of them could ride back home or die here in the mountains. The captain reorganized his men. They buried their dead and then set out to follow the brothers to the end of King Polymius' frontier. They did not know it, but Toma watched every move.

They set out and continued up the mountain until they found a small meadow to camp for the night. They posted their sentinels and set a guard over the remaining horses, all under the close watch of Toma. No moon was out, and right after midnight, Toma made his way undetected into their camp. Waiting momentarily, he crawled over and cut the lines tethering the horses; the guard didn't even know he was there. Toma low crawled out of the camp and then threw rocks at the horses, startling them all, and he watched them bolt out of the encampment. In the dark, he heard the soldiers yelling and running after the horses, but they were gone. Toma could hear curses, but now that the soldiers had lost their horses, the brothers' chances of escaping rose again.

When daylight came, the captain told Qemal that he would not risk any more of his men chasing down the Israelites. "I am not going to pursue them any longer. Besides, the mountains will kill them all. My men will attest to the fact that we saw them all killed in an avalanche, but we were unable to retrieve their bodies as another avalanche was imminent. You are free to chase them down, but we have already lost too much."

The captain rounded up his men to prepare to leave, but one of his men stopped him, "Captain, please allow me to continue with Qemal. These Israelites used their magic to convince my younger sister to abandon our gods and follow theirs. She has brought great shame upon our family and has broken off her marriage to a respected member of our clan. I ask your permission to help hunt these vermin down."

The captain looked at his young soldier, "Do what you must."

Qemal and his young soldier set off to follow Toma and the rest. Now that Qemal was essentially operating alone and most likely in tracking range of Toma, he would be able to use his tracking device to locate him, something he had not been able to do up to this point. Toma, for his part, was watching as the captain and the soldiers turned around and headed back to the north, but he noticed that the man he knew as Quintous and one other continued south. He would have to be very careful of them. He figured he had a good enough lead on him, but they didn't know where he was, so he opted to move and get to the plains as soon as possible. It took another ten days for him to make it over the mountains. The southern Armenian Highlands and plains of East Anatolia were spread before him. Beyond them was the Mesopotamian Plains, and beyond them lay the Syrian Desert. He estimated that he had another three weeks to travel through the desert before getting to the Nineveh Plain, maybe sooner if he pushed himself. However, he would have to be careful traveling through this terrain. Although winter was approaching, the sun could still be dangerous. He was heartened to know that the brothers had made it out of the mountains and were at least three days ahead of him on their way back to Nineveh.

*****

After two and a half weeks, Toma determined he was a few days out of Nineveh. As he continued his walk south, he noticed vultures circling in the sky west of where he was. He broke into a slow trot, and after fifteen to twenty minutes, he saw a figure lying on the ground under a small bush. He approached it cautiously, and then, when he was closer, he recognized the cloak; it was Addai. He ran up to him and turned him over; he was alive but not doing very well. He did a quick assessment, thinking that this could be heat stroke. Addai's skin was somewhat moist, and his skin temperature was hot, but it was not what you would feel with a significant heat injury. Toma took out his waterskin and poured some water over Addai's face. When he began to stir, Toma lifted him, put the skin to his lips, and poured water into his mouth. Addai regained consciousness in a few moments. Toma let him drink some more. When his head cleared, he told Toma what had happened, "When we were coming out of the mountains, I tripped over some rocks and fell on my waterskin. It burst open, and I could not repair it. Japheth and I walked slowly and tried to stay in the shade, but there was very little shade by the time we got down here. We tried to walk at night, but after several days, Japheth's water supply ran out. We split up earlier today. Japheth was going to try to find a wadi to fill his waterskin. He was going to come back and fetch me. I haven't seen him since. I laid down in the shade under that bush and waited. Thank God that you came here when you did. I don't think I could have lasted much longer."

Toma told him, "Don't worry, we'll rest here for a bit, and then we'll be on our way to find Japheth. Can you recall which direction he went?"

Addai pointed to the southwest, "I think that it was in that direction."

"Good, that's heading towards the Nineveh Plain." Then he added, "Let me know when you feel up to moving. We have to stay ahead of Quintous and the other soldier." Addai looked at him with a puzzled look on his face. Toma smiled, "Only two of them are on our trail now; our surprises worked." After a short while, Addai said he was ready to go.

They started walking, and after walking for two miles, they found Japheth's cloak. Continuing on, they began to find more articles of clothing and an empty waterskin until they noticed Japheth off in the distance, walking around in circles. He was wearing very little in the way of clothes. When they approached Japheth, you could hear him yelling at someone or something. Toma told Addai, "He's delirious. He must be suffering from heat stroke." They carefully approached Japheth, and Toma yelled, "Japheth, come here. I have water." Japheth looked over at Toma and Addai without any hint of recognition. Japheth yelled at them and then began to run away. After forty or fifty yards, he collapsed. Toma and Addai ran up to him. As soon as they caught up to him, Toma dropped to the ground and began to assist him. "He's got heat stroke. Stand over him with his cloak to keep the sun off of him." Toma noticed that

Japheth's skin was hot and dry, and his heart was racing. Toma took one of the articles of clothing that they found, soaked it in water, and put this pack under his armpit. He poured some water on Japheth's head, took his own cloak, and began to fan Japheth with it, causing a slight breeze over Japheth's body. Toma poured more water over him and fanned him some more. Addai continued to shade Japheth with the other cloak. After some time doing this, Japheth began to shake, and his temperature started to come down a bit. He lifted Japheth's head and tried to pour some water into his mouth. After some time, Japheth began to come around, but he was still unconscious. Toma and Addai looked across the landscape, looking for some trees or bushes to hunker down until Japheth could recover more. Toma spotted a copse of small trees or bushes off in the distance. "Let's carry Japheth in his cloak and head for those trees." Using the cloak as a makeshift litter, they carried Japheth to the trees, which offered some shade. He then surveyed the area, gave Addai and Japheth water to drink out of the waterskin, and told Addai, "Stay here in the shade. I will go find a wadi and then come back for you two. Do not move until I get back." Addai did not argue.

Toma walked in the direction that he thought a wadi would be. After an hour, he came upon the wadi, walked down the bank to it, filled both waterskins, and soaked his cloak in water. He drank his fill and returned to where he left Addai and Japheth. He put his still-wet cloak over Japheth, cooling him off until the shiver reflex resumed; his temperature was still coming down. He told Addai, "There is a wadi an hour southwest of here. We'll rest here for a bit longer, and then we'll head off in that direction. I have enough food in my bag to last us for another day, but I have to find something for us to eat. When I was walking towards the wadi, I saw some plants that we'll be able to eat, but we need to get more than that. I'll see if I can get something else for us, but I need to tell you that if I catch something, we'll have to eat it raw. We can't risk a fire." Addai was not looking forward to that.

By the following day, Japheth was beginning to show

signs of improvement. Toma told Addai, "We have to get going soon. The two who were tracking us should be out of the mountains by now and will be looking for us. I don't think they plan to capture us and take us back to Arminiya to meet the prince. Let's carry Japheth towards the wadi, and we'll see how he is by tonight."

By the following day, Japheth began to show signs of significant improvement. Toma surmised that his heat stroke, while bad, was not as bad as he had thought initially. Throughout the morning, Japheth continued to improve and became responsive, and by the early evening, Japheth appeared to be over the worst of his heat injury. Toma looked at both men, "Japheth, do you think you'll be able to walk for a while? We're no more than two more days walk to Nineveh."

"I think so, Toma; I know that we need to get to Nineveh as soon as possible; yes, let's get moving." Japheth stood up shakily, "If we can travel by night for a few hours, I think I'll be able to make it." Toma filled their skins again, and they headed south toward Nineveh. They walked until midnight, and then Toma decided that they could rest. Toma and Addai took turns standing watch; by early dawn, they were on their way again.

*****

They were less than a day away from Nineveh when they came across a field where they could forage for food. Toma found a patch of wild tulips and told Addai and Japheth, "These beautiful plants are edible." He pulled some tulips out of the ground and showed them the bulbs, "Some of the people here call these 'melaqa,' here, taste them."

Addai and Japheth tasted them, and Addai said, "They're sweet!"

Toma then found another plant that looked like fennel. He handed the plant to Addai and Japheth, "Try this one, it's called 'dobel.' How do you like it?"

Japheth said, "This is even sweeter."

They foraged for a while, eating tubers and stems. Toma looked to the north, where he sensed movement. He motioned for Addai and Japheth to get down as he scanned the area. About a mile away from them, he saw their two pursuers. Toma was surprised that Quintous and the other soldier caught up to them. He was careful to cover his tracks and to travel in unexpected directions. Toma didn't know that Quintous was using his tracking device to follow him. "Addai, Japheth, listen to me. Quintous and the other soldier are behind us. I need you two to travel to Nineveh, where you will find the others. I will stay back and delay them. They won't be able to catch up with you if you go now. I will see you both in Nineveh."

Addai and Japheth headed southwest to Nineveh while Toma began to execute a rear-guard action. He headed directly south by southeast, keeping Quintous and the other soldier in visual contact while watching Addai's and Japheth's progress. When he was on a slight rise, he gathered some twigs and started a small fire; after it burned for a few seconds, he extinguished it, but it gave off a small cloud of smoke. It had the desired effect: Toma noticed that his two pursuers began to veer to the southeast towards him. He continued his little cat-and-mouse game for several hours into the late afternoon, leading the pursuers away from Addai and Japheth. He had lost sight of Addai and Japheth thirty minutes earlier, but he could now focus all his efforts on his pursuers. As he moved to his next observation post, he didn't notice the saw-scaled viper on the ground off to his right until it was too late. The snake was beginning to stir for its nocturnal hunt when Toma stepped near it. The animal prepared to strike him when he saw it. He moved quickly out of the way, but the viper was able to hit his leg with a glancing blow. Toma was hoping that this might have been a "dry bite" where the animal strikes but does not inject any venom, but the viper *was* able to envenomate him with a small amount of its neurotoxins. Toma moved away from the snake, sat down, and tried to slow his heart rate. As the snake moved off, he tried to position his leg so that it was somewhat elevated, but that required him to lie down, thereby losing sight of

Quintous. He elevated his leg for as long as he could and then got up slowly to check out his surroundings, but when he got up, he could not see Quintous or the other soldier. He thought about how long it would take him to get to his next observation post; if he could continue to delay the pursuers for a while longer, Addai's and Japheth's chances of rejoining the brothers would be assured, so he decided to make his way to the next site slowly. As he got up to begin his low crawl out, he felt a sharp pain in his upper thigh. He thought that the snake hit him again, but when he looked down, he saw an arrow sticking out of his right leg; it was no use; they had him. He looked to his left and saw Quintous standing ten yards from him. The other soldier was to the right, about twenty yards away. As the soldier walked up to where Toma was lying on the ground, Quintous yelled in anger at him, "I told you to leave him to me! Idiot!" Quintous then took his sword and, with unbelievable speed and fury, stabbed the other soldier in the heart, killing him.

"Well, Toma," Quintous said in Latin and immediately switched to English, "Or should I say, Lieutenant Boudagh, United States Navy."

The shock on Toma's face was evident, even in the fading light. He stood up and said in English to Quintous, "Who are you?"

Quintous laughed at him, enjoying Toma's shock and confusion, "Who I am isn't important, but what I'm doing here is. I noticed that when I was with your little group, you always treated me a bit differently. Why was that, Toma? Did you suspect my motives were not as pure as those other sheep?"

"I just thought it unusual that you never participated in our discussions. Now I know why. When did you come through the portal?" Toma began to realize that due to the arrow embedded in his leg, his heart was racing. He tried to block the pain out using his SEAL training. SEALs are taught to endure pain, and their ability to withstand pain is absolute, but the neurotoxins in his system affecting his breathing and his thinking, combined with the blood loss and pain from his wound, he was having a difficult time.

"As I said, who I am is not important, but before I decide to end your life, let me tell you why I'm here and who sent me. Your dear friend, Dr. Edgeton, sent me back here as a bit of insurance. As you know, your being back here with your buddy, Declan, will cause subtle changes to the future. Murray's goal is to stop the spread of Christianity, and he thought that the two of you running around back in time would change the direction of your religion. But why risk it? So, he sent me back here with the mission of killing you and all of your evangelists. I've already got one down. You should have seen the death that Bar Tolomei endured; it was fantastic. Have you ever seen, or better yet, ever *heard* anyone being flayed before? It's quite the experience. He died a horrible, painful death. Sorry that I can't do the same thing to you, but I have to catch up with my other targets. But I'm interested in how I would match up with a famous Navy SEAL, so here is what we will do. I'm going to make this an even fight, well, maybe not that even as that idiot shot you with an arrow, but let's make it as fair as possible." Qemal threw a knife to Toma. "Use that one, and I'll use mine."

Qemal threw off his cloak and approached Toma. Toma picked up his knife, and his training kicked in. He was taught how to fight with a knife: bend your knees and keep your feet flat for balance, crouch down to offer less of a target, and hold your free arm in front of you to ward off blows. He was taught to jab with the knife and aim for the throat and eyes. Toma could fight defensively against Qemal, but he knew that with the toxins circulating and his heart racing to overcome the blood loss, he knew that it was a matter of time before Qemal would overpower him. His best hope was that Qemal was not experienced in knife combat, but that hope was dashed when he noticed that Qemal assumed the same stance as he did. Toma resigned himself to his fate, happy in the knowledge that he saved his brothers. It was over more quickly than he would have imagined. Toma parried off several of Qemal's thrusts, and his shield arm absorbed several other blows, but his strength was gone. Several thoughts were going through his mind: He realized that he would die today, but he would die in his ancestral home.

He was on the Nineveh Plain. He then thought of his family and how he would not see his mother and father and his brother and his sisters in this life, but as he had spoken directly to Christ on the Cross, he knew that he would see his family in the next. He smiled inwardly at that but thought how nice it would be to see his family again. Toma was trying to maneuver to his right when Qemal lunged forward with a fatal thrust into Toma's neck.

*****

Toma was walking through a beautiful open space in the forest. There was a canopy of trees above him with sunlight streaming in, sparkling as it made its way down to the forest floor. He heard the soft sound of a small stream off to the right; birds were calling to each other, and he just stood there, looking up and smiling at the sunlight. Then he heard Bartholomew calling out for him to wait. Toma turned around and saw his friend. Bartholomew looked so young; they talked as they walked together, making their way to the end of the forest where the light was so very inviting.

Chapter Thirty-Five
Mid-Summer, 64 A.D.

Rome following the Great Fire

The Emperor was in a rage once again. Nero called his chief advisor, the Praetorian Prefect Faenuis Rufus, to voice his displeasure at the reports he had been hearing from the Senate. "Don't those idiots realize how much we have done for Rome and our people? How can they even consider blaming us for this fire? We want you to find a way to deflect this blame away from us, and we want it done immediately, do you understand?"

"Of course, my *Imperator,* I am working on this as we speak." Bowing obsequiously as he left the imperial presence, Rufus collected his tribune waiting for him outside the hall. "We have to find a way to fix the blame on this fire on someone else. The emperor will have both of our heads on a *pilum* by the end of this week if we don't find a scapegoat for this that will be acceptable to both the emperor and the Senate. The fire has destroyed what, so far, fourteen of our districts?"

"Yes, Prefect," the tribune answered, "And so far, at least seven additional districts have suffered significant damage. How did this fire become so powerful? Didn't we appease Vulcan at last year's Vulcanalia? My brothers and I fished for days before the festival to offer fish to Vulcan's bonfire. I can't understand how it became so fierce."

"I don't think it was Vulcan as much as it was Septentrino and the other gods of wind," the Prefect mused. "But we have to find an answer, and we have to find it now."

The tribune hesitated but said, "Prefect, I may have an idea. May I speak freely?"

"Of course, Fabius, what is it?

"There is a *speculator augusti* in my cohort who has come to my attention these past two years as he has proven to be exceptional at his duties in gathering intelligence. He is a Roman citizen, but he is from the east in our Illyrian Province. He has some interesting insights into this new Jewish sect, the Christians. He served for several years with our Tenth Legion in Jerusalem, and from what he tells me, this new Jewish sect is unbelievably seditious, even more so than the Jews we have been accustomed to during these past number of years."

The Prefect looked at his tribune with a puzzled look, "How are they seditious? Do they advocate rebellion against Rome?"

"No, sir, not exactly. But they refuse to worship *our* gods, which is the law. They say that worshipping our gods is bizarre. They also refuse to participate in our prescribed sacrifices. They say that there is no need to offer sacrifices. But listen to this, sir, they observe some bizarre rituals in which they perform cannibalism. What could be more bizarre than cannibalism? No, according to my *speculator,* these Christians constitute a very dangerous and superstitious cult. We need to watch them. If the Jews consider these Christians to be seditious in that they will not follow our laws, couldn't it be within the realm of possibility to consider that they may have caused the fire?"

Rufus was considering what his tribune told him, "Fascinating. We may have found our scapegoat. This *speculator* you were speaking of, send him to me."

"Of course, sir. He also said something interesting. It appears that this cult's leader is here in Rome at present. His name is Petrus, but he is commonly called 'The Big Fisherman.' My *speculator* says he has been known to cause quite a bit of trouble within the city."

"Good, let's round him up, let's see how well these Christians operate with their leader in one of our prisons. Your *speculator*, I want to see him this afternoon. What is his name?"

Fabius replied, "His Illyrian name is Qemal, but within our cohort, he is called Quintous."

*****

Declan, known to the Community of Believers here in Rome as "Antoni," talked with two of his friends, a husband and wife called Lucius and Fulvia, regarding the Great Fire that took place the week before and lasted four days. He had been in Rome for two years, working with the Christian community to make converts, and he had become indispensable to the community due to his organizational skills. They had come to depend on Antoni for many issues, and the discussion of how to rebuild a number of their houses was a pressing one. Lucius said, "I have heard from some of my friends who work with the Senate. There is talk among the nobles and others that the Emperor started the fire so that he could have a cleared area for the building of his new palace, the *Domus Aurea*."

Antoni was waiting for this, but he had been busy the past few days rescuing people, "Have you heard anything else, Lucius? Has anyone discussed what they believe was the cause of the fire?"

"No, I haven't heard anything. Why do you ask, Antoni?"

He answered, "Just curious, Lucius. But keep your ear to the ground, and let me know if you hear anything. I have to speak with Petrus about rebuilding our homes and let him know what you have heard."

Lucius turned to leave and then said, "Oh, one last thing. I did hear that Petrus has met an old friend of yours, a Roman Centurion who has transferred back to Rome from Palestine, as he will be retiring from the Legion. I believe that he is visiting Petrus right now. From what I have heard, the Centurion is a Believer, and what is even more amazing is that he was there when Our Lord was crucified. Do you know of this Centurion? What an incredible story!"

Antoni smiled, "Yes, if it's the same Centurion that I met back in Jerusalem, then yes, I know him, and you're right, what an incredible story." Looking over at Fulvia, he continued, "The three of us will have to sit down with the Centurion and have him tell you about The Master." He walked toward the house where Peter, known by the Community as Petrus, was staying. When he arrived at the house, he was greeted by Petrus and an old soldier who was visiting: It was Gaius Valerius Crispinus, the Centurion whose servant was healed by Jesus and the same Centurion who was present at Jesus' crucifixion. Antoni thought Gaius must have been in his late sixties or early seventies, but he still looked strong and fit for his age. He greeted the Centurion, "*Salve, Centurio!*"

The Centurion was shocked to see Antoni, "How can this be?" The Centurion was searching his memory for how he knew him. "I know you; you were there when we crucified The Master, but you can't be; that was thirty years ago. I can see how the years have touched your face, but you still have the body of a young man. It must be that my eyes are failing me. I remember how you and your comrade spoke with The Master when He was dying on the Cross. You had weapons we had never seen before, and you stopped the advance of my soldiers." A frightened look of realization crossed the Centurion's face. "As I said on that hill in Jerusalem, you and your comrade must be angels sent by The Master."

"No, *Centurio*, I am not an angel. I bleed just like you, but yes, my comrade and I were there when Our Lord was crucified."

The Centurion shook his large head, "No, it cannot be. How can you explain those weapons, and how can you explain how the years have not affected you?" The Centurion then looked at Petrus, "Petrus, if he is not an angel, he must be a priest of the dark arts. This is bad magic; he must be from Satan's Legions."

Petrus looked at Antoni and smiled, "Tell our guest what you told *Yimma* when she asked you about Our Lord's crucifixion, and then tell him what you and Toma told John

322

when the three of you were on the road. That should explain things."

He told the Centurion the same story that he told *Yimma,* Mary, the mother of Jesus, and John regarding their tools and how they had maintained their health. Then Petrus spoke up, "Gaius, please understand that Antoni is a most faithful servant of The Master and has been an invaluable addition to our community these past two years. Before that, thirty years ago, he and his brother, Toma, sold everything they had and gave it all to our community in Jerusalem. Antoni is not of Satan's Legions. He is a most devoted brother and is very much loved by all of us."

The Centurion looked at Antoni with a jaundiced eye, "If you say so, Petrus, but I will tell both of you right now, I will be watching you, Antoni, or whatever your name is. I served in the legions for almost fifty years, since I was eighteen, and have seen much of the world. I know that things do not always seem to be as they appear. Until you can prove otherwise, I will keep my eye on you."

Antoni offered a slight bow to the Centurion, "I respect you, *Centurio,* and I know that you have seen much of the world and what the world can do to a man. In light of that, I do not blame you for your skepticism, and to be completely honest, I would also be skeptical. Right now, I hope and pray that I can earn your trust quickly because I believe that we may be in danger."

Always a military man, the Centurion focused all his energies on what Antoni said, "Danger? What kind of danger? Explain yourself."

"I heard from one of our brothers this morning that there has been some talk among the noble class that the Great Fire may have been caused by Nero himself and that—"

The Centurion interrupted, "Why should that be a 'danger?' What has that to do with you, or I should say, with us?"

Antoni answered, "*Centurio,* what do you know of the behavior of the emperor?"

"I have heard that he has some strange tastes."

Petrus said, "Antoni, let me address this. Gaius Valerius, the emperor, has more than strange tastes. He is a murderer and a reprobate. The things that he has done are an abomination to The Lord. He killed his mother, killed his first wife, killed his second wife, and then married a man. This time, the emperor assumed the role of the wife. He does whatever he pleases, and no one is allowed to find fault in anything that he may do. His behavior is such that if he does something wrong, it is impossible to blame him for doing so. Antoni, continue with what you are saying."

Antoni continued, "Thank you, Petrus. *Centurio,* as Petrus has said, the emperor will do horrible things and not accept responsibility for his actions. Here is my concern: The Great Fire destroyed a significant portion of the city and left the rest of the city damaged. If there is talk among the noble class that Nero may have caused the fire, he will place that blame onto someone else. Our Christian community is already being treated poorly by the Roman elite as they consider us a threat to their order. *Centurio*, you are an officer. What do you do with your century if you have cause to believe that a superior force may attack you?"

"First, I would attempt to determine if the threat is real. If it is and we have the time, we would break camp, evade the enemy, and then try to rejoin friendly forces. If we do not have the time and an attack is imminent, we would do what we could to improve our defenses and stand and fight."

Antoni said, "That makes sense. Since the majority of our community has lost their homes, we should attempt to flee Rome. If we cannot flee, and since we cannot fight, we should consider hiding."

Petrus asked, "Should we not try to determine if the threat is real?" Gaius nodded his head in agreement, but Antoni shook his head.

"We can, but I believe we should begin to prepare to get all of us away from Rome. You know how unstable the emperor is. If he gives the word, the Praetorian Guard will swoop down like a hawk on all of us. We should spread the word to our community to prepare what they have to flee the city."

Petrus stroked his beard for a moment, "Antoni, that may cause undue panic with our people, the undue panic that may turn out to be unfounded. No, let's wait and see how things develop. We should ask our brothers to find out if they can learn anything."

Antoni's mind was racing as he knew they were indeed in danger, but he also knew he could not interfere with the natural course of events. "At least let me organize the women and children in case we have to flee at a moment's notice."

Petrus thought about this, "I still think that that may cause a panic, but how would you go about that course of action?"

"I would tell the families to prepare what they need to move out of the city and into the countryside, and that we may have to move out with some haste. We could say there is the possibility of another firestorm, but in the meantime, continue to rebuild what they have and await a word from you as to whether and when we should evacuate. That should keep everyone calm as we're still trying to dig out from the fire, but at the same time, they will prepare to leave if necessary. I will also tell everyone not to discuss this outside our community."

Petrus looked at Gaius Valerius, who sat there impassively, "That sounds reasonable, Antoni, do what you must." Then, as an afterthought, Petrus asked, "Gaius Valerius, what do you think?"

The Centurion answered, "I think that Antoni's plan is sensible. I want to go with him and start spreading the word." Antoni and the Centurion left Petrus' house and went out into the streets of Rome. As they walked, the Centurion looked at Antoni, shaking his head in disbelief, "I still find it hard to believe that you are not an angel. How could you barely age in thirty years?"

Antoni laughed, "As I told the rest of the brothers and Our Mother, along with the balms that our physicians have us use, we also try to stay healthy and keep our bodies strong. Look at you; you must be what, almost seventy right now, and you still look as if you can lead troops into battle and fight all day. You have kept yourself strong, and that will help keep you young."

"Yes, that's true. I can still outfight most of the young *milites* in my century, but how do you *look* so young?"

"Maybe it's because we don't drink wine or beer, *Centurio,* that might be the reason. Does that make sense to you?"

The Centurion was shocked, "No wine? Forget it; I'd rather look my age; it makes me look like I have wisdom and have lived a full life, don't you think?"

Both men laughed as they walked on. They spent the rest of the day telling those of the Christian community to be prepared to gather their belongings in case they had to move out to the fields. The following day, Antoni returned to Lucius and Fulvia's home to help them finish the work they had started earlier that week when they all heard a loud commotion outside. Lucius went outside to see what was happening, and he immediately came back inside, telling Antoni and Fulvia that a squad of Roman soldiers was outside, arresting some of their friends. "Antoni, it looks as if it is happening already. Fulvia, let's grab our bags. We can leave through the back."

They all got up to leave, and Antoni said, "I have to get back to Petrus and ensure he is safe. I will see you across the Tiber, where we said we would meet. Now go as fast as you can. God's blessings be upon you." He ran back to the house where Petrus was staying, where he saw Gaius Valerius standing outside. "*Centurio,* what is happening? Where is Petrus?"

The Centurion answered in a rush of words, "I got here right as a group of soldiers was taking him away. I asked their leader, their *Immunis,* what the meaning of manhandling an old man was, and this snot-nosed brat told me that I had better stand down or I would be joining Petrus. Here I stood in front of this idiot; I told him that I was a Centurion, and he completely ignored my rank. I should have slapped that piece of excrement, but I did not want to make it worse for Petrus. As you know, falling back is sometimes the better maneuver."

"Yes, of course, it is. Is there any way that we can find out where they are taking him and what the charges are?"

"I still have some comrades attached to the Legion's Garrison here in Rome. Let me see what I can find out. In the meantime, let's go to the Forum to see if we can learn anything." He looked at Antoni, "You look like a Roman, and your Latin is better than mine, so I think you'll be able to blend in without any problems. Let's go."

They arrived at the Forum, and a large crowd gathered, listening to an announcement by the Prefect Faenuis Rufus. The Centurion looked closely at the three men on the balcony, "I know Rufus, and I know of the Tribune standing behind him, but who is that third man up there whispering in the Tribune's ear and gesturing to Rufus? He appears to be directing things."

Antoni looked up to the balcony, "I don't know, but look at him. Does he look like a Roman to you? I thought that only loyal Romans constituted the Praetorian Guards." The Centurion just shook his head.

By that afternoon, they had discovered that the Christians were to be blamed for the Great Fire that destroyed so much of the city and that it was to be the duty of every Roman citizen to identify any known Christians as they were to be punished for their roles in this disaster. They also discovered that Petrus was in prison and that no one was allowed to visit him. The Centurion looked at Antoni and said, "Maybe he should have listened to you. We can't do anything now."

Antoni thought for a moment, "*Centurio,* yes, there is. There is something that we can do. There is another leader we need to get out of Rome. I can't believe I didn't think of this earlier; we must leave. One question, how much money do you have with you?" They walked west towards the *Tiber* and followed the river south past the *Collis Aventinus* until they arrived at an older section of Rome. Antoni knocked on the door, and an older woman answered.

"Yes? May I help you?" she asked as she answered the door.

"Thank you. I was wondering if you are selling any fish

today?" Antoni started the formula to identify each other as Christians. Drawing his foot across the ground in front of her door, he drew a small arc.

The woman looked down at the arc and drew its mirror image underneath it; together, these two arcs resembled a fish. "Please come in. Let me see if we have any fish left for sale." They went inside, and the woman turned to Antoni. "Do you have any idea what was happening? I have heard that some of our community members have been arrested."

"Yes, Nero is blaming us for the fire. Gather what you can and leave Rome as soon as you can. Act as if you are on business or going to visit family, but leave immediately. I need to find Paul; I know he came to you after he was released from prison, but I need to get him out of Rome, and we must move quickly. Is he here?" She looked over at Gaius Valerius with a questioning look on her face. "He is one of us and knows The Master personally; do not fear him."

"He knows The Master? He has talked with Our Lord?" And with that, the woman took Gaius Valerius' hand, kissed it, and knelt before him. "You have seen The Master, Blessed be His name, and blessed be you for being close to Him." The Centurion was embarrassed by this gesture of respect and looked at Antoni for help.

Antoni nodded, "Sister, we must spirit Paul away from here; we must leave now, as do you. Please tell me where he is."

"Forgive me, my Brother. It is just that I have met so few of our family members who have talked with Our Lord. Yes, Paul is two houses over. Follow me." The three of them walked to the house where Paul was staying, and when they got there, the woman explained to the other family what was happening. Paul came into the room; he was stooped over from age and the indignities visited upon him in prison, but he immediately joined the conversation.

Looking at the woman, Paul said, "Iulia, let me be with these men for a moment." Iulia walked out the door, and then Paul asked, "I knew something was wrong. Do you know what is happening?"

Antoni explained everything to Paul, saying, "I need to get you away from Rome. Gaius Valerius has retired from the Legions, and with his *praemia militare* discharge bonus, he will be retiring to Gallaecia. We can get passage out of the port of Ostia, but we have to leave now."

Petrus was being interrogated by the Prefect Rufus and his Tribune, Fabius. Petrus did not divulge any information to the Prefect regarding the Christian Community, and the Prefect wanted Petrus to be scourged and then returned to prison. Qemal offered another solution.

"Prefect, my experience in Jerusalem with these cults is that once their leader is eliminated, they disperse like chaff before the wind. After we gather all of these Christians and try them for the crime they committed, we can get rid of this old fool. That should help to prevent any new groups of these people." Qemal stepped back after he addressed the Prefect.

Rufus thought about this and then looked to his Tribune, "Fabius, set up a detail for crucifixion and get this piece of filth out of the city."

Fabius answered, "Yes, Prefect. A large number of crucifixions were done last month across the Tiber on the *Mons Vaticanus*. Will that be far enough out of the city?"

"Yes, see to it immediately. I have to report to the emperor." Looking at both Fabius and Qemal, the Prefect asked, "One last thing, what should we recommend to the emperor that we do with all of these Christians? He is considering imprisoning them for a term yet to be determined, but do either of you have any other thoughts?"

Qemal replied, "If I may Prefect, I may have the perfect answer for the emperor. He might find this very entertaining." He then described in detail what they should do.

Later that afternoon, a detail dragged Petrus across the *Campus Martius* and crossed the *Tiber* at the *Pons Neronianus* towards the *Mons Vaticanus*. By that night, looking at the crucified Petrus, Qemal mused that he had eliminated two of his primary targets.

Chapter Thirty-Six
Spring, 65 A.D.

Gallaecia

The three of them were living on Gaius Valerius' farm in Gallaecia, where Gaius Valerius was enjoying his retirement. He had been stationed in this part of the empire and had purchased this plot of land many years before. His wife had died during one of his postings with the Legions, and at this time in his life, he assumed the role of a widowed "gentleman farmer;" he looked and acted exactly like one. Since they arrived in *Hispania* several months before, all three of them enjoyed working to convert this plot of land into a working farm. All progressed well until the month before when they received several reports from Rome about what had happened to Peter and the Christian community. Paul was still in mourning. He had read the accounts of what had happened to the Christians, the torture that they had to endure before their deaths. He was inconsolable, but as he said, he rejoiced in the fact that they were now wearing the martyr's crown. Paul was especially saddened by the account of the crucifixion of Simon Peter, how he asked to be crucified upside down as he was unworthy to be crucified in the manner of Jesus. The Rock upon which Jesus said He would build His Church had been martyred, but Paul knew that his blood and the blood of all of the martyrs of Rome would be the seed for the growth of the Church, but it didn't stop his anguish.

Gaius and Antoni worked the farm while preaching throughout the northern part of *Hispania,* making many converts. Some Roman soldiers and their families in this western province of the Roman Empire also converted, adding to the growing Church in this part of the world. It took some time, but eventually, Paul began to write again. He wrote several letters to various communities throughout the Roman world, encouraging the faithful not to despair and reinforcing that Jesus was in their midst. By the following month, Paul joined Antoni and Gaius in preaching to the various communities in Gallaecia.

Before the summer began, Paul received word that a number of the surviving members of the Christian community from Rome were planning to join Paul and the new community in Gallaecia. They hoped some of the new converts would return to Rome with them to rebuild the Church. Paul was happy that there were so many converts in *Hispania* and that they could help spread the Word. By mid-summer, the first group had arrived from Rome and were invited to stay at the farm. Antoni and Gaius joined Paul in welcoming the brothers and sisters from Rome and had an emotional reunion. Iulia was there with her husband; they had fled the city as Antoni told them to, but they relayed to Paul and Antoni how many of their old friends had been martyred in Rome.

"It was terrible, Antoni," Iulia was saying. "We did exactly what you told us when you came looking for Paul; we fled to another part of the city and hid. But after a few months, things appeared to return to normal, and we returned to our homes. We were shocked at how few of our community survived, and then we began to hear the stories. We had some friends of ours who, although they never followed The Way, were not opposed to our faith, and they let us live in peace. They were told to inform the authorities of any Christian people, but they never did. They told us that they were in the Colosseum when the horrors began. Nero had informed the citizens that he had an entertainment spectacle scheduled for that day, and the crowd was excited to see what the emperor had prepared." Iulia talked about the events of the day. "After great fanfare, a colossal portcullis was raised on one of the openings of the main tunnels that opened into the arena itself from the *hypogeum*. As soon as the portcullis was lifted, some people ran out of the tunnel. They were all covered in animal skins, but they looked bewildered, as if they did not know what to do. We all thought that this was the beginning of a play, and then we all heard deep roars coming from the tunnel. Then, slowly emerging, we saw several large beasts; they looked like the lions that were paraded through the city a year before.

"The beasts came out of the tunnel. They, too, looked confused until they caught sight of the people scampering about in the middle of the arena. The beasts immediately ran to these poor people and attacked them. The people in the arena thought it was a show, but then they noticed that these weren't armed gladiators fighting these animals but old men and women. They could hear the screams of the people as they were killed, and the people in the stands were 'encouraged' by Praetorian Guards in the crowd to begin to yell and cheer. After a few moments, they did not need any encouragement.

"What happened next was not met with cheers. After the beasts were forced back into the tunnels, a portcullis opened on the other side of the arena. Slowly walking out were hundreds of people, men, women, and even young children. The soldiers led them out, prodding them forward with their *pila*. They were all in a circle in the middle of the arena; the men tried to form a barrier with the women and the children in the middle. My friends told us that the most amazing thing happened. Instead of screaming and wailing, the people all knelt and began to pray, but they did not pray for deliverance; they prayed for their fellow citizens. Then, in the middle of the line of men, our Brother Lucius stood up and began to yell out to the crowd that they were not responsible for the fire; he questioned the crowd, 'Why should the Christians destroy their own homes and businesses?' He then went on to proclaim the glory of the Lord, and that is when two portcullises opened, and many beasts were released. Lucius began to yell to our brothers and sisters to 'take heart for the Lord is with us.' The men tried to fight off the beasts with their bare hands, but it was hopeless. What happened next enraged the emperor. The people in the crowd did not cheer; they began to shout 'NO! STOP!" but it was to no avail.

"As the emperor was so enraged that his people would sympathize with the prisoners, he announced that the most entertaining spectacle would happen at night. That is when the level of his evilness became apparent to all. Nero had a number of our brothers and sisters covered with pitch and then crucified. But that was not the worst part. The worst part happened when darkness fell on the city. It was then that Nero had them set afire. The screams were horrible. The people attempted to leave the Colosseum, but the emperor placed Guards at all the exits. Our friends told us that even when the brothers and sisters were on their crosses, they continued to pray and to praise God." At this point, Iulia broke down and could not continue. Her husband picked up from there and let Paul, Antoni, and the rest know that the week following the horrors, more Romans came to The Way, inspired by the courage of the Christian community.

*****

Over the next few days, other group members began to trickle in, and more emotional reunions occurred. By the end of the week, the number of people who had come from Rome numbered about fifty, but one new group member had them puzzled. None of the other brothers and sisters could recall exactly who he was. Iulia brought this up in passing to Antoni, and he asked her to point this new member out. Antoni casually looked that way and saw the new member. He got up and slowly made his way over to where Gaius Valerius was talking with an old soldier. "*Centurio,* can you help me move something over by our well?" The two of them walked towards the well as if they were going to do some work, "I'm going to point someone out to you, and I want you to tell me if you have seen him before." Antoni casually pointed out the man in question, "Have you seen that man before?"

The Centurion studied the man's face, and then he realized where he had seen him, "Yes, he was who we saw on the balcony when Rufus announced that the Christians were responsible for the fire. I mentioned that it looked as if he were the one telling Rufus what to say." Then the Centurion hissed, "What is *he* doing here?"

"I don't know, but we'll find out."

The next day, Gaius and Antoni made a point of visiting all of the brothers and sisters from Rome, asking if they needed help with anything. Antoni had a chance to approach the new member in the storehouse as he was putting some of his things into his bag; a number of the visitors from Rome were sleeping in this outbuilding. "Good morning," Antoni greeted him. "We haven't had a chance to talk yet. Welcome to *Hispania.*"

The new member cocked his head and replied, "Yes, we have yet to have a chance to talk."

Antoni said, "We're all happy that you all are here. It must have been terrible in Rome after the fire."

"Yes, it was."

Antoni walked over to a workbench and began to organize some of the tools. "I've had a chance to travel to many provinces throughout the Empire and I'm trying to place your accent. I can tell that you're not from Rome. Are you from Greece, possibly?"

He snorted through his nose, "Possibly."

"Well, I'll let you go on with what you need to do. Let me know if there is anything that you may need while you're here with us." Antoni could feel the new member's eyes burning into him as he walked out. He returned to Gaius' house, where he sat down at a table with the Centurion. "Undoubtedly, he is the man we saw on the balcony, and he is none too friendly. He is here to do something; I think that we need to keep a close watch on Paul. After talking with him this morning in the storehouse, I can feel something about this man that is evil. He is staying out there with a number of the others, but I know he is walking around the farm observing everything."

Gaius nodded, "Well, as this is my farm, I can go

wherever I want and 'observe' whatever I like. I'll walk all over my land doing small jobs and checking on things. I can keep a close eye on this one, and no one should be the wiser."

"Just be careful, *Centurio,* this one seems dangerous."

Gaius laughed, "I didn't survive in the Legions for all those years because I was careless. Yes, my Brother, I will be careful."

Antoni was back in the storehouse the following day, inventorying supplies and materials. As he was working, the new member came in, and he approached Antoni. "Are you here to check up on me again?"

Antoni turned around, "No, this is a working farm, and we have work to do. Why would you think that I would be checking up on you? You're our guest here."

The new member sneered at Antoni and spoke to him in English, "Oh, I think you know why you would check up on me, wouldn't you, Lieutenant Declan O'Sullivan?"

Antoni jerked upward like a marionette on a string, "Who are you?"

The new member smiled a malicious grin. "As I told your teammate, Toma, who I am is not important, but what I am here *for* is. If it would satisfy your obvious curiosity, my name is Qemal." Qemal offered a sarcastic bow to Antoni. "To satisfy your curiosity even more, let me tell you why I am here." Qemal began to move so that the sun was coming in directly behind him and into Antoni's face. "You must recall your dear friend, Dr. Murray Edgeton? He was smart enough to send me back through your precious portal to ensure you don't return. At the same time, he gave me another mission: To eliminate all of your Christian leaders. I am happy to report that I have succeeded in eliminating two of them so far, Bar Tolomei and now Simon Peter. But there was a bonus. I was able to give the emperor an incredible spectacle. You should have seen how your Christian friends lit the night sky as they burned on flaming crosses in the Colosseum. That was but one of the sports that I recommended. We had many, many more. Then I strongly recommended that your Simon Peter be eliminated. He died a horrible death, but you already knew that. I am happy to tell you that Nero enjoyed every moment of it. You should have seen him fawning over the little boy he was with; it was so touching, and touch they did. But enough of these little stories, let me do what I came to do." He reached under his cloak, pulled a dagger out, the Roman *pugio,* and threw it over to Antoni. "Pick it up, Lieutenant. This will be a somewhat even fight." Qemal reached back under his cloak and unsheathed a Roman *gladius hispaniensis,* the combat sword used by Roman infantrymen in the Celto-Iberian Wars. "It's fitting, isn't it, that I use a sword immortalized right here in this province? Now pick it up."

Antoni looked down at the dagger. His first thought was that he promised himself he would not fight anymore, but the idea of what this man had done to the Christian community in Rome, Simon Peter, and Bartholomew overwhelmed him. He looked at Qemal and felt the ancient Celt stir in his blood: the Celt who fought the Romans at Numantia, the Celt who fought with Brian Boru at Clontarf; this Celtic warrior rose within him. He roared in rage and rushed forward to pick up the dagger.

Qemal lunged forward, kicked the knife away, and, in one fluid motion, arced his sword through the air directly at Antoni's neck. Antoni side-stepped at the last moment. The strike missed its intended mark but sliced Antoni's thigh. Antoni was seriously wounded, but he forced himself to ignore the pain. They circled each other. Qemal had a malicious grin on his face, stalking Antoni, knowing that it was just a matter of time before he could dispatch him.

At that moment, Gaius appeared in the doorway and yelled, "Antoni!" Qemal stopped and looked back at Gaius. "What is happening here? What are you doing?"

Antoni yelled out in Latin, "Gaius, this man is not one of us. The emperor has sent him to kill me and as many of our leaders as he can. Be cautious, Gaius. This man is extremely dangerous.

Gaius responded, "Move to the bench and throw me my staff." Antoni moved towards the bench, never taking his eyes off of Qemal. He grabbed Gaius' staff and threw it to him.

Qemal had an amused look on his face, "*You* want to fight *me*, old man? A *farmer*? Oh, well, at least two will die today." He assumed a fighting stance as Gaius moved to face him. Qemal reverted to English and began to taunt Antoni, "By the way, *Declan,* your comrade, Toma, was injured when I finally caught up to him on the Nineveh Plain, injured and exhausted, I must say. He successfully delayed me and our troops so that his group of brothers could escape from Armenia. In doing so, he killed a number of my men. Because he fought valiantly, I gave him a quick death, but he's dead nonetheless, as you will be as soon as I get a warm-up in with this relic."

Gaius assumed his fighting stance and moved to his right. This move meant that Qemal would have to reach across his body to thrust at the Centurion. Qemal thought there might be more to this old farmer than he initially thought. He thrust an exploratory jab at Gaius. Gaius parried it off easily with the center of the staff. He then struck Qemal in the head with a downward stroke with the upper part of the staff, throwing Qemal off balance for a fraction of a second. Qemal was not expecting any resistance from Gaius and was genuinely surprised. "Oh my, what do we have here? A farmer who has fought against wolves? Well, now I know I am not up against a sheep." Qemal moved quickly to his left, only to have Gaius strike out at Qemal and move to *his* left, countering Qemal's move. Qemal rushed Gaius with a flurry of rapid and powerful strikes. Gaius was able to parry the majority of them, but his hand took a wicked blow that severed two of his fingers. Qemal pressed the attack again, forcing Gaius back, but this time, Gaius' staff was covered with his blood, and he was unable to hold it well. Qemal feinted to the left. Gaius dropped the staff to parry off a blow, and then, with a swift thrust under Gaius' left arm, Qemal's sword stabbed deep into Gaius' chest. Gaius stumbled back and fell face-first to the ground. Qemal wiped his blade off using the back of Gaius's shirt and walked over to Antoni. "Let's make it an even two, shall we?" He moved forward very slowly and deliberately to strike at Antoni, who stood there unsteadily due to the loss of blood. Qemal raised his

337

gladius to strike when he felt a massive blow hit him on the side of the head. He fell like a poleaxed bull, and when he rolled over to look behind him, he saw a bloody Gaius Valerius Crispinus, Centurion of the Tenth Legion, the *Legio Fretensis*, standing there. His staff had fallen to the ground, and he was swaying very unsteadily. Qemal was blinded by anger and rushed to stand up, only to have Gaius fall towards him. Qemal did not see that when Gaius was on the ground, his hand found the dagger, the *pugio,* that Qemal threw on the ground in front of Antoni. Gaius was holding the dagger in his good hand, and when he fell onto Qemal, he thrust the dagger deep into Qemal's heart. Qemal's face had a look of complete disbelief before the light went out of his eyes. Antoni hobbled over to Gaius and cradled him in his arms. Gaius looked up at his friend and said, "I hope that *Yeshua* will forgive me for killing him, but I had to protect you." He closed his eyes one last time.

Antoni kept holding him. After some time, he got up and looked at Qemal's body. "You were right. Two did die today."

*****

"Who was he, Antoni?" Paul asked as they were preparing Gaius' body for burial.

Antoni's leg wound was deep, but after it had been cleaned and bandaged, it appeared to be healing well. He was still having difficulty walking. "Gaius and I saw him on the balcony at the Forum when Rufus announced that the Christians were responsible for the Great Fire. Gaius thought that this man, Qemal, was telling Rufus what to say. When Qemal came into the storeroom to kill me, he told me that he was responsible for the death of Simon Peter, our brothers and sisters in Rome, and he also killed my younger brother."

Paul considered this, "Do you think we're safe now?"

"No, I don't. We're safe enough here for now, but more agents may be coming from Rome. It's only a matter of time. Paul, you must consider leaving here and going somewhere that is safe. Let me get you away from here safely."

"No, Antoni, I still have writing to do. There is so much more that we have to get done. I have been in prison before, and it's not so bad. It gave me a chance to write. I see myself returning to Rome to strengthen our community with many of those here with us now. No, I do not need to abandon our people."

Declan, he began to think of himself again by his real name; knew what was to happen. Paul would return to Rome, where he would be executed for preaching the Word. Declan decided that his work was done here. He would stay with the community a while longer to help prepare them for their return to Rome, and then he would use his SQQ-38 to determine where he could access the portal. He would return home and outbrief his team. When his work was done there, by the Grace of God, he could return to the Abbey.

Chapter Thirty-Seven
Late Summer – The Following Year

Pasadena

To the team in Pasadena, it appeared that Declan had been gone for over two years. He was in a conference room with Nate and Jill the day after he gave his full outbrief to the team.

"So, Murray has been a psychiatric inpatient for what, almost a year now?" Declan asked Nate and Jill. "What, so he can walk away from all that he has done once he is 'healed?' This guy is responsible for how many deaths, and he'll go free? I'm all for forgiveness, don't get me wrong, but Murray should face the consequences of his actions."

Nate replied, "I'm sorry, Declan, I wasn't very clear earlier. A homicide detective from the Sheriff's Office has been monitoring this very closely. He is still working to finalize the case; he wants a 'slam dunk,' and he's working hard to make sure that happens. Charges were filed against Murray, and he is expected to stand trial for the murder of Richard Hollander once he is released from the psychiatric hospital. You should see him, Declan. He is a shell of who he was. He *is* facing the consequences for what he has done; he is living in his own little hell, and from what we can gather from this psychiatrist, Murray may never recover from this. This horribly sad situation is a waste on multiple levels."

Jill added, "What started as an incredible project, good science and all, was hijacked by the deep-seated emotional troubles of a brilliant mind. Declan, we were all affected by what

Murray did; he played all of us, but a significant lesson has been learned. Murray demonstrated that Einstein was right and that in and of itself is a tremendous accomplishment. But his hubris was his undoing. To send a team back in time with the intent of changing the future was wrong. Jay Agrawal is considering shutting everything down, and we all agree with him."

Nate jumped in, "Declan, Jill also brought up that what Murray did was wrong, but there are a few of us who should also shoulder some of the blame. Arrogance was not restricted to Murray. A lot of us on the project were so eager to see if our hypotheses were correct, we wanted to reopen the portal, consequences be damned."

Then Jill continued, "I could have slowed down on my persistence that chaos theory was just that, a theory, and that we had some 'wiggle room' in what we were doing. That's unadulterated hubris on my part."

Nate nodded at Jill, "Jill mentioned this last year. She said that we should shut the project down. What did you say, Jill? Are we opening Pandora's Box, and the dangers are too real? Something like that, but the bottom line is that we may have demonstrated that Einstein was right, but it's like the vulcanologists are saying: Yellowstone is a huge caldera, and it will be an extinction event if it blows. The vulcanologists are right, but we shouldn't demonstrate how right they are and help precipitate Yellowstone blowing. Same thing with our project, leave those things that are in the past, in the past."

Jill looked wistful for a moment, "We're so glad you're back, Declan, and we all mourn Toma."

Declan nodded, "Toma was a good man, a great friend, and a good teammate. Toma and I talked about this at length before we went back. He said that he belonged back there, he wanted to go back, and from what I gathered from Qemal, Toma died on the Nineveh Plain. He made it back home." Jill and Nate both smiled at the thought of that. "Qemal told me that Toma delayed the large group of pursuers from capturing and killing the brothers that fled from Armenia. Jill, you told me about the Butterfly Effect and how one butterfly flapping its wings can cause a hurricane. What about the forty men Toma saved? How much of an effect could they potentially have? That's a lot of butterflies flapping their wings. What Toma did must have impacted the spreading of the Word. Think about the letters that St. Peter and St. Paul wrote. Qemal didn't stop them; we know how much impact they had. Then, the blood of the martyrs in Rome helped the Church to grow. So, what was the end result of all of Murray's machinations and scheming? It seems that Murray never figured God into his calculations, did he?"

Nate and Jill looked at each other. Jill said, "I never thought about it that way, but it makes sense. Along with Toma being a martyr, we also have to remember that Richard also gave his life. He warned us about the double cross, and because of that, Murray had him killed. So senseless. How about you, Declan? What do you have planned?"

"Great question, Jill. I've done a lot of thinking about this. I'm thinking of going back to the Abbey. I will have a nice long visit with my Abbot as I'm considering entering the priesthood. I think that's where God is calling me. Nate, please ask Friar Anthony to pray for me. Declan got up. "Now, if we're all done, I have to head down to San Diego. I'll meet with Toma's family later this evening; they want to discuss the last two years. They still believe that Toma was on a quasi-military mission, that was our cover. I'll tell them that he died doing what he loved to do and how he had saved many people from being killed. It won't bring him back, but it will hopefully ease their pain."

Nate and Jill got up from the table, then Jill reached out and took Declan's hand, "Declan, we agonized over sending a team back to warn you all, but we couldn't."

Declan smiled at her, "No, don't worry about that. Toma and I both knew that we were on our own. We knew you could not send any more people back through the portal. That would have increased the chances of our altering the future. Toma and I have both been through this before on other missions as SEALs; most times, you're on your own. We both knew the risks, but can't you see what we got out of this?"

"What's that?"

"First, Murray wanted to change the trajectory of history, and because of what we could do, he didn't. Today, the Word of God is being proclaimed throughout the world. But we accomplished something else, too, didn't we? We proved that our faith is not a delusion, as people like Murray would tell us. Toma and I have seen the face of God, and we talked directly with Our Savior. Think about that; we all know what awaits us, now, don't we?"

Jill smiled at him. "Yes, you're right. So, what now, Declan?"

"I'm going to visit Toma's family, but before that, I'd like to see if I can find some closure with this. Is there a way that we can arrange a meeting with Murray?"

Nate answered, "That might be good for all of us. Let me see what I can do."

*****

Murray stirred out of his sleep and looked across the room to see Declan sitting in a chair. "What are you doing here? Oh, I know, you came to gloat."

"No, Murray, I did not come to gloat. I'm simply looking for answers."

"Answers to what, Declan? Why am I locked up in this nut house? Why did Kristin and Toma die? Why did I have Richard murdered? Or the $10,000 prize, why did I fuck everything up?"

Declan stood up from his chair and looked down at this shell of what once was the most brilliant intellect of his time. He thought of Toma, of Abbot Blaise, of Bartholomew. How would they handle this? Instead of looking at Murray with pity, his heart filled with compassion for a tortured soul. "No, Murray, just talk to me. I know that you've spent a lot of time talking with the police and with a bunch of shrinks, but none of them knows what I know about all of this." He sat back down.

"Is this supposed to be a, what do you Catholics call it, a confession? Is that what this is?"

Declan slowly shook his head and then sat back down. "No, I cannot hear your confession, and I cannot give you absolution. But what I can do is listen."

A calmness came over Murray, something he had not felt in a long time. After a few moments, he opened up. "You know, Kristin did that once. When we first met, we were out, ready to have dinner, and memories from my ugly past roared right at me like a freight train. I acted very bitterly toward her. After I calmed down, she just sat there and let me talk.

"Remember when you rejoined the team after you took your leave from the monastery, and I told you how I spent my life shaking my fist at God because of what happened?" Declan nodded his head. "The thought of God doing all of this to me consumed me. I wanted to go head-to-head with him and prove that I didn't need him." Murray shook his head and laughed at himself. "What a moron. Murray Edgeton, big hotshot, bigger than God. You know, I hated God. I hated His followers. How much energy did I waste doing that? Unbelievable.

"Up until the time that you and your team traveled back to Palestine and witnessed the crucifixion of Jesus, I still believed that religion was a fable. But when you all came back with proof of the divinity of Jesus, I wasn't angry. I was scared. I was afraid that my whole life was based on a mistaken belief. And then that charade of sending you all back in time to learn how the Apostles could spread information so quickly. I even told Richard that the whole project was, as I called it, a 'masquerade.' I did what I had to do to stop God." He looked at Declan and then looked around his room. "Yeah, look where that got me. OK, two things. I know now that we should have never embarked on this project. That was a Pandora's box that we should have left closed. Think of what could happen if this got into the wrong hands. Secondly, I set into motion the events that led to Richard's and Toma's deaths. I'm sickened with who I am. You're a military guy. Did you ever see that classic war flick, *The Bridge on the River Kwai*? Do you remember the Alec

Guinness character? What was his name?"

"Col. Nicholson."

"Right. And do you remember what he said after he realized that he fucked up?"

Declan replied, "Yeah, he said something like 'What have I done?'"

"That's how I feel. Look at what I've done. Good people are dead because of me. I can't even begin to think of the damage to the world that could be caused by this fucking project. No shit, what have I done? That's the first thing. Now, here's the second thing, and this is something that I've been thinking about as I spend my hours in this room. I have to make some amends. Going back to my Col. Nicholson analogy, in the end, he did the right thing; he blew up the bridge. He redeemed himself. Kristin always told me about the forgiving nature of God and how His mercy is endless. Well, if I'm going to ask for redemption, He'll need a lot of that mercy for me."

Declan interrupted, "God's love and mercy are everlasting, but don't presume on His mercy. You may have faked me and the others out when you talked about your 'wanting to learn about our faith,' but don't try to fool God on this one."

"I know that, and I know I'll never be able to regain your trust. But Kristin said that redemption requires truth and accountability. I understand that now. As far as the truth goes, I planned to make it a one-way trip for you and Toma. I wanted you dead. You two came back and had proof, actual no-shit proof of who Jesus was. In my fucked-up mind, you two were acting as messengers of God, ready to rub my nose in the fact that God existed beyond any doubt. If I could kill you and Toma, I would be striking back at God. The same thing with Richard. I had to get rid of him. He was ready to blow the whistle on me, but I couldn't let that happen. But you three were people I knew. I could rationalize why you all had to die. But how about those people in the past, Peter, Paul, and the rest? Remember that bullshit story I made up about sending you all back to find out how the evangelists were able to spread the story of Jesus so successfully? I just wanted you all there with them to increase my chances of chaos theory kicking in and affecting the initial condition. Secondly, if you guys were around those evangelists when Qemal got back there, his chances of eliminating them would be enhanced. He knew who you two were. He could follow you and identify his targets more easily. At least that's what I thought.

"Now for the accountability part of it. As far as Richard goes, I will accept whatever the Court decides whenever they get to me. That's the amends that I have to make for Richard. But I need to redeem myself for Toma and Kristin's memory. I need to do this for my sake, and I need to make things right with God. I need to find a way to do this, something concrete that will prove that I'm sorry. If I, in my hubris, thought that I could attack God by trying to alter the past, don't you think that some misguided people could attack some of God's followers? Of course they could. We see this daily. What if I could work to stop some of the religious hatred occurring in the world? Would that help make it right? I don't know what I can do to begin making amends for all I have done."

Declan thought for a moment. "I think you're on your way. But I'm a bit puzzled. As long as I've known you, you've said you don't believe in God. When you tried to portray yourself as wanting to learn about our faith, I detected a sense of insincerity. But now, I don't know. After all of this, do you believe in God?"

"Oh, yeah. I believe in God. He's made sure of that. And I know one thing for certain: He must have a sense of humor. I mean, look where I am. The great Murray Edgeton locked up in a fucking nut house."

"As I said, you're on your way. Just know that God is not a genie in a bottle that will make your problems disappear, but He'll give you the strength to get through this. Trust in God, He'll come up with a way for you to make amends."

The floor nurse stuck his head inside the door, "Time's up, guys."

Declan got up, "One last thing. The project is being

shut down. Not many people knew all that was happening. A lot of our work was done in silos and was fragmented. The team members with a larger view of the project are all signing strong non-disclosure agreements with severe sanctions; these folks won't talk. This will all be tied up tighter than a drum." Murray slowly nodded his head. "Goodbye, and may God bless you. I'll pray for you, Murray." He walked out the door.

Epilogue

Declan visited Toma's family in the San Diego suburb of El Cajon to tell them about the events surrounding Toma's death. Their cover story was that both Declan and Toma were permitted to leave their monasteries to help support the humanitarian effort of bringing food and supplies to the Christian communities on the Nineveh Plain. The story was that their small convoy was attacked by a group of insurgents, and during the attack, Toma stayed behind to delay the insurgents from capturing the aid workers. Toma gave his life to allow the others to escape, and when the group returned to recover Toma's body, they found that his body had been taken. As the humanitarian group was working in Iraq without permission from the government, the story of their attack was not reported by the group to the media, so Toma's sacrifice was not to be covered by any media outlets. Toma's family was grief-stricken by what happened, but as Declan assured them, he died doing what he loved, and he sacrificed himself to save others. Toma's father, Thair, noted that Toma had returned to his ancestral home, so wherever Toma was laid to rest, he would be in the land of his fathers.

Declan was slated to travel back to South Carolina to return to the Abbey, but he received a call from Nate one evening asking if Declan could meet with a small group of people before he left. Declan drove to Pasadena and met with Nate at Nate's house the following day. Walking into Nate's house, Declan noted that the group was small indeed. Nate and Jill were the only people present.

Jill walked up to Declan and hugged him, "Thank you for meeting with us, Declan. We know that you are on your way back to South Carolina, but we have something important that we need to discuss with you. During your outbrief, you discussed Christian persecution under Nero at length. I was having dinner with my brother and his girlfriend one evening, and the old story of Nero playing his fiddle while Rome burned came up. My brother is a professional musician, and he took up the story. He said that 'Nero playing the fiddle' is just an allegory in that Nero fancied himself to be quite talented. He would sing and play music while his people suffered, but the violin family wasn't even invented until the 1200s. Nero couldn't have played a 'fiddle.' But then my brother went off on another tangent. He was telling me that in his studies with musicians from the Middle East and India, Christian persecution is still a big problem in many parts of the world, so that got me thinking. I did some research and found out that it is a big problem. It's actually a huge problem."

Declan asked, "What did your research show you?"

"It showed that the persecution of the Christians in Rome continued until the fourth century. Unfortunately, it continues today, but now it's not occurring in Rome, but worldwide. Several groups are reporting on this, organizations ranging from Amnesty International to the U.S. State Department, and their research has shown that there are some 360 million Christians in the world today who face significant persecution. Currently, one in every eight Christians worldwide faces *severe* persecution, including torture and death. Recent data also indicate that seventy-five percent of all religious-motivated violence in the world today is aimed against Christians, making them the most persecuted segment of the world's population."

Declan sat there, his hands steepled before his face, "That's interesting, Jill, continue."

"Something concrete needs to be done about this. The persecution is one thing, but there is another problem that makes my blood boil. It seems as if no one cares about this, the media don't, I don't know if our government does, and I bet you

349

that the average American has no idea about what's happening to the world's Christians."

Nate looked at Declan with a knowing look as Declan sat there impassively. Declan said, "What do you suggest?"

She looked at Declan and then at Nate. A look of understanding came over her. "You both know about this, don't you?"

Nate replied, "Yes, we know about this, as do several others. Several organizations have been trying to generate some interest in this, but as you say, no one seems to care. Being from India, I have seen firsthand significant religious rivalry and violence between various sects. India has experienced this problem for years, but what is becoming very prevalent in many areas of the world is the wholesale persecution of Christians. But you said something concrete needs to be done about this. What do you suggest?"

She sat back and collected her thoughts for a few moments. "I have put some thought into this. If we could work to raise awareness of this, I think that the American people would demand some action. I'm thinking of taking a two-pronged approach. I don't know if you were aware of this, but my mother is a Daughter of the American Revolution, and she has a lot of contacts. One of her best friends is the wife of one of the congressional representatives from Georgia. I want to enlist his help in working on this issue. The other approach I want to take is similar to what Harry Belafonte did during the African famine of 1985. He contacted some artists, including Michael Jackson and Lionel Richie. They wrote the 'We Are the World' charity single that was performed by many of the top artists of the day. They raised millions of dollars for famine relief. It was incredibly successful. My brother is a professional musician, and he, too, has lots of contacts in the classical, jazz, and popular music scenes that could lend a hand in this project. He thinks that this could really take off. The other thing that I want to do is make this a group comprised of people from many different faiths. I have a framework in mind that I will start working on, but first, I must head back to Georgia, put some things in order, and apply for a sabbatical. I'm hoping that I can get your help on this?" Declan and Nate both smiled at Jill.

Then Declan added, "There's something else I need to tell you regarding my meeting with Murray. He's a broken man, but he's searching for a way to, as he says, 'make things right with God.' He's looking for redemption, and I think it's real this time. One of the things that he brought up is that there is so much religious hatred in the world. He's wondering if he could do something to end this hatred; it might put him on the path of, as he says, making things right with God. Don't you find it interesting that you are looking at the same issue? He has an unbelievable intellect. You may be able to harness some of his energy to help you, even from his locked-down hospital room."

*****

Jill caught a flight back to Georgia the next day, and as she was flying across the continent heading back home, she reflected on all that happened these past few years. Looking out the window, she thought about how Declan and Toma came face to face with Jesus as He was on His cross and the mandate that He had charged them to carry out. She then thought about Toma protecting the brothers in Armenia and on the Nineveh Plain and how Declan worked to save the Christian communities in Rome and Spain. She shuddered when she thought about the dangers they had to face. What she would do would be a complex undertaking but not as difficult as what Declan and Toma had to do. But like Declan and Toma, she would be protecting the faithful. She knew that this was what God had planned for her, and like Joanna and Mary approaching Jesus' tomb, she knew that God would provide her with what she needed to accomplish this.

She smiled as she looked at the farms and the fields below.

Author's Note

There are several organizations that have more information on the issue of Christian Persecution; a few of them are listed below:

For the Martyrs www.forthemartyrs.com

Aid to the Church in Need www.churchinneed.org

Open Doors USA www.opendoorsusa.org

ABOUT THE AUTHOR

Jamison A. Whiteman, the author of *The Quietude of Calvary,* is a retired U.S. Naval Officer, a Vietnam Era Veteran, and a Veteran of the Persian Gulf War. He and his wife, Pamela, reside in their native San Diego. *The Shield Before Me* is his second novel. Visit his website at www.jamisonwhiteman.com